FIRST LESSON

Without warning, the earl pulled Aubree toward him, carelessly sweeping the sheet to the floor as his hand slid warmly over bare flesh.

Aubree raised her hands to hold him off and found them touching the coarse hairs of his chest. He pressed her closer, and her palms flattened over hardened muscle as she yielded to his greater strength. Caught up in the heat of his embrace, Aubree trembled as the earl's lips parted and drank urgently of her own. The shock of this gentle mixing of their breaths weakened her knees, and Aubree fell against him, clinging helplessly.

Placing his finger beneath her chin, the earl tilted her head upward to meet his gaze. "That is something of what passion is about, halfling," he said in a voice that told her that this, her first lesson in love, would not be her last. . . .

PATRICIA RICE is one of the most acclaimed new romance writers. *Romantic Times* hailed her most recent triumph, **Love Betrayed,** as "well-written, fast-paced, complete with engaging characters, searing sensuality, and a believable backdrop."

INDIGO
MOON

Patricia Rice

A SIGNET BOOK

SIGNET
Published by the Penguin Group
Penguin Books USA Inc., 375 Hudson Street,
New York, New York 10014, U.S.A.
Penguin Books Ltd, 27 Wrights Lane,
London W8 5TZ, England
Penguin Books Australia Ltd, Ringwood,
Victoria, Australia
Penguin Books Canada Ltd, 10 Alcorn Avenue,
Toronto, Ontario, Canada M4V 3B2
Penguin Books (N.Z.) Ltd, 182–190 Wairau Road,
Auckland 10, New Zealand

Penguin Books Ltd, Registered Offices:
Harmondsworth, Middlesex, England

Published by Signet, an imprint of Dutton Signet,
a division of Penguin Books USA Inc.

First Printing, February, 1988
11 10 9 8 7 6 5 4 3

 REGISTERED TRADEMARK—MARCA REGISTRADA

Printed in the United States of America

BOOK ONE

. . . he that filches from me my good name
Robs me of that which not enriches him,
And makes me poor indeed.
                              —Shakespeare, *Othello*

1

"Since when does Holland House give entrance to wife-beaters?" the ancient and doddering viscount sniffed with disdain to an equally aged companion, whose head nodded in continual agreement.

The subject of this attack strode stiffly past, head turning neither to the left nor to the right as he entered the throng in the reception room.

". . . a scandal, something to do with his wife," a voice whispered behind him.

". . . mysterious, but isn't he dashing, Mona? Just look how dark he is, like some Corsair."

"Bessie, come away from there. What would Mr. Evans think if he heard you were taking after the likes of that one?"

"But he's a hero, mama, decorated in Corunna, they say . . ."

". . . rutting bounder, I say. All those medals represent is a propensity for violence, if you ask my opinion."

Austin Atwood, Earl of Heathmont, grimaced to himself but continued to ignore the whispers that followed him like a rustling breeze through the anteroom of Holland House. He had only one purpose here, and once it was served, he would remove himself from the hostile society he had avoided these past years.

Though he walked with a pronounced limp, he held his lean figure proudly, and his striking visage, though not handsome in the conventional mold, continued to draw stares as he waded through a tide of pastel debutantes, doting mamas, and bored gentlemen. Though born to this aristocratic society, he moved with a determined stride belonging elsewhere than among this indolent crowd.

Gaining the portals of the ballroom, the earl hesitated just within the archway. Crystal chandeliers danced and glittered over a spectacular array of jewels and costly gowns, interspersed with the more sedate attire of gentlemen in black silk breeches and long-tailed frock coats. But even the gentlemen sported diamond stickpins and gold watch fobs and their black silk and polished leather gleamed subtly in the brilliant candlelight. This impressive array of wealth could scarcely be ignored so easily as the whispers behind him, particularly for one so sorely lacking in funds as he.

Taking the time to orient himself before diving into the unknown, the earl glanced about, noting that friends and acquaintances from earlier days were few and far between. Most of them had survived the marriage mart in one form or another, wed or unwed, and moved on to other, more sophisticated circles. The debutantes and their escorts here tonight were of a younger generation, and his only familiarity with them was through the identity of their watchful parents whose older daughters he had once escorted about this same room. If it were not for the political maneuverings being conducted in the back rooms, he would never have entered this rarefied circle again.

His bored glance fell upon a golden statue nearly hidden by a potted palm and a rather large companion in frilly pink. Blondes seldom attracted his attention, but the still grace and unusual coloring of this particular piece of art gained his passing admiration. In this hothouse of gardenia petal complexions, the golden and rose hues of the young lovely's cheeks glowed like dawn after a moonless night.

Stepping back and lounging against the wall for a better view of this exotic creature, the earl noted with disappointment the girl's extreme youth. It seemed a pity to waste all that extravagant loveliness on an empty-headed child, but it didn't prevent his admiring the sight.

Gowned in some shimmering gossamer that must have cost its weight in spun gold, the girl seemed totally oblivious to the crowd of people jockeying for position around her. Flaxen curls had been neatly coiffed on top of her head and dangled fashionably about her oval face, and she carried the requisite fan to flirt and flutter, but she seemed supremely unaware of this provocative appurtenance. Instead, she seemed to be gazing with nearsighted intensity into the crowd of dancers, her fan all but forgotten in her fingers and her delightfully piquant features frozen into concentration.

A familiar voice hailing him from nearby diverted the earl's attention.

"Heathmont! There you are. I'd about given up on you, though I'd scarcely blame you for avoiding this squeeze."

A slender man of about the earl's own age, the speaker hurried forward, pushing absently at the bridge of his nose, as if adjusting nonexistent spectacles. Running his hand through wispy, exceedingly blond hair, he surveyed his friend's harsh visage with bemusement.

"If you want something, you have to work for it, Averill," the earl replied laconically, focusing his attention momentarily on this one friend who had not deserted him. "Have you found out anything yet?"

The elder son of a younger son of a duke, Averill Bereford—commonly known as Alvan for obscure reasons—held no lands of his own, but his position in society was secure and unquestioned. Enormously liked by all his acquaintances, he never had reason to question the company he kept on his own account, but his anxiety for his sardonic friend gave him cause for pain.

"It's the times, Heath." Averill shrugged apologetically. "The duke is in the briars over this Regency business, being a Tory and all and not knowing when or if Prinny will change his mind about the cabinet. He has to be everywhere at once. My father will reach him sooner or later."

The earl frowned at this news and his attention drifted. Clad in an elegantly tailored coat of black suiting that had been purchased in his younger days, his shoulders moved restlessly within its confines. Though he had lost a stone or so since those grain-fed days of his youth, he had gained an athletic strength that did not fit well in court dress.

With the knowledge that the duke and his cronies

would not attend this reception, the earl lost interest
in the evening. Feeling the black mood coming upon
him again, he softened its arrival by returning his gaze
to the golden child nearby.

To his surprise, the girl's charming features suddenly lit with a candle glow of expectation that completely captivated him. With an unexpected twinge of
envy, Heathmont turned to locate the lucky man who
merited such a smile.

A young gentleman approached the entry with a
self-important tread, his slender frame impeccably tailored to a polished gleam, his immaculate lawn cravat
expertly tied, and his quizzing glass discreetly hung on
a silver chain. He appeared vaguely familiar to the
earl, but this young dandy would have only been a
greenling when Heathmont last attempted London society, and the name escaped him. Still, the youth gave
the appearance of an eminently respectable young lord
and the ideal candidate for a marriage-minded young
miss.

Bored with the commonplaceness of this tableau, the
earl turned to leave, only to be caught by the sight of
two tears sparkling in what seemed to Heathmont to
be enormously wide jade eyes. Long lashes quickly
swept downward over the delicate cheekbones he had
just admired moments before, but not in time to hide
the telltale trace of a teardrop down one golden-hued
cheek.

Frowning at this unexpected turn of events, the earl
sought the young lordling again, only to discover the
cad bowing before the plump miss in pink and deliberately ignoring the golden girl at her side. Heath had
been subject to enough cruel cuts himself to not recognize one when he saw it, and his long-buried anger
asserted itself in the girl's defense.

With haughty aloofness he elbowed aside the simpering miss and her young lord, and with a gallant
bow he smiled his pleasure at the young girl in gold.

"My dance, at last, I believe?" his deep voice murmured with masculine warmth.

Startled, Aubree stared upward into the deepest
pair of blue eyes she had ever seen. That they domi-

nated a weathered face of arrogant sophistication and crinkled at the corners in lines of humor held no small part in the sudden relief sweeping over her at this opportune intrusion. Rashly, she gave the stranger her gloved hand and bestowed a brilliant smile upon him.

"I thought you would never arrive," she announced with false gaiety, ignoring the stares she felt from those around her who listened to their every word.

Heathmont silently applauded her pluck as he led her toward the dance floor but cursed his own foolishness as the musicians struck up a waltz. With a grim set to his lips, he circled her exceedingly slender waist with his arm and began the tortuous movements he had once danced so carelessly.

Sunk in her own serious contemplations, Aubree scarcely noticed her partner's discomfort and thought little of the jerking gait that guided her around the room. The pain welling up inside her overwhelmed everything, and she struggled to overcome the tears that came so easily.

"Smile," Heathmont commanded between clenched teeth. "You'll fool no one with that long face."

In the habit of dancing mindlessly, exchanging only meaningless pleasantries with young men whose features all blurred together, Aubree had forgotten her partner entirely, as was her habit. Startled by the harshness of his command, she returned to the reality of this stranger who held her more tightly than was proper.

Unaccustomed to being forgotten, the earl smiled with satisfaction at this reaction he had drawn from the child. If he were going to torture himself for her sake, he would at least like to be recognized as being present.

"No man is worth tears," he added tersely, in answer to the question shining in those translucent eyes that had now turned darker and appeared to be flecked with gold.

"We were to be married," she replied simply. Now that he had drawn her from her thoughts, Aubree studied her partner more closely.

He was nearly twice her age and obviously out of

place among this crush of the Season's most eligible candidates for the marriage mart, unless he were some miss's older brother, perhaps. Even that possibility did not appear very likely, and she frowned slightly as she turned her considerable concentration on solving this riddle.

"You will have ugly lines upon your brow if you continue frowning in that manner. What do you mean, 'were to be married'? Surely no man in his right mind breaks off an engagement with the Season's loveliest maiden?"

Aubree ignored his flattery, keeping her mind on the subject at hand, the one cutting her insides to ribbons. "My father would not even speak with him. There was an exchange of letters, I believe, but Geoffrey has not spoken to me since. I had hoped . . ."

"That the callow brute would go against your father's wishes? You are naïve, my dear."

She threw him an aggravated glance, but his mocking gaze did not swerve.

"My father promised! He said I might have my choice, so long as I made it before my next birthday. I chose Geoffrey, and my father will not even consider him. He has broken his word!"

Amused by this revelation and the complacency with which the chit accepted the fact that she could have any man of her choosing, the earl drew her out further. It relieved the boredom and he certainly could not complain of the company. She moved like a feather within his arms, almost making the torment of this dance bearable.

"Then, if you love him, you must fight for him. He is being polite and obeying your father's wishes. Make him realize the man you choose must be able to stand up against your father," he stated lazily, humoring her.

A sudden sparkle of light glowed behind green eyes. "Do you think I might? How?" she demanded.

Heath shrugged. "A gentleman's pride is his weakest point. He cannot tolerate being ignored, nor jilted for another. You cannot capture his attention more effectively than to pretend he doesn't exist."

A glimmer of mischief gleamed briefly. "You speak from experience, sir?" she asked innocently.

With a sudden sense of foreboding gained by many years of living on the thin edge of trouble, Heathmont studied the repressed gleam of mischief in merry eyes. "Mountains," he advised sternly.

She peeped up at him through lowered lashes. "Would you, by some chance, know a gentleman willing to help me convince Geoffrey he has been forgotten?"

Black humor turned Heathmont's lips up at one corner at this not so subtle question. He knew the gossip mill better than anybody, how clacking tongues could destroy lives and reputations, overthrow monarchies, and make heroes of villains. In a time when few could—or would—read, gossip took the place of news. He had learned that lesson well. But to use gossip to attain a goal rather than destroy one had a radically different twist to it that appealed to his satiric mood. To turn his scandalous reputation to good use would be an edifying experience, but a rather dangerous game to play, even if it would idle away the tedious hours of cooling his heels at the back doors of the powerful. He shook his head.

"Do not look at me, my lady. Just my presence would be sufficient to ruin your reputation. We both will have a difficult time of it as it is explaining away this dance."

Wide eyes stared up at this dashing stranger with open curiosity. "Are you so terrible a person as that?"

A sardonic curve tilted his lips. "In the minds of men, yes."

The shadow of wariness disappeared, replaced by sudden decisiveness. "So long as you are no danger to me, I don't give a fig for my reputation. Will you help me?"

The earl frowned. "Your reputation is everything. Without it, you are alone in the world."

"Again, spoken from experience?" she replied audaciously. "But then, without Geoffrey, I shall truly be alone in the world. My father will disown me when I refuse to marry one of his hatchet-faced politicians."

Heathmont fought to keep from laughing out loud at this description of the gentlemen he had been pursuing. It might be enlightening to get to know this chit a little better. Just to look upon her would certainly relieve his black mood.

"I will take great care to treat you with the utmost circumspection so no questions can be raised against you, but just the whisper of my name should flush out your young dandy if he has your interest at heart."

A hint of speculation danced in long-lashed eyes as they studied this obvious rake who offered so cynically to come to her aid. "Might I ask what you have done to gain this reputation?"

"You may not," Austin replied sternly. "Suffice it to say that we shall have great difficulty finding anyone to properly introduce us so I might be given the opportunity to call on you. If we are to make your beau anxious, we will have to meet in public places."

Aubree smiled unworriedly. "You were talking with my cousin earlier. Perhaps he could introduce us. My aunt would never object, then."

"Your cousin?" Heathmont raised his eyebrows. He could not imagine how this single-minded nymph could have noticed to whom he had spoken, nor could he imagine anyone condescending to speak with him. Surely she would have been carried off the dance floor by now if either her aunt or cousin had been paying the least bit of attention to their rash charge.

"There he is." Aubree glanced over his shoulder to a point near the entryway where they had met. Then her face lit with a glee that could not be contained. "And there is Geoffrey. Could you not look down upon me with consuming passion or something? He looks positively livid."

The earl chuckled and obliged by pulling her more intimately into his embrace and swirling her in a graceful circle that nearly took her breath away and billowed her skirts out in a most indecorous fashion. Aubree was suddenly all too aware of the steel-hard musculature beneath the disguise of velvet and silk as her new friend bent to whisper in her ear.

"Beware, little one, you play with fire when you play with men's passions."

Aubree caught her breath as the dance came to an end and her partner continued to trap her waist against him. Midnight fires seemed to burn behind his eyes as his gaze raked over the modest cut of her bodice to the hills and valleys hidden beneath the clinging cloth of her gown.

And then his eyes shuttered closed, he dropped her waist and offered his arm politely.

"To your cousin, then, milady."

2

Averill Bereford stared at the approaching couple with outraged dismay, scarcely matched by the Earl of Heathmont's black delight at discovering the identity of the cousin of this enchantress.

He should have recognized the faint resemblance between the nearsighted cousins, but Bereford's fair slimness had not been impressed upon him until he met his friend's female counterpart. And now having some understanding of who this determined young miss might be, Heathmont realized he had plunged into waters well over his head. He raised a cynical eyebrow as Bereford accosted him.

"Heath, have you gone mad?" Averill demanded as he hurried to meet the scandalous couple.

Ignoring this rudeness, the earl answered politely, "The lady says we have not been properly introduced, Bereford. Would you be kind enough to do the pretty?"

If his friend noted the slight touch of sarcasm behind the polite phrases, he ignored them, turning instead to his rebellious young cousin. "Your aunt is looking for you. You know how she is when she thinks she has misplaced something. You had best return to her at once."

Green eyes flashed with sudden fury. "Averill Bereford, how can you be so rude? If you do not make the introductions at once, I shall do it myself."

Averill rubbed his nose, glared at his haughty young cousin and back again to his friend's noncommittal expression. Then, he sighed with resignation—an utterance commonly heard in the presence of this strong-willed miss.

"The sad thing about it is, she would, too," he muttered aggrievedly.

At the earl's quizzical look, Bereford shrugged and made a halfhearted gesture of introduction. "Lady Aubree Bereford—Austin Atwood, fifth Earl of Heathmont." He spoke offhandedly, as if it were already a moot gesture. He glowered again at his wayward friend. "If you have not already surmised, she is the duke's daughter, and a more spoiled, willful brat you will never find. If you retain any sense at all, you will run at the sound of her name."

Serenely accepting these insults, Lady Aubree curtsied slightly to her dancing partner, observing his bemused reaction without comment. "An earl, that is excellent. Geoffrey will be furious." She straightened and smiled sweetly at her cousin. "You are still angry with me for stealing that mare from you. That isn't gentlemanly, Averill. Give Peggy my regards and be certain Lord Heathmont finds my direction properly."

With an all-encompassing smile, she swept away in the direction of a slight, elderly lady who frantically searched the crowd, clutching at the sleeves of all passersby in pursuit of her elusive niece.

The earl followed the graceful sway of slender hips beneath gossamer gold until lost in the crowd, then turned his amused expression to his boyhood friend. "The story of the mare, Alvan?" he demanded.

Averill groaned and ran his fingers through the wispy remains of his hair. "At Tattersall's. She went to Tattersall's, by Jupiter. She went through the stables with only her groom in attendance, and the little witch chose the best damned piece of horseflesh on the market. And she bid it right out from under me. Didn't even know it was her until afterward. Bid it just as cool and calm as you please. The whole damn place was jumping up and down at the prices we were offering, and she didn't twitch a muscle. And you know what she said to me after? Said the damned mare had a nicked hock she wanted to treat. A thousand pounds, I tell you, for a nicked hock! You don't know what you're getting into, Heath."

The earl refrained from smiling as he contemplated his friend's nervousness. He did not mean to strain this one loyal friendship for a passing fancy, but he was a trifle disappointed in Alvan's reaction. Wryly, he offered Alvan the opportunity to back out. "Would you rather this notorious abuser of women stay away from your lovely but exceedingly young cousin?"

Lord Averill gave his sardonic friend a look of exasperation. "Any man who survives the attention of Aubree and the Duke of Ashbrook has received punishment enough for all misdeeds, real or imagined. I'll warn you now, your cause is not helped by standing between the two. They will chop you into mincemeat and stomp on your bones to get at each other."

The earl accepted this warning placidly. "It sounds a good deal more diverting than licking boots," he mused contentedly.

The topic of this conversation arrived home in a swirl of cloaks and laughter, offering to dance with her father's solemn butler and sending her maid into gales of glee as she curtsied prettily and danced with the hat rack when refused the butler's hand.

She was seventeen years old, wealthy and beautiful, and in London for the first time in her life. She had danced with a dashing gentleman who had made her feel as lovely and sophisticated as the elegant ladies she had glimpsed on the streets. She had her whole life ahead of her and the wits to know she could do almost anything she wanted should she put her mind to it.

Why should she bemoan the fate that had made her father a powerful duke who terrorized even the strong-

est of souls? Lord Heathmont was right. Her husband
must be a man unafraid to challenge the duke. If
Geoffrey could not stand up to him over a matter as
important as this, he would not be the man she thought.

A little wistfully, she swept up the three Siamese
kittens that came bounding down the stairs into her
arms. If only the right man could come along before
her eighteenth birthday.

Aunt Clara gazed worriedly upon her young niece
later that evening, though that young lady gave no
indication of being worthy of such concern. Sitting
before her bedroom fireplace in her nightshift, honey-
blond hair cascading in heavy rivulets down her slender back, Aubree Bereford giggled delightedly at her
lap full of playful kittens.

She glanced up in time to catch her aunt's fleeting
expression and made a clown face as she lifted one
kitten to her frail relative. "Aunt Clara, you are worrying again. There is no need of it, really there isn't."

Since she was actually Aubree's great-aunt and at
this moment feeling every bit of her age, Clara lowered herself to the wingback chair at the fireside before taking up the kitten. She continued to contemplate
her great-niece with concern, however.

"Aubree, my child, I know it has been a long time
since I have been part of London society, not since
your mother's coming-out, if I remember rightly . . ."
Her mind wandered to those days of the late century
and found difficulty returning to the present. Thirty
years ago she had been an attractive, ambitious matron who had successfully snared one of the city's most
eligible bachelors for her young charge. After the crown-
ing success of marrying her niece off to a wealthy
duke, she had retired to the country with her laurels.
It had become quite obvious these past few weeks that
she should have remained in the country.

Clara sighed and tried again. "Aubree, you simply
cannot entertain men who have not been introduced
to you. Your family is trying very hard to introduce
you only to the right sort of people. You are much too
young to make that distinction for yourself. And to
waltz with a man you have only just met . . . and at

your age . . ." The shock was almost too much for her, and she shuddered. She could not approve of the waltz, even if the patrons of Almack's had begun to allow it.

Aubree whispered in a kittenish ear and grinned widely at the answering purr before offering any reply to the charges. She loved Aunt Clara, but she had come to realize her high spirits were more than the frail old lady would ever understand. Until now, she had attempted to hide her escapades from her aunt's knowledge, but this time she needed her aunt's cooperation.

"Auntie, I have apologized for worrying you, but you really have no cause for concern. Lord Heathmont is an eminently respectable gentleman, a friend of Alvan's, and nearly old enough to be my father. He is in London only a short time and is looking for some diversion. I am bored to tears with these stuffy assemblies, and since Papa evidently intends to choose my husband for me, I see no reason why I cannot enjoy myself a trifle before I must be shackled to some dull politician for the rest of my life. What can an occasional ride in the park harm, particularly if my cousin attends also?"

Clara had known her great-niece all of the girl's seventeen years and knew well enough that deceptive innocence held a mind as devious as her father's, but she could never penetrate the thought behind the words. She sighed in frustration.

"It would be better had your brother lived. At least, he had the talent to make you mind and served as a buffer between you and your father, but now . . ." She halted, thinking of the cataclysm to come when the duke discovered the identity of his daughter's latest wounded creature. The maimed bear had been the outside of enough, but a lame earl . . . ?

A flicker of sadness shadowed Aubree's eyes as she remembered the proud young lord who had been her father's only heir. Perhaps she modeled her suitors after him, and no other met the standards. Even Geoffrey fell short of her memory of the young marquess, but who could live up to such a hero? Even the powerful duke had not been able to stop his only son from fighting at Nelson's side—and dying for a cause that was not yet won, even five years later.

Cursing the foolishness of men and war, Aubree placed the kittens in their box and rose to stand beside her aunt. "I can never be Henry, Aunt Clara. I have tried, but I only disappoint Papa more. Soon, I will be married, and you need not worry about me anymore. Can you not allow me this little bit of freedom now?"

The affection between these two was real and strong, and the older woman sensed the plea that was not spoken. She nodded sadly, stood to hug her niece, then walked to the door.

She paused for one final shot, however. "I trust you, Aubree, but that earl of yours is no gentleman, I fancy. Remember the injured hawk whose broken wing you set?" At her niece's thoughtful nod, she continued, "He bit your finger and flew away when he needed you no longer. I'll not allow that to happen again, Aubree. You keep your cousin with you."

After her aunt departed, Aubree climbed into bed and buried her face in the pillow, trying to hold back the tears. How could she make her aunt understand that the cynical earl offered a cure for her own wounds and not the other way around? Geoffrey's cut had injured deeply, more than she would willingly admit. Her father's rejection of her had shadowed her entire life; to be rejected by the man she had chosen to marry was a humiliation too deep to be borne.

But never would she let anyone know it.

The earl arrived as promised, his aged Hessians gleaming with new polish, his biscuit-colored trousers snug and revealing the trim hips and flat stomach of a man accustomed to vigorous exercise. The deep blue of his square-cut coat accented the similar coloring of his eyes, and though the thick mass of chestnut curls falling upon his brow had not been deliberately styled in the classic mode, he succeeded in resembling any statue of a Greek god Aubree had ever seen.

She smiled hesitantly as he entered the salon, dominating the delicate Sheraton pieces with his athletic grace and air of the outdoors. If it had not been for his limp, she might have frozen in panic at her foolishness in inviting this stranger here. As it was, she rushed to his side to urge him into the most comfortable chair.

Averill's eyebrows lifted at this maneuver as he entered behind his friend, but he bit his tongue and kept out of the fray. This was only a polite social call of twenty minutes and no more. Surely a tempest could be avoided in so short a time.

Though he should have known better.

Aubree opened innocently enough, politely introducing Aunt Clara, who immediately sought to place the earl's ancestors in relation to her own. Delighted to learn the earl's mother was the younger sister of a close friend of her youth, Clara succeeded in occupying the first five minutes with her chatter before the tea arrived.

Averill paced nervously up and down the room, narrowly avoiding tripping on the Aubusson carpet, accidentally upsetting the Sèvres snuffbox on the mantel, and nearly colliding with the new Hepplewhite table, until Aubree grew exasperated with his obvious anxiety.

"For pity's sake, Alvan, either put your spectacles on or sit down and have some tea. My father is not about to stroll in on us anytime soon, and he will not cut the throat of his future heir in any event. Why didn't you bring Peggy? She must certainly grow bored sitting at home while you're out gallivanting about."

The earl hid his amusement as the future Duke of Ashbrook obediently lowered himself to a tapestried sofa at the command of a tiny chit of a girl. Though she lacked the polished sophistication of her London-bred peers, Lady Aubree Bereford obviously had learned the lesson of power and command. He would do well to remember that for the future. Relaxing, Heathmont spread his long legs out more comfortably and waited for the Punch and Judy show to begin.

"Peggy stays home for a very good reason, as you well know, Aubree. A lady in her condition does not show herself in public," Bereford explained, as if to a very slow child.

"Stuff and nonsense, Alvan! Is all the world to pretend women don't have babies? Perhaps we are to believe babies come from heaven, delivered directly to the doorstep of good little girls and boys? If that's the case, heaven is enormously fond of those poor creatures down by Covent Garden and the docks."

"Aubree!" Aunt Clara intruded, aghast, but she awarded the floor to the young heir-apparent's quick retort.

"Aubree, we are not animals to parade ourselves as nature made us! I don't know how you grew up to be such an uncivilized little heathen, but even you must admit the necessity of clothing ourselves." Although the argument was an old one, Averill threw himself into it as heatedly as ever.

At the dangerous gleam in golden-flecked eyes of green, the earl hastened to interrupt. Bereford had left much too wide an opening for this opinionated youngster to jump through, and Austin had no interest in being spectator to the result.

"Lady Aubree is correct in some respects, Averill. Why should we hide away our women as if we were ashamed of them, while the men strut and preen like roosters over their accomplishments? But I doubt if this is a topic for the tea table, my lady. Perhaps you should apologize to your aunt and find a more suitable subject for our minds?"

"Apologize?" Aubree stared at the stranger as if he had developed two wings and horns, but his frown warned her that she needed his help, and she complied with an alacrity that astounded both cousin and aunt.

"I do apologize, Aunt Clara. I shall learn to speak with more circumspection." Until after she was married, she vowed silently. "Perhaps Lord Heathmont would do us the favor of describing his home and neighbors? You are from Devon, I believe you mentioned, my lord?"

Since this was the next-to-last topic he wished to discuss and Austin suspected from the mischievous gleam in her eye that the little minx knew it, he felt himself aptly repaid for his coercion. He steered clear of the subject of his neighbors and launched into the topic of the sailing to be had from the coast.

The remainder of the visit passed innocuously enough, and their callers were rewarded with the promise of Aubree's company for a ride in the park on the following day. As they left, Aubree watched their departing backs from the window. She surmised that even the earl's closest neighbors shunned him and wondered what mystery in his past had put him beyond the pale of all society. Except for the bitterness that occasionally accompanied a sharp word, he seemed completely indifferent to his status as pariah. But no man could live completely inside himself. It would be interesting to see how much she could pry from him during his short stay in society.

Outside the duke's fashionable Park Street residence, Alvan turned on his companion with vehemence. "Devil take it, Heath! You cannot mean to court a chit nearly half your age. Even if I know there is no truth to the gossip about you, you have no cause to taint Aubree's reputation with any hint of scandal. She's a greenling—and a willful brat, admittedly—but a gentleman . . ."

"I have long since resigned the position of gentleman, Averill," Austin replied wearily. "The young lady knows what she wants and I am only helping her to obtain it. Courtship plays no part in it. With the proper handling, I believe I can help my own cause as well. The young lady and I understand each other to that extent. You need not fear any further involvement on either of our parts."

The nearsighted young man looked dubious but resigned. Though he was more than half a score her senior, Aubree always had that effect on him. He prayed fervently his own offspring inherited none of the Bereford ambition.

"You had best know what you are doing, Austin. I'll not be in the briars over that tyke again. I'm too old for it."

The earl snorted disrespectfully and climbed into the waiting phaeton. "You have a wife and child to keep you young, my lad. Allow me my few eccentricities."

Knowing something of his friend's troubles, Averill grimaced, but kept to his own train of thought. "What you need is a good woman, Austin, and I don't mean that high flier you were with the other night. Pity Peggy's not up to the mark right now. She'd match you up with just the thing. A sizable dowry can always make a man's coffers sing a different tune."

The earl's dark face grew darker. "I have nothing to offer a wife, and I'll not be indebted to anyone. The subject is closed, Alvan."

If his companion's expression grew slightly mutinous, the earl ignored it. Women were no longer a part of his life—not the marrying kind, leastways. Other problems were uppermost in Austin's mind as he made his plans for the courting of the duke's only daughter. The girl herself scarcely came into it.

3

The Duke of Ashbrook tapped his quill impatiently against the desk, his piercing gray eyes looking through and past his caller. The golden Bereford hair had faded to a dull beige and gray, but age had not robbed him of much of his energy or ambition. Both were thwarted by the necessity of sitting still and listening to this prattle of his daughter's latest jingle-brained escapade.

He had sired his youngest child at a late age, too late for both himself and his wife. The duchess had died in this final effort to bring forth a second son. The duke had left the upbringing of the brat to a succession of nannies and governesses and plunged into the volatile world of politics to hide his grief and disappointment. He fully realized now the folly of leaving a malleable child in the hands of fools, but he'd had no choice then and very little now. If only Henry had lived . . .

This was an admission of weakness, and the duke shoved his pen aside, standing up and striding angrily to the window overlooking his northern estate. He straightened his shoulders against the tendency to sag. He would never convince Aubree he only wanted her happiness, and he certainly had no intention of revealing the reason for his need to see her safely settled. Physicians could be wrong, and there was no point in worrying her needlessly. He might yet live to see his grandchildren. Still, he would feel the responsibility relieved only when he knew his rebellious daughter had a husband to look after her in the extreme case the physicians might be right for a change.

Cursing to himself, the duke wondered what devilment she was up to now, for he knew of a certainty that his quick-witted daughter had not taken up with a scoundrel out of innocence.

"The Earl of Heathmont? Is he not that rapscallion they accused of—what? Beating his wife? Murdering her? Some such nonsense. Bitch probably deserved it." He swung around to confront his unwelcome visitor.

"So they say, but he was never brought to trial." The solicitor surreptitiously eased his weight from one leg to the other. It seldom occurred to his grace to offer a visitor a seat. The duke seldom sat himself. "They also say he is a war hero, cashiered when he nearly lost his leg at Corunna."

"Corunna." A little more than three years after Henry's death. Henry would have been thirty this year. He wondered how old this Earl of Heathmont might be.

The duke turned and stared at the dumpy little man who was the most astute solicitor he'd ever had the fortune to acquire. "Find out everything there is to know about this bounder. I'll have his throat slit if he's up to no good."

The little lawyer didn't doubt that for a minute. He bowed out, hat in hand, praying for the earl's sake that Lady Aubree knew what she was about.

*   *   *

"There goes Lady Driby, Heathmont. Look how she stares at us. Shall we smile and wave? Perhaps she will assume my father encourages your suit. She will be groveling at your doorstep within the week, if so," Aubree observed disdainfully.

"Aubree!" Alvan objected vehemently. "Someone should have taken you over their knee and thrashed some sense into you long ago."

"It's true," she replied defiantly, tossing her hair, forgetting her maid had carefully coiffed it in pins and curls atop her head to make her look older. She succeeded in bringing the arching feather of her hat into her eye and she brushed it away impatiently. "Ever since I arrived in London, I have had people fawning all over me in hopes of pleasing my father. I should have no acquaintances at all if I were merely Miss Bereford from Hampshire. I am glad he left me in the country all these years. At least I had some real friends."

A trace of adolescent defiance lingered in her voice, and the earl threw her a quick glance. Garbed in a fawn riding habit that provided a perfect foil for golden complexion and jade eyes, her honey-blond hair stacked in intricate curls and balanced neatly on a proudly held head, this child-woman possessed all the attributes of a worldly princess. Yet, sometimes when she spoke, he heard the fear and insecurity of a lonely child. In a few years, she would quickly gain the poise and maturity and social acceptance, but her father asked too much to marry her off now.

"Your wealth and position entail a certain amount of responsibility, Lady Aubree. You should not mock it," Austin responded calmly before Alvan could launch another tirade.

"And I assume you have shouldered your responsibility admirably, my lord," she taunted. "However, you will forgive me for doubting. Every flapping tongue in the town has come to call these past days. If you have committed half the crimes of which you have been accused, you must lead a very busy life. Whatever lies at the bottom of them cannot represent a great deal of responsibility."

Though couched in hints and subtle terms, the gossip Aubree had heard of this man over the tea table had been nothing less than horrifying, as she was sure her sources had intended. They whispered of the earl's ways with women that left them ruined forever, though never clarifying how that was possible. Others brought up the tales of the earl's first wife and her tragic death, making it seem Heathmont was somehow responsible. They recited his many and varied duels with a great deal of relish, and warned that he was head over heels in debt, but Aubree disdained their warnings. A man with a limp did not fit her image of a rakehell.

"I am not perfect," Heathmont responded stiffly to her earlier accusation and not her thoughts. He wished for the opportunity to urge his mount to a greater pace than this sedate one. He had the desire to gallop open fields, or strangle a certain ivory throat. "I have eluded responsibility in the past and I am paying for it now. I simply meant to remind you of your position."

Aubree immediately regretted her mocking words. She would have sooner kicked an injured animal than puncture the pride of this man who had so patiently aided her cause. Even now, the proof of his gallantry rested in a safe place next to her heart. She wished she dared show it to him, but she could not. Instead, she sought a safer subject.

"Have you any brothers or sisters, my lord?" she asked softly.

Startled and vaguely suspicious of this turnabout, the earl turned to gaze upon her deceptive innocence, but he could see nothing more than simple curiosity in her eyes. Averill, however, stiffened and threw his cousin a look askance.

"I have a younger sister," Austin replied cautiously.

"Then you do not have to worry about her going off to war. That is very fortunate," Aubree sighed, her thoughts momentarily taking flight and not noting the relief of her companions.

"Yes, quite," he replied wryly, avoiding looking to Averill.

"Aubree's brother was lost with Nelson," Alvan explained, *sotto voce*.

"I am sorry; I did not remember." Heathmont reined in his horse until he rode beside the youngster. He should have remembered the death of the duke's heir, but he'd had his own problems at that time. This child would still have been in the schoolroom then. The gap of age widened between them, only to be quickly shortened by her reply.

"I did not mean to solicit sympathy," Aubree informed him a trifle tartly. "I only tried to relate your lecture on responsibility to the world I know. Henry had an enormous responsibility. He was heir to all my father's estates, overseer in his absence, yet he chose to run off to the glory of war. Still, I am not certain he lacked responsibility."

"Many of us thought we were assuming a greater responsibility by protecting our country from invaders. I am certain your brother was one of those," Austin replied absently, still remembering the bleakness of that time and of his own foolishness. It was hard to believe he had been as young as Aubree once. A million years ago.

"And you, my lord? They tell me you were decorated at Corunna. Is that where you injured your knee?"

Averill had fallen behind and he could not see the mixture of curiosity and compassion upon his cousin's face or he might have foreseen the future. Instead, he kept silent, not wishing to intrude upon this personal subject.

"It was a mad, drunken rampage, and I feel no great pride for my part in it. Only at the end, when we turned upon them and drove them back before they drove us into the sea, did we show our true courage. Too many died for our carelessness. Yes, that is where I injured my knee. Now let us find a less morbid topic for this beautiful day."

Aubree obediently tilted her head and applied her not inconsiderable intelligence to the matter. The day was indeed a lovely one. The thick canopy of foliage above shaded them from the warmth of the sun, and their spirited mounts tugged at their bits, eager for a run. But the most interesting part of the day was this man riding beside her. His shoulders strained at the seams of the worn, cinnamon-colored coat, and the powerful muscles of his thighs clad in tight buckskins bulged as he kept his restless stallion under tight control. Aubree had never noticed these physical attributes in any other man, but she assumed it had something to do with her awareness of his lame knee. She suspected it pained him to ride for any length of time, but his stern demeanor revealed no sign of it.

The object that held her interest longest was the sword he carried at his side. Gentlemen carried walking sticks, not swords. Why did Heathmont feel compelled to carry this protection with him on the civilized pathways of Hyde Park?

"Tell me in what way I can repay your kindnesses," she blurted out, surprising even herself. "I would very much like to force society to accept you back into its good graces, but I fear Geoffrey may not be very receptive to the suggestion."

At this ingenuous remark, the earl gave a bark of laughter, startling his mount into stepping sideways. Smiling, the harshness of his features dissolved into an almost puckish expression beneath the curls on his forehead. Blue eyes twinkled delightedly as Austin leaned forward to contemplate the self-important child from whom such generosity flowed.

"My lady, you are an education unto yourself," he stated admiringly, ignoring Alvan's snort of derision. "I take it this means your reluctant swain has returned to the fold?"

Aubree sent him a secretive smile and touched the place where the sacred letter lay. "Soon, I trust. But you have not answered my question."

Heathmont sat up again, smothering a small frown of regret. This had been a pleasant diversion, but he had known it would not last. Another foolish miss off to Gretna Green to shackle himself to some silly lordling. Somehow, he had thought this one might be different.

"I thank you for your thought, but once my business here is complete, it is not likely that I shall return soon. Just keep your young lord from challenging me for my presumption in accompanying you. I would

regret having to put an end to what we have endeav-
ored so hard to bring about."

Alvan made a rude noise at this stiff-necked reply.
"Spare me the platitudes, both of you. If the duke
hadn't been up north this past sennight, you'd both be
brought to task by now, and if this Geoffrey person is
not in his grace's good graces, you're likely yet to
come a cropper. I'd suggest you save your mutual
congratulations."

The earl's expression grew thoughtful. "If my sources
are correct, his grace has neatly shaped a few straying
northern members into line behind the Regent. He
should be back in town shortly."

Austin bent a grave stare to the slender creature
riding beside him. In her elegant riding habit with her
golden curls caught up and neatly hidden beneath a
jaunty hat, she appeared older than her seventeen
years. The calm, but very determined gaze he received
in return did little to reassure him.

"You are certain your fiancé will stand firm this
time?" Austin asked. He thought little of any man
who would cry craven at the first hint of resistance,
but he kept his thoughts to himself. Talking sense to
young lovers was akin to banging your head against a
Chinese gong—noisy and painful. He ought to know
as well as anyone.

A trace of doubt flickered briefly in eyes that had
become more brown than green. But resolution quickly
firmed full lips. "If he loves me, he will not let my
father stand in our way."

Alvan gave his cousin an odd look. "That is like
throwing a man to the lions and promising your hand
if he survives. I should think the duke would have a
little more wisdom in these matters than you. Wouldn't
it be better to heed his advice?"

Aubree threw her well-meaning cousin a scornful
glare. "It is my father who insists I must marry before
my eighteenth birthday. I see no insight or wisdom in
that."

Alvan grunted. "I do. Once you come into your
mother's inheritance, you will be totally impossible to
control. He's better off finding you a husband to sit on

the purse strings or you are likely to turn all of Hampshire into a haven for every mistreated animal in the kingdom."

The earl chuckled at the irate glare this riposte rated, but he strongly suspected Alvan came close to the crux of the matter. He covered his grin with a look of solemnity when the young lioness turned upon him.

"I suppose you, too, consider a female totally incapable of managing her own affairs?"

"Affairs, never," he assured her cheerfully. "I cannot imagine a woman alive not capable of contriving an affair, if she so desires it."

Aubree cast him a look of loathing and with sudden impulse spurred her mount into a gallop. She tired of the sedate pace required of city grounds and longed for the fields of home. For just a little while, she would like to feel the wind in her hair again.

Her smaller mare easily outdistanced their larger mounts on narrow park paths and the advantage of surprise gave her an even greater lead. With the wily expertise of a country-bred rider, she cut across carefully kept lawns and through a grove of trees before her guardians came around the curve, losing herself entirely from their sight.

Satisfied she had jarred their male complacency, Aubree eased into a canter along their usual route. They would catch up with her eventually. In the meantime, she had the opportunity to go over in her mind again the note that had been delivered the previous day.

My dearest love,

Your father convinced me it was in your best interests for me to refrain from claiming you as my own. However, recent events make me doubt that your interests are best served by the neglect of those who love you. I shall make your father see he is wrong about me. Do not fear, my love, I shall be with you soon.

Your adoring,
Geoffrey

An odd letter, to be certain, but the words of love warmed her heart. She should have known Geoffrey would never have hurt her unless he had thought it best. She wondered what her father could possibly have said to him to make him avoid her as he had. Still, it seemed Lord Heathmont's suggestion had worked admirably. Now Geoffrey could see for himself that her father had no real interest in how she fared.

The line about being with her soon made Aubree's heart beat erratically. Where? When? She wished he had been more specific. The adventure of it made her blood boil with excitement. Soon, very soon, Geoffrey, she prayed. The tedium of waiting for escape from the confining box of her life had become almost too much to bear. Proof of that came from the fact she had almost begun to enjoy these outings with that infuriating rake, Heathmont. The scandal she was causing was almost half the fun.

Her mare pranced nervously as they rounded a bend and encountered a closed barouche halted in the middle of the roadway. It seemed strange for anyone to ride these lovely park grounds in a closed carriage, stranger still that they had chosen to halt in the middle of this popular thoroughfare. Aubree glanced over her shoulder to see if her riding partners had caught up with her yet.

She saw no sign of them and very little of anyone else. It was not the fashionable hour to be out. A curricle raced along the roadway farther ahead and a few strollers meandered among the bushes. Undoubtedly the stopped carriage was innocent enough.

Aubree eased her skittish mare forward, intending to circle the carriage. It had halted in an extremely inconvenient spot between parallel rows of shrubbery, and of necessity, she must go slowly to edge between them.

So it was no major difficulty for the man to step from the concealing bushes and grab her reins, forcing her horse to a halt.

"Lady Aubree, we have been waiting for you."

He appeared in every way a gentleman, from the stylish cut of his copper curls to the polished gleam of his Hessians. Only the sword at his side and his man-handling of her mare brought a frown to Aubree's brow.

"Release my reins," she demanded coolly, tapping her riding crop significantly against her thigh.

"There will be less commotion if you hurry into the carriage before your friends see you. I can explain all . . ."

The sound of approaching horses and Aubree's stubborn expression convinced the stranger time was of the essence. With only a polite "Beg your pardon," he jerked Aubree from the horse and shoved her into the hands of the carriage driver.

Aubree screamed more in fury than terror as she was lifted bodily from her horse and thrown into the waiting carriage. The gentleman's face at the door as it closed behind her did little to alleviate her anger.

"You will be safe. You are in good hands." He jumped from the step and swung his sword in a signal to the driver, who immediately lashed the team of four into a gallop.

Clinging to the window, Aubree unlatched the door and leaned out, but they were already traveling too fast to jump. In the distance, she saw Heathmont and Alvan riding furiously after her, and watched in horror as the swordsman stepped into their path, rapier drawn.

Her last sight of her cousin and the earl before the coach dashed around the bend was of Heathmont throwing himself from a galloping stallion, sword in hand, and Alvan dashing for the shrubbery.

And then the trees cut off all vision and the force of the wind slammed the carriage door closed.

The clash of silvered steel rang clearly in the early-afternoon silence as Austin met his opponent's thrust with an experienced riposte and turned the play against him. The rapiers flashed viciously, sparkling in the sunlight as the two men met with equal skill but different purposes. Heathmont had to keep the other man alive if he hoped to discover the girl's abductors.

Gritting his teeth, Austin tackled the task, and the clink and flash of silvered metal swirled in the dusty path. He had met stronger opponents before, but his knee robbed him of the swiftness necessary to win with ease. His challenger had an arm of steel and a sure knowledge of how to use it.

For a fleeting moment, Heath wondered if this were the elusive Geoffrey, but a good look at the younger man convinced him this was no young dandy. He bent to his task with renewed vigor, knowing the longer he delayed, the farther the carriage carried her away from him.

Bereford returned, empty-handed, just in time to witness the earl's wicked feint and jab that had brought down many a more experienced combatant. The young abductor sprawled in the dust, his coat sleeve slashed at the shoulder, but alive by the grace of Austin's deliberate restraint.

Pointing his sword at his opponent's throat, Heathmont waited for Alvan to dismount, a worried question in his eyes as he met his friend's.

"They escaped me. A fruit cart overturned in the street at the entrance and the carriage disappeared before I could make my way through the riot. I doubt if Lady Driby will ever speak to me again. Her phaeton's lost a wheel in the melee and I ignored her." Bereford cast a glance at the young gentleman waiting stoically for his death in the dust of Hyde Park.

"Where are they taking her?" Austin demanded coldly of his victim.

The young man remained silent, whereupon Heath skewered his sword a little more painfully against the skin beneath the elegantly tied cravat.

"You'll not die neatly, I assure you. Abducting young ladies is not a gentleman's habit, so I feel free to treat you as the scum you are. I think I will pluck your right eye first, then begin upon your left. What remains of you, if we have not found Lady Aubree, will be given to the duke to do with as he pleases. I don't imagine it will be a pretty sight."

Gray eyes snapped coldly. "It will be a sight prettier than what you would have done to that poor girl." He turned his gaze to Alvan. "Your cousin is safe, but you would do well to take better care in your choice of friends."

Bereford rolled his eyes heavenward in mock prayer. "By gad, Heath, it is another young knight come to slay the dragon. Shall we save him and set the fair maiden upon him when we find her?"

Austin's grim expression did not reflect Alvan's humor. The point of his sword drew blood as it pressed harder. "You little fool," he cried bitterly. "That girl is out there now without protection of friends or relatives. Have you any certainty where that coachman takes her? Or to whom? Who set you to this?"

The figure sprawled in the pathway had grown pale, but defiance still flared in his eyes. "I'll never tell. I could not save my sister, but so long as I am alive, you will not destroy another innocent."

Beneath his dark complexion, the earl grew pale. He moved the point of his sword to the young man's chin, holding it still as he studied the long-lashed gray eyes and shock of auburn hair. Austin's mouth grew dry as he removed the sword and gestured for the man to rise.

Alvan gave his friend a questioning glance, but not until the young swordsman had risen from the road and begun to dust himself off did Austin offer any explanations.

"Harley, I presume?" the earl asked wryly, keeping his own sword firmly in hand while standing on his opponent's weapon.

Steely eyes met his. "Correct. If you will give me my sword, I will be more than happy to continue where we left off."

Heathmont did not move his foot. "When we left off, you were sprawling on the ground, at my mercy. I'll not kill your father by killing you. My concern is for the girl. If you do not tell us where she is, she has some rather persuasive relations who will wring the information from you. Spare your father that disgrace."

Harley glanced at Averill Bereford, who regarded him with cold amusement. He spoke to this man, the girl's cousin, and not to Heathmont. "I will speak to his grace or Lord John, but not to this criminal."

Sadness and anger mixed in Heath's face as he gave a nod of agreement over Harley's head, but the matter had already left his hands. He mounted his stallion and waited impatiently for the others to follow.

4

By the time they reached the countryside, Aubree had exhausted every stratagem conceivable for escape or rescue. That last slam of the door had jarred some hidden lock, preventing her from throwing herself onto the mercy of the teeming streets of London. She had attempted crying for help as the carriage rolled slowly through jammed roadways, but she met only the stares of strangers. Little had she realized how very few people she actually knew in this terrifying city.

With the safety of the crowd behind her, Aubree collapsed against the seat and put her mind to work. She had no intention of despairing like some wailing miss in a romance novel. The young gentleman who had halted her horse had seemed kind, and if Heath and Alvan had not come riding up when they did, he might have explained what this was all about.

The letter in her bodice crackled suggestively and Aubree felt a leap of hope. Perhaps this was Geoffrey's way of "saving" her from Heath. Perhaps this carriage even now carried her to Geoffrey's arms. The thought made her bounce with excitement as she carefully took note of the direction they traveled.

They were definitely headed north. Surely, if he meant to take her to Gretna Green and put an end to her father's resistance, he would join her soon. But the thought of her father brought another ugly, nagging suspicion.

What if her father had heard of her dalliance with Heath and this were his way of removing her from trouble? The occurrence was not without parallel. The duke had whisked her away from a stay in Brighton once when she had offered to treat the Prince's headaches. The duke had been in London at the time. She had no idea how he had learned of her very circumspect offer, but she had found herself in a carriage bound for Hampshire the very next day. Prinny's dubious morals and the impropriety of a young, unmarried girl treating his complaint personally had never occurred to her and did not now.

Grimacing at this possibility and the knowledge that her father was in the same direction as she was traveling, Aubree settled herself in for the ride. Even if she could throw herself from the coach, it would be a simple task for the driver or footman to catch up with her. She might as well resign herself to waiting to discover which fate lurked around the corner. She supposed she could consider herself kidnapped, though her father would scarcely sell her off as a servant as kidnappers did their small victims. The slang simply seemed apropos.

The countryside they rattled through as the day grew longer became increasingly familiar and an uneasiness settled in the pit of Aubree's stomach. She had only visited her father's ancestral home upon occasion, preferring the cozier Hampshire estate of her mother, but the road signs and the increasing density of forest warned of the direction the coach took. It would not be a welcome homecoming that awaited her, she felt certain.

As Aubree contemplated her father's terrible anger, a young man sat comfortably ensconced at his usual table in White's, sipping leisurely at a glass of wine. His companion twitched irritably and grimaced at his rich surroundings while surveying the young lord with a certain amount of annoyance.

"It's a harebrained scheme, Geoff," the surly, older man finally spat out. "She would have run to Scotland with you and you'd be wed within the next days. The duke wouldn't let his only daughter starve once it was done."

The slender young man set his goblet on the table and carefully adjusted his cuffs, removing a tiny piece of lint from the otherwise immaculate blue of the cloth. He regarded his country cousin with immense patience.

"He informed me in no uncertain terms that we both could starve if we were bacon-witted enough to elope. The old bastard is tough enough to mean it. No, this is a much better way, cuz. I thank you for your aid. You will be well rewarded, I promise."

The older man's impatience grew as he watched the young fop's precise adjustment of cravat and collar. He had never benefited from the education in dress and deportment provided by his cousin's city-bred family, and he despised the effeminacy of such niceties, but they had their benefits if they gained a wealthy dowry. He curbed his irritation. "The chance to cut in on Heathmont is its own reward. Stupid wench to fall for the likes of that one, but still, it makes me wonder if there's any truth to the rumors."

The young man's sharp gray eyes looked up quickly. "Which rumors?"

"The ones about her ladyship possessing a fortune of her own. They say it's a close-kept secret, except among the family, of course, but if that blackguard is a friend of the family . . ." His voice tapered off insinuatingly.

For the first time, the dapper young dandy appeared a shade nervous. "Harry, you're just afraid that cad Heathmont will make a cake of you again. The duke ain't about to let a bounder like that into family secrets." He shifted uneasily in his seat, picturing Aubree's innocent expression and wondering if she would have kept such a secret from him. Remembering his own pose as a wealthy baronet, his uneasiness grew. It might never have occurred to the gudgeon that her dowry mattered a whit, spoiled brat that she was. His finger went nervously to his tight cravat and tugged at it. "Do you think . . . ?"

"Don't wait for your congratulations when you win her, I say." Harry threw back a gulp of ale. "Go in the conquering hero and carry her off to Scotland. The duke can be just as grateful after you're wed as before. Don't take any more chances."

Geoffrey nodded and summoned another bottle of wine. "Damn good thing you knew that chap who hates Heathmont. I'd hate to come up against that fellow tonight." Lifting his glass to his cousin, he toasted, "To the lady's rescue."

Harry held up his mug and leaned back. "To the lady's bed. May it be a rich one."

He tipped his cousin a wink and roared at his own wit. Old Heath would never know who to blame. Until too late.

The carriage rolled to a halt in the drive of a small but well-built hunting lodge somewhere on the outskirts of Ashbrook. In the deepening twilight, the shadow of the trees disguised the warmth of the stone, and Aubree puzzled over its familiarity. The rough, vine-covered walls reminded her of Castle Ashbrook, but she did not recognize the lodge. Why would they bring her to this hunting box and not to her father's home?

When the driver opened the door, he found Aubree primly sitting in the center of the carriage seat, her gloved hands clasped, her jaunty hat a little the worse for wear, but her expression definitely not one of a terrified miss. She regarded him with a haughty lift of her brow.

"Ma'am, if you will come down, there's dinner waiting." The driver waited uneasily. He had been ordered to treat the lady with respect but he knew enough of ladies to know the impossibility of making one do what she didn't want to do. And even this chit of a girl made it very evident she was a lady.

"I am not in the habit of dining with strangers," Aubree replied in odious accents learned from an ancient dowager aunt on her father's side.

"Mayhap somebody you know will be along right enough," the driver offered hopefully.

The growling of Aubree's stomach warned that she hadn't eaten since brunch and that to continue resisting was the height of foolishness, but submission was not a talent she had inherited.

"If they are not here now, then I most certainly cannot enter. There's an inn back in Ashbrook where I am known. I wish to be returned there." Aubree did not bother to look at the driver but sat looking forward, waiting for her orders to be carried out. Not that she truly expected them to be, but pride has its place, and it kept her from falling to pieces now.

A man who appeared to be a groom came from the direction of the stable and watched this confrontation with a smirk on his face. The driver's lips closed in a tight line as he eyed Aubree's petite figure with something less than compassion.

"If you don't come down out of there, miss, I'm going to have to carry you out, and you ain't goin' to be likin' that a bit."

Aubree bit her lip and turned her head sufficiently to judge the likelihood of this threat. The man stood easily six foot four and appeared twice Heathmont's breadth. He had thrown her into the coach with ease, he would have no difficulty removing her. Pride would not allow any further mauling and common sense told her the wisest choice was to comply, for the moment.

Delicately placing her toe on the step, she waited impatiently for assistance, refusing to step forth without the required aid, though she frequently ignored this civility with her own footmen. Beaten at his own game, the burly driver politely offered his hand and assisted the arrogant young miss from her high perch.

Once inside, Aubree hastily searched for familiar faces but heard only coarse laughter in the back rooms. A young woman hastened to guide her toward the stairway, and relieved to find at least one other female in this masculine habitat, Aubree willingly followed her.

Galloping the horses in the turf beside the road to muffle the beat of their hooves, Heathmont and Bereford turned down the road into the forest.

Bereford cursed under his breath. "Why in the name of Jupiter would any man kidnap the duke's daughter and hold her right under his nose? It makes no sense, Heath."

"That depends on the purpose of the kidnapping, I suppose," the earl replied shortly. His mind had already traveled these roads and concentrated now on the outcome. His leg ached abominably from the long ride and the hard leap he had made earlier, but his fury and his anxiety carried him at a relentless pace. If anything happened to that child as a result of his company, he would never forgive himself. He had to get there in time.

"Ashbrook's only an hour's ride from here, maybe we should seek reinforcements first." Averill brought his mount apace with the earl's thundering stallion. As winded as his horse, he had difficulty keeping abreast of Heathmont's furious pace.

"Your father should not be far behind if he received our message. He'll bring reinforcements enough. In the meantime, we must locate Aubree."

He did not explain his haste and Bereford had no reason to ask why. They had pried the coach's destination out of the conquered swordsman, but not the motive. Despite assurances that she would come to no harm, they placed no faith in the inherent gentlemanliness of kidnappers.

The formidable walls of the stone hunting lodge loomed darkly against the piece of night sky opening overhead. Light flowed from a back room, but the remainder of the house slumbered still and gloomy.

They dismounted and tethered the horses in the tree's shadows, creeping forward stealthily on foot toward the pool of light. The sound of raucous laughter and a woman's scream brought an exchange of glances. Heathmont's hand went automatically to the hilt of his sword, his face set hard and grim, but Bereford's hand stilled him.

"Look, up there," he whispered urgently, pointing toward an upper story as they came around a corner of the lodge.

A single candle flame flickered in a darkened window, and then a blur of white moved across the open pane. Bereford's poor vision only caught the color and movement, but Heathmont's sharp eyes recognized those golden tresses at once.

He eyed the ancient vines covering the stone walls beneath the window and knew what he would do, but for politeness's sake, he consulted the future heir.

"There must be a half-dozen men in the kitchen, from the sounds of it. Do you wish to risk breaking in and carrying her out, or shall we wait for your father?"

Averill gazed uncertainly at the slender form outlined by the frames of mullioned windows. She did not seem in any grave danger, and knowing Aubree, she could easily have planned this herself. He voted for caution.

Austin accepted his decision without comment on its wisdom. Instead, he began to make his way through the underbrush toward the house.

"What are you doing?" Averill demanded, following close at his heels.

"Making certain that she's safe," the earl replied firmly, not breaking his stride. "How good are you at climbing ropes?"

"Climbing . . . ?" Alvan gazed up at the vine-covered walls and gulped. "Henry used to, at the castle, but I never could."

Impatiently, Heathmont tugged at one of the wider trunks. It didn't budge, and he gave a grim smile of satisfaction. "I've been climbing the rigging of ships since I was a tad, and scaling cliffs worse than this one. You had better signal her I am coming up, or I'm likely to terrify her."

Bereford grunted cynically. "Terrify? Aubree? Would you care to cast a wager on why her guards are belowstairs drinking themselves under the table?"

Austin threw him an unreadable look and began the task of pulling himself hand over hand up the rough stone walls.

The rustling of leaves alerted Aubree. She glanced downward, unable to detect the cause immediately. Though her vision was infinitely better than Averill's, the heavy blanket of darkness blotted out distinctions, limiting the scene below to form and shadow. Before she had time to recognize the figure signaling her from the shrubbery, a heavy hand closed over the window-sill and Heathmont emerged from the night.

Aubree gasped as his heavy male figure suddenly straddled the sill where she sat. In this proximity, deprived of genteel distance and the safety of daylight and polite company, he seemed to loom above her with frightening massiveness. But the painful manner in which he lifted his bad leg over the sill removed all foolish fears.

"My lord, what are you doing here?" she whispered hurriedly, catching his sword before it clanked against the stone while he carried his leg into the room.

"Cursing my idiocy, mostly," Heathmont replied through gritted teeth. Righting himself finally, he turned to study Aubree's pale face in the flickering light. "Are you safe? Have they harmed you in any way?" he demanded curtly, successfully reading the flash of fear behind her unwavering stare.

"I am fine. I have barred the door from the inside so no one can enter. How did you get here?" She glanced dubiously downward, judging the possibility of escaping the same way.

Glancing in the direction of the door and remembering Averill's wager, Austin was glad he hadn't accepted it. With the door barred, there was little more her abductors could do but drink themselves under the table. The little brat would only need his help if the men came wielding axes.

Still, he was in no hurry to make that climb down, and even drunken men could find axes. He preferred to stay. He shrugged in reply to her question. "No matter. Your uncle should not be far behind, and then we'll get you out of here. Have you recognized any of the men?"

Aubree shook her head, turning her gaze to the earl's worried frown. The anxiety creasing his brow she understood well enough, but the smoldering anger beneath gave cause for concern.

"Could we not leave the same way you came?" she asked uncertainly. The scent of lathered horses clung to Heathmont's clothing, reminding her again of his nearness. He made no attempt to move a polite distance away, but kept his place at her side, nursing his injured knee while he watched her with curiosity and concern.

"I'll not risk your neck unnecessarily. If the door is barred and I am here to guard you until your uncle and his men arrive, you should be safe enough. Unless you have some objection to this arrangement?" He lifted one eyebrow in cynical questioning.

Aubree hurriedly shook her head. "No, don't leave me here alone is all I ask. You do not think it is my father who has carried me here, then?"

Austin had not realized the tension that held him until she released it with her innocent plea. She was no more than a frightened child after all, and no mad scheme lay behind this abduction on her part. He relaxed and rested his shoulders against the window frame.

"I have not had the occasion to meet his grace, but no one has given me cause to think him mad. I thought perhaps your Geoffrey might have concocted some plan . . . ?" He ended on a questioning note.

Aubree shook her head vigorously, sending another of her troublesome curls cascading down her neck. "I would have come up to meet him anywhere he requested. He knows that. There would be no need to go to such great lengths."

"Then there are only two other possibilities, neither of them pretty. You are either being held for ransom, or my enemies have followed me to London. In either case, I intend to put a permanent halt to the perpetrators."

The earl glanced about the room much as a general surveys a battleground. Only a bed and a washstand occupied the narrow cubicle. They would not obstruct his hand, but neither would they protect his hide. It would be best for all concerned if Aubree's uncle arrived before anyone attempted to open that door.

Not voicing this conclusion, Austin attempted to rise to work the painful kink from his leg. The knee resisted his weight and he stumbled, nearly falling, until saved by a soft shoulder and steadying hand.

"You had best sit on the bed and raise that leg, my lord. The stiffness will work out once it's rested."

Accustomed to vehemently protesting any assistance, Austin bit his tongue and rested a small part of his weight on slender shoulders. To reject her offer would only raise her angry defenses, and he had no wish to come to verbal blows with a frightened child. He suspected there was much they could teach each other, had they but the time. Patience and sympathy came first to mind.

Attempting to shift his weight from her shoulders to the bed, Austin caught his scabbard in the heavy cloth of Aubree's skirt. Tripping over this impediment, Aubree lost her balance, and in a tangle of swords and skirts and arms and legs, they tumbled onto the down-filled mattress.

Austin's curses as he attempted to disentangle himself and remove his heavy weight from her slight frame brought a gurgle of laughter from below him. Propping himself on one arm, he gazed down at tousled golden tresses and laughing green eyes.

"Are you accustomed to laughing at every man you fall into bed with?" he asked wryly.

The giggles increased, and Aubree had to slap her hand over her mouth to muffle them. In between bursts, she gasped, "I meant to ask if this is what is called a tumble in bed, but I think you have answered my question."

Another outbreak of mirth had Austin biting back laughter of his own. Gently extricating himself from the tangle, the earl finally gained a sitting position and eased Aubree up to sit beside him.

"It is a wonder I did not break all your bones. A gallant knight I make," Austin reflected ruefully.

Pulling her legs up beneath her skirt and sitting in a decidedly unladylike cross-legged fashion, Aubree grinned saucily at her errant knight. "I always preferred Don Quixote to Sir Lancelot."

"I may be aged, but I do not have the excuse of poor vision to tilt at windmills. I shall leave the quest to you and your cousin." Austin stretched his long legs out before him and regarded his impish companion with a mixture of curiosity and admiration. "Shouldn't you be in tears by now? Most young ladies I have known cry buckets if their favorite bonnet is crushed. You have been carried off and locked away and then nearly crushed by your would-be rescuer *and* your bonnet has disappeared, but all you do is giggle. You aren't considering hysterics, are you?" he asked with some degree of suspicion.

Aubree suppressed a smile at the masculine anxiety lurking behind his dry humor. He could duel with kidnappers, ride until he was lame with pain, and scale stone walls, but she dared say he would fall to pieces at a woman's tears. The monster Earl of Heathmont had a heart somewhere beneath that insouciant exterior.

"They threw me out of school before I could learn such ladylike tactics. You will have to bear my odd sense of humor, instead." She grew quiet and listened to the sounds from below. "You don't suppose they have heard us, do you?" She tried to keep the anxiety from her voice, not wishing to be tarred with the brush of fear, either.

"They would not hear the chimney if it fell upon their heads. If that door is unlocked, we could possibly walk out of here, and none be the wiser."

He shifted as if to rise and inspect the door in question, but Aubree gestured for him to remain seated. "They locked it with a key from the outside. I have already tried it. I still think my father must be behind this. Why else would they bring me here? And they have all made every attempt to be courteous, under the circumstances."

Austin shrugged and searched for some comfortable position for his aching leg. "The man who put you in the carriage would only tell us where you were being taken, and that, only after much persuasion. He seemed to be of the opinion that I was out to do you harm and that he was only rescuing you from a fate worse than death. We had some difficulty convincing him otherwise, else we'd have been here sooner."

Seeing his difficulty, Aubree jumped from her perch

and lifted the earl's leg so he could swing it onto the bed where she had been sitting. She reached for a pillow to prop under it, but Austin gestured her away.

"It will be fine," he said curtly. "Now sit down and don't flutter about me." Propping up his good leg to make room for Aubree beside him, he draped one arm over his raised knee and waited patiently for his command to be followed.

Aubree perched obediently on the edge of the bed, but her gaze continued to stray to the stiff leg encased in tight buckskin breeches. "Does it swell or get feverish when you exert it like this?"

Austin had to choke back a bark of laughter. The elegant, exceedingly wealthy Lady Aubree Bereford, daughter of one of England's most powerful nobles, sat unconcernedly on the bed of one of the most notorious men in society, inquiring after his injuries. The improbability of place was only outdone by the ludicrousness of their conversation. He wished Bereford were here to appreciate it.

"Occasionally, but I am lucky to have it at all, so I'll not complain." Austin gestured toward the open window. "You had best signal your cousin that all is well, or he will begin doubting his judgment in sending me up here."

A wicked gleam leapt to green eyes as she understood the implications of his words, but she did as told and rose to peer out the window to the shrubbery below. Outlined by the candlelight, she hoped she could be seen better than she could see into the darkness. Eventually, she detected a movement at the base of the wall and caught sight of a hand waving in a signal from their childhood. She returned the gesture, then turned to her "patient."

"Alvan can be exceedingly stuffy at times, but he has uncommon good sense. I doubt that he will attempt to scale the wall to protect my virtue. I am surprised that he even helped to subdue your swordsman. Did he run him down with his horse?"

Aubree perched again on the bed's edge, this time studying the earl's face and not his knee. In the dim light, she could read little of Heathmont's expression, but she sensed the strength and self-confidence in his posture, and relaxed a little. She was more than grateful for his company after the happenings of this day.

The earl chuckled. "He left me to deal with your swordsman while he chased after the carriage. But a fruit cart had been upset by your coach's hasty departure, and Lady Driby's carriage had become entangled with the carter's animals, and the ensuing mob prevented any further chase. He returned in time to threaten our captive with your father's name."

"I missed all the fun," she sighed wickedly. She found it astonishingly easy to be herself with this man she had known no more than a week. She did not understand the reason but was grateful for it. To play the part of demure miss at this moment would stretch her patience to the breaking point.

"I daresay you will see the best part when your uncle arrives," Austin replied wryly. "I shall have to scurry back down the wall to lend my hand so he has no reason to think you compromised."

Aubree frowned. "That is foolishness. There is no point risking your neck in such a manner. Alvan will simply have to tell them you were protecting me. I shall sit on the windowsill if it will prevent you from making such a foolhardy attempt."

The earl smiled at such naïveté but kept his thoughts to himself. There seemed no point in worrying her now. He would do as need be when the time came.

"Sitting on the windowsill would effect nothing if you should fall out of it, and it would make conversation exceedingly difficult. Unless you are inclined to sleep until your uncle arrives, we shall have to regale each other with our wittiest tales to pass the time."

Aubree brightened. "Let us play Question and Answer. I will go first."

Heathmont looked dubious. "I never heard of such a game. How do you play?"

"It is also called Honesty. We each take turns asking one question and the other must answer it as honestly as he is able. If he cannot, or will not, he loses. I'll show you how. I'll start with an easy one. It's more fun with strangers. I can stump Alvan within two questions, he's so pompous." Aubree settled herself more comfortably on the bed, totally unaware of the impropriety of playing parlor games while sitting on a bed in a room alone with a strange man, let alone under these circumstances and with this particular man.

After searching her brain briefly, Aubree opened with, "What does your mother call you?"

"My mother?" Austin grinned as he gathered the gist of this game. She had gone easy on him, if the point were to embarrass the other the most. "She calls me fool, frequently, but Austin when she wants something. If I play this game, will you call me Austin?"

"Of course, Austin. My turn again. What is the most embarrassing thing that has ever happened to you?"

Heathmont roared in protest at the speed with which she had hoodwinked him, but her giggles brought laughter to his lips and he accepted the lost point.

"I can see already, you are too good at this game. My most embarrassing moment . . . Probably the time at school when I so carefully glued all the pages of the professor's text together, then turned around to find him watching me. It may have been one of the most painful, too, now that I think about it."

Heath watched her expectant face light up with approval. The sophisticated coiffure of earlier had disintegrated into a tumble of tousled curls by now, but it in no way detracted from her loveliness. If he were being fair, he would have to admit that those long-lashed eyes were much too wide for her small face, and that the fullness of her lips was too ripe for the delicate structure of her jaw, and that her coloring was too wholesome for perfection, but he had no desire to be fair. She might not suit society's standards, but she suited his gaze well enough. Too bad she had to come along ten years too late.

"My turn. Why did your mother leave her wealth to you and not to your father?"

If Heath thought to stump her with that one, he was disappointed. She lit up like gaslights on a London street at this opportunity to tell her tale.

"My grandmama entailed it, just like a man would

do for the eldest sons. She lost her first love when her father refused to allow her to marry a poor man. He sailed off to make his fortune and never came back. When her father died and she came into his wealth, she tied it all up neatly so her daughter and her daughter's daughter and so on would inherit on their eighteenth birthdays. That way they did not have to marry for money or marry at all, if they wished. When she did marry, her husband was wealthy enough not to argue over the entailment, and my father certainly had no need of my mother's wealth, so he never seriously considered the entailment until I got older and presumably more troublesome."

Austin watched the shadows play across her face as she recited this tale without emotion or thought. She was too clever not to see the opportunities missed if she followed her father's wishes. He could only assume she either loved this Geoffrey so much she willingly sacrificed her freedom by marrying now, or she loved her father too much to refuse to obey his desire. The wistful look on her face when she was done was his undoing.

Without thought to his action, Austin leaned over and brushed a kiss against her lips. He had wanted to do this from the first moment he had seen her, but common sense had prevailed. Here, now, in this semi-darkness, with her childlike figure curled carelessly next to him, he could no longer recall his reasoning.

It was a gentle kiss, without demand or need for reply, yet Aubree tasted the heat of his lips against hers and felt a stir of emotion she could not quite comprehend. She should be angry at his presumptuousness, but it was not that kind of kiss. Instead, she needed to know more to understand what she felt. When his mouth moved lightly across hers, she turned her head to meet it with firmer pressure.

Austin's lips closed tightly against hers then, and his hand came up to rest at the small of her back, steadying her within the circle of his embrace as his head bent to sample her response more fully. Giddy excitement raced through Aubree's veins as his kiss grew heated, and she melted slowly beneath the smoldering fire.

Never before had she experienced such sensations, and she knew little of how to react to them. She craved more as the heat of this fire spread rapidly, but the fear of the unknown and the knowledge of her rashness held her back. She had no reason to fear this man who held her; she trusted him as she did Averill, but she feared what he did to her.

Still, it did not prevent her from raising her hand to his chest and bending like a willow to the heavenly bliss encompassing her. Heathmont's mouth was firm and hard against hers, and beneath her fingers, his heart beat a tattoo to match her own.

5

Austin knew the foolishness of his action even as he embarked upon it, but the fragile softness filling his arms felt too good to set aside, and his blood came alive at the warmth of her response. He wanted only some small token of affection to lighten his load, but he found himself holding an armful of easily ignited explosives.

With a great effort of will, he placed his hands firmly around her supple waist and moved her to a safer distance, where his lips would not so easily be tempted to stray.

Aubree stared up at him, green eyes wide and questioning as they took in the tender slant of Austin's mouth, the flicker of some hidden emotion behind the deep blue of his eyes. She felt the urge to brush the dark curls back from his face, but she feared she had gone too far as it was. She kept silent, waiting for his verdict.

"Your turn, I believe," he murmured, keeping her at a distance but not releasing her. She had discarded the jacket of her riding habit in the warmth of the evening, and he could feel her breathing through the fine lawn of her shirt. He could not let go, not quite yet.

Aubree felt the emptiness of the gap between them, but recognized relief that he had the sense to stop what she could not. She began to develop some vague understanding of why unmarried couples must not be left to themselves, but she had so much more to learn. She wondered if Geoffrey would teach her, and if it would all be as pleasant as this. A small smile of delight began to replace dazed wonderment.

"I claim two questions as a forfeit for your behavior."

This return to her lighthearted banter removed the cloud of despair that had threatened to overcome him, and Heathmont gladly returned to his role, releasing her waist to lean back and cross his arms and stare at her boldly.

"Fire away. I shall accept my punishment."

"How many girls have you kissed and is it always as pleasant as that?" she demanded, the teasing glint in her eyes warning his answer had best come up to par or a dire fate awaited him.

Austin grinned and feinted a grab, but she dodged and moved farther from his reach, perching warily at the side of the bed in preparation for flight.

"I have never kept count of the girls, but there has only been one lady, and yes, it is almost always as pleasant as that, particularly with a lady."

This roundaboutation left Aubree too flustered to reply, unable to determine if she counted as a lady, and Austin took advantage of her silence.

"Did your Geoffrey never kiss you?"

A slight flush crept to Aubree's cheeks, and she was grateful for the darkness, but she suspected he guessed her reaction, anyway. "Not like that," she replied almost shyly. Then, regaining some measure of her composure at admitting this indignity, she added a trifle tartly, "He only kissed me politely as a proper gentleman should when a lady agrees to be his wife."

"Of course," the earl answered, the words drying on his tongue at this mention of marriage. He had momentarily forgotten her intention of marrying the young puppy. It seemed a waste, but there had been worse mismatches through the ages. He certainly should know.

He sat up and started to throw his leg over the side of the bed, but Aubree darted to her feet and blocked his path.

"You are supposed to be resting that leg. I will go sit in the window and behave properly. I promise."

Before he could protest, she put words into action and leaned out over the sill to locate Alvan. If her cousin could see her clearly, he would have cause to raise the roof, Heathmont reflected, watching Aubree's slender form outlined against the panes. Her hair had fallen into a disheveled mass of curls and her stiff shirt had pulled from her waistband and wrinkled in a suspicious manner. He would be lucky to get out of this one without a bullet between his ribs. Luckily, Alvan could not see well enough without his spectacles to tell a cow from a horse. Wrinkles and ribs were beyond him.

"Wave at Alvan and then come sit yourself back down here. I may not be much of a gentleman, but I'll be damned if I lie here in comfort while you stand."

Aubree located her cousin's figure, scanned the horizon for signs of rescue, then turned to regard the man in the bed. He seemed so hale and hearty, his broad shoulders straining at the seams of his shirt, and his bronzed features telling the tale of outdoor life, yet his lameness somehow equaled their positions. She did not fear his greater strength as she might another in his place.

Still, she approached him cautiously. With his shoulders propped against the headboard and his long legs sprawled across the covers, Heathmont fairly well occupied the whole of the narrow bed. She aimed for the foot of the bed, where some small space remained.

"It's too late for that now. You may as well come sit beside me and make yourself comfortable since we have done away with propriety." He gestured toward the space he had made beside him, less room than the width of a love seat, and she had been warned about those.

Aubree hesitated. Up until now, she had considered this dark earl to be a fortunate circumstance and little more. If she thought of him personally at all, it had been as one of her cousin's many and assorted friends, far removed from her life. But she had some inkling now of the danger he presented.

"Aubree, I will not bite, I promise." Echoing her words of earlier, Austin raised his hand to assist her. "If you prefer, I will sit on the windowsill myself, but I will not sit in comfort while you pace about. It may be a longer night than I expected. You must get some rest."

She bit back the irresistible tilt of her lips as she settled gingerly within the curve of his arm. Austin pulled her closer so she was in no danger of falling out and his shoulder made a comfortable pillow for her head.

"The thought behind that grin, my lady?" he asked mildly.

"Are you asking me to sleep with you, my lord?" A hint of a giggle underscored her words.

"That is what one normally does after a tumble in bed," he commented without inflection.

Her giggling response reassured him. He had no intention of seducing young girls or of being accused of trifling with their affections. He had more than enough problems without involving himself with susceptible adolescents. He should have known better than to agree to this mad charade with a volatile miss like this one. Neither one of them had any sense of propriety, and the result could only be disaster. As the elder, he had only himself to blame. He ever was one for acting without thinking. He would see her delivered safely to her uncle and be far gone before another day passed. There must be other means of accomplishing his goals besides playing with fire.

"How will you know when Uncle John arrives?" A soft voice murmured sleepily from beneath his arm.

"Alvan has a very distinctive whistle. He'll let us know."

"Us, and half the world." She smiled softly, remembering the piercing shriek she had so admired when she was younger.

When she said no more, Austin let the subject rest. He kept his ears tuned for any change in the sounds below. A bar across a door was very little protection should anyone decide to force an entrance. He felt inclined to believe they were safe, but he had learned to take no chances. He would remain on guard until help arrived.

After a while, Aubree's even breathing told him she slept. He smiled to himself as a small hand curled upon his chest, and she shifted her position to rest more comfortably against him. It had been a very long time since he had held a woman like this. He had not realized how much he missed the gentle give and take of genuine affection. The women he had held these past years had only one purpose, and affection had no part in it. Perhaps he needed to reconsider his solitude. There were women enough out there who would be glad for a roof over their heads and a man in their bed. He would just have to refrain from choosing among the better classes of society.

That thought angered him no small amount, and he deliberately stopped thinking. He listened for the sounds of the night that would warn him of another's approach and prepared for the confrontation to come. A bloody battle would serve his mood nicely.

Toward dawn, Austin's vigilance was rewarded. The sound of a horse galloping through the woods gradually intruded upon his consciousness. He puzzled over the fact that he heard only one horse and waited impatiently for Alvan's signal, but none came.

Cursing to himself, he gently lay Aubree's sleeping figure against the pillows and rose from the bed. He had no intention of being caught in this compromising position. If help had arrived, he would make his departure now.

Despite his lameness, he moved silently, Austin judged from the lack of sound below that all slept. Perhaps Alvan had taken it upon himself to seek the key that would free them and had deserted his post.

Austin could find no sign of Alvan in the shrubbery

below, but the faint whicker of their horses in the
woods told him he couldn't have gone far. The galloping hooves came closer, from somewhere on the other
side of the house where he could not see.

He had expected Lord John to ride to Ashbrook
and gather men there. That would mean coming in by
the north road he could see from the window. Whoever
this rider was, he came from the south, from the
direction of London.

His fingers clenched the hilt of his sword. Perhaps
he would be lucky enough to come face to face with
the bastard who had engineered this little plot. He
grew tired of fighting nameless tormentors. It would
be extremely pleasant to run this one through with
steel.

An explosion of noise from the direction of the
kitchens warned of the horseman's arrival. Austin sent
one last glance in the direction of the shrubbery and
the road. He thought he detected some movement at
the corner of the house and a cloud of dust farther
down the road bore promise, but there wasn't time to
follow it. The sound of a gun barking and running
footsteps drew him away.

Aubree raised up on one elbow as Austin strode
toward the door. A quick gesture warned her to silence, and following his silent command, she dropped
behind the bed. Austin stationed himself behind the
door where he could not be seen immediately by anyone attempting to enter.

The room had grown gray with dawn, and the sounds
below echoed noisily through the old lodge. Loud
voices, a scuffle, falling furniture, followed by the
hasty tramp of two pairs of boots up the wooden
stairs. Steel clashed on steel and a loud, rather dra-
matic scream bit the air.

From the window, Aubree recognized the piercing
shriek of Alvan's whistle and realized he had been
signaling for several minutes now. Austin seemed totally oblivious to the sound, his concentration bent on
the battle beyond the door. His sword was already out
of the scabbard and she held her breath as his fingers

closed about the bar. Surely, he did not mean to join the fray!

Over the mayhem outside the door, a welcome voice reached her. "Aubree! Let me in!"

"Geoffrey!" Aubree bounded from behind the bed and ran to help Austin slide the bar.

"Not so fast." Understanding more of the sounds outside the door than she, Austin caught her wrist and held her away. "There's something not right here."

"Austin, it's Geoffrey! They could be murdering him!" Aubree struggled frantically against his hold, her nails scratching at his impervious arm as she tried to reach the bar.

The thunderous tread of seemingly a thousand boots spilling into the downstairs hall served as background to Geoffrey's urgent cry. "Aubree, what are you doing? Open the door!" A fist beat against the wooden panel.

Muttering curses, Austin threw a swift look to the window, a million miles away.

"Austin, let me go!" With a sudden twist, Aubree jerked free and flung the bolt, and all thought of escape was lost.

The roar of a commanding voice echoed up the stairwell. "Who in hell is that stripling and where is my daughter? John, send men after those cowards running out the back. Aubree, where are you?"

"Oh, my word," Aubree barely squeaked out as the door flew open and she shrank back against Heathmont at the sight revealed.

Resigned to his fate now that Pandora's box was open, Austin caught her by the wrist, and sword still in hand, came face to face with the handsome Geoffrey as the door swung wide.

"You!" The handsome features turned cold with astonishment as he took in a disheveled Aubree caught familiarly in the arms of the notorious Earl of Heathmont. The earl's stony expression as he pointed his sword downward sent a shiver of dismay down the guilty young man's back.

"Aubree, what in hell is this?" The duke arrived at the top of the stairs and gave Geoffrey a look of disdain. Several powerful hands reached out to remove the younger man from between his grace and his daughter. His grace then turned a cold glare on the man holding his daughter with one arm and a sword in the other. Midnight eyes remained implacable as Austin made no attempt to relinquish either burden.

Hiding her fear, Aubree stepped bravely away from Austin, allowing him to sheathe his sword as she confronted her father.

"I can assure you, I do not know what happened below," she spoke clearly and without hesitation, "but you have no right to treat Geoffrey like that. He has only come to rescue me."

Silence reigned in the direction of the young lord, who hung between the heavy hands of several of the duke's gamekeepers. His grace cast the culprit a contemptuous glare.

"Let the whelp go. If he follows his playmates out there, I'll not press charges."

Free from painful grips, Geoffrey stood his ground and protested vehemently. "What about *him?*" He pointed at the earl lounging lazily against the door frame, his weight resting heavily on his good leg, though none but Aubree noticed.

Austin's eyes swept insultingly over Geoffrey's elegantly costumed figure, not a cuff out of place for all his loudly fought havoc. With contempt, they left the young lord's spotless waistcoat and turned to meet the duke's condemnation without flinching.

"That's obvious. He'll be standing before an altar by sundown tomorrow," the duke replied scathingly, holding the icy-blue stare with ease.

Aubree's shriek of outrage drowned out Geoffrey's feeble protests as he was peremptorily guided toward the stairs. Austin and the duke, however, made no move to end their battle of wills. They glared at each other impassively as Aubree broke through them and ran after her suitor.

"Averill, catch her," the duke commanded to the young man hovering in the background, not bothering to follow his daughter's flight.

"I suggest we talk." Austin unfolded himself and stood upright, putting his gaze on a level with the duke's.

Averill took one look at the grim set of two jaws and fled after Aubree, leaving his father to deal with the tempers that would soon flare.

Geoffrey had disappeared by the time Aubree reached the front drive. With no other goal in mind, she ran toward the nearest horse, determined she would not stay in this madhouse a moment longer. Her father had no intention of listening to reason. She had seen that mood in him before. She felt no guilt in deserting Austin. He could deal with her father easier than she, and even better if she were not there.

A horse not equipped for sidesaddle presented certain problems, but she managed to mount herself with the help of a low lying wall. Averill's shout behind her only served to spur her on.

She had a good lead on her cousin as she turned down the road bearing south, but her mount was already winded by the run from Ashbrook. She urged it on, but Averill obviously had discovered a fresher horse and quickly gained on her.

Still, there was nothing he could do to make her turn back. Aubree relented her pace somewhat and stared coldly at her cousin as he caught up with her.

"I'm not going back, Alvan. You are wasting your time."

Averill studied his young cousin with sinking heart. He recognized the wildfire in her eyes and knew better than to combat the flames before they died out of their own accord. Once her temper was roused, Aubree became impossible to handle.

"You would have done better to waste *your* time with a brush and comb before you opened that door back there," Averill informed her hotly.

Aubree's hand flew to the curls tumbling wildly down her neck and her gaze traveled downward over the remains of her wrinkled riding habit. She looked as if she had slept in her clothes. As she had.

She hid her dismay as she looked up again. "I fell asleep. There is nothing wrong with that."

"Explain that to all the men who saw you open the bedroom door with Heath's arm around you. You gave your father little choice."

"Nothing *happened*, Alvan," she wailed desperately. "Geoffrey would believe me. Why did he have to send Geoffrey away? Surely Geoffrey would be a more suitable husband than Austin."

Even as she said it, she felt a prickle of doubt, but she managed to squelch it by kicking her horse to a more spirited canter. She was starving and weary and dirty, but she had no intention of ever turning back.

Averill kept apace with her. If she would not turn back, he must follow to keep her safe. The question about Geoffrey left him groping for words. He had seen more of that inane performance than anyone, but how did you explain to a lovesick child that the man she loved had her kidnapped by playactors? That was the only conclusion he could draw from the performance he had witnessed.

"I wouldn't be too certain of that," he replied gruffly.

Aubree sent him a look askance at this unusual tone of voice from her studious cousin, but she did not question him. Turning her chin up stubbornly, she continued riding toward home.

Averill continued doggedly at her side. She had to stop sometime. She couldn't go on like this forever.

It seemed very much like she meant to as the morning wore on and the stubborn glint in her eyes never once dimmed. They passed through one small village, and Averill offered to stop and buy her some eggs, but Aubree made no reply. She had her heart set on returning home to Hampshire and nothing would sway her.

The furious gallop of a horse down the road behind them drew a worried look from Aubree as she glanced over her shoulder. She had not seriously considered pursuit since Alvan was with her. But the sight of only one rider reassured her. Her father would have sent half an army.

Guiding her horse to the edge of the road to allow the other rider to pass easily, she continued her pace. She wished she knew where Geoffrey had gone. If he hadn't disappeared so quickly, they could have headed north to Scotland together. She felt a twinge of disappointment at Geoffrey's lack of perseverance.

To her surprise, the rider behind them seemed to be slowing his pace, and when Alvan did the same, she grew immediately suspicious. Turning, she spied Heathmont bearing down on them.

Her first thought was to spur her horse on rather than face him again, but common sense told her it would be to no avail. He was riding that huge bay stallion of his, and it had had all night to rest and graze. Her nag was thoroughly winded already. She came to a halt beside Alvan and silently awaited her fate.

Austin gave his friend a furious glare as he jerked his mount to a halt in front of them. "I thought you had more sense than to help the little brat."

Alvan grew indignant. "Did you truly think the brat would listen to me? She's had her way for too long to listen to reason. I figured the best I could do was keep her from more trouble."

This admission that a seventeen-year-old child was more than a grown man could handle did not lessen Austin's aggravation, but he turned it to another direction.

Facing Aubree, he demanded, "What did you think you would gain by running away? This is nonsense. Your father is in even a worse humor than before, if that is possible. Let's go back and get this straightened out before he has us all thrown in the dungeons."

Aubree glared at him mutinously. "You do not know him as I do. When he makes up his mind, there is no swaying him. You would do better to find a ship and sail for distant shores. I, for one, have no intention of returning to listen to him prate nonsense. I am going home."

She kicked her tired mare into a canter, a spurt of dust flying up at her heels as she rode off. Austin cursed and spurred his horse after her.

Grabbing Aubree's reins, Austin brought her tired horse to a halt, and leaning over, he lifted her kicking, squirming figure from the saddle.

"Austin, you can't do this," Aubree screamed as he plumped her down over his knee, his arm firmly planted about her middle so she could not escape his iron hold.

As Averill rode up, Austin threw him the reins of Aubree's horse. "Here. You take this nag back while I take the other."

In a fury of frustration and outrage, Aubree beat against his chest. Austin merely spurred his stallion into a canter back the way they had come. Deprived of transportation and aid, hungry and tired and with nowhere else to turn, Aubree had no other recourse but tears. They fell furiously as Austin continued to ignore her pleas.

When she finally collapsed against his chest in gulping sobs, Austin's arm gentled its hold, but his voice still held the sting of scorn.

"You are behaving like a child, Aubree. If you mean to marry anyone, you had best grow up quickly. Running away never solves any problems. I speak from considerable experience, so I hope you are listening."

In between sobs, she gulped, "I don't want to marry anyone! I want to go home to Hampshire and my pets. I hate London and I hate my father and I hate society. Why can't they all just leave me alone!"

Her fury came through even through the tears, and Austin had to smile at the tirade. There had been times when he felt very much the same, but he had never been given the pleasure of venting it in such a manner. Perhaps he would have been better off if he had ranted and raged instead of retaining a gentlemanly stoicism until all his anger exploded at once, always too late for all concerned. With this virago about, he might soon have the chance to find out.

"If you will calm down and stop acting like a silly child, that very well might be arranged, but I doubt if you will enjoy such isolation for long. Can you not trust me to explain things to your father?"

Aubree threw back her head and stared up at him through the glitter of tears. The shock of meeting his midnight eyes at this proximity jolted her into realizing her position. Austin's sun-darkened face beneath the tumble of chestnut curls viewed her dispassionately, as very well he should. Despite his reputation, he was a dashing lord of more years and sophistication than she could claim. To think her father could force a man like this to marry a green girl like herself was the height of lunacy. She forced a wobbly smile to her lips.

"Can you? Make him see reason, I mean? No one ever stands up to him, and when he sent Geoffrey away . . . It was my last chance," she explained, somewhat hazily.

Austin set her more comfortably in the saddle, well aware of the slightness of her waist in his arms and the full curve of a breast that had curled so softly against him moments before, while she appeared oblivious to any such feelings. A virgin and a lady to the core. How had he paired up with such innocence?

Knowing the fury that awaited them and remembering the amateur performance of swordsmanship he had heard outside the door that morning, Austin felt his way carefully over uncertain ground.

"This Geoffrey, do you truly love him enough to marry him? Or is he just your means of escaping your father?"

"Oh, I don't know." Aubree pouted, curling up closer against the strong chest shielding her from the world. "He is fun to be with, and he doesn't mind when I say things I oughtn't, and he has an estate in the country and would not expect me to entertain London society if I did not want. I think I could love him well enough if Father would let me."

That was not the answer he sought, but the one he expected. It in no way made things easier for him. The sound of Alvan galloping up behind them did not relieve the tension, either.

Austin sent his friend a questioning look at the absence of the mare he had been assigned.

Averill gave his cousin a meaningful glance. "I left the other nag at the inn. If you are going to carry her back like that, I thought you might prefer a more legitimate excuse."

Alvan's sarcastic tone caused Aubree to sit up and stick her tongue out at him. Austin nearly fell from his horse with laughter at this childish but—to him—highly appropriate response. Alvan's answering scowl produced a wider grin.

"You are both behaving like a couple of pampered brats. I don't suppose you thought to trade the nag for some food while you were there? I could eat the damned thing about now."

Instead of being shocked by Heath's profanity, Aubree giggled and watched her cousin expectantly. Despite his slenderness, Alvan had been known to consume vast quantities of victuals at every meal. And his last meal must have been some while ago.

Alvan gestured to the pouch slung over his pommel. "Fresh bread, meat, cheese, and ale. I thought perhaps you two had other things on your mind besides your stomachs."

While Aubree reproachfully cried, "Alvan," Austin quickly located the nearest grassy hillock and not so gallantly dropped her on it. Before she could protest, he was off his horse and appropriating the bag of food from his fickle friend.

As they all tore ravenously into the simple delicacies provided, Heath managed the last word through the crust of bread he chewed vigorously.

"I crave the simple pleasures of life, Bereford. Ravishing as she might be, your lady cousin here is far from simple. Now close your dirty mind and eat quickly. I fancy I have some hard talking to do."

6

Aubree paced up and down the parlor floor, occasionally checking her hairpin in the gilded mirror above the mantel. She had scrounged up a brush and comb and put it into some semblance of order, but without a ribbon to hold it back, she feared it would never meet her father's standards. She stuck her tongue out at the childish image reflected there, wishing for a proper nose so she might look down it like a real lady, instead of the pert slant that made her appear even younger than she was.

She tucked her shirt in more tightly and checked the buttons of her jacket one more time. She could do nothing about the wrinkles in her skirt, but at least her jacket had survived safely unrumpled. Perhaps if she could give the appearance of responsibility and maturity, her father would listen to her pleas.

A knock at the door gave cause for one further hasty pat before she gave permission to enter. Heathmont had been closeted with her father for hours, and from the angry voices that occasionally reached her ears, the interview did not go well. Judging by the politeness of the rap, she thought that perhaps some equitable settlement had been reached. Surely her father had calmed down enough to see reason.

Heathmont entered at her call, his dark face drained of all emotion as he sought her slender figure in the dusty dimness of the curtained parlor. With her hair falling down her back in that fashion, she looked no more than a schoolgirl, and his lips tightened in anger. Striding stiffly into the room without a coat, his cravat untied, he looked the part of rake or worse.

Aubree held herself rigid. "What is it, my lord? Surely he believes you. Alvan can vouch for us."

"He believes me, I don't doubt." Heath limped forward, his eyes nearly black with anger. "You were right when you said he refuses to see reason, however. He is insistent that your reputation has received irreparable damage. I have been sent here to ask you formally for your hand in marriage."

Aubree heard him in terror, not believing his words. The grim expression on Austin's face verified her worst fears, and she lashed out at him with the fury of helplessness.

"How much did he offer you?" she demanded scornfully. "What is it worth to take a troublesome daughter off a duke's hands?"

Her scorn stung like a whip, but Austin did not

flinch beneath it. He deserved whatever she meted out. His anger was as much at himself as with the man waiting in the other room.

"He has offered sufficient to keep you comfortable for many years." He strode toward the window, avoiding the pain in Aubree's pale face. He had been offered whole new worlds, at her expense. It wasn't fair, but very little in this world was fair. He stared glumly out upon the landscape.

Aubree felt the cold chill of fear creeping along her spine as she stared at Austin's stiffly erect back. She had been warned of his reputation, but she had not heeded the warnings. She still could not believe this stranger standing there was the man who had held her so tenderly last night. This man was cold and callous and she could not marry him, not ever.

"Well, I am sorry to disappoint you, but I cannot accept," she informed him coldly.

"You have no choice, no more than I." Austin swung around to find her slight figure in the gloom. She hovered like a ghost in the shadows of the far corner, her fawn riding habit only a blur against the wooden furnishings. "Your reputation has been compromised whether or not anything went between us. Your father is right in that. My reputation is of the sort for society to expect the worst. I cannot think that marriage to me will right the wrong, but I am compelled to offer."

"And I am compelled to refuse."

He had expected this, but he had no easy argument prepared. "Aubree, I will give you the choices that have been given me. At least listen before you give me your answer. The choices are not pretty, but I will respect your decision. I cannot do otherwise, for I have nothing at all to offer you."

Aubree started at this admission, her gaze searching for the truth in Heathmont's face. He did not plead with her, but stated his case baldly. She read his anger, but recognized his honesty.

"That is a curious proposal, my lord. How is it my father chooses a man with nothing at all to offer me?"

Heath's fingers clenched into a fist as he gazed into

her questioning face. He preferred to face her fury to her reasonableness. "I don't know. I have tried to talk him out of his foolishness, but he is convinced your happiness is at stake. He knows he has not raised you as he ought, and he has somehow got it into his head that a husband is what you need. After last night, it seems likely mine will be the only offer you will receive."

Unsteadily, Aubree sank into the nearest chair, not bothering to remove the Holland cover. She still had not come to terms with how she had come to be in this place. How would she ever make sense of this new development?

"Perhaps you should explain our . . . choices," she ventured fearfully.

The earl began to pace, unmindful of the halt in his gait as he strode from mantel to door and back again, his fists clenched and his jaw muscle twitching.

"First, I must tell you what I told your father." Austin straightened and glanced about, finding a straight-backed chair and dragging it in front of her. Sitting, he strove desperately for the words to explain his plight.

"It is not just a matter of age. Your father was considerably older than your mother, and they got along tolerably well, as he pointed out." That wasn't how he meant to start, and he waved a hand to dismiss the point and bring forth another. "I have been married before. You knew that, didn't you?"

Aubree gazed at him steadily, her heart pounding in frightening knocks as she studied Austin's face. The skin over the sharp angles of his nose and cheekbones strained in a fierce expression that frightened her, but she nodded sagely.

"My wife died within two years of our marriage. We were both very young. Too young. I can assure you there is no truth to the rumors about us, but there are exceedingly few who will believe me. It has ceased to matter to me, but any wife of mine would bear the brunt of my shame. I cannot ask a child such as you to live as an outcast, as I have."

Since he evidently did not intend to enlighten her on

the matter of the rumors, Aubree could say nothing. A scandal from years ago seemed ancient history and could scarcely affect her as the one threatening her now.

Wrapped in his own concerns, Heathmont did not expect a reply, but continued, "My father left his estates threadbare; the coffers empty, the land ruined. I was only a few years older than you when he died, but I tried to make the lands pay."

He rose abruptly, pulling at his cravat as if he would rip it from him and throw it aside. He did not, however, but his expression grew fiercer as he attempted to finish his tale while pacing the room.

"My wife went through her dowry and what little I made very quickly. When she died, I scraped together enough to buy into the cavalry. Every cent I could squeeze out of every opportunity offered, I sent to my father-in-law to repay his daughter's dowry. After Corunna, I returned home, but there has not been time enough for me to rebuild what was lost. There have been . . . mishaps that have destroyed everything I have done. The place is in rack and ruin, Aubree, no place for a gently bred lady."

Aubree had to succumb to a wry smile. "You do not have to convince me of your unsuitability as a husband, my lord. I am quite willing to cry off, if you are."

A raw grin broke through the pain of Austin's recitation as he turned to the young girl perched on the edge of her seat. She never *sat* properly on anything; she always seemed in position to take flight. It did not relieve the pain of his decision, but lightened his mood. She always succeeded in accomplishing that.

"If it were only that simple, my dear, I would not have bored you with the details. However, now that you know some small part of my plight, let me show you our choices."

He returned to the chair and studied her anxious features. He was unwilling to paint the picture as black as her father had made it, but he had to make her see the impossibility of any other choice.

"Your father insists I have ruined your reputation

and as a gentleman I must offer to marry you. If I in any way thought I would be helping you by doing so, I would jump at the chance, but as I have pointed out to you, and to your father, marriage to me would scarcely settle your problems."

"What about Geoffrey?" She grasped at straws eagerly.

"I suggested that, but he has taken your Geoffrey into dislike. There is no persuading him on that ground." He did not mention his own doubts on Geoffrey's suitability. To antagonize her would serve no purpose. "Your father has suggested a sizable dowry and your inheritance might go a long way toward recouping my losses." At the angry retort he saw forming on her lips, Austin frowned, and for once, she kept silent. "I told him no amount of money would buy my agreement to what I considered to be a travesty of justice for you."

Hope leapt to her eyes and Aubree clasped her hands eagerly in her lap. "Then that settles it. He cannot force us to marry if we neither agree to it. This is not the Dark Ages, after all."

A sad smile crossed the earl's bronzed features at her eagerness to be quit of him. "It is not quite so simple as that, halfling. Your father has seen fit to have me investigated thoroughly. He knows everything about me, including the reason I have been attempting to contact him these past weeks."

Instant suspicion appeared behind her glare. "You were using me to reach my father, just like all the others!"

"Just as you were using me. That is not the point." Austin waved aside her protest. "The point is that if we marry, he will help me gain my goal. A man's life is at stake, a man with a wife and small children."

"But my life is at stake, too," Aubree protested heatedly. "Why should I trade my life for someone I don't know? You may agree to this madness, but I will not! He cannot force me to take those vows. I will not!"

Austin sighed. He had hoped to avoid what he must tell her now. He had not handled this very well, perhaps because it was a little like waking to find all his dreams had come true. He still felt dazed by the swiftness of this reversal in his heretofore ill fortunes—at this child's expense. He still could not accept that, but he had been cut off at every corner. He had nowhere else to turn.

He delayed telling her the worst by appealing to her better nature. "You have not even asked what man's life you would be saving or why. You have a rather distracting habit of leaping over details without surveying the ground beyond. It will get you into trouble one day."

As it already had, Aubree had the sense to realize. She shrugged aside this warning, however. "It must be someone important to you for you to seek out my father. I'm sorry."

There wasn't a repentant note in her voice, but Austin understood that. "I realize it is of little concern to you, but my family is very small, and my mother and my sister are very important to me. I have been a disappointment to them in many ways, but now, in this, I feel I can help. If there is no other choice for you, you might at least consider what your answer means to my family."

She looked puzzled. "I do not understand. Besides my inheritance, in what way can I help your family?"

Austin's lips quirked upward at one corner. "I fear my mother is beyond our help. She lives in her own world and my concern is not for her, although she would greatly approve if I should bring home a wife. It is my sister who needs my aid."

He rose again, limping to lean on the mantel and stare out the window. "I have been involved in several shipping ventures with an American with British ties. On one of his journeys over here, he met my sister, and they were married not long after. They are a few of the lucky ones who marry for love without regard to anything else, and they have been singularly blessed to remain that way."

He turned and Aubree could almost feel the sadness she read in his face. Her heart went out to him, but she had no knowledge of how to show it. She kept silent, thinking he and his sister must have been very close.

"Her husband was born here, but he was raised and has his home in Virginia. He is by all rights a citizen of the United States and not England. Yet, after an encounter with a press gang from a British frigate, he was impressed into the service of His Majesty's Royal Navy."

Aubree stared at him, trying to remember what she had heard of this old argument over the right of the navy to impress able-bodied men to service. She seemed to remember her father viewed the policy with scorn and had grown rather vehement about its effects on relations with the United States, but she had never clearly understood the consequences.

"Impressed, my lord?" she inquired, covering her confusion.

"Shanghaied, abducted, forced into slavery in the stinking galleys of rotting frigates where no sane man would go willingly. That is why they must sneak through the streets of coastal cities and carry off the dregs of humanity to man their ships. It is a criminal policy for British citizens, but to apply it to Americans is grounds for war. We will see one soon enough if Parliament does not have the wisdom to put an end to it."

"You mean, they have abducted your brother-in-law and forced him to work as a sailor for the navy?" Puzzled at how this outrage could be allowed, Aubree sought interpretations.

"He is a sailor, and a fine one, but it is doubtful if they will make full use of his talents. Adrian has a singular knack for making trouble. He is hotheaded, stubborn, and rebellious as only a Virginian knows how to be. By now he will have promoted mutiny and been thrown in the brig or worse. My sister fears for his life and rightfully so. The conditions aboard some of those ships are inhuman. My sister is left with two small children in a foreign land with no idea of whether she will ever see her husband again. Your father is almost our last hope."

Aubree understood this part well. Her father had powerful connections within the navy. With only a

word from him, the ship could be found and returned
to port and the sailor released. A stirring of uneasiness
began in her stomach.

"My father has agreed to find this Adrian if we
marry?"

"He will use what powers he has to do so, or give
me a warrant to locate the ship and seek Adrian
myself. You see why I am torn by this decision he
forces on us." Without breaking stride, Austin finished, "I have agreed to his terms."

He met her gaze implacably. He would have married a penniless hag if he could accomplish his friend's
freedom and his sister's happiness. His life was worthless to anyone else. It would have been better if she
had been a penniless hag. As it was, he feared he
would destroy the life of this golden child in the process of saving another's.

Aubree's lips tightened as she realized what her
father had done, and rebellion simmered beneath the
surface calm. "But I have agreed to nothing, milord.
There may be other ways of obtaining the aid you seek
for your sister, but there is no other help for me. My
father cannot force this marriage if I refuse."

Austin gazed at her sadly, knowing the time had
come to give her the final blow. He could delay no
longer. "We both have the right to refuse, halfling,
but the cost is so high you will have difficulty meeting
it." He watched as those wide green eyes turned questioningly on him, and he broke the news gently. "You
have told me of your home in Hampshire, part of your
mother's estate, I believe. Your Aunt Clara resides
there when she is not with you?"

Aubree nodded wonderingly, the uneasiness in the
pit of her stomach growing more painful. "It is her
childhood home. She returned there to raise my mother
after my uncle died. She stayed on to look after me. It
is a beautiful place, though less grand than my father's
home."

Still not daring to touch her, Austin returned to his
seat and sought for words to make this final blow a
little easier. "As I understand it, the Hampshire estate
came to your mother through your grandfather, not

your grandmother, so it is not part of the inheritance that comes to you on your birthday."

With sudden clarity, she saw the path he took, but she refused to believe it until the words were spoken openly. "No one has ever explained to me what I will inherit. I never considered it of great importance."

Austin nodded approvingly. Born to wealth, she had no grasping instinct as did his first wife. Greed had no part of Aubree's nature. "The Hampshire estate became your father's upon his marriage to your mother. That is the way the law reads. He can do with it as he will."

Pain struck with a forceful blow that nearly bent Aubree in two. He could not do this. He would not. She raised her eyes hopefully to midnight-blue ones, and the pity there nearly put an end to her composure. Unable to speak, she waited for the deathblow.

Austin could not resist any longer. He took Aubree's hands between his before reciting patiently, "He claims he will sell the Hampshire estate and refuse you entrance to any of his other homes. He has the power to make it very difficult for Alvan or your uncle if they tried to take you in. They might disobey him, but the consequences of such a family feud would not be pretty."

"He would not sell Aunt Clara's home. I cannot believe that. After all she has done." Aubree's voice went flat, displaying none of the emotion the words described. Her gaze wandered into space and she seemed unaware that he continued to hold her hands.

Austin watched her with concern, fearful the tragedies of this day had been too much for the child. The color had fled her cheeks and, with it, the indomitable spirit he had thought her to possess. For the first time, he realized how delicate she was. The bounding zest for life that seemed so much a part of her served to disguise the frailness of her slender figure. He remembered how weightlessly she had drifted in his arms when they danced and understood why. She seemed created of some fragile porcelain, too delicate for one such as he to touch. The long, slender fingers captured within his palms could easily be crushed, there seemed so little strength in them. He stroked them gently, waiting for her reply.

Of a sudden, the light returned to her eyes, and Aubree turned lanterns of maliciousness toward him. Unsmiling, she asked, "What do you know of annulments?"

It was Austin's turn to feel uneasy. "I am not a solicitor. I cannot tell you details. But I believe there must be extenuating circumstances involved."

Aubree skimmed over his evasive politeness. "If we do not live together as man and wife, would that not be grounds for annulment?"

"Possibly so, Aubree, but your father . . ."

"Will do everything in his power to see the marriage consummated. But he would certainly not stoop to the practice of having us watched, like royalty." She spoke daringly of topics of which she should have no knowledge, but the effect on her listener was instantaneous.

Austin dropped his hands and stood up, beginning to pace nervously as he followed her thoughts. He had contemplated allowing her to remain in Hampshire while he returned to his home and made it ready for her, but not once had it occurred to him to sacrifice his marital rights. He wanted children, but even more, he now realized, he wanted Aubree. That painful realization shattered his thought processes, leaving him open to suggestion.

"I would not put that past him," Austin stated roughly, angered at this new position he found himself in. "But even so, there are other means of knowing. Your father is no fool. If this has occurred to you, it will occur to him, also."

"But he thinks I am a silly miss with no knowledge of these matters. And he must know you would never suggest such an alternative. He must be reasonably confident of success or he would never have gone this far. If we can make him believe what he wants to believe . . ."

Austin interrupted with abruptness. "I see now what Alvan meant when he warned me not to stand between the two of you. You have a mind just like his, Aubree, and I am not at all certain that I like it."

"All the more reason you should agree with me," she replied tartly. "We scarcely know each other. The difference in our ages alone is enough to foresee disaster. I daresay you prefer more sophisticated, experienced women than a country girl who prefers animals for companions. I will not interfere with your affairs, if you will but agree to an annulment when I turn eighteen. By then, surely your brother-in-law will be returned to you, and if my father threatens to sell Aunt Clara's home again, I will have the means to buy it. It is perfect and will serve him right."

Austin glared at her smug expression. "Have you given any thought to your reputation if you go through with this? The scent of scandal will scare off all but the fortune-hunters. You will never live it down. The gossip might give you entrance to society again, but only as a curiosity. You will be eighteen years old with no future ahead of you. Aubree, think what you are saying!"

Jade eyes turned mutinous. "I am saying I will live my life as I choose and not as my father wishes or society dictates. If you are worried about losing the dowry, I will repay it myself. You will gain all he has promised and be relieved of the nuisance of my presence within half a year. Surely that is a better bargain than my father offers?"

This interview was not going at all well. Heath felt he had handled the duke better than this treacherous little she-devil. If it were not for his background, he would take her over his knee and beat some sense into her. Frail, indeed! She had taught him one lesson this day: strength of character outweighed any physical weakness.

"I do not need your charity, thank you," he informed her icily. "In six months, I can more than double your dowry, with any luck at all. I am only thankful that I will not have a lifetime to spend pulling you out of sordid scrapes. I am grateful for your consideration, milady." He bowed sarcastically, his shoulders straining at his shirt seams. "May I return to his grace and say you have accepted my offer?"

Stung by his sarcasm, Aubree replied coldly, "As

long as I can trust your word as a gentleman to keep our agreement."

A sardonic smile lifted the earl's lips as his gaze raked over her proud figure. "As a gentleman, my dear, I give you my word."

Why did she feel, as he strode out, that he had got the better of this bargain?

7

Before the day was out, the marriage arrangement had been hammered out to the satisfaction of both men. With Castle Ashbrook close at hand, they prepared to remove there to await the final details before the marriage could take place. The wedding might not be carried out by sunset of this day as threatened, but certainly within the week.

Messengers flew north and south, carrying directions for special licenses, newspaper notices, solicitors, relatives, and of course, a suitable churchman to carry out the formalities. Before Alvan departed, he stopped to see if Aubree had any missives to be sent.

He found her sitting in the window of the upstairs room where she had spent the night. Her golden hair fell forward over her rumpled shirt as she sat pensively staring at the shrubbery below.

"Aubree?" When she did not look up, Alvan stepped farther into the room. "Is there anything I should tell your Aunt Clara? Some gowns you want sent? Men have no notion of how to plan a wedding, and I fear they will forget something of importance to you."

When she looked up at this, he could see the glitter of tears in her eyes, and he nearly fell backward in astonishment. Aubree had been a hellion since she was old enough to toddle, but always a happy one.

She had taken her share of scrapes and bruises and suffered the blame for her escapades without batting an eyelash. Occasionally, he had caught her crying over a dead bird or some such, but never for herself. Guilt colored his reaction.

"I don't suppose anyone considered love or affection, did they?" she asked wryly, through a veil of tears. "Do you think they can be bought in time for the wedding?"

"Aubree . . ." Alvan stepped forward, offering his hand helplessly. "If I could help in any way . . . You are welcome to stay with Peggy and me, you know you are. I would not see you unhappy. But I thought you and Heath . . . I mean, you seemed to *like* each other so well."

She grimaced and waved away his hand. "He likes me well enough as a plaything to keep him amused. I suppose we shall suit. Do not worry over me. Just tell Aunt Clara to send whatever she thinks necessary. I trust I will find a few things at Ashbrook so I will not have to wear this"—she made a face at her ruined riding habit—"much longer. Give Peggy my love and tell her I wish she could be here. She would make a lovely matron of honor."

Alvan vowed silently never to raise a word of complaint against his cousin again. She might have more temerity than a pride of lions, but she had equal amounts of courage. He offered a tentative smile for her benefit.

"I told Heath he needed a good wife like mine. He did me one better, I think. He's a good man, Aubree. Don't wear him down."

Remembering the earl's scorn of this afternoon, she thought it might be a little late for that advice, but it made no difference now. She gave Alvan a smile, and after a brief hesitation, he left.

Below, he discovered Heath lying in wait for him. Tired lines etched the earl's face and Alvan suspected his friend's game leg was paining him, but Austin made no mention of this as he handed Alvan several sealed messages.

"I am not allowed to venture beyond the duke's

boundaries," Austin explained with a twist of his lips. "If you would carry these to my groom, he will see them delivered."

"Of course, but I thought all these things went out with my uncle's men." Alvan hefted the lengthy missives before slipping them into his coat pocket.

"There were a few things I preferred to see to myself. His grace has only one thing on his mind at the moment, and his daughter's desires aren't among them. You won't mind a few extra passengers coming back?"

Alvan grinned, beginning to follow the drift of this conversation. "I can round up enough carriages to transport half London if you'd like."

"I had Hampshire more in mind. You would know whom to call upon . . ."

A gleam devilishly similar to Aubree's danced in Alvan's eyes. "I'll see it done. It may not be a proper courtship, but it will be one hell of a wedding."

They parted on an amicable basis, but Austin's mood did not carry over to their departure from the lodge for the castle. The hired hack that had carried Aubree here was brought out and surrounded by a half-dozen of the duke's men. Austin scowled at this entourage and turned in time to catch the rebellious expression on his fiancée's face as she, too, spied the carriage.

Her father spoke some word to a gamekeeper and strode rapidly across the lawn to join them. The sun had lowered well into the west and shadows prevented reading his expression as he approached, but Austin felt Aubree's jerk of indignation beside him. Before he could say anything, she was off and down the stairs, aiming for a horse that had been left riderless.

"Aubree," the duke shouted, gesturing for one of his men to interfere with her path.

"Leave her be." Angrily, Austin jerked down the steps and appropriated the reins of his own mount, swinging himself up effortlessly as he returned the duke's glare. Aubree had managed to seat herself and now urged her horse into a canter.

"You'll be chasing after her half the night again," his grace sputtered furiously.

"You don't know your daughter very well," Heathmont replied quietly, following the path of Aubree's escaping horse with his eyes. She rode exceedingly well, even in the awkward position forced upon her by a man's saddle.

"I think I'm in a position to know her better than you, sir," the duke answered harshly.

The earl glanced downward at his irate father-in-law-to-be. "Then you should know she keeps her word. She may not like it, but she has promised to marry me. She will be there waiting for us."

"She'll keep her word, no doubt," the duke fumed, "but the manner in which she keeps it is what worries me. You promise to get her to that altar and I'll trust in that."

"I promise." Heath sent a worried look in the direction Aubree had disappeared. He, too, had doubts about the manner in which she would keep her word.

By the time they reached the castle, Aubree had returned and retired to her chambers, leaving word for her meal to be sent up to her.

In the ancient grandeur of Castle Ashbrook, the earl could better glimpse the royal upbringing that had been Aubree's. The hall that formed the main entrance was regally adorned with heavy tapestries woven by Bereford women of long ago. Vaunted arches and stained-glass windows dated to a time when soldiers wore the suits of armor now guarding stately corners.

Servants scuttled to and fro, silently anticipating the duke's every need as they brought messages from London, lit fires, and poured wine. Excusing himself, feeling exceedingly grubby after spending two days and a night in the same clothes, Heathmont followed a housekeeper to an elegantly furnished upper-story chamber.

Staring at the paneled walls and velvet draperies, the earl felt a moment's foreboding. Aubree might call herself a simple country girl, but she had never known an instant's discomfort in her life. She was accustomed to luxury well beyond his means. Her father had assumed he would use her dowry and inheritance to simulate this wealth in her new home, but he had assumed wrongly. That money belonged to Aubree, not Atwood Abbey. Austin intended to invest it wisely so it might return sufficient income to ease his financial crisis while leaving the sum intact to return to Aubree six months hence. That would not pay for elegance.

Dissatisfied with the path of his thoughts, Austin stripped off his soiled shirt and began to wash. Half a year, she had said. With any luck, that would take him into October. He would do well to pin down the exact date of her birthday.

The following day, Aubree went out of her way to avoid everyone. The energetic hustle and bustle below told of the preparations being made in her behalf, but she had no interest in them. The activity in the stable yard was no less with messages going to and fro, carts of food being unloaded, and packages arriving from hither and yon. Her father had evidently stirred up quite a hornet's nest by his haste for this wedding.

Staring out her window, she watched Heathmont's well-set figure ride out. His coat had evidently been cleaned and pressed since she had last seen him, and he had apparently located someone's shaving gear, but that was not what impressed her. He seemed to suppress as much energy as his barely controlled stallion as he kept to a canter for the sake of the groom accompanying him. He seemed ready to burst at the seams with the need to vent all that pent-up vitality, yet he retained a remarkably steady composure. Aubree envied him that ability. She would have outdistanced the groom before the first bend in the road.

Aubree's self-imposed isolation ended that evening when the duke sought out his daughter in her chambers and discovered her staring over the moonlit landscape of the gardens below. She recognized his presence with an absentminded nod, then returned her blank gaze to the window.

"I know you think I am being cruel and unreasonable in forcing this marriage upon you, but it is your happiness I have in mind, Aubree. Your Aunt Clara and I have grown too old to chaperone you as you need to be, and you are much too young to look after yourself. This incident could have been much more tragic. I would prevent your coming to any harm."

Aubree turned to stare at her father searching for some sign of warmth and affection behind his effort to be reasonable, to no avail. He had learned to hide too well any emotion he might feel. He could be speaking with hatred as easily as love. She hung her head and stared at her slippered toe.

When she made no reply, the duke tried again. "From all reports, your Earl of Heathmont is a man of strong character and courage. Wellington has only praise for his actions in the years he spent over there." He held back the fact that the general had also said that Austin entered battle like a man who did not care whether he lived or died. That he had survived at all was a gesture of Divine Providence. "A man like that can protect you and keep you safe, Aubree."

Aubree sent her father a curious look. "Is that the basis for marriage then, Father? Protection?"

The duke shrugged. "It is as good a basis as any. You already possess a title and wealth. You need only someone to look after you. I think Heathmont has learned his lesson in that area."

A spark of interest entered jade eyes. "Learned his lesson? In what way?"

The duke smoothed over this *faux pas*. "It's no matter now. My only concern is that he make you happy. I think he can. Once you have a brood of children around you instead of your abominable animals, you will understand what I mean."

Aubree blushed and looked away. To have children by that man down there spoke of an intimacy she could not bring herself to consider. He was a stranger and would remain so, if she had anything to say about it.

Hesitating, the duke sought words of warning that would not frighten her. He could negotiate with men whose language he could not speak, but he could barely find the words with which to talk to his own daughter.

"Aubree, one thing: if you are not happy, if the earl offers you harm in any way, you are to return to me at once. Do you understand me?"

Remembering the hints from gossips about the earl's

reputation, Aubree met her father's gaze coldly. "You mean, if he beats me, I have your permission to leave him?"

Anger kindled at this response to his attempts to offer solace. "If he so much as lifts a hand to you, you have my permission to leave him. But if I discover you have given him some reason for his brutality, I will beat you myself. You are not too big yet for me to spank some sense into you."

"Thank you, Father, for your loving concern. I look forward most eagerly to this marriage with a man whose only recommendations are that he fights viciously in battle and has a reputation for beating his wives."

Stung more than he cared to admit by her hostility, the duke replied in fury, "Good. We've set the time for tomorrow at sunset. You will go to bed the Countess of Heathmont on the morrow."

Swinging on his heel, he strode out, leaving Aubree to stare panic-stricken at the closed door to her gilded chambers.

8

Trapped in this cage of her own making, Aubree had not the nerve to venture out the next day. She had given her word to Heathmont that she would go through with this mock ceremony, but the horses down by the stables had almost become a fixation with her. She longed to ride out of here and never be seen again.

She flung a lace-bedecked pillow against the satin-covered wall, allowing rage to take the place of tears. Since she had turned seventeen last September, she had been carried about from one party to another, introduced to more people than she had ever cared to know, and gowned and coiffed like some fashion doll from France. She had not had one moment to herself, and now she felt like the entire time had been one headlong rush down a precipice, gathering momentum for the crash to come.

Tonight would be the culmination of that precipitous fall. She did not even know the man she would stand beside and promise to love and obey. She had not even been told by whom or why she had been abducted in the first place. For all she knew, Heathmont had planned it all. She wouldn't put it past him. She felt quite certain he was capable of anything.

By the time the knock sounded on the door, she had almost persuaded herself that escape was essential. When she opened the door to find Aunt Clara on the other side, she threw herself into the older lady's arms with hysterical sobs of misery and joy.

"Aunt Clara, you came! I thought nobody would come. I thought he'd marry me off and send me away and I'd never see anybody ever again," she wailed, releasing just a few of the fears she had kept bottled up inside.

"My goodness, child! What fustian! Did you think I'd raised you all these years to see you wed and then miss the wedding? I cannot understand your father's haste. It is a lot of nonsense, of course, but if this is what everyone wants, well, we must do it proper."

Clara patted her niece's hand and led her to the bed, hiding her doubt and dismay from her distraught charge. "There, now, dry those eyes. We cannot have a bride with red eyes. It's just nerves. I almost hid in the attic on my wedding day. Absolutely terrified, and my Charles the sweetest thing alive. I would have been here sooner, only Alvan needed the carriage and Peggy wanted me to go with her and we've been at sixes and sevens trying to get all your things packed."

"Peggy? Is Peggy here?" Joy wrote itself across golden-hued features.

"Yes, of course. When she heard you wanted her here, a team of four couldn't have kept her away. She's lying down right now, but she is as eager as I am to thank—"

Another knock on the door intruded and Aubree leapt from the bed, trusting this surprise would be as pleasant as the last. She had feared her father had been so ashamed of her he would not invite anyone, but Alvan must have taken her side. Bless Alvan. She must remember not to be so hard on him.

A parade of footmen and maids carried in box after box from every dressmaker in town, it seemed. The last to arrive carried a familiar basket with three tiny heads peering eagerly over the side, and Aubree screamed with delight.

"My kittens! You brought my kittens! Oh, thank you, Aunt Clara. How can I thank you?" She raced to hug her aunt and back to the basket and danced about the room with glee, holding one tiny kitten after the other.

"Well, I'd thought, knowing how your father felt about animals, that perhaps it would have been better . . ."

But Aubree had already dived into the largest dressmaker's box and paid no attention, and Aunt Clara subsided. The young man evidently knew what he was about. The misery she'd seen on her niece's face had disappeared like magic, and she was wreathed in smiles as she pulled the gown from its wrapping of tissue. This was Aubree's day and the duke would simply have to endure a little bending of the rules for a while.

"How did you have a gown made so quickly, Aunt Clara? Look at these pearls—it must have taken days." Aubree spread the ivory satin across the covers, admiring the intricate detail of the seed-pearl design that wound through the bodice of satin and lace. The delicacy of the lace spoke of French origins, and she wondered in amazement at this. French lace had become impossible to obtain. How ever . . . ?

"Well, you remember we had already given orders for the ivory satin. Madame simply replaced the primrose netting with the lace and made a veil to match."

Another box lid opened to reveal acres of frothy lace, enough to carpet the room, certainly. Aunt Clara had not inquired too carefully into the origins of this wedding gift. Smuggling had become a necessity for these luxuries, but surely the young man . . .

"Oh, my!" Awestruck, Aubree lifted the delicate material from its bed of tissue. She had never owned anything so fine, and the elegance of it brought a lump to her throat. From this day forth, she would be entitled to wear silks and satins when she chose, instead of missish pastels and muslins. The lace was her first step into the world of womanhood.

Before she could cry again, a maid appeared in the doorway, waiting respectfully to be acknowledged before speaking. At Aubree's questioning look, she bobbed a curtsy.

"There's some come to see you, milady, but they have a package his lordship says is not to go abovestairs. Would you be so kind as to come down, he says."

Not knowing to which "lordship" the maid referred and not particularly caring, Aubree bounced happily into the corridor carrying two of the kittens, prepared for any number of surprises. Except the one meeting her at the foot of the stairs.

"Alexa!" she screamed, flinging her arms around the nervous girl standing in the hallway, her pelisse still over her shoulders and a small case at her feet.

The kittens meowed pitifully beneath this embrace, until unseen hands hastened to claim them.

A smile of relief flooded the older girl's undistinguished features as she returned the hug. "Oh, Aubree, I scarcely recognized you, so fine you've become. When his lordship said you would like us here, I worried."

Stepping back, but still clasping Alexa's hands, Aubree grinned her exuberant delight. "I never thought you would come all this way to see me, and on such short notice! Did your father object mightily?"

"He could not much object after the invitation he received from his lordship," a deep voice intruded, causing Aubree to spin about and give another cry of glee.

The stout young man looked mildly surprised as the slight feminine figure flew into his arms, but overall, he seemed quite pleased with himself when he returned Lady Aubree to her feet. A shadow lounging behind the stairs observed this scene with a mixture of disgruntlement and pleasure as he set the kittens loose upon the floor. Whatever had once gone between the young squire and the lady had been set aside with childhood. The two stared at each other now with pleasure and embarrassment.

"Everett! I cannot believe it! I knew you promised to dance on my grave, but you said nothing of coming to my wedding." Aubree giggled at the look of chagrin crossing the young man's face.

"I've played the husband's role enough to your nagging wife to enjoy watching some other poor gudgeon walk you down the aisle. I'll not ever forgive you that nettle tea you served me last time."

Both girls went into gales of laughter at the memory returned by the look of discomfort on Everett's round face. The shadow in the corner fidgeted restlessly over these childhood reminiscences. He nudged away the purring kittens. He had no desire to intrude, but he could not escape without being seen. Besides, he wanted to see Aubree's face when she spied the last of her visitors.

"Did Everett escort you all this way, then? How very gallant!" Aubree exclaimed with a secret smile to Alexa. The minister's daughter had harbored a secret *tendre* for the squire's son for years. Such an occasion as this seemed auspicious.

"His lordship's groom acompanied us to London. Then we stopped to pick up your maid. She has been highly insulted that you have been out adventuring without her skills. If Lady Clara had not insisted you could not do without Matilda to dress your hair for the wedding, you might well have been without any maid at all."

"Umph," Everett grunted at this excessiveness. "Besides, we have had a most effective chaperon in that useless spaniel of yours. She has sat in Alexa's lap all the way here."

"Lady?" Aubree squealed, her eyes growing wide with wonder. "You have brought Lady? Where? Where is she? I haven't seen her in forever and ever."

A staccato barking just outside at the sound of this

name sent Aubree flying to the door, followed by two kittens consumed with curiosity. At the same time the door flew open, the eager spaniel broke loose of her restraint and bounded happily up the stairs to greet her mistress.

Nearly bowled over by the dog's ecstatic leap, Aubree quickly dropped to the floor to gather her pet in her arms. The smile of joy upon her face satisfied the man lingering in the shadows, and while she was thus occupied, he took the opportunity to slip out the back way. He did not reckon on the pursuit of the two kittens who had befriended him.

Spying the kittens scurrying through the hall, Lady took up a frantic bark and, leaping from Aubree's arms, dashed gaily down the marble floor in hot pursuit. Just like old times.

Aubree screamed a warning, and Everett and Alexa, quite accustomed to this chaos, set chase, but too late for the man walking unsuspectingly away. Both kittens made flying leaps upon his back to escape the terror stalking them, and the spaniel did her best to follow. With his game leg crumpling under the weight of this final blow, the earl went sprawling across the polished floor.

Having heard the commotion, Alvan came racing down the stairs and whooped with glee at his friend's undignified pratfall. Nervously, Alexa and Everett hurried to help, but it was Aubree who firmly lifted the yelping spaniel from Heathmont's back, handing the animal to Everett for removal. The kittens had already scattered for parts unknown as she leaned to assist the earl to his feet.

Garbed only in linen shirt and buckskins now neatly coated with dust, Heathmont presented far from a formidable figure as he rose and bowed stiffly to the newcomers. The laughter in Aubree's eyes as her friends stood with curiosity before this stranger did not warn them. She shook her head at Alvan as he approached, and she proceeded with the introductions as her cousin looked on with interest

"I'm so sorry, Austin. We did not know you were about. I'd like you to meet Alexa Carlisle and Everett

Smith, from Hampshire. They're my oldest and dearest friends." Blithely ignoring Austin's title and his relation to herself, Aubree hurried on. "I trust you are not hurt. Poor Lady has been confined too long and is overeager for a romp, I fear."

"Lady isn't the only one, I surmise," the earl commented dryly, bending a suspicious glance to the imp clinging to his arm. Turning, he bowed politely to the country youngsters.

"Austin Atwood, at your service. Perhaps, Mr. Smith, we might remove this mangy mongrel to more congenial quarters and find a sip of something to quench our thirst while the ladies address more important matters." Lifting one eyebrow as he regarded Aubree, he played along with her charade. "By your leave, milady?"

Both Alexa and Everett relaxed at this end to the havoc Aubree's pets had created. Not many of the duke's household were so understanding, and they warmed to him instantly.

"I say, that's a capital idea," the squire declared jovially. Then more respectfully, he turned to Alvan. "Averill, will you be joining us?"

Giving his mischievous cousin a laughing glance, Alvan shrugged his shoulders and joined the "commoners." "Why not?" he declared, and slapping the backs of the two larger men, led them away.

Alexa watched them go with worshipful eyes, then turned her beatific gaze upon Aubree. "This is beyond all dreams, Aubree. You must tell me all about it. I never thought I'd be here, but to be here for your wedding, and with Everett . . ."

Laughing, Aubree led her toward the stairs. "I don't know how Alvan did it, but I shall be forever grateful."

"Alvan?" Dreamy eyes considered this and accepted it. "Yes, of course, without the Ashbrook crest on the carriage, it is doubtful if my father would ever have let me go." Her delicate features grew thoughtful. "But there was not time to have a new gown made. I fear I shall shame you in front of your Lord Heathmont. An earl! I cannot imagine you married to an earl. I know you are the daughter of a duke, but you never seemed like it. And now you will be marrying some grand noble who will carry you off to his glittering castle. It is just like a romance from the magazines."

Aubree's giggles had multiplied by the time they reached her chambers. Austin had taken his fall remarkably well, she admired him for it, but he should never have been sneaking about the stairs, spying on her and her friends. Whatever could he have been doing? She would take him to task for it soon enough, but for now, she hoped he enjoyed Everett's company. She stifled another giggle.

Peggy awaited them nervously, but at Aubree's laughing entrance, she relaxed and threw her arms around her husband's cousin. "Oh, Aubree, I am so happy for you. After everything Alvan has told me, I've been so worried."

Wearing a full gown that hid any sign of her pregnancy, the matron of honor stepped back to better study her friend and relative. Of the same height as Aubree, Peggy Bereford had always been plumper, and she sighed wishfully as she observed the bride's slim waist.

"Oh, to be so young again." Then hastily slamming the door, she chased Alexa and Aubree into the room exclaiming, "Why are you dawdling about? We have work to do."

Matilda appeared next, scolding like a magpie as she directed the laying out of gowns and petticoats and supervised the dressing and tucking and pinning. Aubree insisted that Alexa be garbed in one of her gowns as a member of the wedding party since Peggy refused the honor of standing up with her, and maids were hastily sent hither and thither to gather the necessities for the alteration.

The afternoon flew by before Aubree knew it, leaving her no time to fear the night to come. The arrival of what appeared to be hundreds of elegant carriages below made her increasingly nervous, but she channeled her energies into seeing Alexa transformed into a fashionable lady. If Everett's eyes didn't open this day, they never would.

Aunt Clara and Peggy took turns spying on the arrival of the guests, declaring the entire *haut ton* had most certainly taken a day's diversion from the Season's activities to see Aubree wed. By the time the final finishing touch had been found to adorn Alexa's slender throat and Aubree's curls had been arranged neatly beneath her veil for the thousandth time, the guests had already been ushered into the chapel or reception hall, depending on the level of their importance.

Events left Aubree with no time to contemplate this step she took. Perhaps this had been her father's intention, but as she gazed wistfully at the image in ivory in her mirror, Aubree wished there had at least been time for romantic courtship. No flowers, no rings, no whispered words of love, she'd scarcely even danced with her intended. And now they were to be wed.

Holding back her tears, she straightened her shoulders and turned for a final inspection from her eager assistants.

"Oh, my, Aubree, your earl will be so proud of you when he sees you walk down that aisle," Alexa whispered, awestruck by the vision of Aubree's golden hair encircled in a halo of flowing ivory lace. "I wish I had the nerve to thank him in person for arranging for me to be here. He must be a wonderful gentleman," she sighed dreamily.

Aubree paid little heed to Alexa's ecstatic gratitude, but turned at the sound of Peggy's prosaic comments. "Well, I wouldn't make him out to be a Corinthian, but Heath does have his finer moments. If he hadn't sent that letter to Lady Clara asking for her aid in bringing me here, Alvan might never have let me come. I shall certainly give him a hug for that, and one for you, too, Alexa."

Aubree's eyes widened. "Heath! Heath brought you both here?"

Before she could question further, Aunt Clara began shooing everyone from the room. "It's almost time to take your places. They will think we have all run away if some of us don't put in an appearance."

Espying the Duke of Ashbrook approaching his daughter's chambers, Clara turned for one last word with her niece. "Your Lord Heathmont might not be a gentleman in every sense of the word, my love, but he is very much a man. It is not young Everett or your Lord Geoffrey waiting down there for you, but a man who is trying to please the woman who will be his wife. Behave like that woman, Aubree, and he will have no reason to regret his decision."

She entered the hall, exchanged a few words with the duke, and then followed the others, leaving Aubree to face her father alone.

He stopped in the doorway, his proud figure discreetly but elegantly garbed in his official court dress, the black making him appear even more slender than usual. Shadowed gray eyes met his daughter's, and at the glistening tears he found there, he winced. He closed the door and offered her a lace-edged handkerchief. "You will not wish to walk down the aisle with tears in your eyes."

Aubree accepted the square of lawn, dabbing it at her eyes.

"Has anyone said aught to make you cry?" he asked gruffly.

A shy smile appeared from behind the lace edging as she removed the last trace of moisture. "Is a man who sends happiness instead of expensive gifts less than a gentleman?"

The duke looked mildly perplexed as he tucked away the handkerchief she returned to him. "I didn't know it was possible to send happiness. Does he bottle the stuff?" He offered his arm. "But expensive gifts do not a gentleman make, that I can tell you. Now let us proceed. In time, perhaps we'll discover the answer to your question."

Aubree accepted his arm and gracefully followed his lead, the train of ivory satin and lace swishing luxuriously along the carpeted hall as they walked toward the chapel. The thought that Austin had been the one to bring her friends and pets here held her steady. A man with the insight to anticipate her fondest desires could not be the man gossip made him to be.

She did not know how she would thank him, but she knew what she must do now. Her lips curved softly upward as they entered the candlelit chapel.

A hushed gasp of awe whispered around the vaulted chamber as the guests turned to crane their necks for a better view of the bride. In the half-light of dancing candles and sunset glow through stained-glass windows, Aubree's shimmering gown created the impression of etherealness. Beneath the delicate lace, luminous green eyes shone with splendid intensity, framed by long, dark lashes that never flickered as her gaze focused upon the man at the end of the aisle. Wisps of golden curls danced about her face in the draft from the open door, and the rosier hues of her golden skin brightened as her gaze touched upon the one she sought. No one watching could doubt this bride went any less than willingly to the altar.

Garbed in a deep-blue swallow-tailed coat and matching breeches, Austin's rigid figure stood imposingly at the aisle's end. The midnight blue of his eyes burned darkly against the bronze of his lean features, and the cluster of dark curls upon his brow gave his stern visage a devilish cast. Yet the smile that slowly bent his lips as he followed his bride's stately approach nearly sent every woman in the room into a swoon.

Aubree's own heart fluttered as she drew closer and felt the intensity of Austin's gaze, but nothing could frighten her on this day. She heard her father's words giving her away, and accepted Heathmont's hard fingers without hesitation. They closed tightly around her hand, not relaxing as the minister's voice droned on with the solemn phrases of this ceremony.

Whispers behind them failed to break their concentration as they repeated their vows. When it came time to produce a ring, Aubree held her breath, uncertain that anyone had taken this into consideration. But behind Heath, Alvan produced a small box and handed it to the minister as directed, and Aubree let out a small sigh of relief.

With a wry twist of his lips at his bride's exhalation, Austin carefully slipped two bands upon her finger, one a delicately filigreed heirloom of emeralds and diamonds, the other a simple band of twined gold strands surrounding a single diamond. Aubree gazed at them in awe until the minister's words prompted her to repeat her pledge of love. She looked up to meet Austin's eyes as these words passed her lips, and the heavens seemed to come to a standstill as their gazes locked and held.

The whispers and rustlings behind them grew louder, but the bride and groom had no eyes or ears for anything beyond each other. The minister murmured those words binding them together until death did them part, but not until Alvan nudged Austin into action did he hear the final instruction.

Bending to kiss his bride, Austin heard the contented purr of a feline just as a small, furry body wrapped itself around his ankle. Aubree gasped as a second ball of sleek fur discovered the delights of fragile lace and began to climb upon her veil, with disastrous results. A titter of laughter from close behind was echoed in muffled snorts and gasps throughout the chapel.

Still shaken by the vows she had just made, Aubree could do little more than grasp futilely for the kitten entangled somewhere in the yards of lace behind her. Alexa, all thumbs, attempted to extricate the now-terrified kitten, but succeeded only in earning a scratch. Austin grabbed the pet at his feet before it could join his adventuresome companion and handed it to Alvan, who stared at it with incredulity. Then slipping the pins holding Aubree's veil in place, Austin uncoverd her golden curls, allowing the yards of lace and a frightened feline to drop gently to the floor.

To smattered applause from their audience, Austin bent to claim his kiss, his mouth firmly staking his claim for all to see. She trembled in his grasp, and he held her reassuringly, chasing away her fears. Before he released her to meet their guests, however, a teasing glint appeared in Austin's eyes, and his fingers clasped Aubree's securely.

"I have taken you for better or worse, my dear, but do you remember if he included the animal kingdom in that list anywhere?"

Aubree gave a brilliant smile and reached for the kitten in Alvan's hands. "Whither I go . . ."

"They shall follow," Austin groaned mockingly, and to the tune of an ancient processional, the earl led his new countess—and her cat—down the aisle.

9

Aubree's normally cheerful grin tightened into a thin mockery of itself as she forced a smile and ignored yet another not so subtle offer of protection, this time from a lord old enough to know better. The military gentleman ignored the earl on her side and moved down the line, uttering imprecations to her Uncle John and off-color jests to Averill and Peggy.

She decided hell would be an eternal reception line as she waited for the next arrogant Corinthian to offer his sympathies or his aid while directing a look that dared the man at her side to challenge him. She scarcely dared look Heath in the eye herself by this time. She knew he must be furious, but no sign of it touched his calm authority as he held his place beside her.

The irony of these so-called gallant offers did not escape Aubree, although she wasn't certain Austin was fully cognizant of it. She had met all these young bachelors sometime during her hectic stay in London, but not one of them had shown any more than the slightest sign of interest in a green seventeen-year-old when she was free. They had paid their calls and taken their requisite share of dances and gone their ways, wenching and gambling and drinking. Now they gallantly flocked to assure her of their undying devotion should she ever be in dire need of help. Reminded of her conversation with her father about Austin's reputation, she felt a sour taste in her mouth and grimaced.

"Lady Aubree." A swaggering young gentleman bowed politely before her. She recognized him as a friend of Geoffrey's, though they had never been introduced. She offered her hand almost fearfully, but his next words held no insults.

"May I have a moment of your time later?" he asked softly, for Aubree's ears alone.

He must carry a message from Geoffrey, but she was no longer certain she wanted to hear it. Twice now, he had deserted her, bowing to her father's demands. It was too late to try again.

She smiled pleasantly, squeezed his fingers, and merely answered, "It's a pleasure to see you," before turning to the next guest.

Austin noted this exchange with suspicion. Aubree had not the experience to hide her emotions well, and he had felt her nervous jolt at the man's murmured words, but he was in no position to demand explanations. He carefully memorized the man's face and returned his attention to the farce of being reintroduced to society.

If the duke had hoped to force society to accept his new son-in-law, much as his daughter had threatened to do earlier, he had misinterpreted his powers of persuasion. These people would come because they were required or because it amused them, but they had no intention of accepting a man who abused and murdered his first wife and kidnapped his second. And the earl had no intention of taking this opportunity to explain himself to anyone. He felt sorry that Aubree had to suffer through this, but it might make her father easier to convince when the time came to leave her behind. As it most certainly would, judging by this reception.

Alexa and Everett were almost the last of the guests in line, and they hung back sheepishly as they drew closer. The duke shook their hands and quickly ushered them on, but even Aubree's happy grin did not ease their embarrassment.

"Aubree, why did you not tell us?" Alexa whispered heatedly, sending a nervous glance in the direction of the formidable earl, who was presently bent politely over an elderly lady, listening to her chatter.

"I wanted you to *know* him." Aubree grasped Everett's hand and dragged him into the conversation. "I really wanted you to like Austin, so you would not refuse me when I ask you to come visit us. Say you will," she added eagerly.

Austin straightened and returned his attention to his wife in time to catch this part of the conversation, and he felt a moment's uneasiness at Aubree's naïve invitation, but he revealed none of it as he warmly acknowledged the two.

"I say, dashed unfair of you not to say who you was," Everett protested, taking Austin's hand and shaking it. "Thought you was the duke's secretary or summat. Aubree's always quizzing the poor fellows. Never dreamed, you know—"

"Everett!" Alexa hissed, putting an end to this embarrassing monologue. Then curtsying prettily beneath the earl's complete attention, she announced, "Aubree is my best friend in the whole world, but she is a trifle impetuous at times, milord. I trust you will forgive us for not recognizing who you are."

A rare smile of genuine delight lit Heathmont's bronzed features as he bowed gracefully over the girl's small hand. "Miss Carlisle, my wife is blessed beyond her knowledge to have such friends. I am pleased you were able to come."

"Oh, come now, Austin, that's doing it up a shade too brown," Aubree declared, reddening at this gracious end to her little jest and his reference to her as "wife." "Could we not all go find some punch? I think I shall perish of thirst if I must stand here much longer."

The suggestion seemed to appeal to all within hearing, and chattering merrily, the reception committee dispersed to seek refreshment from their torturous ordeal.

Overflowing the main salon, the wedding guests had already formed into small cliques and groups throughout the reception area. Well-meaning ladies, young and old alike, hurried to surround Aubree and Lady Clara with eager questions.

Unable to politely separate herself from the conversation, Aubree sent Heathmont a despairing look. With a faint grin, he nodded toward the refreshment table, indicating he would return shortly. In truth, he felt relief at leaving her thus protected. The punch bowl had apparently become the gathering place for a conspicuous number of unattached gentlemen, and their mood did not appear to be one of jollity.

Alvan drifted along at Austin's side, supremely unaware of the possibility of trouble in paradise. He rambled on of some scheme to invest his income in a fool contraption that operated wheels with steam just like Fulton's boat did paddles. At any other time, Austin would have been interested, but at the present he could see no future beyond the next few hours.

Most of the young gallants were younger than he, the earl observed as he served himself from the punch bowl. He had probably gone to school with their older brothers, who were conspicuously absent from this assembly. He recognized one or two, but they blatantly kept their backs to him, continuing their conversation as if he were not present.

"You don't call out a bounder like that," one voice protested recklessly. "You horsewhip him through the streets."

"After what he did to his first wife, no decent woman would look at him. The only way he could have caught her was to compromise her. Too bad her brother's not alive to punish the cad."

Coming down out of his clouds, even Alvan caught the meaning of this last, and he cast a nervous look at Heath's taut face. The earl continued to pour a second cup of punch.

"I heard she's no better than she should be, throwing herself at the lecher's feet," another voice spoke scornfully. "Then after he'd spoiled her, he demanded a ransom to wed her."

This last caused Austin to very slowly and carefully set both cups of punch back to the table. Midnight eyes flashing, he casually tapped the speaker upon the shoulder. Alvan made as if to interfere, but he moved too late. When the young gallant turned, Heath's fist connected squarely with his jaw, and the obnoxious speaker crumpled to the floor.

The crowd of young gentlemen eagerly pushed one another aside in their attempts to confront the earl's furious gaze first. Both sides totally ignored the gasps and warning whispers circling around them. Angry mutterings came from the back of the group of Corinthians, but all waited for the fallen man to rise.

The golden-haired giant rose rubbing his jaw, his steely gaze focusing on the darkly arrogant man waiting calmly for his reprisal.

As the man staggered to his feet, Austin informed him, "You may say what you wish of me, but you will apologize to my wife."

A muttering of surprise and approval arose at this declaration, but a rustle of stiff petticoats and the scent of lilac warned Austin of an unwanted intrusion. Without taking his eyes from his antagonist, he ordered Alvan, "Take her away from here."

"Why? So she won't know you for the cowardly bounder that you are?" the giant forced out from between bruised lips. "Meet me outside and she need not worry over you again."

Aubree dodged Averill's hand and placed herself between the two men, hands on hips as she stared at this friend of Geoffrey's. "Go away and play your little boy games elsewhere. If Geoffrey sent you, tell him he is far and away too late, as usual. This is my wedding, and I'll not have it ruined."

"Aubree!" Alvan spoke tersely, jerking her from the ring of men, aware of the disapproving twitch of Heath's jaw. "This is not your affair. Let Heath handle it." He hauled her toward the nervous women gathering nearby.

Disdaining the look of warning in Alvan's worried eyes, Aubree wriggled free and ran back to the group of men just as a second man offered his challenge. A third and fourth echoed their demands, and Austin regarded them all with cold acknowledgment.

"Very well, gentlemen. If that is the way it is to be, I believe this gentleman has the right to choose his own weapon. After that, I will be glad to meet you on my terms." He frowned as Aubree dashed between them again, and his black glare raised to meet Alvan's apologetic one.

"Austin, if you go through with this, so help me, I—"

"Madam," Heath interrupted coldly, "if no one else can teach you how to behave, I will most certainly be obliged to do so."

The sight of such black fury turned upon her from eyes that had always regarded her with respect sent shivers of fear up Aubree's spine, but she had never learned the meaning of retreat. Only Alvan's whispered words in her ear made her change her tactics.

"Aubree, Heath cannot refuse this fight and still consider himself a gentleman. You can do nothing."

Green eyes flashed in anger at such nonsense, but this time she tore her gaze from Austin's rigid fury to the insolent pups behind her.

"Fine, then. If this is such an honorable cause, why don't all of you take him at once? Lord Heathmont, the master swordsman, the hero of Corunna, can most certainly fight all of you at one time. It would be a much more gallant display than wearing a man down one by one until the last one of you wins simply by reason of exhaustion."

Austin's grim smile reflected nothing of amusement as he regarded this petite, towheaded fury in their midst. "Well, gentlemen, will you allow a woman's tongue to defeat you, or are you ready to step outside?" His glare challenged them.

"Pistols, at twenty paces," the golden giant affirmed readily.

Aubree's furious glance swept them all, waiting to see who spoke next.

The first challenger stepped forward. A stray lock of hair fell smoothly across his brow as he bowed politely before Aubree, a look of concern in his eyes. "This is for your own good, milady. You had best go with your cousin."

Aubree's scathing glare swept from his beautifully folded cravat to his polished boots and back. Looking him in the eye, she deliberately trod upon his toe. When he did not flinch, she kicked him in the shin. Then, smiling sweetly at his pained expression, she curtsied and replied, "My aim will be higher if you come looking to me for thanks."

She turned and swept away, leaving a flurry of covered grins and muffled chuckles behind her.

She walked away so furiously, Alvan had to maintain an undignified pace to keep up with her. Out of the corner of his eye, he caught the meaningful jerk of the duke's head in his direction, and he hesitated. Aubree hurried on, but the duke nodded his approval as Alvan made his way through the crowd toward his father and uncle.

Aubree had no awareness of the sympathetic gazes turned toward her, or the clucking murmurs in her ears as helpful hands tried to lead her away. She shoved them all aside and, lifting her skirts, ran recklessly down the wide hall to the stairs. No one dared stand in her way as she flew up the graceful mahogany staircase.

Gaining her chambers, she found a startled Matilda laying out some frothy gown of sheer gossamer upon the turned-down covers of her bed. Disregarding the meaning of this scene, she turned her back to the maid.

"Unfasten me, quickly, Mattie," she demanded.

The maid hurried to do as told, thoroughly confused by the command. Was the bridegroom in such a hurry his bride feared damage to her gown? Or the bride in such a hurry that she wished her maid to be gone before the groom arrived?

Not daring to question, the stout woman hurried to do as told, her gnarled fingers firmly locating and unfastening the row of tiny buttons. She helped Aubree struggle from the folds of confining satin, but stood back in amazement at her next command.

"The breeches in the bottom drawer, Mattie. Get them while I take off these petticoats." Aubree's fingers tugged nervously at the recalcitrant ties.

"Milady, no. I'll not complain if you want to keep summat of your brother's, but it's no place to be callin' for them on your wedding night."

Aubree dived impatiently for the drawer and pulled out the ancient pair of buckskins herself. She had wanted something of Henry's, true, but she had other reasons for keeping these about. She pulled them on and hurriedly worked at the buttons beneath the shocked stare of her maid.

The shirt from her riding habit followed next. By this time, someone was pounding on the door, and she did not dare hesitate. No inane group of masculine hotheads would mar her day with bloodshed. If she wanted their defense, she would ask for it. Until then, they mounted a filthy game she could never condone.

Fastening the shirt, she ran to the window and, to the maid's scream of horror, dropped out of sight.

Heathmont grimly selected his pistol from the pair offered and stepped back a pace, flexing his muscles as he accustomed himself to the weight of the long-bored gun. He had expected this result to his return to society's notice and had warned the duke of it, but his father-in-law had declined to discuss it. He did not fear for himself, but the lives of others were at stake.

He sought Alvan in the circle of men on the side lawn. No one had deemed it necessary to go any farther for this brief encounter. A guard had been posted to prevent any unwarranted interruption, but Alvan had been allowed through. He responded to Heath's look and came forward.

"The duke has made promises to me that I would see carried out, Bereford. My solicitor should have a copy of the agreement by now. Should anything happen, you will see it is kept in full?"

Alvan's thin face set in a grim line as he nodded to this request. "I wish I had never introduced you to Aubree. I warned you . . ."

Heathmont looked away, checking the pistol's sight against a distant tree. "I am responsible for my own actions, Alvan. Leave Aubree out of this."

One of the older men stepped forward to act as judge and Heathmont and the blond giant joined him in the center of the circle.

As they received their instructions, a slight figure slipped from an upstairs study window and ran silently along the castellated roof of the remaining ancient fortress. This oldest section of the castle jutted out into the side lawn, forming a protective barrier from the remainder of the grounds, making its base the ideal location for a secluded rendezvous. The shadowy figure halted at that point nearest the guarded meeting below and lifted a slender arm between the crumbling battlements. In the moonlight, the silver barrel of the shotgun in her hand gleamed dully.

"My lords!" a young voice rang sharply through the cool night air, echoing against ancient stone walls.

Engrossed in their deadly task, the antagonists failed to hear the cry, but several onlookers glanced about, searching for the source of this ghostly emanation.

"I have a clear aim, but I would suggest you gentlemen below remove yourselves to a distance to prevent any mishaps," the voice rang mockingly.

This warning brought Austin's head up sharply and caused the circle to shift uneasily away from the wall, closer to the shrubbery beyond.

Austin's eyes quickly located the glimmer of the shotgun barrel and its shadowy wielder, and he cursed. Turning back to his challenger, he spoke harshly. "We had best do this quickly, or she'll blow us both to hell."

The blond giant glanced nervously upward, then nodded, signaling his readiness to the judge. The pace count began.

"I'm an excellent shot, gentlemen, but I cannot guarantee the shot will only shatter your guns. If you value your fingers, you will drop the pistols now." Cool and authoritative, Aubree's voice sang clearly over the now-silent night.

The judge stopped counting and glanced nervously from Austin to the waif on the rooftop. "It ain't proper. She can only shoot one at a time, which gives Lord Heathmont an edge."

Austin gave the military gentleman a dark look. "You don't know my wife very well, General." Resigning himself to this farce, he turned to face the slight figure on the battlements. Golden hair gleamed in the moonlight, and he wondered what in hell she wore that she could have climbed out there with such ease, but he preferred to remain ignorant.

"Aubree, put that gun down or I'm coming up there after you."

"Do that, milord, and I will shatter that fool's hand as you try. Send someone else up after me, and it is your hand you endanger. Go elsewhere, and you'll not find me waiting for your return. If you gentlemen are so determined to destroy my wedding night, perhaps you might consider the consequences when my father finds me gone, and he has only the lot of you to blame."

A triumphant note rang in her voice as she watched the uneasy stir among the crowd around the combatants.

"By George, if she don't blow us to pieces, the duke certainly will," one young lord whispered to another. "It's a wonder he ain't already out here taking names to turn in."

Utterly livid at her disobedience and interference, Austin ignored the murmurs around him, continuing to stare up at his defiant young wife. "Aubree, go back to your room or you will regret this night for as long as you live, I swear it!"

"I already regret it, milord," she taunted, "but you are welcome to come up here and try."

"I'd be willing to take up that challenge," one wit declared, observing Aubree's slender figure with admiration.

"She's eager for your bed, it seems," the blond giant sneered, watching the earl's reaction closely. "Shall we not keep the lady waiting?"

Austin returned his black glare to his opponent. "If you do not value your life, it is your choice. Let us continue."

Aubree nearly cried as they called her bluff and began pacing again. She had tried, but she did not dare carry out her threats. She had practiced target-shooting with stationary objects, but she could never aim at a living one, even if she could see them with any clear precision, which she couldn't. It had all been for naught. In moments, one man would be dead and the other would be running for his life. Such senselessness!

Both men had doffed their coats, and their white shirts gleamed against the dark shadows of the high hedges behind them as they paced the remaining steps. Austin's chestnut curls and distinct limp stood in sharp contrast to the young giant's golden looks and graceful stride. In frustration, Aubree lifted the shotgun to her shoulder and took careful aim.

"Aubree! Put that gun back in my study and go back to your room. Sheriff, escort these gentlemen off the grounds. All except that one." Appearing in a far corner of the fortress, followed by a string of grooms and village constables, the duke gestured to single out Austin from among the others. Under the duke's hostile gaze and enforced by the local constabulary, the crowd hastily dispersed. With a look of disgust, Heath handed his pistol to the military gentleman and, turning sharply on his heel, approached his father-in-law.

The duke observed Austin's scowl implacably. "Heath, I apologize for intruding, but I'll not have my daughter locked in the Tower for murder. Her aim is not so good as she claims."

Austin sent a quick glance toward the battlements, but the slim shadow had already disappeared into the darkness above. She had won this battle, but he had not yet begun to fight. He returned his attention to the duke. "Sir, with your permission . . ."

His grace took one look at Austin's murderous gaze and shook his head. "Not like that. Lay one hand on her and I'll have you hung."

Austin's thin lips turned upward. "A cane is what she needs, but a thrashing is not what I had in mind. You did mention a desire for grandchildren?"

The duke sent his son-in-law a dubious glare, but the earl met it without flinching. The matter was no longer in his hands. He had chosen this man because he had the strength of character and firmness of resolve that no younger man could possibly wield. If he had chosen wrongly . . .

He nodded, and Heathmont strode quickly toward the castle.

10

Aubree crawled through the window of her room, coming up on the other side to meet Aunt Clara's terrified gaze.

"Aubree! My word, child, what are you doing?" she cried, staring at the apparition in boy's breeches that not an hour before had worn angelic white.

"My father has run the clothheads off. I never thought I'd see the day . . ." Aubree shook her golden curls to retrieve the loosened pins barely holding it in place.

"Just look at you," Clara declared with shock, then turning to an equally terrified maid, she ordered, "Have them send up a bath, at once."

Matilda hurried to do as ordered, leaving Aubree to struggle alone with her recalcitrant curls and her frightened aunt.

"Aubree, what on earth have you been doing? You look like a chimney sweep! Where's Lord Heathmont? This is supposed to be a wedding party, and the bride and groom are out playing hide-and-seek. I've never seen the like in my life. Wherever did you find those clothes?"

Clearly no longer able to reason with the night's happenings, Clara scolded haphazardly, and Aubree listened with only half her mind. She had infuriated Heath beyond all measure this night. She had no idea of what action he could take. If he tried to beat her, she would scream the house down. There were enough guests left to come to her rescue. And he had given his word as a gentleman that he would not take her as a wife, so she need not fear reprisal in that way. Perhaps he would call the whole thing off, go to her father and demand an annulment, and she would never see him again. That seemed the most logical conclusion.

After Aunt Clara's panic had worn itself down and the bath arrived, Aubree found herself blessedly alone. Matilda deserved this chance to gossip with the maids of their guests, and Aubree sent her away. There would be no further use for her this night; the lovely wedding gown had already been tucked away. Aubree breathed a sigh of relief as she sank into the warm water, fragrant with the bath oil Henry had sent to her from abroad long ago.

The strain of this day soaked out of her as she sank among the bubbles. She deliberately blanked out all memory of Heath's black glare. He would go away and leave her alone, and in time this day would only be one more infamous incident in her history. She must remember to thank her father for arriving in time. She did not like to think what might have happened had any of those triggers been pulled. Her eyes drifted closed.

The slam of her bedroom door sent Aubree shooting upright, spraying water across the Turkish carpet. She grabbed for a towel, but a bronzed hand snatched it away. She rubbed at her eyes to remove the splashed soap, straining to see this brash intruder, though in her heart she had little doubt of his identity.

"Did you require this, madam?" Heath's voice grated icily as he dangled the towel before her.

She snatched at the corner he allowed her, rubbing her eyes with the cloth while attempting to sink lower beneath the water. She had the miserable feeling she failed to disguise herself, and crimson tinged her skin as he continued to hover over her.

"Go away," she muttered, hiding her embarrassment in the towel.

"I asked you to do that on several occasions this evening, milady, and you chose to ignore me." Heath jerked the towel away, once satisfied she had dried her eyes and could see him well.

Aubree crossed her arms over her breasts and wished her knees would bend backward as she cowered beneath the thinning layer of bubbles. She glared up at Heath's lean face, his eyes almost black beneath dark curls.

"I was trying to save your fool life," she retorted. "I see nothing honorable in dying. But since we are so obviously unsuited, why are you not downstairs appealing to my father for an annulment? Go talk to him instead of invading my privacy. Give me the towel and go away."

"Is that what you thought you were doing? How generous." Austin dropped the towel on the floor where she would have to reach for it, then sat down on the bed and began tugging at his shoe, ignoring her stare of horror. "However, I have no intention of asking for an annulment until your father has carried out his end of the bargain. And in the meantime, I will look after myself, thank you."

"What are you doing?" Aubree whispered wildly, watching as one shoe fell to the floor, revealing a well-muscled leg beneath a silk stocking. She did not dare grab for the towel while he faced in her direction.

"If you will get out of the bath before it grows cold, I will spare the maids a second trip." Heath threw down the next shoe beside the other.

"You can't come in here like this . . ." Aubree panicked as she realized no one below would agree with her. She had just vowed before all those people to surrender all her rights to this man. She realized now it was an act of madness.

Heath raised a sardonic eyebrow. "Would you care to place a little wager on that?" Standing, he went to the mirror to unfasten his stickpin and cravat.

Aubree took this chance and dived for the towel, but catching this movement in the mirror, Austin turned, to be rewarded with the fleeting glimpse of fair white skin and rounding curves before she dived beneath the water again.

At her irate glare, Austin shrugged. "If you care to look, your father has footmen posted at either end of the hall. If I had not come in here, it would have been reported, and would not augur well for our agreement. However, if I should thrash you as you so roundly deserve, they would be in here within an instant to flail my hide. So if you truly value my life as you proclaim, you will keep your voice down and attempt to obey my orders, for a change."

"I cannot step out of this bath until you leave the room," she insisted, gritting her teeth at even this much capitulation.

Austin ripped off his cravat with a flick of his wrist, midnight eyes returning her glare full force. "Madam, you have made enough of a fool of me this evening. I do not intend to stand meekly outside the door of my marriage chamber until my bride decides to let me in. You should have thought of that *before* you rewarded yourself with that bath."

Weary of this argument, Aubree conceded the point and waved in the direction of a dressing screen in the corner. "At least have the decency to place the screen around me so I might dry myself. I cannot believe my father meant for us to share this chamber so soon."

Austin met her stare with incredulity, but satisfied she did not mock him, he moved toward the screen. "What did you envision us doing on our wedding night?" he asked in curiosity as he lifted the screen and carried it back to her.

Aubree shrugged in embarrassment as she felt him staring down at her. If it were not for the protection of the water, she would sink right through the floor and die.

"I don't know. I thought we could have separate chambers, at least. Surely, in a *mariage de convenance*, the husband is not expected to attend to his wife every night?"

Austin choked back a sharp retort at this naïveté and arranged the screen around her in silence. He had to remember she was naught but a child, though there were moments . . .

Finally adjusting the screen and his thoughts to his satisfaction, he replied, "If that is what you think we have, my lady, let me disillusion you."

He returned to the bed and began removing his

stockings, listening to the splashing sounds she made as she rose from the tub. He would very much like to see through the stiff fabric of that screen but was too much the gentleman to trick her any further than he had. He sighed at the opportunity lost and continued speaking, as she evidently had no intention of replying.

"I have had one wife who felt called upon to make a cuckold of me; I will not have another. So long as we are considered man and wife, I shall take care not to insult you by consorting with other women. I will expect the same respect in return. Do you understand me?"

Aubree nodded thoughtfully, forgetting he could not see her. She considered his words as she dried herself and nearly screamed when Austin jolted her back to reality by rattling her protective barrier.

He sent her gown flying over the top of the screen. "Put this on and come out here and answer me, Aubree Elizabeth."

Her eyes widened at this use of her given name, but she hastened to slip the gown over her head before he came barging in after her. She gasped as she realized the indecent amount of flesh left still uncovered. The pale-green silk formed a scallop over each breast and came up at an angle to cover only a very small portion of her shoulders. Full sleeves fell back at every movement, giving tantalizing glimpses of bare arms despite the covering. The bodice clung to her waist and hips like a second skin, and only the full train of the skirt offered any protection at all. She wondered whose idea it was to buy this gown and prepared to chastise them firmly when she found out.

Biting her underlip in vexation, she asked nervously, "Austin, would you please fetch my shawl?"

Pacing the floor in irritation at her silence, Austin scowled at this request. "Madam, I am waiting for your answer. I am in no mood to scour your drawers for fripperies."

With her hair still partially pinned but tumbling down over one shoulder, Aubree lifted her skirt and held her chin defiantly high as she stepped from the privacy of the screen. "I understand you, milord."

Austin swung around and the blue of his eyes brightened to twinkling gleams as he gazed over the golden fairness of unblemished skin and feasted upon the high curves of young breasts. He caught his breath as his gaze slid lower to discover the reed slimness of a long waistline and marveled at the smooth swell of round hips below. As he imagined what more could be seen should that gown be stripped away, he felt a surge of heated blood in his loins, and reluctantly, he forced his gaze away.

The flash of long-lashed jade eyes did nothing to relieve his state, and Austin moved toward the dressing screen as he pulled his shirt from his breeches.

"The gown looks better than I expected," he muttered gruffly, disappearing behind the screen.

Aubree's cheeks flushed scarlet. "From you, milord?"

"My name is Austin, if you will recall," he answered dryly. His shirt fell upon the screen, followed by his breeches.

As she heard him step into the water, Aubree's cheeks grew brighter, and she dashed behind the curtains of the bed, lowering them hurriedly. That a man had purchased this shockingly intimate apparel was bad enough, but that he now bathed completely naked just behind that screen was more than her senses could bear. The darkness provided by the velvet bed hangings helped close him out, but the softness of the mattress beneath her recalled another point.

"Mi—Austin," she stuttered out.

A splash was her only answer.

"D-does this mean we must share this bed tonight?" she finally braved to ask.

Austin dunked his head and came up sputtering, cursing himself for three sorts of a fool before replying. "Yes, madam, it does, and every night until we escape your father's attention. So you had best begin practicing obedience as soon as possible."

Aubree's head popped from between the curtains at this pronouncement. "Obedience?"

"You have read Shakespeare?" he questioned wryly from behind the screen.

"Of course. I am not completely ignorant." Indignantly, she perched on the bed's edge and began to remove the remainder of the pins from her hair.

"You remember the *Taming of the Shrew*?"

Aubree flung a hand full of pins at the screen. "I am not a shrew!"

"Not enough experience." Austin stood in the bath, water running in rivulets down his lean body as he reached for the damp towel Aubree had discarded. "But take a lesson from Katharina. When I say the moon is blue, comment on the lovely shade of indigo."

"What flummery! What will that gain us?" Aubree pattered across the room for her brush, then perched cross-legged upon the bed again.

"Atwood Abbey, with any luck." Austin gave up on the soaking towel, then glancing up, came to a sudden realization. With a mild curse, he inquired, "I don't suppose you had the same consideration in my night-wear as I did yours, my love?"

She detected the sarcasm, but his meaning threw her into panic. "No, I'm sorry. I did not know . . . I mean, can we not send for some?"

Austin sighed and reached for his tight breeches. There were pluses and minuses to this business of wedding virgins. "I have none to send for, my dear. I am as unaccustomed as you to this business of sharing a bed." He reworded his thoughts more politely.

"Austin, you cannot!" Aubree dropped her brush and dived between the curtains again, avoiding the sight of her husband reappearing from behind the screen in this state of undress.

With water still running down the dark line of hair over his breastbone, Austin made no attempt to don his shirt, but used it for a towel. He eyed the shivering bed curtains warily, but there was no escape from it. The day had been a long one, and he'd be damned if he intended to spend the night upon a chair.

On silent feet, he went about the room, snuffing out the candles. The scent of hot wax blended with the faint aroma of lilac blossoms, and he moved to throw open the latticed windows. A good dose of cold night air might help.

Aubree slid as far away from the side of the bed he

approached as she could. The bed scarcely seemed
large enough as a draft of cool air blew over her bared
skin. The silk against her breasts did strange things to
her insides, and she knew an ache she had never
before experienced. Remembering Austin's kisses of
not so many nights ago, her heart began to pound
unevenly. Surely, he wouldn't?

Austin's heavier frame weighed down upon the bed
as he crawled between the curtains. Aubree avoided
the tempting tilt of the mattress as he situated himself
comfortably, keeping a distance between them.

She could only see the vague outline of broad shoulders against the pillow, but she would have sensed his
presence without the use of sight. He exuded a virile
warmth and energy that could not easily be contained
by these feminine surroundings, and the masculine
scent of him seemed to permeate the closed air of the
draped bed. Beside him, she knew her own smallness,
and she cowered further against the edge of the bed.

"You are still angry with me?" she asked timidly as
his silence continued.

Crossing his hands beneath his head and staring at
the canopy, Austin considered this. "I am angry that
you felt it necessary to interfere with my affairs. I am
not angry that you prevented me from shooting the
vulgar fellow. I am a better shot than you, I wager,
and I did not intend to kill him. So you have simply
made a spectacle of yourself for naught. In the future,
I would thank you to remember that I know a little
more about what I am doing than you do."

Aubree sighed and curled the pillow up under her as
she turned to stare at his silhouette. "I cannot abide
bloodshed, milord. If you are prone to involving yourself in these unnecessary duels, I cannot promise to act
the part of bystander."

He knew he had only to turn his head to see the full
curve of her breasts and the swell of her hips so close
to his. His hands ached to reach out for the solace he
could find in the soft body that by all rights was his to
possess. Yet he lay without moving, keeping his hands
beneath his head.

"Then I shall make certain to keep my activities

hidden from you in the future, my lady," he answered stonily. "Now let us get what sleep we might."

Aubree grew silent, but she could not sleep. She sensed he, too, lay awake well into the small hours of the morning. She did not disturb his thoughts, however, and eventually, they both fell into a restless slumber.

Cool rain pattered against the open casement, filling the morning air with the damp scents of saturated earth and May flowers. Aubree tossed uneasily in her sleep, sliding instinctively closer to the source of heat between the covers. She warmed her backside against Austin's hip and his lips curled in amusement as he considered turning to warm all of her against him. His loins leapt eagerly at just the thought, and had he not worn breeches, he would have had some difficulty extricating himself from this position without embarrassment.

As it was, he chose caution over temptation, and tugging the covers more securely around his wife's sleeping form, he slid from the bed to close the window.

Hearing the stealthy movement beyond the heavy draperies of her bed, Aubree stretched sleepily, trying to orient herself. Something seemed lacking, though she could not put a name to it as she drew the sheets up under her chin. The brush of the covers against her nearly bare breasts enhanced the feeling of emptiness, but now she remembered her place, and her eyes opened in shock.

Austin chose that moment to lift one of the draperies and lean in, and Aubree nearly shrieked with alarm at the sight of his bared torso. When one muscular arm reached for the covers, she quickly rolled to the far side of the bed.

Blue eyes regarded her with amusement from beneath a shock of tangled curls, but instead of reaching for her, he only rubbed his forefinger along the bottom sheet, leaving a smear of blood.

At her wide-eyed stare, he shrugged. "There is some bloodshed that cannot be avoided, my lady, particularly if we wish to convince your father we are well and truly wed." His eyes watched her with curiosity as she absorbed this information.

Continuing to hold the sheet loosely against her breasts, Aubree stared at him with growing understanding. "You mean . . . what happens between man and wife . . ." She shuddered at the prospect, throwing his bronzed chest a covert glance before asking, "Is it painful?"

"Only the first time." Then, seeing she looked toward his finger, Austin grinned. "This? Not to notice."

He tied back the other curtain, allowing light to flood in and illumine the tender morsel between the sheets. Disheveled golden curls fell deliciously over the soft ivory of her shoulders, and Austin felt the need to receive some reward for his good behavior.

" 'Tis time to begin your lessons, my love," he announced cheerfully, standing with hands on hips as he grinned down at her. "It would be best if we appeared at breakfast together and I am mortally starved. So let us rise and begin the day."

Aubree stared at him with suspicion. "When you are gone and not a moment sooner."

Without his shirt and coat and cravat and all those things that kept him civilized, she could very well visualize this man as pirate or worse. His skin had the bronzed coloring of a man well-accustomed to baring himself to the weather, and the ripple of muscle over his wide chest made it obvious he had the strength to do as he wished with her. She had to rely on her memory of him as a gentleman to keep from quaking with fear.

Blue eyes sparkled with mischief. "The moon is blue, Countess, and I wish to see you out of that bed before I leave."

Remembering his words of the night before, Aubree swept the covers around her and dangled her toes over the side of the bed farthest from him. "I've always hated indigo," she stated crossly. "And I cannot see what I have to gain by agreeing with you."

"Your privacy, my dear." Austin eyed the straight line of her slender back with admiration. "Until your father is firmly convinced that we are lovers and that I have you under control, he will not allow us out of his sight. The number of nights we spend in this bed together is directly related to the amount of loving obedience you show each day. Now come around here and practice a little before I go."

Aubree threw him a look over her shoulder, but there appeared to be no mockery in his expression. He waited patiently for her compliance, and she sighed, flinging a corner of the sheet over her shoulder as she slipped to the floor, wrapping the linen around her.

"This is complete fustian," she complained. "I have seen men ignore their wives for weeks on end and no one suspects that they are any less than married. The only obedient wife I can recall offhand is the vicar's wife. Surely you cannot expect me to behave like the vicar's wife?"

She came around the bed trailing the sheet, jade eyes regarding him warily. "I am up. Are you satisfied?"

"You are not supposed to glower at me like that. Lovers are supposed to look at each other with passion," he stated critically.

Aubree gave him a venomous glare. "How am I supposed to know aught of passion? You and my father have successfully stood in the way of my ever finding out."

"Then, by all means, let me show you what you are missing."

Without warning, Austin grasped her shoulders and pulled her toward him, carelessly sweeping the sheet to the floor as his hands slid warmly over bare flesh. Before Aubree could protest, his mouth closed over hers, and the sensation of being drawn into a whirlwind possessed her.

Aubree shuddered as she raised her hands to hold him off and found them wrapped in the coarse hairs of her husband's chest. He pressed her closer, and her palms flattened over hardened muscle as she yielded to his greater strength. His lips plied hers with gentleness, and she felt no fear as she responded tentatively.

The shyness of her response warmed Austin's blood,

and he cradled her against him, pressing for that passion he had found once before in her kiss. Her hands prevented him from feeling the full curve of her breast against him, but he would be satisfied this first time with simply rousing her passions.

Caught up in the heat of his embrace, Aubree trembled as Austin's lips parted and drank urgingly at her own. She learned from him and, under his encouragement, met his kiss fully. The shock of this gentle mixing of their breaths weakened her knees, and as his tongue took bold possession of her mouth, Aubree fell against him, clinging helplessly as he claimed her for his own.

Reluctantly, knowing how far to test his control, Austin released her lips, spreading his kisses upward to her cheek and temple, giving her time to grow accustomed to his hold.

Still shaking, Aubree rested against his chest, fearful she would be unable to stand should he release her now. Placing his finger beneath her chin, Austin tilted her head upward to meet his gaze.

"That is something of what passion is about, halfling. Keep that look in your eyes, and all will know we are lovers."

He kissed each lid gently, then set her from him, his eyes so blue as to be almost black as he gazed upon her.

Then, grinning broadly, he strode from the room, leaving Aubree to stare openmouthed after him.

11

Plagued by the spate of messages from London, the duke threw them back on the desk as he heard his guests welcoming the bridal pair in the hallway. Standing in the door to the small parlor, he watched with suspicion as Aubree clung, giggling, to the arm of her gallant husband as they traversed the distance to the breakfast table. Austin's wide smile as he proudly escorted his young wife through the small crowd of early-morning risers returning to London told the duke nothing.

Garbed in their traveling clothes, Aubree's friends from Hampshire approached, and his daughter flung her arms around Alexa while Austin genially shook Everett's hand. From the looks and laughter between the two couples and the pretty blush of color on Alexa's plain cheeks, the duke surmised another romance was in the making. But those simple children had not the experience at deception possessed by the earl and his new countess, and he continued to regard them dubiously.

The duke strolled out into the corridor just as Lady Clara joined them. Aubree exuberantly hugged her aunt while Austin dutifully greeted his father-in-law. The two men exchanged glances, the one searching, the other politely noncommittal. The duke shook his head and turned to his less-reserved daughter.

Releasing her aunt, Aubree smiled at her father and took Austin's arm as if he would protect her from all harm. The duke frowned slightly at this indication of her preference, but after all, this was what he had intended.

"Good morning, Father. Have you eaten? Will you join us?"

"I ate hours ago. The news from London gives me indigestion. I will have to return today."

Heathmont frowned. "I trust it isn't bad news?"

The duke shook his head. "The news from Spain is all good. Wellington progresses nicely. No, the Prince Regent has decided to make a royal fool of himself as usual and I am persuaded to return and plague him out of it. I have sent maids to pack your trunks. We will be returning sooner than anticipated."

Aubree could not hide the hope in her eyes. "Surely you do not intend Heath and I to return with you? Many of the guests came expecting to stay some weeks. Someone must remain to entertain them."

"Alvan and Peggy are here, so's John, for all the entertaining he does. No, the two of you will come with me. There are matters pertaining to the dowry that have not been settled yet. You have not had time to purchase a trousseau. I am certain your husband will have no objection to seeing you garbed as should suit his wife." The duke sent a wry look to the expressionless earl.

"Of course, your grace. I am at your disposal," Heath replied dryly.

Aubree watched in disappointment as her father walked off. "You are right. He does not mean to let us out of his sight. That's not fair."

"I will not argue with it so long as he is making efforts to keep his word." Austin calmly watched the duke depart.

Aubree looked at him askance, but she could discern nothing in her husband's expressionless demeanor. He had learned to hide his thoughts too well. Remembering what he had done to her with his kiss, she looked away in embarrassment. He had evidently only plied his more-than-expert skills to teach her a lesson, as he had said. The kiss meant nothing to him, or he would not be regarding their future with such dispassion. The idea of spending nights untold in this man's bed frightened Aubree more than she would willingly admit.

Holding her head high, trying not to remember how her husband's unclothed arm had felt against her not an hour before, Aubree proceeded grandly into the dining room.

In London, a trio of gloomy faces contemplated their coffee with various degrees of disgruntlement. Only the blond giant offered any hope to this mournful gathering.

"She didn't appear too eager for rescue, seems to me," he offered tentatively. It was little-enough excuse for his failure, but he felt comfortable with it. If the lady hadn't interfered, he would certainly have accomplished his goal.

"Bahh, what do you know of women? They never know what's good for 'em. She'll be regretting your failure by now, I reckon."

Geoffrey threw his older cousin a bleak look at this reminder of how Lady Aubree had spent the night. "Well, it is too late to help her now. He will be carrying her back to the abbey, I suppose. Rutting bounder," he added dismally, his dreams of grandeur rapidly crumbling.

The blond giant rose from the table. "Heard a lot of tales about Heathmont, but he seemed a decent sort. Looks to me like he's shackled a wildcat. Never saw a lady holding a shotgun. Better off without her, Geoff." With that parting remark, he ambled off, satisfied his mission had come to its best end.

The older man followed his departure with a look of scorn. "Fair enough for him to say. He never lacked for blunt. Your gentlemen ain't got the backbone, Geoff." He hid his scorn as he turned back to his young cousin. "It may be best this way. She'll come more willingly to heel after a few months at Atwood Abbey."

The fair-haired dandy sent his country cousin a despairing look. "But she's *married*, Harry. It's too late for me now."

A smug look settled on Harry's heavy jowls. "As I hear it, she ain't coming into her money for some time yet. Knowing his noble lordship, he'll be taking her dowry and slipping off on that smuggling sloop of his before long. The bride will need a bit of consoling in his absence. I think a lengthy visit with me will cheer your spirits, cousin, and if the earl should meet an untimely end in his endeavors, well, you'll be there to console the grieving widow. Much better this way, I daresay. Dallying after married women is much more profitable than virgins, if you catch my meaning."

Doubt and hope mixed equally in Geoffrey's expression as he listened to his more experienced cousin. Polite courting bored him, but the possibility that he might gain more than a kiss for his efforts cheered him considerably. He succeeded in dismissing his cousin's hints at Heathmont's demise. A man like that deserved to die but seldom did. Still, if there were any way he could gain a wealthy widow . . . The role of offering consolation suited him well.

Aubree stared bleakly out the carriage window as it rolled her toward London. With Alvan and Peggy staying at Ashbrook and Aunt Clara returning to Hampshire, she would be cast adrift in London alone. More and more it seemed like her father and husband were two of a kind. Petting the spaniel sprawled across her lap, she watched as these two men rode side by side, arguing vociferously over some point. Neither one of them cast a glance in her direction.

So much for romantic daydreams. She began to have some understanding of why women sought wealth and titles instead of love. Love didn't exist in the real world. It was a myth perpetuated by writers to feed the fancies of their readers and their own pockets.

Lady's soulful brown eyes stared up at her mistress sorrowfully at her absentminded caressing. When Aubree finally turned her attention to the dog, the long golden tail thumped eagerly, and she licked joyfully at the hand holding her. Aubree's smile brightened. Human affection might be fickle, but she was not without friends.

They returned to Ashbrook House by midafternoon. While Aubree saw to the unpacking of trunks and pets, the two men disappeared into the city on business of their own.

She spent a lonely evening conversing with the kittens and dining alone. There had been invitations she could have accepted, but it did not seem proper to go without her husband, or at least, his permission. Instead, she found a book and retired to her chambers.

Aubree gave a cry of dismay as she entered her chamber to find Heathmont's trunk at the foot of the bed. She thought she had ordered his things carried to the gentleman's wing, but evidently someone had countermanded her wishes.

She glanced around the room that had been hers alone these past months, and her gaze fell upon the *chaise longue* in the far corner of the high-ceilinged chamber. Her lips curved up in a perfect bow, and by the time Mattie came to help her undress, she was singing softly to herself as she unbound her hair.

Mattie clucked in protest as Aubree chose a high-necked gown of heavy lawn for her bed attire, but she knew better than to argue with the stubborn miss. Instead, she helped pull the girlish gown over golden curls with silent disapproval, then gazed in contempt at the result.

Aubree admired the way the stiff material fell straight to the ground without any hint of the womanly curves beneath and laughed at Mattie's frowning expression. "You don't think his lordship will approve?" she asked teasingly.

"You look no more'n a babe straight from the nursery. His lordship will think he's robbed a cradle and go lookin' elsewhere for his comfort. You ought to be ashamed of yourself, miss."

Aubree listened to this prejudiced speech from her loyal maid with curiosity. "You are on his side, Mattie? Do you not fear he will beat me as they say he did his first wife?"

"That's just gossip, my lady, and I know better than to put faith in gossip. He's a gentleman, your lordship is. He's even asked me personally, himself, if I be willing to come with you and stay in his household. He even asked should I have anyone to recommend for other positions, since his is a bachelor household and not much attended to. He wants you to have people you know about you."

That piece of information did not startle Aubree in the least, since she suspected Atwood Abbey suffered from a dearth of good help. The fact that the earl employed only one man to act as valet and groom spoke volumes, even had she not known of the deplorable state of his finances.

"Well, Mattie, and have you volunteered to follow me into exile? Or must I meet my fate alone?"

Mattie's round face puffed up with indignation and her white cap bobbed vigorously. "And did you think I would leave you to the hands of some poor wench with no skills at all? Why, who would know better than me how to fix them stubborn curls of yours? And I've sent to ask if me niece and nephew will come out. They be willing workers and will look after you as if you were their own."

Remembering the pair to whom Mattie referred, Aubree smiled happily. She would not be completely alone in a strange place, and the mischievous twins would comply willingly to all her requests. This had the makings of a merry jaunt, if she could only escape her father's scrutiny and Heathmont's proximity.

Dismissing Mattie, Aubree hastily assembled sheets and covers and wove a cocoon of comfort upon the chaise. Since he had said he was unaccustomed to sharing a bed, surely Heath would not object to this arrangement. Come morning, they could hide the sheets and no one would be the wiser. It made the possibility of sharing this room for an extended period of time more comfortable.

Entering the chamber well after his wife had time to find sleep, Austin gazed upon their new sleeping arrangements with dispassion. Removing temptation from his grasp would certainly make sleeping easier, if not at all as satisfying. How they would survive these next six months was open to conjecture.

12

With the excuse of pressing political matters preventing him from completing the final documents of their agreement, the Duke of Ashbrook succeeded in keeping the newlyweds in London for several days.

Austin itched impatiently for a return to his home so he might set the wheels of fortune in motion, but the duke had successfully tied his hands. Instead, he passed the days escorting Aubree about town, purchasing a trousseau she did not want and he did not expect to see.

Invitations continued to arrive from those who craved recognition, but Aubree's name had been dropped from the guest lists of the *haut ton*, where Austin's had been banned long ago. Out of a sense of duty, the earl offered to escort his wife to those invitations of her choice, but after enduring an evening of whispers and innuendos and outright stares, Aubree showed a disinclination to accept any others.

Instead, she rebelled against any further civilities at all.

"I want to see the lions and I want to see Vauxhall and I want to go to the theater," she insisted when Austin suggested she might accept an invitation to tea at Lady Driby's. "This may be my only chance to see London and I want to see something besides over-decorated drawing rooms. If you will not take me, then I shall go myself."

She did not need to stomp her foot or pout to make her meaning clear. The flash of green in a deceptively serene visage warned of a storm ahead should any interfere. Not having any desire whatsoever of parad-

ing himself as an ogre for the delight of Lady Driby's
guests, Austin agreed readily to this change of plans.

Actually, the earl's dry sarcasm and wry wit prevented the day of sightseeing from being a severe
disappointment to Aubree. The sight of those poor,
caged animals nearly ruined her day at the outset.
Austin's comparison of the various beasts to mutual
acquaintances forced a giggle from her. When he carried the parallel further to envisualize Geoffrey as a
noisy peacock and Alvan as a silent owl, she could not
take offense but retaliated by calling Austin a black
swan.

Somewhat taken aback by this strange description,
the earl bent a quizzical glance to his slight companion. "And how might I rate such a comparison?"

Aubree smiled sweetly. "They are said to be both
beautiful and vicious, my lord. Or would you prefer to
be a strutting gander?"

Gulping back his laughter, Austin eyed her with
grave displeasure. "Then you should have to be a
foolish goose. Take care, my lady, or you will be
served up in sauce one day."

The day improved as they relaxed and sharpened
their wits upon each other and the world in general.
By the time they returned home from a rather poor
performance at the recently rebuilt theater at Covent
Garden, Aubree was riding high on a cloud of eupho-
ria produced solely by her companion.

As the duo came in, laughing and chattering as if
they had only just met after a long separation, Aubree's
father stepped from the study to join them. Piercing
gray eyes noted the way Aubree's gloved hands clung
to her husband's arm as Austin gazed down into her
laughing eyes with evident amusement. They seemed
so enraptured with their nonsense that it was some
moments before they noticed the duke's presence at
all.

"I take it the performance was a success?" the duke
asked dryly when the pair finally turned to greet him.

"On the contrary, Mr. Sheridan tried to disguise a
pig as Ophelia and a—"

Austin interrupted hastily, knowing the epithet he

had attached to Hamlet would shock all within hearing when rolling from a lady's tongue. "Suffice it to say we found comedy disguised in a tragedy. Did you wish to see me, sir?"

The duke's tired frown relaxed slightly as he observed the protective manner in which the earl sheltered his wife at his side and the easy camaraderie that allowed Aubree to accept this protection. Whatever else might be between these two, they had accepted each other as friends, and many another marriage had survived on worse.

"Yes, if you don't mind, Heathmont. I know it's late, but I have to be leaving for Norfolk in the morning. There are one or two pieces of business remaining to be settled before I go."

Instantly, Heathmont sobered. Taking Aubree's hand, he bowed over it formally, blue eyes searching her face as he did so. "You will excuse me, my dear, if I do not follow you immediately?"

Aubree wanted to giggle at such formality, but understanding how much this might mean to Austin, she curtsied prettily and returned his request with gravity. "I will be waiting for you impatiently, my lord."

He smiled at that and watched her trip lightly up the staircase before turning to his father-in-law. Bowing politely, he murmured, "At your service, sir."

Not even attempting to follow this absurd performance, the duke gestured Austin toward his study.

Aubree stared restlessly out her bedroom window, watching the fading moonlight on the garden below. She could not curb the disquieting energy that flowed in her veins, making her want more than she could see, more than was there.

Heath had been the perfect gentleman these past days, not complaining when she moved her bed to the *chaise longue* or attempting to force his attentions on her in any way. If anything, he had held himself as aloof as she, except in the presence of others, of course.

It was those disturbing moments when he presented her to the world as a new husband should a wife that kept her pacing restlessly now. Or so she thought. He made an attentive husband, always there to offer her an arm, catch her shawl, or just smile at her conspiratorially at some private jest. Most men barely acknowledged their wives, and she thought he would infinitely prefer the company of men his own age rather than her immature chatter, but he showed no sign of impatience as would many another man. The incongruity of his behavior worried her.

Aubree clutched her arms beneath her breasts and tried to shut out the memories of those times Austin had held her in his arms and treated her as a man does a woman. He was a man, with a man's needs, and she was available. She felt certain, given the opportunity, he would take her without thought to his promise or the consequences. That did not mean he thought of her as a wife or woman, or even thought of her at all. He would simply ease his needs and face the consequences on the morrow.

So it was up to her to see that their agreement was kept or they would end up married, in truth. Unless, of course, she decided this loveless marriage more suitable than loneliness. If she were only old enough, more experienced, she might even make Austin love her a little, but she had no idea where to begin. After all, she actually knew very little about him.

Unable to settle down to sleep, Aubree slipped barefoot down the gallery to the stairs, aiming for the library below. A good book might take her mind off these nonsensical notions.

Outside the study, Heath's raised voice halted her. She caught her name and could not help but linger briefly. Heath seldom raised his voice, but she could hear him plainly now.

"That is not fair to Aubree, sir," he exclaimed heatedly. "She needs to be given this chance to make her way in society. She is too young to be isolated in a strange place with none of the comforts to which she is accustomed. At the very least, allow her to stay with her aunt until I can make the abbey livable. I cannot take her with me, surely you must see that."

Aubree's heart stopped cold and she quickly retraced

her steps without hearing her father's reply. He meant to be rid of her, already! She had thought they were learning to be friends, that he might even take her as a wife if she encouraged him, but no! He would dump her on friends and relatives and return to his home alone as her father had done. How dare he! He had promised to give her protection until she came into her inheritance, and now he wanted to abandon her to the mockery of all!

Hurt, humiliated, and enraged at the discovery that Austin wished to be quit of her, Aubree stormed into her room and threw the bolt. Let him find his own chambers this night. Perhaps her father would let him sleep with him, they were such good friends.

She heard the slam of the door as Austin stormed out into the night, obviously infuriated by her father's refusal to allow her to remain in London. Tears of anger and self-pity wet her pillow at this knowledge that she was not wanted by either man in her life. And only moments before she had been so confident of her new position as wife!

Later that evening, Heathmont swayed slightly while contemplating the polished dark wood of the locked door confronting him. In his muddled state, he could remember no reason for this sudden disbarment. He had begun to think of Aubree as his one ally in a hostile world, and now she, too, had turned her back on him.

Thoroughly disgruntled by this new turn of events and determined not to lose this battle of wills with both father and daughter, Heathmont went in search of a footman.

With as much dignity as he could muster under the circumstances, Austin rewarded the silent footman as the bedroom door listed open, pried from its hinges. The footman nodded his thanks and disappeared into the darkness as Austin found his unsteady way through the opening and shoved the door back in place. The humiliation he had suffered at the hands of this domineering family demanded vengeance, but his head was not clear enough to seek a sensible solution.

Remembering the woman's arms from which he had

just come, Heathmont seriously considered returning to them. His former mistress had accepted his purse and his excuses without complaint. He did not think she would be averse to sharing her bed one more time.

But remembering his reason for severing that relationship in the first place, Heath straightened his shoulders. He had been given this one last chance to do things properly. He would begin by teaching his errant wife her duties. He would suffer no further humiliation at a woman's hands, particularly not those of a spoiled, willful brat.

Staggering slightly, he lifted his candle to locate Aubree's sleeping figure on the chaise. He would begin there.

Successfully negotiating the distance between door and Aubree, Austin blundered against her low-lying bed, knocking his shin and nearly dropping his candle. Swearing softly, he collapsed on the cushion, his bracing hand instantly coming in contact with something soft and malleable that began to wriggle and scream in surprise.

At the precarious tilt in which he held it, the candle flame drowned in molten wax and doused the room in darkness. Still cursing, Heath set it aside and hastened to halt the commotion below him. The scent of lilacs guided his movements.

Aubree squealed and tried to escape Heath's heavy weight as he leaned over her, but he trapped her beneath the covers. The smell of brandy filled her nostrils, but it was not that scent that enraged her as she wakened fully. A heavy, musky scent of expensive perfume permeated the air, a feminine scent she had never used in her life.

Aubree's screams would bring the whole household running if he did nothing to halt them. Fearing he had nothing to lose, Austin bent to quiet them in the only manner that occurred to his sodden brain.

His kiss suffocated her with the potent intoxication of brandy and anger. Aubree raged against it, twisting and turning and beating against him with her powerless fists. At the same time, she melted beneath the heat of his body against hers and the passion of his lips as they pressed hungrily for some response. She could not believe he was doing this to her, or she to herself.

When at last her hands clung to him rather than repulsing him, Austin felt safe in allowing his kisses to travel farther, to whisper along the soft line of her jaw and trail over her earlobe to her temple. Painfully aware of the yielding body below him, Austin sought for some easing of his needs, some understanding for his actions. His hand drifted to the tempting swell of her breast pressing against his chest, and he gasped as he encountered more flesh than expected. The hideous lawn shift she had worn these past nights would never have slid so easily through his fingers as this.

The touch of his heated hand against her bare breast shocked Aubree back to sensibility, and when Austin sat up to stare at her incredulously, she reacted violently. In one lithe movement, she freed her trapped hand and slapped it soundly against his jaw, before fleeing the confinement of her silken prison.

Even in the dim moonlight, Aubree could see the shock and fury written across her husband's countenance, and she sought futilely for some protection. She had run in the wrong direction to escape by the door. Now his tall frame towered between her and any possibility of escape. As he began advancing on her, Aubree snatched a hairbrush from the dresser to wield as weapon.

"Get out of here, you monster," she whispered fearfully, clutching a sheet around her and extending her miserable sword threateningly.

"Not until you learn your lesson, brat." The alcohol had not entirely dissipated from his brain, but his pride could never have reacted in any other way. They had made an agreement, and he would see that she abided by it, willing or no.

"I'll scream," Aubree threatened as he snatched the brush from her grasp and flung it across the floor.

"And I'll silence you the same way I did before."

She had backed up against the window seat and could go no farther. Austin stood before her, all his anger and pain shouting for expression as she cowered beneath his glowering stare. He reached for the sheet that protected her from his sight, ripping it from her fingers and flinging it aside while his gaze absorbed the lovely form revealed.

In the moonlight, her skin glimmered like silver above the froth of green silk. She wore the gown he had given her—which she must have donned for his benefit—and Austin suddenly felt a fool. He had spoiled everything, again, with his hasty actions. The last of the alcohol fled, leaving a throbbing ache behind his eyes.

"You barred the door," he accused her.

Shivering without the protection of covers and beneath his icy glare, Aubree clung to what anger she could. "You reek of cheap perfume," she returned curtly.

Stunned by this observation, having forgotten that brief encounter aeons earlier, Austin hesitated. Golden hair fell in thick waves across her shoulders and down her back, and he longed to wrap his fingers in it, but now was not the time. Never might be the time.

"Actually, I believe it was very expensive perfume. I certainly paid enough for it." He walked away, leaving her standing there. Sitting down upon the edge of the bed, he began to remove his shoes.

"You bastard!" Aubree exclaimed at this admission of guilt. Without bothering to grab for the sheet, she strode determinedly toward the door.

"Touch that door and I'll come after you so fast you won't know what hit you, Aubree Elizabeth," he warned.

She halted and turned to find him calmly throwing his coat over a chair and reaching for his cravat.

"You wouldn't dare!"

"Wouldn't dare what, my dear?" he inquired politely, dropping his cravat atop his coat. "Risk a scene chasing you through the house in our nightclothes? Yes, I'd dare that."

That wasn't what she meant, and he knew it. Aubree glared at him impotently. "Do you expect me to stay here after you attacked me like that? And while still stinking of another woman's perfume? You've broken your word!"

Dropping his shirt on the pile of discarded clothing, Austin deliberately advanced in her direction. In the pale gleam of moonlight from behind him, Aubree could only discern the silhouette of his bronzed torso against the window, and the darker shadow of the line of rough curls across his chest. Yet this sight of his nakedness frightened her even more than the well-lighted display of their wedding morning. She edged closer to the door.

"We will be fortunate if the whole household does not know you locked me from our chambers this night," he admonished sternly, coming to a halt just before her quivering figure. "Did you expect me to seek a bed in the attics?"

"I certainly didn't expect you to seek your mistress's bed!"

If his head hadn't hurt so badly, if he hadn't been so confused and angry over the night's events, he might have laughed at this small spark of jealousy. Instead, he grabbed her by the waist and hauled her close to him where his hand could travel over silken curves.

"Are you offering to exchange your favors for hers?"

His hand located the tempting tilt of her breast and rubbed sensuously against the tautening peak beneath the smooth silk.

Aubree caught her breath and almost wept at the sensations sweeping through her at this knowing caress. She leaned against him as his hand skillfully taught her the impossibility of resistance.

"Austin, you promised," she whispered tearfully against his chest.

He drew his hand down between them, touching briefly at her flat stomach and rounded hip before coming to rest near the place where her passions centered. He rubbed lightly at the silk and heard her small cry of surprise with satisfaction. She would learn, with time.

"I owed her some explanation of my desertion, halfling. I broke no promises. Now come to bed before I regret keeping this one."

He lifted her easily and carried her to the bed. Aubree stared in fright as he joined her between the covers, but he did no more than lie on his back with his hands beneath his head and stare at the canopy. She jumped nervously when he spoke.

"I gave you my word as a gentleman that I would not touch you, Aubree, but there are times when I forswear any claims to that status. Beware that you do not drive me to that, my love."

He grew silent after that, and Aubree held herself tensely until his breathing grew even and she knew he slept. Her body still ached and tingled from those sensations he had brought to her and they did not lessen when the cause of them lay pressed against her side. Her body warned her more clearly than his words. She had made a bargain with the devil.

When Aubree woke in the morning, Austin had already departed, but Mattie and several of the maids were frantically packing what must have been every trunk in the attic. Aubree peered at them from behind the bed curtains, trying desperately to calm her quaking nerves.

Just as she gained the courage to step from her bed, Austin stormed the portals like a wayward wind, scattering maids in every direction as he stalked into the room. His mop of chestnut curls had evidently been trimmed and arranged in some attempt at order, but they still managed to look modishly disheveled. His tan features contrasted well with his elegantly tied white cravat, but the rough, brown kerseymere coat and fawn-colored riding breeches indicated a lack of elegance more suited to the country. Aubree stood up to him daringly.

Ignoring her dishabille, Heathmont proceeded to give curt orders to the maids, then turning to Mattie, he demanded, "See she is ready within the half-hour. Anything that is left behind you can carry with you on the wagon."

Finally acknowledging his wife's presence, Austin turned an aloof gaze to her proud stance. Suddenly seeing the golden enchantress he had first met in this slight figure with tumbling curls nearly hiding her lovely curves, he gentled his voice.

"It is time to go home, my dear. The coach will be waiting at half-past the hour. I would like to make this journey in as short a time as possible. Please be ready when I come for you."

With that, he turned on his heel and departed as swiftly as he had come, leaving Aubree staring after him in gaping astonishment. Home? His home? After last night, the thought suddenly terrified her.

She was not given time to think. Mattie whisked her out of her nightclothes and into a traveling dress of dusty blue, embellished with a fall of lace at her throat. The matching pelisse and hat were sent to the door to await her departure while Mattie hastily smoothed thick golden tresses into a simple chignon. A few rebellious curls still escaped about Aubree's pale face, but satisfied with the result, Mattie sent her charge down for a hasty breakfast.

Before Aubree knew what was happening, her father had kissed her good-bye and Austin was handing her into a spanking new landau emblazoned with his coat of arms and pulled by four matching chestnuts. She did have time to throw him a quizzical glance at this extravagance, and Heath shrugged nonchalantly.

"The journey is a long one, and I had no intention of chasing you halfway across the country on horseback. They can easily be resold later." He fastened the door securely after her and strode away.

Maids came tumbling out of the house with last-minute packages and instructions. The horses pawed restlessly at the dirty cobblestones, while Heath's stallion reared and protested after his long idleness. Mattie's capped curls bobbed vigorously as she ran up and down the mansion steps, directing the placement of food baskets and comforters and clean sheets should they stop at inns along the way.

The duke, in his beaver hat and carrying his knobbed walking stick, appeared momentarily on the doorstep, but a crowd of street urchins clamoring at his feet drove him to find his own coach.

With a cry to the magnificent chestnuts, the landau rolled out into the street, Austin's groom handling the reins and one of the duke's footmen clinging to the back. The wagon carrying luggage and pets and servants lingered behind. Alongside the carriage, Austin held tight rein on his prancing stallion. His gaze swept the street of neat, palatial mansions nearly devoid of any sign of human life, then returned to the rumbling landau and its lone occupant. Her fingers pressed against the glass, his wife waved tearlessly to the servants standing upon the steps.

They waved back, aprons clutched to their faces to wipe away tears, even the men dabbing inconspicuously at watery eyelids, long after the carriage disappeared from view.

BOOK TWO

Things base and vile, holding no quantity,
Love can transpose to form and dignity.
Love looks not with the eyes, but with the mind,
And therefore is winged Cupid painted blind.

—Shakespeare, *A Midsummer Night's Dream*

13

Aubree lifted the moth-eaten drapery from the window of Atwood Abbey's main salon and stared out over the desolate expanse of yard and drive leading down to the main highway. Not a single neighbor had ventured up that path since she had arrived a week ago, so she knew better than to expect any visitors now. She watched for some sign of Austin's arrival from the shipyards in Exeter, but that hope was even more futile this early in the day.

She turned away and lifted the disintegrating cover from another piece of rotting furniture. She understood now why Austin had fought to keep her from his home. The once-grand Gothic structure of Atwood Abbey had deteriorated to little more than a ruin after decades of neglect. All the good pieces of furniture, the paintings that once must have adorned the walls, the tapestries, and the candelabra had all been sold to cover mounting debts. The pieces that remained were barely in a state to be used, except for those too large to be moved, such as the massive Jacobean bed in Austin's chambers. Or his former chambers.

Aubree thoughtfully stuck her finger in the mouse-gnawed hole of the once-lovely Queen Anne winged chair. Austin's mother had been quite upset when she discovered her son's intentions of keeping a separate bedchamber for his wife, but after her first attempt to sabotage his plans fell through, she had wisely kept her silence on that subject.

Aubree smiled in remembrance of her first meeting with the incorrigible dowager. Aware of her new position as countess, she had attempted to dress herself with some dignity, donning a fragile yellow muslin the dressmaker had assured her was the latest mode, and then she had let herself from the room to search for breakfast.

She found it without too much difficulty by following her nose. The aroma of scorched rashers left a distinctive trail. She glanced at the sideboard displaying runny eggs and blackened slivers of meat and a bowl of something congealed, and shivered. When she glanced up again, Lady Heathmont had stood in the doorway, her merry eyes laughing silently at the expression of distaste on her daughter-in-law's face.

"I trust, my girl, that you are well-versed in the manner of running a household. My son is woefully negligent in that department, not entirely of his own fault, I will admit. I recommend the tea and think you may have more luck if you ring for toast. Only Austin could make a meal of that other slop."

With gratitude, Aubree did as bid. The dowager joined her in a cup of tea and watched with interest as Aubree inspected the cobweb-bedecked ceiling and the threadbare linen on the table. The pewter tea set and spoons did not shake her, but the mouse darting out from beneath the sideboard left her visibly mortified.

Aubree dropped her cup to the saucer and stared after the creature with incredulity. Lady Heathmont tapped her hand comfortingly.

"I am glad to see such things do not send you into the boughs. It would be most difficult to bring this house to order if we must continually pry you off the ceiling. You seem a good, sensible type. Your servants will be following shortly, I trust?"

Aubree nodded, still staring at the place where the mouse had disappeared. Tearing her fascinated gaze away, she turned to her table companion. "I have only my maid and her niece and nephew. That will scarcely be sufficient to set this house in order. Is there no one here beyond Austin's groom and that creature in the kitchen?"

Lady Heathmont made a slight gesture of distaste. "There was Blanche, but Austin gave her her walking papers before you arrived. Which was only proper." She did not linger over explanations. "The Dower

House has a cook and maid, but they refuse to work for Austin. Stubborn creatures, I should sack them, but I'd never find others. Perhaps you should come stay with me and let this place fall to ruin. I would not condemn you at all for your choice."

This stream of information had left Aubree floundering then and still had her wondering. Who was Blanche and why had Austin turned her off? Why would the servants at the Dower House not work in the abbey? Did the countess truly want the abbey let to ruin? Aubree did not trouble herself with such mysteries for long. There were too many other things to do.

Matilda and the twins should be arriving soon, but even a full staff could scarcely tackle the task of cleaning the decades of cobwebs and dust. To renovate the moldering ceilings and floors would take the abilities of an army of carpenters. Aubree gazed in dismay at the thick webs of dust hanging from the massive chandelier. Whatever had made her think she could save this room?

If only she could have a staff to tackle one room at a time, but no amount of persuading had been able to entice anyone local to work in the abbey. Austin had sent one of his ship's carpenters from Exeter to repair the mouseholes, but he could scarcely set about all the other tasks that needed doing.

Aubree took a cloth to the stained glass carefully preserved behind wooden shutters. If only she could talk to Austin, she might not feel quite so helpless in these matters. But since that last night in London, he had maintained a careful distance between them that she could not breach no matter how hard she tried. She supposed she had bargained for no more than that, but although she hated to admit it, she missed him.

He had promised to let her keep her animals and had even stopped at Southridge so she might bring her guinea pigs and tame raven and favorite mare with her, but the company of her pets was no longer enough. How would she possibly survive until fall with no one to talk to but Mattie and the twins?

Staring out the deep blue of the glass, Aubree had a
sudden vision of Austin's eyes as he stared down at
her prior to taking her into his arms and kissing her.
The memory of those muscled arms around her still
had the ability to make her tingle, and she threw
herself into the task of cleaning with renewed vigor.
Never would he know what he had done to her with
that kiss.

Cheeks rosy with the ride she had taken before
dinner, hair tousled and tumbling about her shoulders
in its usual disarray, Aubree wheeled her mount
toward the roadway and home. The mist had let up, and
now the sun threatened to peer out from behind the
clouds. She would have liked to explore farther, but
the possibility of Austin returning before she did made
her hasten homeward.

A shout and a galloping of hooves behind her made
her slow the mare and glance over her shoulder. An
auburn-haired young man on a gray gelding raced
toward her, and her heart leapt to her throat in fear.
Surely, it could not be . . . She forced herself to steady
her mount until she could see his face clearly. She had
no wish to insult Austin's neighbors, but as the other
rider drew nearer, she could not fail to recognize that
hard, squared jaw and determined expression. They
had been imprinted in her memory since those strong
hands had swept her from her horse and thrown her
into the coach that had carried her to disaster.

With wide-eyed panic, she whipped Dancing Star into
a gallop and tore down the road toward home. Contrary
to earlier, she prayed Austin had arrived home already. With no one there to protect her, she had no
idea of how to escape the madman closing in behind
her. The pounding hooves grew closer and his shouts
more frantic as she guided her steed unerringly toward
the low stone wall that separated the abbey from the
roadway.

Clearing the wall with ease, she raced her powerful
mare down the faint traces of a path between the
overgrown woods and shrubs of the grounds. Tree
limbs whipped at her face and towering rhododen-

drons bent out to grab her, but she reached the stable yard without accident.

Only to find him there waiting for her. He had lost his hat and his auburn hair had fallen forward across his forehead, but there was no mistaking the determined cut of his jaw.

"Lady Aubree . . ."

He reached for her reins and Aubree struck at him with her crop.

"Not again, you won't," she hissed, trying to maneuver past him and closer to the side door. Perhaps if she could get inside . . .

He jerked his gloved hand hastily away. "I must apologize, please, if you will but give me a chance . . ." he pleaded, holding his mount still so that he did not send her flying again.

"Apologize!" Aubree screamed. "Apologize for having me carried off by a band of cutthroats and thieves and ruining my life in the process? Get out of here, sir, before I seek the sheriff."

Gray eyes grew wide with alarm. "By gad, they did not harm you? He promised me you would be in good hands. Or is it Heathmont . . . ? Please, Lady Aubree, you must trust in me. I will do anything to make right the wrong I have done you."

Aubree stared at him in incredulity and eased her horse toward the mounting block. He did not seem to be armed, but she had experience in his strength. She must be in a position to run for her life.

"You are far and away too late, sir," she informed him coldly, keeping him talking while her boot sought the block. "I would suggest you leave at once before Lord Heathmont returns. He will not take lightly to your presence."

Again, an expression of sincere distress crossed mobile features. "Surely he does not hold you prisoner here? If he is due home, I must speak with him. I cannot leave you like this, not knowing how you fare because of my rash stupidity. I will take you away, if you request it. Anything, just name your wish."

Aubree found the mounting block and hastily climbed down, clinging to her riding crop as she kept Dancing

Star between herself and the young madman. He did not appear mad, but his words and prior actions labeled him so. At the moment, however, he seemed harmless.

"I wish you to leave, at once," she replied firmly, watching hopefully to see if he would obey.

An expression of regret instantly appeared in his eyes, and he dismounted, coming forward with hand held out to her. "I cannot leave you here without knowing that you are safe and in good hands. Heathmont is fearsome, but if he has harmed you in any way, he will feel the wrath of those greater than he. Please, will you not talk to me?"

As she finally understood the basis of his ravings, Aubree felt the hysterical urge to giggle. The slide from panic to relief was too great for a more sensible reaction. Had he truly thought he rescued her from Heath when he thrust her so rudely into that coach? She ought to ring a peal over his head, but she knew Heath had done a fair job of that already.

Harley stared at the girl in disbelief as the corners of her mouth turned up in evident merriment and jade eyes began to dance with unmistakable devilment. He had come to offer rescue to a maiden in distress or, at best, apologize profusely to an outraged lady, but he had never once contemplated being laughed at.

"Sir, we have never been introduced, but you have caused me more trouble than I shall readily forget. If Austin has not carved your heart out, it must be for a reason, so I will not chastise you for your foolishness, but I suggest you depart before he has reason to change his mind."

He stood before her in dismay and disbelief and a growing sense of relief. But before he could reply, a familiar tall figure sauntered lazily from the stables, and the young man's face fell.

"It's a little too late for that, my dear," Heath's voice carried clearly from behind Aubree.

She spun around in delight and Austin caught her by the waist, holding her quite familiarly as he confronted their unexpected visitor. He kept an eye on Harley as he continued speaking to his wife. "Is he bothering you? Shall I order him never to darken our doors again?"

Something in his tone of voice told her he was not serious, but Aubree studied her husband's face carefully before answering. The pressure of his arm around her sent other signals, different from the tone of his voice, but these she could not translate. Finally deciding she found no fear or alarm in his questions, she smiled up at him.

"It is not often a gallant knight rides to my rescue. Can I keep him?"

Heath smothered an explosion of laughter at Harley's startled expression. "Like one of your pets? Would you stable him in the barn? He might fare better there than in the house."

Thoroughly mortified by this amused discussion, the young man attempted to protest. "I say, now, if I've made a cake of myself, say so to my face. I'm prepared to take my measure like a man."

With straight face, Heath acknowledged, "Harley, you've made a cake of yourself. And a crumpet or two, I fashion. Have you more to add to that, my dear?" He turned to Aubree with lifted eyebrow.

Feeling sorry for the man by now, Aubree shook her curls lightly. "I think I prefer some explanations and an introduction. He has just given me the fright of my life, and I think I'm due that much."

Harley swallowed and adjusted his cravat nervously as Heath's piercing blue gaze shifted questioningly to him. "I only wished to apologize, but she ran. I had no idea you hadn't explained . . ." He gave up, fearing he only dug his hole deeper.

Austin contemplated him gravely. "My wife does not frighten easily. If you have harmed her in any way—"

Aubree interrupted impatiently. "On the contrary. I hit him with my riding crop. We ought to have his hand looked at. Now, if someone will please explain, I would appreciate it more than watching you behave like two bulls in the same pasture."

Both men stared at her with incredulity, but Heath's lips began to twitch and any remaining tension dissipated.

"Your metaphors leave a good deal to be desired, halfling," Austin informed her with amusement. Before she could ask why, he continued smoothly, "I'd like to introduce you to Harley Sotheby. Harley, I assume you know my wife, Lady Aubree."

The young gentleman bowed cautiously over her hand, keeping a suspicious eye on the lady's husband. "I am most happy to meet you, my lady, and I must apologize profusely for all the grave harm I have done you."

Aubree eyed the wide stripe in his leather gauntlet where the riding crop had struck him. "Perhaps you had better remove your glove, Mr. Sotheby, and let me have a look at that hand. I would not be held responsible for inflicting both wound and infection."

Harley looked up uncertainly to his lordship's face and, finding only amusement there, floundered helplessly. "The hand is fine, milady. The damage is not serious, I assure you."

"Fine. Then you must come inside and take potluck with us. Perhaps then I will get more explanation from the two of you than has been forthcoming." Aubree picked up her skirts and prepared to lead the way back to the house, but Heath caught her arm.

She turned quizzically to discover Mr. Sotheby gone red with embarrassment and Austin regarding her with a mixture of amusement and frustration.

"I am sorry, Lady Aubree, but I must return home. I only came this far to assure myself of your . . ." He caught Heath's sardonic look and hastily amended. "To offer my apologies. But I would hear no end to it if I did not invite you to our home. My sisters are much of your age, I believe, and they are most eager to meet you. If I could persuade you to visit, I would gladly come fetch you myself."

At the knowledge there were others nearby with whom she could make friends, Aubree brightened perceptibly, but as the gentleman's speech grew nervous, a strange suspicion took root in her mind. When he finished, she regarded him coolly.

"I would be most happy to make the acquaintance of your sisters, Mr. Sotheby. If my husband would be so kind as to take me there one day, I should like to call upon them."

Harley glanced nervously to Heath's impassive face. "Well, you see, my father is old and set in his ways. It would be better if I came for you. Perhaps his lordship could explain . . ."

"There is no need of explanations, sir," Aubree replied with deceptive softness. "I will not go where my husband is not welcome. Please send my regrets to your sisters."

She spun around and began to stalk off, but Austin's abrupt call halted her irate retreat. She spun around and glared at them.

"Don't be foolish, Aubree. Maria and Anna are intelligent, extremely likable young ladies. You will enjoy their company."

She lifted her chin proudly. "Then I am most sorry I shall not have the opportunity to meet them. Good day to you, sir." She nodded a regal dismissal to the auburn-haired young man and strode away without another look back.

Affection and irritation shadowed Austin's eyes as he followed her graceful sway across the rough terrain. He turned back to meet Harley's gaze with a shrug. "If you have not noticed, she is an extremely opinionated young woman," he murmured in explanation.

"She is right, you know," Harley offered apologetically. "Still, I had hoped . . . It's going to be damned difficult, Heathmont," he finished almost angrily.

"So is Aubree." Heath grinned and offered the young man his hand. "It's not your worry, Sotheby. I appreciate your concern."

Harley glanced at the offered hand and with sudden decision shook it firmly. "I owe you an apology, sir. It is very difficult to overcome habit, but I intend to mend my ways."

Heath shrugged wearily. "I daresay you can live down your reputation without great difficulty. I am sorry you cannot dine with us. Good evening."

Harley watched the proud earl's straight back as he marched away, the limp more pronounced than he remembered. He had given Heathmont every opportunity to savagely retaliate against his insults, but the earl had nobly overlooked his faults. He could not believe the man a coward, not after he had fought so viciously when he had thought the lady endangered, but he could believe him to be a gentleman to the core, despite rumors to the contrary.

It seemed a pity he should be so tarnished by rumor as to put him, and his lovely young wife, quite beyond the pale.

By the time Heath reached the upper hallway, he could hear Aubree chattering with his mother's maid and assumed she would be preparing for dinner. He could not intrude upon her now. Explanations would have to wait for a more opportune time.

As he entered the neglected surroundings of his own room, Heath could hear the splash of bathwater coming from his wife's chambers. He threw off his soiled coat and wished for even a pitcher of warm water in which to wash. John would be rubbing down the lathered horses; he tended to put his animals before his master at the best of times. The earl's need to bathe regularly seldom occurred to the groom.

Austin sat down and removed the hot boots from his weary feet, then threw off his sweat-soaked shirt. He had worked as hard as his men at repairing the dry-docked ship, but it would be some weeks before it would be seaworthy again. He had six months in which to repair and stock the ship and hope it returned with a cargo sufficient to repay Aubree and line his own pockets. It would have to be a short trip and a risky one if he were to gain his goal.

A soft scratch at the connecting door startled Austin from his reverie. Unthinkingly, he barked a command to enter. Not until Aubree's golden head peeked around the door did he realize he was half-dressed.

Pink tinged Aubree's cheeks as she breached the privacy of her husband's chambers to find him stripped to the waist and obviously prepared to wash. He had sheltered her from much of these intimacies, she realized, but she rather enjoyed this one. Except for their wedding morning, she had never truly seen her husband half-naked, and the sight sparked her interest.

She had no idea his shoulders were so broad even without the padding, and the bulge of work-hardened muscles across his chest and arms made her shiver with some pleasant emotion. Her cheeks grew pinker.

"The bathwater is still warm, my lord. I thought you might find it more pleasant than cold water in a basin. And Delphine says you have a mirror in here we might use while you bathe." Despite her pink cheeks, she spoke boldly, and her gaze did not falter as he sauntered closer and leaned against the door.

She smelled of fresh lilacs and rainwater, and drops of moisture still clung to the hollow of her throat where her robe did not close. Austin gazed in silent delight at this sight before replying with a nod.

"That seems fair exchange, my dear, one mirror for one bath." He continued to gaze upon her until her creamy cheeks blushed a deep pink.

Not certain how else to act in the presence of a half-dressed male, Aubree turned and gestured for the little French maid to bring her combs as if she had full access to her husband's chambers all the time. The maid cast Austin a wary glance as she passed by him, but imitating Aubree, she managed to ignore him and turn her attention to golden curls.

Lips curled in amusement, Austin exchanged his new chamber for his old one and closed the door between. He possessed no screen to protect a maiden's modesty, though at this point he was none so certain Aubree needed protecting. She had the curiosity of a young kitten and the active mind of a budding connoisseur. It would be a privilege to teach her the differences between a man's body and a woman's, but it was a privilege he had not yet earned.

Realizing the near impossibility of ever earning the privilege of possessing a wife like Aubree, Heathmont slowly lowered himself into the bath water. He wanted many things, and he had full confidence that one day, he would have them all. But Aubree . . . Aubree was the golden sun of his day. What man could hope to attain the sun? It would not do to dwell for long upon it.

14

Having succeeded in persuading the dowager's cook to expand her efforts to include the abbey's residents, Aubree chose to keep the woman happy by providing those expensive condiments a limited budget had denied them before. It was still awkward for Patience to carry the cooked dinner from the Dower House to the ancient warming ovens on either side of the abbey's huge kitchen fireplace, but Aubree had not found any means of overcoming that problem yet. The small remainder of her last quarter's allowance would only cover minor inconveniences.

She smiled at John as she mounted her frisky mare, and the taciturn Welshman offered a tentative tug of his forelock in return. Small and wiry and uninclined toward conversation, the groom had served Austin for a score of years or more, and the two men got on together well. The presence of a woman in the bachelor household made the man fidgety.

"I am sorry Austin thought it necessary to leave you behind to tend to me, John, but my servants should be arriving soon and then you can return to your usual duties. Since he has been so generous as to leave you here, however, I hope you will show me the way to the village. I have some shopping I would like to do."

A loud "caw" and the flap of black wings behind them caused the groom to turn a wary glance over his shoulder, but Myna settled complacently on Aubree's shoulder, uttering only a "caw" of triumph from his perch.

"Yes, mum," the groom muttered before climbing into the saddle of his own horse. Throwing the crow another suspicious glance, he spurred his mount into a trot.

Just outside of town, a familiar gray gelding raced toward them and reined to a sudden stop as its rider espied Aubree and her groom.

"My lady, I am in luck! I thought to ask if you would go riding with me, but you must rise earlier than my sisters." Harley held his horse steady as Aubree rode to join him.

"I have come to do some shopping, sir. Pleasure will have to wait for another day, unless you wish to accompany me?" she inquired innocently. It would be a good deal easier to encounter the curious stares of strangers with someone she knew, however vaguely, at her side.

Harley's face brightened. "I would be delighted. I shall be able to make a round of visits for a week simply on the subject of your introduction to county society. Where would you like to start?"

Though he made light of it, Aubree suspected he spoke the truth. Heath had warned her that his standing with his neighbors was not a good one, and the village folk would be even less forgiving than the gentry. It would help if she knew the stories behind the rumors, but Heath had not seen fit to provide her with that information. She walked blindly into unknown territory.

"I need someone who deals in spices, I believe," she answered politely. It would be necessary to muster her forces before storming the citadel. Before this day ended, she would have the village know that she meant business.

Harley directed her to a small shop in the center of the village's main street and helped her to dismount. With the auburn-haired young man's arm beneath her fingers, Aubree felt well prepared for battle, and she dismissed John to tend to his own amusement. Myna had already flown off to circle the town in search of crow delicacies.

Inside, the scent of dried herbs mixed with the odors of camphor and liniment, and Aubree blinked to adjust her eyes to the dim interior. A doughy-faced proprietor watched her suspiciously while an elderly customer swaddled in ancient black bonnet and innumerable shawls peered at them with open curiosity.

Aubree presented her list and inquired politely, "Will you be able to supply me with these, sir?"

By now, the black-garbed woman had digested the expensiveness of Aubree's elegantly tailored fawn riding habit and judged the quality of her speech and recognized her companion. With a nearly toothless smile, she asked, "You be from the hall, then? Not one of your sisters, eh, Master Harley?" She winked.

Aubree turned the full effect of her smile on the old woman. "I'm from the abbey. Mr. Sotheby is good enough to escort me on my errands this morning." Properly, she should not have acknowledged the old gossip, but she had plans of her own, and there was no better way of setting them in motion than gossip.

Both the proprietor and the old woman stared at her as if she had claimed residency on the moon. The man behind the counter turned and slowly began replacing the spices she had requested on the shelves.

"Sorry, miss, we don't extend credit to the abbey." He spoke gruffly, not rudely, simply stating a fact of life.

Aubree pressed her lips together tightly and opened her purse of coins. "I am prepared to pay for my purchases, sir," she informed him firmly.

The old woman cackled happily. "She's got you there, Barnaby. Ain't you heard? Our earl's gone and wed a rich wife. You'd best spruce up your manners, boy."

She peered from Harley to Aubree and back again, finally addressing her question to a familiar face. "How comes it you're consorting with the abbey again, Master Harley? Does your papa know?"

Harley had held himself stiffly aloof throughout the entire conversation as a proper gentleman would, but at this direct inquiry he replied quite forcefully. "My father holds no complaint against the countess, Mrs. Green, and I suggest we would all do well to show her our welcome."

He turned his glare on the shopkeeper. "I'll vouch

for the lady's credit, Barnaby. I'll not have the countess carry gold about like a common moneylender. Send her package to the abbey. Lady Aubree, if you are ready . . ." He held out his arm in dismissal of the shop's occupants.

The shopkeeper had already noted the glint of coin and the depth of the lady's purse and obliged willingly. He might disapprove of the carryings-on of the nobility, but he had no objections to taking their coins.

Startled at the realization that this young girl must actually be the new Countess of Heathmont, the old woman bobbed a hasty curtsy as Aubree accepted her escort's arm. She was rewarded with a warm smile in return before the young couple departed for the next stop on their tour.

By the time Aubree had worked her way through half her list of purchases, the entire town had learned the new countess was in their midst, and her treatment thenceforth was deferential and just a bit wary. Aubree heard the whispers and caught their stares of curiosity with aplomb, diverting their attentions with questions and leaving hints that the abbey would be hiring if any wished to apply. She did not expect immediate results, but planted the seeds for thought.

Before they had time to enter the dress-goods shop, a light curricle clattered down the street and came to a smart halt in front of them. The two well-dressed occupants called a greeting, and grinning widely, Harley introduced them.

"Lady Aubree, I would like to present you to my sisters, Anna and Maria. If they were not so slow in rising, they would have joined us much earlier."

Aubree couldn't prevent a grin at this obviously well-planned attack. If she had set out to conquer the village, the Sothebys had set out to conquer her.

"It's my pleasure," she murmured as Harley helped one after the other from the vehicle. Anna was apparently the taller, older sister, a few years younger than Harley, perhaps. Where Harley's hair was a deep coppery auburn, Anna's was a bright carroty orange. But her smile was pleasant and her voice well-modulated as she acknowledged Aubree's greeting.

Maria hopped from the curricle with little help from her brother. More Aubree's age than either of the others, she beamed with self-congratulation at succeeding in this plot to meet their new neighbor. Though still showing distinct evidence of the Sotheby red coloring, her hair tended toward a more subtle hue of strawberry blond. She spoke with less propriety and more eagerness than her sister.

"I am ever so glad that Harley hasn't made a complete cake of himself yet and that you're still on speaking terms with him, Lady Aubree. I would have just died if I'd known there was someone my own age at the abbey and I couldn't speak with them. Have you just come from London? Did you visit King's Theatre? Did you go riding in Hyde Park? Of course, you did. How foolish of me."

She cut off her flow of chatter abruptly after a stern look from her older sister. Their indulgent brother had already taken their places in the curricle and called to them now.

"I'll just take these around to the stables. Tell the girls where you want to go and they'll take you." He whipped the horses into a trot and rolled off.

By the time Harley ambled back to join them, the "girls" were already deep in animated discussion over the merits of Sir Walter Scott's novels and the benefits of chamomile when feeling sickly, a combination he did not fully comprehend. However, they changed the subject immediately to the necessity of purchasing a carpet Aubree had discovered in the mercantile shop and the best means of transporting it to the abbey intact, since the day had begun to threaten rain.

Harley neatly solved that problem by suggesting the use of Heath's new covered carriage, so relieving the shopkeeper that he forgot to remind the countess that he did not extend credit to the abbey. The young people walked out, leaving the shopkeeper jubilant that he had finally sold the extravagant carpet and terrified that it would never be paid for.

As they strolled toward a small tea shop tucked away in the front room of a cottage at the end of the street, an oddly familiar figure came riding through the village. By the square cut of his coat and the polished gleam of his boots and hat, he was obviously a wealthy gentleman, and Aubree and her companions weren't the only ones to stop and stare.

"Geoffrey?" Aubree murmured in astonishment as the young man reined to a halt in front of them and gallantly doffed his hat.

Her companions did not find his appearance so astonishing and welcomed him into their group as if they were old friends. Geoffrey's pale eyes sought Aubree's, and he made a slight nod in her direction before succumbing to Anna's chatter.

Geoffrey fell in between the two sisters while Aubree accepted Harley's arm as they entered the tea shop. Not understanding in the least how or why Geoffrey had come to be here in Devon, far from the civilization of London he preferred, Aubree kept silent.

Though the two men obviously knew each other, there seemed to be some constraint between them that kept them from being easy in their speech. Geoffrey's cousin was inquired after and the length of his stay determined by the two sisters anxious to plan the summer's activities.

The young man lifted his blond head and looked directly at Aubree as he replied to the latter question. "I shall stay for so long as I am needed here, however long that might be."

The directness of his stare made Aubree grit her teeth and Harley fidget restlessly, but Maria and Anna didn't seem to notice. A young gentleman added to their limited circle was excitement enough without looking for meanings behind words.

Aubree had to wait until everyone had drunk their tea before she could make her excuses and rise to leave. To her relief, Harley signaled his friend to remain behind while he escorted Aubree to the street in search of her groom.

John was already waiting outside, horses in hand. Heavy clouds had moved in overhead, and he looked relieved at Aubree's appearance.

Harley, however, held her back a moment longer, his sympathetic gray eyes searching her face as he spoke. "Lady Aubree, I know you were affianced to Geoff before my fiasco in Hyde Park. I cannot help but think his arrival here now is at a most inopportune time. Your husband is some five years my elder. He and I were at school or war at different times and never had the opportunity to know each other well, but I know something of his history and I cannot believe he will take kindly to Geoff's presence. Will you give me permission to warn Geoff off? It would be better should it come from me than Heathmont."

Aubree stared at the rutted dirt of the road and contemplated his question. Once, she had used Heath to make Geoffrey jealous, and the result had been unmitigated disaster. She had no desire to turn the tables now. But Heath had not married her for love or in any expectation of staying wed, so she doubted very much if jealousy would play a part in his behavior. Pride might, however, and she did not think pride would allow him to give Harley the task of chasing off Aubree's suitors. No, that would be a task Heath would prefer to do alone. She shook her head negatively.

"No, Harley, you are not my brother nor my husband. It would not be proper for you to speak to Geoffrey as if you were. I doubt if I will see much of him, since I gather Austin attends very few entertainments in the area." Her lips turned upward in a melting smile as she finally turned to face him. "I thank you for introducing your sisters. Whatever lies between Heath and your father, I pray we can someday set aside. I should very much like to be friends with your family."

He bowed formally over her hand. "As you will, my lady." He straightened and a glint of mischief twinkled in his eyes. "You'll not be lacking in friends, or I miss my guess."

She returned his smile gladly. "My friends call me Aubree. I trust I will see you and your sisters again soon."

With a wave of farewell, she allowed John to assist her into the saddle, and not finding any sign of Myna, she rode off. The raven would follow at its own pace.

The first sprinkles of rain began halfway down the

road to home, but the heavy clouds held their worst moisture while Aubree urged her mount to greater strides. A streak of black came squalling from the treetops, screaming obscenities learned from the grooms in the stables where he resided. Myna landed on Aubree's shoulder just as another rider appeared from the woods.

Ignoring the groom and giving the raven a strange stare, Geoffrey reined his mount into stride beside Aubree.

"We need to talk, Aubree."

Aubree waited for Myna to quiet before replying. "I have told you before, Geoffrey, it is far and away too late for talk. You can only cause me trouble by pursuing the matter. Let us just be friends."

"I should hope we are that and more, Aubree." Aware of the silent man riding behind them, Geoffrey did not elaborate further. "Will you allow me to call?"

Aubree sent him a look of surprise that caused Myna to flap his wings in protest. "The abbey is scarcely prepared for visitors, but I should not turn you away. Have you met Heathmont?"

"It is not Heathmont I wish to see." Pale eyes searched her face sadly as he slowed his horse to a walk.

Aubree remembered the pleasant times they had shared, the jests and dances and walks together that had convinced her she might share her life with this man. A pang of sorrow crossed her face as she looked up into his troubled eyes, but more recent memories kept her course steady.

"But it is Heathmont you must see if you wish to be friend to me," she declared before spurring her mount to outpace him.

The raven flew off with a squawk as Aubree raced on and Geoffrey remained behind. John, the groom, watched with secret delight as the bird circled the young dandy and delivered a message more forthright than his usual incoherent obscenities. The Welshman offered no assistance as he rode by the cursing young gentleman wiping angrily at the ugly splotch upon his elegant black riding hat.

When Heath rode into the stable that evening, his long redingote dripping from the downpour, John greeted him with his usual solemnity. The two men wiped down the steaming stallion together.

"Well, John, did my lady lead you a merry pace today?" Austin inquired genially as he threw the soaked saddle across the stall frame.

"Just to the village and back, milord."

Austin's eyebrows raised at this piece of information. "To the village? I trust she was treated with respect." This last was said in a tone bordering on anger.

"Of course, milord. Young Mr. Harley accompanied her, and the ladies," he hastened to add before his employer's black frown could spread.

Heath's brow cleared immediately. "Good. Anna has a good head on her shoulders. She will keep the little witch out of trouble."

With a self-satisfied smile on his face, Heath gave the stallion one last rub and began to walk toward the door. Remembering his sodden condition, he halted and turned a quizzical look to his groom. "Did Harley or the ladies return with her? I may need to send them home in the carriage."

"No, milord, just the other young gentleman, and he returned before the storm broke." John had debated whether or not to impart this piece of information, but faced with a direct question, he could not lie.

"Other gentleman?" Puzzled, but not concerned, Austin simply asked for enlightenment.

"Blond gent with fancy clothes," John explained to the best of his abilities before returning to his duties. He had not liked the haughty young man and felt better for warning his master that such a one lingered about. Remembering the raven's mutual distaste of the chap, John threw a few extra oats in the direction of the loft.

Guessing at once the visitor's identity but refusing to believe it, Heathmont turned and strode out the door. He could not imagine the spoiled little dandy going out of his way to track Aubree down to this remote abode, particularly after she was wed. Could he have mistaken the bond between these two?

Deciding not to jump to conclusions, Austin hurried for a dry roof over his head and change of clothing.

A clatter of boots on the stairway made Austin look up in surprise as he entered the hall. A towheaded young boy carrying an empty pail in each hand came to a startled halt, attempted to touch his forelock, remembered the clattering pail, and made a jerky bow, before scurrying off into the kitchen. Bemused by this apparition in his front hall, Austin came to a complete halt in the upper corridor at the approach of a tow-headed maiden of tender years carrying an assortment of towels and soaps. When she entered the portals of his room, he had no choice but to venture on to Aubree's.

At Austin's entrance, Aubree leapt from beneath Matilda's gentle administrations and flew to his side.

"You're soaking wet! Didn't Jamie see you? I sent him to take this dreadful redingote from you." She helped him to shrug out of the dripping layers of cloth.

"Jamie? The tall, thin lad with pails for hands?" Austin wished for some excuse to hold her still so he could continue enjoying the soft scent of lilacs drifting to his nose, but Aubree had already confiscated his coat and condemned it to hang at the hearth, and he had no reason to follow.

"You *did* see him! I shall have to give him a talking to. He's not accustomed to working in the house, but he'll learn."

The young maid popped through the connecting door, her arms bereft of towels. "It's all prepared, mum. Be there anythin' else to do?"

"The countess is addressed as 'my lady,' Joan. You must forget the dairy and prepare yourself for better things," Matilda instructed impatiently. "Now take the master's wet gloves and dry them by the fire in the kitchen and tell that widgeon brother of yours to hurry back and assist his lordship. He'll have a death of cold before you two nodcocks get the fire made."

As the young maid scurried out with his gloves,

Austin turned a questioning glance to his wife. "The twins, I presume?"

Aubree suppressed a' giggle as she nodded. From beneath the bed, a long golden tail waggled tentatively, followed shortly by a moist black nose and soulful eyes. Aubree hastily spread her skirts and perched on the edge of the bed to hide the evidence, but tired of confinement, Lady whimpered pleadingly.

A smile tugged at Austin's lips. "We've accounted for Matilda and the twins and the dog. Aren't we missing something?"

Brilliant green eyes grew even brighter. "You don't mind? She cried so when I tried to leave her in the stables, I couldn't bear it. She's awfully good." She bent over and snapped her fingers at the spaniel cowering beneath the bed. A moment later, a ball of golden fur came bounding out, leaping directly toward the delightfully smelly man in the center of the room.

Austin caught himself on the back of a chair and lowered into the seat so he could bend over and pet the friendly animal. "She can scarcely do much damage to this place. The carpets were cut to rags years ago." He eyed the brightly colored floor-covering lying beside her bed but refrained from asking its source.

"Oh, thank you, milord," Aubree cried ecstatically, throwing herself on the rug at his feet and hugging the spaniel. "Papa would never allow Lady in the house, and Aunt Clara did not like it. I shall teach her not to chase the kittens." Remembering his earlier question, she turned a cheerful smile up to him. "They are in the kitchen helping Patience. If there are any mice left after the carpenters leave, they will chase them off."

Austin relaxed, enjoying the simple pleasure of drying out before a blazing hearth while listening to the welcome chatter of a lovely woman and petting a dog at his feet. "Then Patience will have no meat to add to her stew. You had better keep close count of your kittens."

Aubree stared at him in disbelief, then noting the laughter in his eyes, relented. "Patience will only be delivering your meals. Your mother's cook has agreed to cook your dinner in the Dower House. I think the kittens are safe."

His hand traveled of its own accord to stroke golden curls glimmering in the firelight. The rain beat heavily against the shuttered windows, but the room was cozy and dry. "So that is how you arranged it. Those harridans my mother employs are loyal only to her and refuse to enter my portals. You must have charmed them with some Hindu chant."

"Only if Hindus resort to bribery. Now you must take your bath before it grows cold. Your mother is joining us for dinner, and I gather she does not like to be kept waiting."

Austin was reluctant to rise from his comfortable seat. His comforts had been few and far between for as long as he could remember, and this particular comfort held an attraction for him he found hard to fight. Still, he could not luxuriate here forever.

Rising, Austin gave his hand to Aubree and helped her to her feet. "You have had a good day, then?" he asked, studying her closely.

"A lovely one, milord. I have met Anna and Maria," she added eagerly, as reluctant as he to end this moment. "They are everything you claimed and more."

"Good. Then you will have some friends to keep you occupied." He watched her face, waiting.

Suddenly conscious that Matilda continued to putter about the room, Aubree offered no more of her thoughts. She continued to hold his hand, aware of the strength and warmth it contained, wishing she could transmit messages through this silent connection.

Instead, she only smiled.

Austin felt his heart twist in his chest at the tantalizingly aloof light in her eyes. He wished she had mentioned her encounter with Geoffrey, or even with Harley, but he had no right to confront her with it. He had no rights at all, except to wait for that day when he had an unsullied name and a fortune to offer her.

He might as well wait for the cliffs of Dover to crumble to the sea.

15

Austin flung himself so vigorously into his work at the shipyards that Aubree scarcely saw him from one day to the next. He was gone before she rose in the morning and seldom returned before dark in the evening. She saw to it that a bath and a warm meal awaited him, but their limited exchange of words extended only to the happenings of the day or preparations for the morrow.

Aubree knew better than to complain. Her father had the same single-mindedness of purpose, and she had learned to entertain herself quite comfortably, but each sundown found her waiting eagerly for the sound of horse's hooves in the cobbled yard. She told herself she longed only for companionship, but those nights when she produced a gleam of approval in bleary eyes or a smile to tired lips were her happiest.

While Austin went about rebuilding and restocking his ship, Aubree turned her time and talents to increasing the comforts of his home. The task was not an easy one since Austin had diverted all funds and the only available workmen to his project, but Aubree was not without resources.

The carpenters from Exeter left Austin's chambers in an unfinished state upon being ordered back to the ship, and local workers stubbornly avoided the abbey. Understanding only that gossip had painted her husband as some kind of ogre and that lack of funds encouraged this attitude, Aubree resolved to make wrong things right again. Lack of funds might hinder restoration of the abbey, but she would not allow gossip to stand in her way.

With the help of Mattie and the twins, rotting draperies and wall coverings disappeared. Colonies of spiders and cobwebs were driven back to their natural habitat, and walls and floors were swept and washed clean of grime. Little could be done about damaged paneling and crumbling stone at this stage, but a careful arranging of furniture and remaining tapestries and portraits accomplished miracles. One room at a time underwent a slow but steady transformation.

Knowing she was limited in what she could do with one lady's maid and two pairs of unskilled hands, Aubree never lost sight of her goal to clear Austin's reputation and return workers to the abbey. From various sources she learned of the excesses of the previous earl and understood some of the grudge between the village and the abbey, but the more serious charges lay somewhere in Austin's own past.

The dowager refused to speak of the past but surrounded herself with the comforts provided by a small trust her late husband had been unable to touch. Not unintelligent, she had learned long ago to accept what could not be changed. She watched Aubree's eager efforts with amusement and encouragement, but offered no hint of the family scandals.

Aubree found an unlikely source of information in Patience, the cook. Mentally incapable of comprehending or judging the actions of others except as they applied to her, Patience spoke of the years of abusive behavior suffered under the previous earl as if they were yesterday. She recounted tales of drunkenness and wild parties with the slow wonder of a newborn babe. Her main grief appeared to be the loss of friends as one by one, the servants left for better-paying, less-degrading jobs, or were sacked for various and illusory wrongs. Once only a lowly scrub maid, Patience eventually found herself the only remaining servant in the kitchen. The promotion to cook had come as a result of the process of elimination and without benefit or reward.

But there still had been servants employed at the abbey when Austin inherited the title after his father's death. Aubree learned this much from Patience, who spoke of Austin's first wife with an awe that reflected fear as well as admiration. Perhaps after his wife's death, Austin had let them all go, but that did not explain their reluctance to return. Aubree vowed to get to the bottom of this mystery if she had to confront Austin himself with it.

She found the villagers and tenants to be taciturn, but not unfriendly as she came to know them. They watched her warily and often with open curiosity, but treated her with respect. Still, all her hints of available positions seemed to fall on deaf ears.

One particularly discouraging day she succumbed to disgust and ordered the lowering of the crystal parlor chandelier with only the aid of Jamie and Joan, only to discover the three of them could not raise it again after washing and polishing the myriad of tiny prisms. Irritated and impatient, Aubree donned her riding habit and rode into the village again. Surely somewhere in all of Devon there ought to be one able-bodied man willing to work to feed and house his family. She could not offer a large salary, but there were rooms aplenty to provide housing, and the kitchen garden flourished. They would not starve. With that thought in mind, she aimed for the one place she had not been, the village tavern.

Jamie accompanied her to town and, realizing her intent, tried ineptly to dissuade her, but he held Aubree in too much awe to argue well, and she ignored his protests. She stepped from the humid summer heat into the musty dimness of the tavern interior with a determination that did not bode well for any who interfered.

At this time of the afternoon, there were very few occupants at the heavy trestle tables along the walls. A man with an open-necked and rather grimy cotton shirt polished mugs behind the rough-hewn bar, and several loungers sprawled in a far corner, nursing their cups of ale. They all looked up with interest at Aubree's entrance. Despite the fact that she had simply gathered her hair at the nape of her neck and wore a rumpled and dusty riding habit, she held herself with the proud stance of a well-born lady and none mistook her for any less. They all recognized the Earl of

Heathmont's new wife and watched her with a mixture of suspicion and interest.

The bartender moved first, hurrying from behind the bar and wiping his hands on a well-used apron. A man in his thirties, with some claim to looks and an athletic build, he was known to be popular with the local female population, but his interest was purely professional now.

"My lady, I am honored by your presence, but I have no tea room to offer. Might I show you the way to Mrs. Croft's? She would be delighted . . ."

Aubree made a gesture of impatience. "I know how to find Mrs. Croft's, thank you. You are Mr. Weston, are you not? I was told you might be able to help me."

The few idlers in the room began to move closer, their curiosity unable to withstand the possibilities of this opening. The bartender looked uncertain, but not uncooperative. Aubree addressed them all as one.

"I have need of aid. I am seeking able-bodied men willing to come to the abbey and work for me. I have coin and you will be paid. Is there anyone here, or do you know of anyone, who might help me?"

Fear and distress flickered momentarily in Weston's eyes and the men behind him began to murmur among themselves. Aubree felt them studying her, but she could not understand their expressions. If they wanted to work, why did they not step forward and say so? Or if they did not, why didn't they return to their tables and ale?

"She's just a wee bit of a thing," one of them murmured with what sounded like sympathy.

"Sure, and she is that, but it's none of our affair," whispered another angrily. "He's like to murder us all if we stand in the way."

"If we say her nay and aught happens . . ."

Weston snapped this speculation off in midsentence. "There ain't a man among us, milady, who wouldn't be willing to lend a hand should you come to us, but we'll not be interfering with his lordship and his affairs at the abbey. You'd do best to go to those of your own kind and not bring trouble to the likes of us."

Thoroughly puzzled by this reply, Aubree opened

her mouth to protest, but the loud clatter of boots in the entranceway intruded. An auburn head ducked under the low timber of the doorway, followed shortly after by Jamie's anxious features.

"Lady Aubree! What in heaven's name are you about?" Harley nodded a brief greeting to the gathering of men. "Gentlemen, if you will excuse us, I believe the lady has gone astray."

To the relief of his audience, he firmly captured Aubree's elbow and led her from the tavern, followed close behind by Jamie. Outside, Aubree shook him off and glared at Harley with frustration.

"Who appointed you my keeper, Mr. Sotheby? I'll thank you to explain this outrageous behavior!"

Smoky gray eyes regarded her with a mixture of bemusement and curiosity. "Your groom came to me for aid, and rightly so, I expect. I cannot believe his lordship would approve of your frequenting taverns."

Aubree's fists knotted in a rage of helplessness. "And what do you know about anything? Austin is busy and has not time to concern himself in my affairs. If I want something done, I must do it myself. Unless, of course, you are volunteering for the position."

Harley gave her an odd look and signaled for Jamie to bring their horses. "Let us go somewhere where we are not quite so visible. I have no desire to hear the tale that would develop if we come to cuffs here in the street."

Aubree contemplated telling him that problem would most easily be solved should he leave her alone and go his own way, but she resisted. She had so little company in this forsaken spot, she could not bear to drive off one of the few friends she had. Reluctantly, she obliged.

They rode out toward the abbey and halted in a copse of trees beside the road. By this time, Aubree could find very little to say to him, and she resisted Harley's insistence that they dismount.

"You are the stubbornest wench I've ever had the misfortune to meet," Harley complained ungallantly as he reached up and lifted her from the saddle.

"I am not one of your sisters to be ordered about in

such a manner," Aubree exclaimed indignantly as he
settled her on the turf.

"It is because of my sisters that I dare treat you in
such a manner." Harley pulled off his coat and spread
it upon the grass. "Sit. Pretend I am your brother.
Tell me why you felt called upon to enter a tavern
seeking help."

Refusing to sit, Aubree stared at him in perplexity.
Though less than half a score her senior, Harley acted
with the maturity and wisdom of a much older man.
She found it easy to look upon him as an older brother,
but she could not forget that he had once attempted to
"rescue" her from Austin's company for reasons beyond
her understanding. Perhaps now was the time to seek
comprehension.

"I will tell you that when you tell me why you feel
so compelled to interfere in my affairs," she demanded.

"Are you going to sit?" Harley crossed his arms and
watched her patiently.

Feeling that he had learned much too much from
Austin, Aubree flounced her skirts crossly and settled
in the place indicated. "There."

"Good." Harley found a seat on a rock across from
her. "You first."

This was worse than playing Questions and Answers, and Aubree felt grossly put upon to be in the
position of answering instead of questioning, but she
made the attempt in hopes of gaining something in
return.

"I cannot see where I did anything so wrong. I
merely needed someone stronger than I am to lift the
chandelier back in place and do other odd jobs about
the house. I was not trying to hire a butler or any such
thing in that place. I am not quite so giddy as that."

Harley stared at her in growing amusement. A
slight breeze tossed a lock of his hair across his forehead, and the sun caught the rich satin of his yellow
waistcoat as he sat upon the stone in the field of grass,
watching the beautiful, spoiled child at his feet.

"You went in a tavern looking for someone to lift a
chandelier?" he asked incredulously, laughter lighting
his eyes as he began to understand her predicament.

"What on earth possessed you to lower those ghastly, monstrous creations in the first place? Were you planning on giving a ball?"

Aubree sent sent him a look of irritation. "Of course not. I haven't even a butler to answer the door or a maid to polish the floor. How would I give a ball? I just wanted them *clean*. But I can scarcely expect a man to understand that. Now will you tell what is wrong with that and why you persist in interfering with my affairs?"

Harley sobered. It was one thing to offer help when help is needed but quite another to explain why he offered when it was readily apparent she had no need of it. But he had promised, and something needed to be said.

"You should have sent Jamie or John on that errand. It is not proper for a lady to enter that kind of tavern. The men did not understand what dire peril had driven you to seek their help."

"Dire peril?" Aubree looked at him as if he had gone mad. "One can only enter a tavern in dire peril? That's exceedingly odd, I must say."

Harley gazed at her in exasperation. "A lady of your circumstances would only enter a tavern in dire peril. And they had reason to believe you might be in such a state."

Aubree gave up this futile argument. "That makes no sense to me. Did you, too, think I was in 'dire peril'? Whatever on earth for?"

Harley sighed, realizing he was in over his head now. "Do you not know anything, Aubree? Surely Austin did not carry you here without some explanation of what you would find?"

Aubree made a face and plucked a daisy, unconsciously tearing off the petals one by one. "Oh, he was quite honest with me. And the gossips in London certainly didn't lose time in informing me of his reputation. But I cannot see where Heath's lack of fortune and evil gossip should lead to this excessive caution on your part. You must know he is the kindest man who ever lived, even if he is slightly irascible at times." She punctuated this last with a mischievous smile, remembering Austin's irked response to her cobweb clearing.

Shirtsleeves billowing slightly in the breeze, Harley rose and paced to a nearby tree, not daring to meet the clear-eyed innocence of Aubree's expression. She was right and he was wrong, but she must understand the point of view held by the majority. Heath obviously had never cared to enlighten her, curse his stiff pride.

"Aubree, your husband has been known to be a good deal more than irascible in the past. He has learned to control his temper, but in his youth he was involved in more duels than justified by the quiet life we lead here. There are men to this day who bear the mark of his wrath." Harley turned to see how she took this information.

Aubree absorbed and digested the news quietly and nodded in understanding. "That may be so. His father treated him cruelly. The gossip and scandal concerning his family would have burned at the pride of a much more placid temperament than Heath's. He would have fought for his mother's and sister's reputations, even if he could not respect his father's. That explains nothing." She remembered guiltily the two duels Heath had involved himself in since meeting her, one with the man she spoke to now. No wonder he had not wished to marry. The burden of upholding his family's reputation must be a heavy one.

Harley slid to the grass beside her and braced his head upon his hands. "That is just the beginning, Aubree. You must know there are those who say he carried his temper into marriage with him."

"I have heard it said, but I do not believe it," she replied scornfully, moving as if to rise from his contaminating presence.

Harley caught her hand and held her still, gray eyes pleading for understanding. "I was just a school lad then, Aubree, but Louise was my elder sister. I adored her. She was reckless, full of life, and had a temper to match Heath's, I suspect, but I loved her. I came home one summer and saw the fading bruises on her face. If Heath had not been gone to sea, I would have killed him then."

The shock in Aubree's eyes was more than he could

take, and Harley turned away to give her time to collect her thoughts. He needed time to calm the jumble of emotions stirred by this recitation.

The knowledge that Harley's sister had been Heath's first wife struck Aubree more powerfully than anything else. While the woman had been a nameless, faceless figment of the past, she had presented no problem. Knowing now that Austin had married a young woman of wealth and breeding and intelligence like Anna and Maria made her too real for comfort. The knowledge that this woman of a loving family had died in Heath's care hurt more than it did before.

"I did not know, Harley. I am sorry," she whispered, responding to his grief and not his implications. She still did not believe Austin could hit a woman, and she did not think Harley believed it any longer, either.

Harley continued as if she had not spoken. "Louise never told us how she acquired the bruises. She tried to hide others, but you know how gossip flies. She and Heath did not get along well. She liked to spend money and Heath had none. We were poor once, and I once heard her vow she would never go without again. She must have thought marrying an earl would make her wealthy forever. Whatever silliness went between them, the whole county heard sooner or later. I wouldn't have wanted to be in the vicinity when both of them got their tempers up. War would have been quieter."

Aubree tried to imagine this scene and found it very easy to do. Austin was a forceful man who acted on the strength of his beliefs. She would not have him any other way. Although they had exchanged cross words upon many occasions, she had never deliberately tried to interfere with his goals, and he had likewise respected hers. But should she ever step out of line, he would let her know it, in no uncertain terms. If Louise had tried to persuade him to act differently than he had expected of himself, the fireworks would be plentiful, indeed.

"Harley, you need not tell me this. Whatever happened then is over and done. I cannot believe Heath would hit a woman, but I can understand where others might think it. He is not like that now, I can assure you. You need not worry for my sake."

He turned and studied her face thoughtfully, noting the delicate jaw that would bruise so easily, the fair skin that would show every smudge or mar, and the brilliant light of green eyes that bore no glimpse of sorrow. She was much smaller than Louise had been, much daintier and more fragile. Louise had come from sturdy peasant stock and would have fought back tooth and nail. Aubree would have crumpled beneath the first blow. But she spoke with the assurance and authority of centuries of noble breeding, and he smiled in admiration. Should Heath ever lift a hand to this woman, he would most likely find it severed by dawn.

"You are right, of course. I cannot know the truth of it, but now that I've had the opportunity to get to know your husband, I know he is a gentleman. He may have felt called upon to thrash Louise for her behavior, my father did often enough, but he would never strike her in a manner that would leave such bruises. No, I am not worried on that account, but only explaining the attitudes of people around here."

"And your father? He would believe he married his daughter to a man who would beat her?" Aubree couldn't resist asking.

Harley lifted her hand and studied it rather than face the directness of her gaze. "He and Heath were once the best of friends. But the manner of Louise's death and my father's gradual blindness has made him a bitter man. We have never discussed it, but I am certain he blames Heath for everything."

"How did Louise die?" Aubree knew better than to ask, but she had to know, had to get to the bottom of this barrel of misinformation and rumor that blackened their lives.

"I was away at Cambridge. I know only what I have been told, and I carried it like a burning torch of anger for too many years. I wanted to kill Heath, but he would never have accepted a challenge from a schoolboy. Besides, he was gone to war before I came home. I spent many years learning to fight as well as he so I might kill him when the opportunity came. And he still bested me. He could have killed me then, but he did not. That was when I knew he could not have killed Louise, either, no matter what she did to him."

Aubree's eyes grew wide with horror as she heard these words. "Killed Louise? You thought he killed your sister? Whatever made you think such a horrible thing?"

"It is what they all think, Aubree. That is why Heath is not welcome anywhere in polite society. There can be no proof, he cannot be brought to trial, but he has been found guilty by word of mouth. I am sorry, I thought you knew."

Dazed, Aubree stared into the dappled sunlight playing over the lush grass. So many things became clearer now, but she gave no thought to them. She must prove the whole world wrong to free Heath from the prison they held him in. The task seemed enormous.

"How did she die?" she asked quietly.

Harley would have preferred not to be the one to spoil the innocence in the childlike face upturned to him but something in the manner in which she looked at him told him he had gone too far to back down now.

"There was an argument, a particularly violent one, from all reports. Louise ran from the house and Heath followed her. Louise was an expert horsewoman, and her mount had just been saddled. She apparently rode off in a fury. Heath had just come home and his horse had not yet been unsaddled, so he followed her. I have never heard Heath's side of the story. All I know is that Louise was a skilled rider and knew every inch of the abbey grounds. She would never have tried to jump the quarry that they found her in. By the time Heath found help to carry her out, she was dead. So was the child she carried, a child that must have been conceived while Heath was at sea."

A thick silence fell between them, a silence broken only by the mournful call of a dove. Harley had never before spoken this knowledge out loud, and the pain of admission quelled any other urge to speak. Aubree continued to hold his hand, sensing his pain but lost in her own dizzying whirl of discovery.

Heath was a proud man, younger than Harley at the time of his wife's death. He had worked to overcome the ruin and decadence of his father's life, fought with hands and wit to keep his family alive and together, had every reason to believe he could carve his own future and happiness. And his wife had killed it all, bankrupted and cuckolded him, made the heir to his title a bastard. What sane man would believe he hadn't thrown her off that cliff? Perhaps it had not been intentional, perhaps they had argued and he had hit her and she had fallen, but her death was at his hands, nonetheless.

A great sadness permeated her heart. By whatever means Louise had died, Austin had suffered enough for her death. She could not bring herself to believe that Austin was directly responsible, but she understood why it lay heavy on his heart. What chance had she to throw off that burden and make him live again?

She touched a gentle hand to Harley's cheek. "Thank you for telling me, Harley. Your sister and Austin cannot be faulted for marrying for the wrong reasons or loving where they shouldn't. It happens every day. It is not our place to judge them."

Harley's frown relaxed a little and he bent a brotherly kiss to her forehead. "You are right, of course. Now, if only you could spread the gospel . . ."

From a small rise behind them, a solitary figure watched this tableau with pain and understanding. Harley was a good man, much better for her than the insipid Geoffrey, though Harley could claim no title or noble breeding. He had wealth and youth and would make an excellent husband for her one day. The scandal of an annulment would not scare him away. He could not wish for a better development than this.

His mind knew all of this and approved. So why did he feel as if a stake had pierced his heart and the coffin lid closed in on him?

Setting his jaw against the pain ravaging his heart, the Earl of Heathmont turned his horse back to the path. He had returned early to consult with John about the sheep disappearing from the back field. He still needed to make some decision about the thatching of the hay barn. It was time he began considering the state of his lands.

16

A few weeks later, with the ship nearly finished and ready for sailing, a torrential rain gave Austin the excuse he needed to stay home and catch up on the mounting bookwork. By keeping his distance, he had succeeded in driving a wedge between himself and Aubree that she did not dare disturb. She left him alone and went quietly about her own tasks as he settled himself at the desk with its musty ledgers and stacks of yellowing bills.

But even in the silence of his study with the rain pounding against mullioned windows and a fire licking happily at the grate, Austin could not concentrate. A pair of laughing green eyes danced before him as he dipped the old quill in ink and set it to paper. A small chin tilted and full lips pouted as he scratched across the faded lines of old ledgers. He stared at the fire and saw honey-blond hair floating in the breeze, and he wondered what she was doing now.

The silence began to make him uneasy. While he was away from home, he knew others looked after her. Each day he heard reports from John or his mother or even passing neighbors on what Aubree had done that day. He knew when she went with the Sothebys on picnics, knew when Harley came to take her riding, knew of her attempts to hire servants and patch old quarrels. He heard disapproval in some of the reports, laughter in others, but affection in all.

The little brat was slowly worming her way into the hearts of the entire county.

The little brat and her pets, he might add, as one of the Siamese kittens leapt to his lap and butted its head against his stomach, begging for attention. He could hear the dog lunging down the steps in search of its prey, but the cat did not seem in the least disturbed by the sound. Austin had noted a runt lamb in the stable with Dancing Star and a brood of tiny yellow chicks about the kitchen door, but he had made no comment on the growing populace. Aubree had too much love bottled up inside her with no other outlet but these animals.

The thought made him even more restless, and he rose from his chair and went in search of his errant wife. He could not contain his curiosity on how she would spend a day like this one. She had wrought miracles on this musty old manor, but surely there was little more she could do without help.

Carrying the kitten, stroking its head until it purred like the machinery of contentment, Austin wandered aimlessly through the downstairs halls. He had thought to hear the sound of voices or the clatter of cleaning or at least Aubree's idle chatter as she spoke to her animals. He found himself very much wanting to hear the sound of her laughing voice right now.

Only persistence discovered her whereabouts. The library door was slightly ajar, and he glanced into the unlit interior, almost believing it empty until the fragrance of lilacs wafted toward him. Gently pushing the oak panel aside, he stepped into the dusk.

Gowned in fragile white muslin, Aubree's slight figure presented an ethereal wisp of light against the gloom of dusty shelves of moldering books. She stared pensively upward where the rain trickled through a flaw in the rotting woodwork and ran in a stream down the backs of some ancient religious tracts.

"Whatever you're thinking, I can't afford it," Austin announced mildly, his voice echoing in the carpetless room.

Startled from her revery, Aubree glanced toward the doorway, and a smile turned up the corners of her lips. Garbed informally in waistcoat and shirtsleeves, his buckskin trousers rather the worse for wear, Austin still managed to appear very much the lord of his household. Only the purring kitten sleeping in his arms gave the image a note of incongruity. The deep blue of his eyes warmed the sun-darkened coloring of his features, and she felt a sudden urge to brush aside the curls cluttering his high forehead.

"Thoughts do tend to be expensive, don't they?" she answered impishly, ignoring her desire to cross the room to him.

He grinned at this jab. "Yours do. Everytime I see that frown upon your forehead, I hear the sound of coins falling."

It was a gentle criticism. He had said nothing when the carpet appeared on her bedroom floor and the hangings on his bed had changed. He knew the spices in his food had not come free and the new linens cropping up on beds and table and sideboard were not the result of charity. He did not know whether they came from her purse or his credit, but he did not begrudge her these comforts. They were little enough in light of what she had given up to be here. He just wished her to be aware of their cost, for he intended to repay every cent.

Her frown deepened with concern. "I did not mean to cost you money, Austin. I only meant to make you comfortable. The chickens will soon produce egg-laying money, and I will have my quarterly allowance shortly. I did not think . . ."

Austin strode into the room and deposited the kitten into her arms. "Little fool," he muttered warmly, "I am not complaining. But if all you have to do is think up more ways to squander your time and egg money on this ruin, perhaps I can put you to more profitable use."

Aubree took the kitten and searched his face eagerly. "Do you mean it? Can I be of some help to you?"

His heart lurched in his chest, and he knew better than to involve himself further, but he could not turn his back on her eager gaze.

"It's about time you learned the worth of money. Instead of my sitting there poring over columns of figures, you should be learning where it goes. Come, I will teach you how to keep books."

If he had said he would teach her to dig graves, she would have gladly followed. The distance he had forced between them had eaten at her heart and soul, though she had strived desperately to understand his reasoning. She sought only his companionship, but he must think of her as a childish nuisance. That she could be of use to him lightened her day.

Somehow, it was easier to work through the stack of bills when a golden head bent at his side, diligently recording them in the ancient ledgers. Austin showed her the income he expected to make this fall on the harvest and the worth of the sheep in the back field. She commented on the high price of bringing in labor from outside the county, but even so, the profit would be a good one. Austin felt better about the state of his finances after explaining them to her. If all went well, he would be out of debt within a year.

The scent of lilacs hid the musty odor of old ledgers, and it wasn't the flickering fire that took the chill from the room. They worked well together, and the task was done sooner than expected.

Austin stared out the rain-spotted window while Aubree copied out the final set of figures in her firm, fair hand. The rain had stopped and a golden sunbeam strayed from behind a dark cloud. He spied a piece of a rainbow and turned to ask Aubree if she wished to walk outside and find its end, but the sight of her slender back bent over his desk twisted the words in his mouth.

"How are you and Harley going along?" he asked, without any conscious intent of forming the words.

Aubree looked up at him in surprise. "Harley?" She could scarcely remember the name, so far had her mind strayed. Her entire being had focused on this room and the man beside her, and she was quite content to remain there. The mention of Harley intruded upon the cocoon of security she had woven.

He could tell by the surprise on her face that he had

startled her, but the memory of the loving scene he had observed had haunted his nights these past weeks. He could not help but wonder what other scenes had taken place without his knowledge. Soon, his ship would be ready for sailing. Would he come back to find her completely lost to him?

"I spoke to him last week. He sounded rather evasive. I wondered if you and he had a tiff." He tried to keep his voice casual.

Aubree lay down the pen and stared at him. Sunshine had begun to fill the window, and she could see only his outline, the dark tumble of curls and square jaw, the broad shoulders beneath loose-flowing linen. He had not held her in his arms since she had slapped him, she suddenly realized, and the longing generated by the thought triggered other emotions.

"Why did you not tell me he was your brother-in-law?"

The question caught Austin completely by surprise, and he did not answer immediately. Instead, he lowered himself to the comfortable chair beside the fireplace, his game leg held out stiffly before the fire to absorb the heat.

"I did not know you were in need of history lessons," he answered almost curtly.

Aubree ignored the curtness of his tone, instinctively sensing his vulnerability. She might never have another chance, and she wanted the subject out in the open between them.

"Harley tells me he has never heard your side of the story, yet he believes you innocent. Can you not speak of it now?"

She did not coax, but the seductive softness of her voice held the same effect. He could get up and walk out and ignore her plea, but Austin found himself wanting to talk. He would have her understand what others did not. There could be no harm in telling her, as there would be to those most directly affected.

He began much further back than she expected, voicing a story that had played inside his head countless times, never with complete understanding. "Louise and I grew up together, but we never knew each other. Her father was a merchant in Exeter when I first met her. He made a fortune at the beginning of the war in '93 and bought one of the old manor houses my father sold off the abbey estate. Whenever I was home, Louise and I rode out together. She seemed more real, more accessible than the powdered, simpering misses of London. I wasn't her first lover, but I didn't mind. Marriage didn't occur to me until after my father's death, and I saw myself floating down the River Tick.''

Austin leaned over and grabbed a poker, jabbing at the crumbling embers of logs in the grate. He had his back to her, and the high back of his chair separated them, but Aubree could see his face in her mind. The pain of memory etched itself in the tired lines about his mouth.

"Louise wanted too much out of life, more than her father could give, more than *I* could give, as it turned out. Sotheby was losing his eyesight by then. His wife was frail, and he had three younger children he wished to raise among the gentry. He never said so, but Louise's behavior was almost beyond his control and endangering all the plans and dreams he had made. The opportunity to marry her into the nobility was too good to be ignored. Much to my shame, I allowed him to buy me.''

The self-disgust was well hidden but there. Aubree wanted to shake him, make him see that he had done no less than generations before him, but she did not dare interrupt the story that poured from him, pent-up for so many years.

She could only gently spur him on. "I think you must have loved her a little, at first, didn't you?''

Austin contemplated the question, easier than thinking of what came next. "It's easy to love when one is young and your whole life is ahead of you. She was beautiful and she made my nights happy, for a time. I could have loved her, yes, but it didn't last.''

He thought of Aubree's youth and understood more clearly his instinctive urge to keep her separate from him. She was so very young, he could make her think of love with only the gentlest urgings. But she was too young and inexperienced to know her own heart. He could take her and keep her without earning her love or respect, but he would despise himself for it, and soon enough, so would she. No, he was better off waiting until he had earned the right to take a wife like Aubree. The chance that she might wait for him was a small one, but one he must take. Only then could he be certain that love would grow instead of becoming the stunted, deformed thing he had experienced once before.

He sighed and shifted his position to ease the ache in his leg. He was in a hurry to get it over with now. "Louise wanted to be introduced to London society. The idea of being a countess was fascinating to her. I tried to please her, but I had not the wealth to buy her the place in society that she craved and that her breeding denied her. After she went through half her dowry trying to please the unpleasable, I made her return here. From there on, everything went sour.

"I put a large sum of money into a ship and did not dare let it out of my sight. I was gone six months. When I returned, Louise had spent what remained of the dowry and my cash and had run up my credit all over the county. I never knew what she spent it on. Very little went into the abbey, I know."

He cursed mildly and Aubree slipped from her seat, finding the small stool he had misplaced and sliding it under his foot. It seemed strange that so vigorous a man could be laid low by so simple a thing as an aching knee, but he had refused all her offers to poultice it at times like these. She knew better than to offer again.

"You do not have to tell me this, you know," she murmured, hating to add to his pain.

Austin ignored her. "Things rapidly went from bad to worse. When we were together, we fought continually. I think she looked for excuses to argue with me." He wondered if Aubree understood what this meant between man and wife, but he did not explain. He knew now that Louise had taken a lover and fought to keep him from her bed, but the truth was ugly enough without this addition. He glossed over it.

"I took to staying in Exeter much of the time. Sotheby accused me of keeping a mistress and neglecting his daughter. In a way, he was right, but Louise seemed to prefer it that way.

"About that time, I noticed she had taken to wearing more powder than usual. She wore only long-sleeved, high-necked gowns in my presence. I didn't understand it at first. I was young and ignorant. But when I came back from sea that last time, I learned the truth. If I could have pulled the man's name from her tongue, I would have killed him. He destroyed her, literally destroyed her, and I still do not know who he is."

The anger and anguish that twisted his thoughts rang clearly in his voice, and Aubree wanted to cry out to him to stop, to stop torturing himself, to stop bearing a burden that was no longer his. But she could say nothing. He still protected Louise, still avoided calling her adultereress, but she knew the man he wished to kill could be no other than Louise's lover. Sorrow engulfed her, but she was in no position to offer comfort.

"I fully believe that last day she was mad. I don't know what had happened, but when I came to the door, she flew at me in rage and tears. She was hysterical. I tried to calm her and she screamed. I yelled at her and she hit me. I offered brandy and she threw it in my face. I should have called for a doctor, but I was too far out of my mind to think rationally. I hit her, thinking to return her to her senses. It was the worst thing in the world I could have done."

Aubree suddenly had full understanding of Austin's reaction when she had hit him that last night in London. She shuddered at the memories that must have brought back, the rage that he had controlled. She knew now that he would never lift a hand to another woman. But he would undoubtedly walk out if ever confronted with such a situation again. She breathed a prayer of relief that he had not left her behind.

In a flat voice, Austin continued his recitation. "She ran out of the house and I followed. She had a head start and her mount was fresh. Mine was exhausted. I would have been better off if I had let her go. Then I wouldn't have to live with what happened next for the rest of my life. I could remain as ignorant as everyone else as to what happened that day."

His last words were so tortured, Aubree could no longer bear the pain of them. Without a thought to propriety, she slipped into Austin's lap and slid her arms around his neck. He pulled her close, as one with a chill hugs a blanket, but he did not allow her to distract him. He would have her know why he had allowed gossip to label him murderer, and how difficult it would be to prove him otherwise.

"Louise was too fine a horsewoman to endanger her horse on the edge of the south crevasse. She wasn't on her horse when I found her. She was balancing on a boulder above the highest point of the ravine."

Austin's voice softened to a low murmur, as if speaking his thoughts to himself. "When she saw me, there was a terrible expression of sadness on her face. I'll never forget it. It was worse than what happened next. I think she died then, not a moment later. She lifted her hand in farewell, then before I could take a step toward her, she dived into the ravine."

Pain crackled and tore at his voice, and Aubree could see the image just as he must be seeing it now. Her eyes welled with the tears and anguish that must be his, the helplessness and guilt that haunted his memory. They spilled down her cheeks as he held her against him and the moisture mixed with the wetness of Austin's cheeks.

With a mutual craving for comfort, they turned to each other, and Austin sealed her lips with his. He tasted of their saltiness and drank their comfort, burying his pain in the welcome softness of a gentle caress.

The kiss deepened until Austin became physically aware of the pressure of young breasts against his side and soft thighs arousing hungers that had nothing to do with comfort. He craved the solace she offered him, but not at the cost they would have to pay. Sighing, he moved his kiss to cover her cheeks, realizing her tears were for him, and kissing them away.

"Don't cry, halfling. I am not worth your tears."

Aubree shook her head, burying her face against his shoulder. "I feel so sorry for her." Her muffled words were barely audible.

Austin's eyebrows went up slightly at this unexpected viewpoint. "You did not even know her, little goose. How can you feel sorry for someone you do not know?" he asked gently.

"But I know *you*," she cried. "She must have seen what a fool she'd been, throwing you away for a man who would beat her. That is why she did it. At the last, she knew she could only save you by killing herself. She could never have known that you would be blamed for her death. It's so awful, Austin. Why are people like that?"

Her incredible insight followed by her childish plea left Austin momentarily speechless. He had never seen Louise in quite that light before, but he knew at once that she was right. Louise had never been bad, but spoiled and selfish. Maybe, at the last, she had understood what she had done, when it was too late for everyone. The knowledge hurt, but not as much as the confusion he had felt before. How this child-woman could have seen it was beyond his ken.

"We're all human, Aubree, we make mistakes. I think you're giving me more credit than I deserve, but it's too late to do anything but avoid making the same mistakes again."

He could not set her from him just yet. He cradled her in his arms, breathing the scent of lilacs and enjoying the soft pressures of her supple body against his. They had been married nearly two months, and he had not had a woman since before that time. Desire lay very close to the surface, but he kept it in ruthless control. Shortly, he would sail away and be gone for months. Now was not the time to initiate actions that might never come to term.

As if reading his mind, Aubree shyly disentangled herself from his embrace. "Am I another mistake?"

A raw grin curled one corner of Austin's mouth as he lifted her from his lap and set her firmly on her feet. "You're a mistake, I don't doubt, but I didn't make you. Not yet, anyway."

She threw him a dubious look but avoided questioning him further on that subject. She tackled a related one. "Have you heard from my father? Has he found your brother-in-law yet?"

Austin lowered his leg from the stool and rose to stand beside her, ruffling her hair with his hands as he gazed down into her pensive face. "They know what ship was in the vicinity at the time Adrian was impressed, and they know its route. It will take time for messages to be left at all ports and for the ship to return to London. We can only hope now, halfling. You have done your share. I must learn patience and do mine."

That puzzled her even more, but she did not question it. She suspected he was being deliberately ambiguous, and she would not give him the pleasure of laughing at her. "Have you written your sister? She must be dreadfully worried."

Blue eyes smiled upon her fondly. "I have written. There was very little I could say, but it is better than nothing. Is there any other information you wish to pry from me? As you can see, I am quite willing to tell you all today. Tomorrow might be a different story."

His hands rested on her shoulders and she was loath to end the closeness. It had been so long since he had spoken to her in such a manner, she could not desire an end to it.

"Did you tell her of our marriage?" she asked with curiosity, half fearful of his reply.

The smile slipped away and he regarded her with seriousness. "I have told her of our marriage and your father's help. I have told her nothing of the circumstances. I see no need that she should know that."

Aubree nodded, not understanding her sense of relief. It had just suddenly seemed important to her that he acknowledged their marriage. How foolish to think that he would deny it.

She smiled and pressed a kiss upon her finger and laid it across his lips. "That is one secret that shall remain sealed forever."

"Minx." And because he could not help it, Austin took her in his arms again and sealed it with a kiss.

17

Austin could still taste that kiss like a fine wine some days later as he returned home early from Exeter. The ship would be ready to sail on the morrow, and he must find some way of telling Aubree. The scenes Louise had created upon his sailing burned indelibly on his mind, and he had no heart for the task. Various alternatives raced across his mind as he guided his stallion into the courtyard.

He should have known he wouldn't find her in. The fields had just begun to dry, and though the sky was overcast, it did not threaten immediate rain. John informed him she had ridden out with Jamie well over an hour earlier.

Wearily, Austin slid from his horse. His leg ached abominably from the long ride, but he had no desire to lounge about waiting for his wife to reappear. He had hoped to spend a pleasant afternoon with her before breaking the news; he felt entitled to that much. Now it seemed he would have to work even for that small pleasure.

"Saddle up the mare, John. In which direction did they go?"

"Out toward the Shaughnessys', milord," John volunteered with more alacrity than usual. "Their young un's been down ill."

This was a new aspect to his wife's activities, but entirely in keeping with her character. He should have known his few lackluster tenants would soon be adopted into Aubree's menagerie. Austin mounted his fresh horse and rode off in the direction indicated.

The crumbling cottage that housed itinerant field hands had held only one family for some years. The head of the family, Tim Shaughnessy, had worked two summers in the abbey fields, then drank himself into a grave during the second winter. Austin had not the heart to tell the impoverished family to move on, and they had squatted there ever since, eking out an existence on odd jobs wherever there was money to be found.

Austin felt a brief uneasiness at Aubree's involvement with the ramshackle brood, but his own guilty conscience, and not her safety, inspired the twinge. With relief, he noted Jamie holding the horses some distance from the cottage and none of the occupants within sight. He saluted the young lad, handed over his reins, and swung his stiff leg in the direction of the cottage.

Aubree looked up in startlement at the large shadow blocking the light from the doorway, but her surprise quickly led to joy. She leapt from her place on the floor beside the small pallet and flew into Austin's arms.

"Oh, I am so glad you have come, Austin. I have been at my wit's end. I have tried everything, but there is no help for it. We must have a physician. Mrs. Shaughnessy says there is none to be had, but that can't be possible, can it? An apothecary won't do, I fear. Is there not a physician somewhere we can call on?"

She clung to his arms as if he could produce solutions simply through the strength of his presence. Austin bent her a wry smile and slid an arm around her waist, turning her so that they faced the tired woman sitting dejectedly at the crippled table.

"How do you do, Edna? I take it young Michael is not well?"

The woman sent a blank stare to the gentleman in her doorway, then turned it back to the labored breathing of the thin youth upon the pallet. " 'Tis God's will to take the good when they're young."

An expression of pain and annoyance crossed Austin's bronzed features, but he held his tongue as he bent over the fevered youth on the filthy pallet. It was true, Michael was the best of the lot, an eager youth willing to work at whatever given him, but he had never been strong. With healthy food and rest, he might have had a chance. As it was, Austin shook his head in discouragement.

But Aubree clung to his arm in hope, wide eyes watching his every expression, and he could not let her down. His gaze took in the linen-covered basket of food that must have come from his kitchen, and he wondered how much of it would ever cross the lips of the sick youth, but he did not express his thoughts out loud.

"How long has he been like this?" he demanded gruffly, rising to glare at the child's mother. His head barely cleared the low beams of the cottage and he carefully avoided the lamp hung on one wall.

"Don't rightly know. He been sleeping in the fields, come warm weather. The rains done for him, I reckon."

The woman's speech was a strange amalgamation of accents. Austin had often wondered what dock Tim had found her on, but he had never inquired into her antecedents. She did not drink and she struggled her best to feed the squalling mouths around her. Her pessimism sprang from a natural source.

"And where are the others?"

The woman sent him an odd look. "Out and about. They be home sometime."

Aubree tugged lightly at his arm. "I think it's pneumonia, Austin. I have tried everything. We must have a physician."

He doubted if the money spent would produce results, but gazing down into those dark-lashed eyes brimming with tears, he knew he would have to try.

"I'll have John come carry him to the abbey, where you can keep an eye on him. There's a physician in Exeter I'll fetch in the morning."

The relief spreading across Aubree's face was sufficient payment for the fruitless task he had set himself. Accustomed to having the best of everything at her beck and call, Aubree had no idea of the true difficulty of rural life. Physicians were few and far between out here, and what few existed were in all probability quacks. Austin did not know the quality of Exeter's one physician, but he did know the man catered to the wealthy. He would not come without the promise of a healthy purse.

The weak sunlight seemed stronger for their having been in the dismal cottage, and they stood blinking in the graveled dirt of the yard before returning to their horses. Their lingering gave the rider down the path time to make her presence known.

"And it's time you stepped forward, my lord."

Aubree glanced up to the speaker with surprise. She had seen nothing of this person in her previous visits, and she studied the girl with innocent interest. Riding an ancient donkey, wearing some lady's discarded raiments, the girl held herself proudly upright as she greeted the visitors with a suspicion of a sneer. Hair that once must have been yellow was stacked in imitation of her betters above a narrow forehead and pale eyes of cornflower blue.

"Good afternoon, Blanche," Austin replied mildly, gripping Aubree's elbow and steering her toward the horses without further intention of carrying on the conversation.

" 'Good afternoon, Blanche'! . . . Is that all you've got to say to me?" The girl slid from the donkey and stepped quickly to confront them.

From this position, Aubree could see that Blanche was more woman than girl. Hard lines etched a pattern across her forehead and the thinness of her face sharpened the silhouette of her nose to an extreme. Despite the wasted look of her features, her breasts were full and high and exposed loosely beneath the frail covering of open muslin. Aubree gulped back a swallow of apprehension as her gaze traveled lower and found the certain signs of pregnancy beneath the fullness of faded skirts.

Austin did not seem visibly disturbed by the confrontation, though he drew Aubree closer to his side and farther from Blanche's spiteful glare. "I did not think there was more to be said, Blanche. Did you not find the position I found for you satisfactory?"

"You expect me to work like this?" she demanded shrilly, indicating her distended belly. "I didn't last long enough for it to take some silly twit to carp to the mistress on me. You'll have to pay for my shame, my lord. No one else will."

Aubree smothered a gasp as Austin's fingers tightened on her elbow and the implication of Blanche's words struck home. This was the maid he had sent packing before she arrived. And the reason was evident enough. She tried to twist from Austin's grasp, but he held her firmly.

"I paid you fair wages, Blanche, and asked no more of you than you were willing to give. If that child were mine, I would acknowledge and support it, but I can count, too, Blanche. It has been nearly a year since I've spent time with you. You must find someone else to blame for your trouble." He eyed a large, fading green bruise above her elbow. "Perhaps if you gave me the man's name, I could persuade him to take proper actions."

Cornflower-blue eyes grew suddenly fearful and she backed away. "It could have been yours, milord. You owe me that."

Disgust and horror welled up in Aubree's throat, and some other emotion she could not quite name. She knew better than to blame either Austin or the maid for succumbing to physical needs, but she could not control the violence of her reaction at meeting this woman who had served him so intimately. She jerked forcefully from Austin's grasp and strode hastily to her waiting mount without further word to the pair.

Blanche watched her go with a certain amount of satisfaction. Cursing, Austin swung on his heel and followed.

So much for the leisurely afternoon of pleasure he had planned.

Austin made no attempt to catch up with her. She had every right to be angry, and he would do better to wait until she cooled off. He had confidence in Aubree's rationality once her emotions were out of the way. That he had once lain with a slut like Blanche served even to disgust himself. He could scarcely imagine the reaction of a gently bred lady like Aubree. His anger with Blanche was diluted by his curiosity over her lover. Had he been the one to leave that vicious bruise on her arm?

Deciding someone like Blanche could have as many lovers as trees do leaves and there need not be any significance in the old bruise, Austin left the subject alone. He had no great desire to speak with Blanche again. What he wanted to do was to speak with Aubree and reassure himself that he had not ruined any chance he might have with her. His chances were slim enough as it was. He could not afford to lose any of them.

He rode into the stable yard in time to catch sight of a small urchin slipping through the kitchen hedge to the back door. A quick glance found John engrossed in brushing down Aubree's mare and no other of the servants in sight. Instant suspicion raised its ugly head, and Austin hastily dismounted.

Very few of the villagers came to the abbey for anything. He did not recognize the urchin as belonging to any of his tenants, but there was a vague familiarity about him that made Austin hasten his step.

The boy eased himself into the open stone archway to the kitchens and looked around as if searching for someone. Since Patience was the only one likely to be in the kitchens at this hour, Austin could only assume she was his ultimate goal. But the poor, slow-witted cook could be of little use to anyone, except as a conduit to the others in the mansion.

With a surprisingly soft tread for a man with a limp, Austin came up behind the lad and caught him by the collar before he could make his escape. The youth yelped and wriggled, but quickly gauged the firmness of his trap and grew silent.

"You have some business here?" Austin asked with deceptive mildness.

The boy clutched desperately to the corner of a vellum letter sticking from the neck of his shirt. "Yes, sir—I mean, no, sir. Is Patience t' home, sir?"

Ruefully, Austin realized his presence in the kitchen garden and his ungentlemanly attire had labeled him as one of the staff and not master of the household, but he had no need to assuage his pride at the boy's expense. Any rank would be sufficient to pull authority over the child.

"What's that you have, lad?" He jerked the envelope from its hiding place despite the boy's sharp cry of protest.

"It's for the lady, sir. He says to put it in the lady's hands and no other, sir. Please, sir, he'll thrash me if I don't."

Austin ignored the lad's cries as he examined the sealed message. The handwriting addressing Aubree was unfamiliar but unmistakably masculine. The seal meant nothing to him. But his fingers tightened in fists as he realized the implications of this secretive delivery.

"I'll see that the lady gets it," he stated peremptorily, dropping the boy's collar and sliding the paper into his shirt.

"But, sir . . ." Wild-eyed, the boy met Austin's steady gaze and subsided.

"I give you my word the lady will receive it. You need not tell your master more, but I suggest you discourage him from sending any more messages in such a manner. The master does not approve of strangers sneaking about his back door." Austin flipped the boy a coin and entered the kitchen, closing the heavy door behind him.

The vellum scorched his skin as Austin leisurely made his way through the cool stone and marble corridors to the front of the house. By all rights, he should take the letter directly to Aubree without questioning. He owed her that much. She had never done anything to deserve his distrust. But he had lost so much in the past due to neglect and ignorance, he could not afford to let history repeat itself. He had to know.

Once in the seclusion of his study, Austin had no great difficulty in prying loose the seal. His hands shook as he unfolded the heavy paper, and he had second thoughts about actually reading the black lines scrawled across the page, but he could not turn back. Slowly, agonizingly, he began to read.

Aubree, my love,

I can wait no longer. You cannot doubt my devotion after all that has gone between us, and tomorrow I am prepared to prove it. I have learned your husband sails in the morn, with provisions for two months' journey or more. You cannot love a man who has stolen you from me. Now is the time to right the wrong that has been done. We will be far gone before he returns. Say you will, my love. I will give you everything your heart desires, if only you will come to me. I will be waiting for you in our special place tomorrow. Hurry, my love. We have been denied each other too long.

The large scrawled "G" across the bottom left no secret as to the writer.

Austin's gaze slowly reread the lines that tore at his heart. "After all that has gone between us" and "our special place" held hints of passion that only a lover knew. He could not believe that she had been unfaithful to him, but he did not doubt that Geoffrey had tried to seduce her. He must have judged himself successful to write a missive such as this.

Austin had thought his heart long since dead of all emotion, but the cold bleakness opening within him now warned of worse to come. After today's fiasco, he could scarcely blame a loyal and lighthearted girl like Aubree from fleeing to the devotion of her former fiancé. Geoffrey's timing could not have been better. And his own could not have been worse.

Facing the bleakness of a future without Aubree's lively chatter and warm affection, Austin was tempted to crumple the paper and burn it. But he had given his word, and he could not live his life wondering what decision she would have made had he not interfered. He had to know her feelings about the treacherous little pup. Then he would decide what to do with the scoundrel.

With that decision made, Austin refolded and re-sealed the message. With a casualness he did not feel, he handed the paper to Joan as she scurried through the hall.

"This just came for Lady Aubree. Take it to her, please," he commanded. He watched as the little maid hurried up the long stairs to obediently deliver the sword that could slay him.

Aubree was quieter than usual at dinner, but she gave no evidence of holding him in total reprobation. Austin made no mention of Blanche but reiterated his promise to send a physician for Michael. At this, wide green eyes turned to him as if waiting, but he said nothing more.

Aubree concealed her emotion and returned to her plate. He made no mention of leaving her. Could Geoffrey's sources be wrong? Surely he would not disappear for two months without some explanation, some farewell?

Perhaps he meant to send a letter. Maybe he feared a scene. That would be in keeping with Austin's character as she knew it. Louise had probably staged some fairly lively scenes upon his decision to sail with his ship. She didn't understand how he could think she would be like Louise, but men sometimes developed strange notions.

Instead of moping over this piece of information, Aubree found new use for it. Two months was not such a very long time. There was so much to be done, and two months would barely begin it. If Austin left as the letter promised, she would have to hurry.

The memory of Blanche slowly faded into the background as this new development took priority. After all, she had known Austin had never been a monk, and she certainly had no right to protest what he had done in the past. But she did have this opportunity to change his future, and sulking would not solve anything.

With that in mind, she made a concerted effort to be pleasant. Austin did not exactly make it easy. He remained taciturn throughout most of dinner, and even after he finally responded to her chatter, his mind seemed elsewhere. Aubree would willingly have hit him over the head with the lovely soufflé sent over from the Dower House, but she had vowed to stay on her best behavior.

To make matters worse, Austin insisted on returning her pleasantries by walking with her in the garden after dinner. After months of barely sparing her the time of day, he seemed to have time on his hands to share with her. Aubree felt nervous and uneasy under her husband's calm scrutiny, and she wished for the easy camaraderie of before.

At long last, it grew twilight, and they turned their steps back toward the abbey. In the privacy of the rose arbor, Austin halted their pace, turning her to face him.

"Aubree, I have been as honest with you as I am able. Perhaps it was a mistake to let you see all my faults, but I cannot live a lie. I hope you feel you can be just as honest with me. We have been thrown together against your wishes, I realize, but there is no reason we cannot still be friends."

Vaguely startled by this sudden declaration, not understanding what turmoil had led to it, Aubree stared up at him searchingly. His eyes appeared troubled, but she could discern no immediate reason for it. Could he fear this trip he was about to make? Surely it would not be a dangerous one?

Alarmed, but unable to voice it because he had given her no opening, Aubree touched his cheek as if memorizing its texture.

"I should hope we are more than friends, my lord," she whispered with a trace of bewilderment. "You know all that I am and more than most. Have I done aught to make you doubt that?"

Relief washed over him in great, pounding, deafening waves. He could not doubt her innocence, not when she looked at him like that. Austin slid his arms around her and pulled her to him.

"No, halfling, sometimes I just terrify myself," he whispered against her hair. Vowing to keep it that way, he bent to taste of her willing lips.

She came to him readily, and he rejoiced in the heady sensation of her trusting lips parting beneath his. He took what she had to give and returned it threefold, feeling the growing urgency of her passion with guilt and joy.

On the morrow, she might hate him, but tonight, he would have her trust.

18

Austin reined in his prancing stallion on a curve overlooking the abbey, ignoring the look the portly physician gave him. His entire future hung on what he found waiting behind those stone walls, and he had need to gather his thoughts before he descended into the courtyard. If she were preparing for flight, she would not greet his unexpected arrival with pleasure.

The decision not to sail with his ship had not been as difficult as Austin had thought. The ship's captain was loyal and honest, and if he could trust the man with his life, he could certainly trust him with his cargo. It was the treasure he kept in the abbey that Austin could not leave unprotected.

With a curse at his own cowardice, Austin kicked and sent the stallion galloping down the road toward home.

Impatient to judge Aubree's reception of his decision, Austin dismounted in the stable yard. Throwing his reins toward John, he strode hurriedly toward the room that housed Aubree's patient.

"Is Lady Aubree with Michael?" he called out as John hastened to hold the reins of both horses and follow in their footsteps at the same time.

"No, milord. When she saw he slept comfortably, she went out. We did not expect your return . . ."

Refusing to acknowledge the pain knifing through him, Austin swung his furious gaze to the groom. "How long has she been gone?"

He had trusted her, and she had not even waited to be certain of his departure before running off. Well, she would learn the folly of trying to make a fool of him. He would not suffer that torture again. Not waiting for John's answer, he stalked back to his stallion.

"Upward of an hour or more, milord. They were heading for the village. The boy was with her . . ."

Before the staring eyes of the physician and the groom, Austin vaulted back into the saddle. "Did she send any messages before she left?" The words were curt and heavy with anger.

The groom swallowed as he realized the path his employer's thoughts had taken and his own guilty involvement. It had never occurred to him that those notes were any less than innocent. "To the gentleman, milord. There was no reply."

Austin did not need to hear more. Jerking the reins, he swung the stallion around and raced down the abbey drive, leaving the two men in the courtyard to stare after him as if he were demented.

Harley watched with alarm as a small crowd gathered around the box beneath Aubree's feet. It was market day, and the village had filled with travelers as well as the occupants of the outlying countryside. She could not have chosen a wider audience for her soapbox plea, but he doubted if the earl would approve. Harley had half a mind to reach up and snatch her down, but Aubree had already made it clear she resented his interference. She only wanted him here to add substantiation to her words.

"I cannot offer high wages, but honest work and a roof over your heads and food in your bellies. I'll pay you quarterly, so you need not doubt whether the coin is there. I know the times are bad and there are many of you who need work. Why should the jobs go to strangers from outside the county when you have your own to feed?"

Aubree had preached these words over and over in many variations, without great success in the past, but Harley sensed the people had begun to listen to her. It was nonsense for a girl of seventeen to be down here among this rabble, utter heresy for a countess to do so, but they listened to her. She spoke with an authority that commanded attention, but her feminine grace softened words that might have been harsh or scornful in the mouth of others. The crowd listened and rumbled with varied interest.

"Won't get me to work for no murderer. I'd rather starve," Harley heard one man mutter behind him.

"It's her we'd be workin' for, didn't you hear?" another replied. "The earl's gone off again and her pa's a rich nob."

A third man snorted cynically. "He'd do better to buy her protection from that husband of her'n. And she just a poor mite of a thing."

Harley felt a general stir of agreement along those lines, and a small twitch of mischief caught at his thoughts. If the only way he could get Aubree off that box was to hire workers for the damned abbey, he would find her workers.

Nonchalantly, he answered the cynical gentleman's assessment of the situation. "Seems to me the best thing a man could do is hire on and look after the lady's interests as well as his own. I daresay the duke would be more than grateful to any man who protected his daughter. And at the same time, you'd feed your bellies. What more could a man want?"

He repeated this commentary in different words at every opportunity, until others began to repeat them for him. Before long, his casual remarks seemed to be the consensus of the crowd, and it needed only a slight impetus to push them forward.

Austin halted on the hill above the village and groaned aloud at the melee swarming below. How would he ever find trace of her in a crowd like that? He did not even know where to begin. There was no inn, no coach hire, no place he could go to start his questioning. But there was only one road toward London. They would have to follow that wherever they were headed.

Fury settled into grim determination as he eased his horse down the rocky path toward the confusion below. The thoughts of what he would do to that lordly young pup when he caught him occupied Austin's mind more than doubts as to whether he would catch them in time. He had no room for doubts.

As he edged his mount through a street thronged with fruit and vegetable carts, meat-pie and cider vendors, horse traders, and sideshow barkers, Austin discerned a small crowd gathering before Mrs. Croft's tea room. Knowing this to be the village's one claim to gentility, he found that an oddity. Local farmers did not generally crowd into tea rooms.

And then he caught sight of a bright-golden head raised up above the swarm of rough-garbed men and women, and his heart leapt to his throat and became lodged there. At the same time, she looked up at the mounted gentleman winding his way through the jammed street, and green eyes grew wide with joy.

Not once did Aubree consider Austin's anger at her undignified speech-making. That he had come home to her and not sailed off without explanation was the only thought in her head as she met the wild flare of midnight eyes.

Following Aubree's gaze, Harley groaned inwardly, however. The steely control of the muscles along Austin's jaw warned all was not well, and his stiffly erect posture held all the authority and command his nobility and breeding required. Austin wore no hat, and he had abandoned the high collars of city dress, but his gleaming white cravat and tailored frock coat set him well above the country gentry. For the first time in over half a decade, the earl had come to town.

Silence fell on the small crowd in front of the tea shop, and a path widened before Heathmont. He maneuvered his horse between the staring townspeople and up to the box where his wife waited.

A small flicker of fear wavered in Aubree's eyes for a moment as they regarded Austin's grim expression and she finally grew aware of the impropriety of her position, but she defied his anger with boldness.

"My lord, you are returned!" She held up her arms for him to take her. "Did you find the physician for Michael?"

Instead of lifting her to the safety of his saddle as he ought, Austin swung down amid the murmur and rumble of the crowd. All ears strained for his reply, though none understood the question.

Austin was at her side in a single stride, his arm circling her waist and lifting her easily from her incongruous perch. "By Gad, little wench, I ought to throttle you," he replied loudly enough for all to hear.

And before the crowd could gasp in shock, Austin pulled his troublesome wife against his chest, and her arms flew to circle his neck, and there before all the town, they greeted each other with the passionate response of lovers long separated.

Gasps turned to titters and murmurs of approval and outright laughter. Their earl had caught a rare, wild bird, indeed, and it seemed he knew well how to tame her. Those who had moments before been eager to stand in the lady's defense now wondered if it might not be more appropriate to offer a hand to the earl. The countess had played on their emotions, but the earl returned them to reality. Women belonged in the kitchen and bed, not on street corners. The men cheered lustily as the earl made his point clearly.

Harley watched in wry admiration as Heathmont succeeded with one gesture in doing what he had spent the morning bringing about. Aubree was not only off her soapbox, but the crowd was surging forward eagerly, putting their pleas for employment to the man who had just ridden into their midst. He would do well to learn from his superiors.

Keeping his hand firmly about his wife's waist, Austin looked out over the eager crowd with a sudden lifting of his heart. For the first time in seven years, they turned to him for guidance, instead of away in disgust. He knew the reason for this, of course, but he could not allow the brat to think she had the upper hand.

With a wicked grin, he announced to the waiting crowd, "Somebody has to look after her if Heathmont is to have another heir. Any who wish to hire on in my employ need apply to me."

Laughter and cheers drowned out Aubree's embarrassed gasp of outrage.

Above the town, on the same hill Austin had occupied not minutes before, two riders watched the touching scene below with less than pleasure.

The older of the two turned to his fair-haired cousin with ill-concealed disgust. "You seem to have set your cap for a singularly fickle flirt, old boy."

Geoffrey could not hide his dismay. He had been thoroughly convinced only Aubree's good breeding had created the reserve that kept her from acknowledging his pleas of devotion. This public display of affection certainly overturned that theory. A slow anger burned within him, and he replied more harshly than was his wont, "I thought you said the bastard sailed this morning. Is that his twin?"

"Or the devil, himself, straight from Hades. That's the only explanation I can find. The bastard has more lives than a cat."

Geoffrey gave his cousin an odd look at this rough growl. The livid scar streaking down one side of Harry's face strained in a rigid contortion as he stared down at the loving couple below. Geoffrey stirred uneasily at the expression of hatred behind those narrowed eyes, but his own plight was too real to worry about that of others.

"My debtors will have me in Newgate if I go back to London, cuz. What in hell am I to do now? Is there any use trying after the Sotheby sisters? The younger one's not so long in the tooth, and they say the old man is worth a fortune."

The older man turned him a look that made Geoffrey pale. "You'll leave them alone. They're mine. That one down there is yours. I'll take care of the earl for you. It's up to you to bed your countess. They're all whores underneath. Once she tires of the games her husband teaches her, she'll be ready enough for you. Play your hand right, boy, and we'll both be wealthy men before year's end."

The thought of bedding a wealthy countess—particularly a beautiful, dainty one like Aubree—so excited Geoffrey that he paid little heed to the implied threats in his cousin's words. The Sotheby girls were mere peasants and more Harry's style. He wanted to take

London with Aubree on his arm, and in his bed. A jaunty grin sprouted upon his lips at the thought.

"Lead on, Macduff," he brayed.

Happily, he ignored his cousin's baleful glare.

With orders for all petitioners to apply to his office at the abbey on the morrow, Austin disentangled himself and his wife from the mob and, with the help of Harley and Jamie, got her safely back on the road toward home.

"Harley, I could cheerfully wring your neck for allowing her to get away with this stunt," Heathmont complained as they came to the crossroads between Atwood Abbey and Sotheby Manor.

The younger man threw Aubree an apologetic look and shrugged before Heath's ire. "I'd heard you sailed this morning, or I would have warned you. I have no authority to rule her."

"You sound just like Alvan," Aubree pouted. "Why does everyone feel it necessary to tell me what to do? My plan worked, didn't it?"

Austin and Harley exchanged looks of exasperation. Reining his mount toward the road to his home, Harley made a parting gesture. "I'm damned glad you're staying, Heath. I was seriously contemplating offering my services to Wellington rather than ride guard on that one until you returned."

With a wave, he rode off, leaving Austin to contemplate his young bride with a mixture of relief and frustration.

"Why, Aubree?" he demanded.

She gazed at him with wide-eyed innocence, belied by the mischievous smile of happiness on her lips. "Why, what, milord? Have I displeased you? Should we not be returning to the physician and Michael?"

"That is where I expected you to be when I returned home this noon. But you could not wait for me to be gone to be up to your mischief."

Aubree set her mount toward home. "I had need to go before the market grew rowdy. Matilda had instructions for caring for Michael. I had no idea you would be returning with the physician."

Austin rode beside her, uncertain how to chastise her behavior when his had been twice as reprehensible. How could he tell her he had read her letter and expected her to be halfway to London by now? How could he ask why she had not gone? He gave up the argument.

"We are both too inclined to act without thinking, I fear," Austin mused aloud. "But you are young enough to learn better behavior."

Aubree made a rude noise. "If I thought before I did everything, I would never do anything. If it is a prim-and-proper wife you want, look to Miss Sotheby. She is so proper she will not even look twice when a gentleman favors her with a glance. But do not expect such a wife to be happy with you when you go off sailing without a word to her, or return without warning and scare her half out of her wits."

A grin twitched at one corner of Austin's mouth at this haughty outlook. "But I did not go off sailing, so there should be no need to warn of my return. You have been listening to gossips, I fear."

Aubree's ears grew crimson, but she did not retreat. "And what brought you riding into town as if you meant to tar and feather the population? Was your concern for Michael that great that you must chase after me to bring me home?"

She was much too sharp to fool, but Austin had no intention of admitting the error of his ways. Let her think what she might. "You will have to become accustomed to my presence. The ship sailed this morning, and I have nothing better to do than plague you."

Aubree sent him a quick glance, but she could read nothing in his placid countenance. A warm feeling of relief stole over her, and she smiled contentedly. "An extra pair of strong arms is always useful," she murmured wickedly.

And he had no choice but to grin in agreement.

The physician disdainfully wiped his hands on a lace-edged handkerchief and regarded his lordship with near contempt.

"The boy is scarcely worth the waste of my entire

day. He still stinks of the cow pasture. There are important people dependent on my services, I'll have you know. Next time one of your filthy tenants becomes ill, do me a favor and call the local apothecary." He carefully folded the dainty linen and placed it securely in the pocket of his elegantly tailored coat.

Aubree had been bent over the boy's pallet when the doctor began speaking, but she was at Austin's side before he finished, her delicate features flushed with fury.

"I will do everyone a favor and report you to the Royal College of Surgeons. In the meantime, I shall send for my father's physician and ask for recommendations for someone more suitable to tend this area. I'll not soil the air with the stink of quacks such as you, sir. Those given the gift to heal use it for all, not just for their own selfish purposes. I'll nurse the boy, and someday I hope he becomes a great physician and you must come to *him* for healing!"

Aubree flew off as quickly as she had arrived, and Austin made no attempt to apologize for her behavior. Coldly, he handed the doctor a small purse that clinked gratifyingly.

"My wife is hasty, but she is right. We'll not need your services again, sir."

After the doctor left in an outraged huff, Austin returned to the pallet beside Aubree. "Is there any improvement?" he asked quietly.

"I have been applying heat to his chest, and it seems to be a little clearer. The doctor suggested he would breathe easier in moist air. Do we dare trust him?" She threw him an uncertain look.

Austin felt his heart constrict within his chest at the sight of those wide hazel eyes brimming with worry in a small face flushed with the room's heat. Her concern for this child she scarcely knew was evidence of the woman hidden behind the childish facade she presented to the world. In time, she would love her own children even more fiercely. He desired very much to be there when that happened.

"I cannot see that it would hurt," he answered gently. How long would he have to wait before fortune turned his way and he could claim her for his own? And should he ever earn that pinnacle on which she stood, would she accept him?

At times like these, when they worked together, Austin thought she might accept him. But there were hidden depths he had not explored and childish shallows that might develop into dangerous shoals. And when he looked at himself, his doubts multiplied. Once, a decade ago, he might have had the confidence necessary to carry her off regardless of consequences, but experience had taught him caution. He would bide his time. She could not leave him yet.

John offered to look after the boy through the night, and after slipping down for one last peek to make certain Michael's breathing improved, Aubree returned wearily to her chambers later that evening. To her surprise, she found Austin waiting for her beside the fire.

He caught her expression with a wry grin. "You are going to regret that I did not sail with my ship. I grow restless already. Since I lack a billiard room, would you care to join me in a game of chess?"

She glanced toward the bathwater cooling in the corner of the room and back to the tall man lounging in his dressing gown before the small fire. His curls were damp and plastered to his high forehead, and the faint aroma of his shaving soap wafted through the air. The look in his eyes decided her.

"It has been a while since I played, but I am willing to test your skills, sir. Where do you hide the set?"

Austin smiled in approval, tracing the outlines of her curves beneath the frail muslin of her gown with his gaze. He would drive himself to madness with this constant proximity, but he had made that decision when he had turned his back on his ship. He could only go forward from there.

"I will fetch it while you undress. Do you need any help with the fastenings?" he inquired politely, straightening and moving away from the grate.

Aubree's hand flew to her drawstring neckline, and she shook her head, flustered. "No, I am fine. It is not necessary . . . I mean . . ."

Austin stopped before her and removed the ribbon from her hair, running his fingers through it until it fell loosely about her shoulders. "I am a fairly strong player, so I will give you a handicap. Bathe while we play and I will be so distracted I cannot concentrate."

Aubree could not help but giggle at this outrageous ploy. "That strikes me as highly improper, indeed, sir. And I cannot think it much of a handicap. Sacrifice two pawns and wait outside until I have changed."

Austin grimaced. "You drive a hard bargain, milady. Agree to a forfeit should I win, and I will accept your terms."

Just the way those penetrating midnight eyes looked at her set Aubree's insides into turmoil. The touch of his hand upon her hair sent warning signals of alarm all up and down her spine. But his kiss the prior night had been warm and strong and full of the affection she craved, and she could not fear him now. Bravely, she lifted her hand to the brocaded robe above his heart.

"The nature of the forfeit, sir?"

"A good-night kiss, no more," he replied simply, though his eyes burned through the frail muslin of her gown to the woman beneath.

Aubree understood, in that moment, what it meant to be a woman desired by a man. Her stomach contracted and a burning flame flared into life and spread its warmth throughout hidden recesses of her body. She had not known the sensation before and desired more of it, though she knew she played with fire. Austin had no more principles than she.

"A kiss, then, milord," she answered softly, but her eyes spoke more.

Austin read her message easily, smiled, kissed her nose, and departed. He did not play an honorable game this night, but the scare he had received that morning seemed to justify this revenge. He might never gain her heart, but he would have the pleasure of teaching her the secrets of her body.

Aubree bathed quickly and fastened her robe snugly around the lace nightgown she had donned. She was very much aware of the lack of covering over her nakedness. Each step she took swung the robe to reveal bare ankles and limbs scarcely disguised in filmy lace. But she enjoyed the thought of teasing Austin with this display, and possibly distracting him into losing.

Austin forced his starved body into control as she met him at the door with a wicked gleam in her eye. The robe she had chosen did little to conceal the swelling globes of young breasts beneath revealing lace, and his hands ached to drop the table he carried and find instead the softness that beckoned him. He eyed the feast so carefully hidden from him and sighed exaggeratedly.

"Madam, I can tell right now you play dashed unfair. You'll not find me such an easy mark in the future."

He was not far off in his estimate. The heady scent of lilacs distracted him even when he closed his eyes to the beauty displayed before him. If he opened his eyes, she made it a point to lean teasingly over the table to study the board. Austin groaned and bent his mind to the game, goaded on by the promise of winning his forfeit. He was not at all certain that he had made the right move in opening this gambit.

But when he finally held her king in check, every moment of suffering preceding it was worth it. Austin rose from the table and commandingly held out his hand. Aubree took it without protest, rising gracefully to stand before him.

He feasted on the splendor that was his until Aubree lowered her lashes shyly, and a rosy hue flushed slightly across her skin.

"My lord, I forfeit a kiss, but no more," she pleaded.

"There are many kinds of kisses, halfling, you would do well to learn them and be wary. Come here, and put your hands around my neck, and I will stare no longer."

Austin guided her into his arms. The bracket of candles on the table flickered across the pale shadow of her gown as she approached. And then she was enveloped in the circle of his arms and the room faded from view.

Aubree felt the hot flesh of his neck beneath her

palms as he pressed her closer, and her fingers wrapped instinctively in the thick, smooth curls of his hair. As he bent to kiss her, her breasts pressed longingly against the hard musculature of his chest, and she was very much aware he wore no hampering shirt beneath the dressing gown. The heat of his flesh seared hers at those points where they touched, and the rough hairs spreading across his skin beneath the loosened neckline of his robe teased at her breasts.

She gasped as Austin's hand slid below her waistline to press her hips next to his. When his lips touched hers, a heated rush of warmth invaded her body, and no thought became coherent anymore.

This kiss was like no other he had given her, and Aubree surrendered herself totally to the giddiness of it. Austin held her as if she were a part of his body and he sought to complete his possession. His mouth was hard and relentless, and she gave way beneath his insistence. Her lips parted and his tongue scorched its triumphant claim, branding her forever.

Melting beneath the heat of these demands, Aubree was scarcely aware at what point her robe parted, but as Austin's hand came between them to caress the flesh thus exposed, a shudder shook her from head to toe and the flame of desire grew stronger. Strong fingers brushed aside useless lace and laid claim to a quivering peak. Aubree moaned and fought weakly to escape this trap he laid for her.

"Don't, Aubree," Austin muttered huskily against her hair, holding her tightly with one arm while stroking her into passion with his free hand. "I'll not harm you."

She lay weakly in his hold while he blindly explored the soft swell he had discovered, easing the pain of his hunger with this small gratification. Her shudders became increasingly frequent, and Austin smiled softly to himself. Passion would come easily to her—when the time came.

Austin pulled her robe closed before releasing his tight grip and brushed a gentle kiss across her hair. "I would tuck you into bed, my love, but I fear I would climb in after you. Close your eyes, and I will go."

She did as told, hugging her arms around herself at the coldness created by his departure. She heard the door close and stood there a moment longer, a tear trickling down one cheek.

So this was what it meant to be in love.

19

She did not tell him that, of course. Aubree stared out her bedroom window as Austin crossed to the stables with several of the new men he had hired that morning. He was as at home in his shirtsleeves in a barnyard as he was at the dining tables of dukes. He was a man of much intelligence and ambition with varied interests that made him all the more fascinating. She could not see where a man like that would have much interest in a schoolgirl like herself, outside of the fact that he had no one to share his bed at the moment. To tell him she loved him would be to terrify him into sending her away, for her own good.

Turning away from the window, Aubree pressed her lips together in determination. Austin thought of her as a ticket back to wealth and a lifeline for his brother-in-law, but she would force him to see that she had other advantages. She could be a wife to him; she knew she could, if he would but give her half a chance.

This thought gave her actions impetus. A home and children of her own were sufficient reward for surrendering what limited freedom she might attain on her birthday, but to gain a husband like Austin was a goal she had never thought to achieve. Now she knew she could only live half a life without him, and every act must work to win his heart.

By day's end she had discovered she had set herself no easy task. Austin disappeared for the day as thoroughly as if he had gone with his ship, though he left traces of his passage wherever he went. She found Jamie boiling water over a makeshift fire to moisturize the air in Michael's room, a stranger hoed at the straggling plants in the kitchen gardens, and a new maid appeared downstairs, waiting for orders—all undoubtedly at Austin's behest. But of her husband, Aubree saw nothing until late that evening.

When he finally returned to sit himself down to a cold meal, he listened attentively to Aubree's lively details of Michael's recovery and work accomplished, but he made no effort to repeat the prior night's lovemaking. When Aubree indicated she intended to retire and watched him with hope, Austin merely kissed her forehead and said he had work to do on his books.

He watched her depart up the stairs with an ache in his heart. She was so damnably young and impressionable. He had done her no good by playing on her affections as he had. She wanted more of what he had given her last night, but he had not the strength to control himself so well this time. Her smiling face and happy chatter eased the burden of the black cloud that had overtaken him again, but Austin knew if he followed her up those stairs, she would not come down again a maiden. He would not risk losing her happiness forever.

Instead, he turned his feet toward his study. Someone, or something, had ripped out a line of fences in the sheep pen. He would have to see if there were sufficient cash to mend them or if he would have to use his new marital status to seek an extension on his credit. He did not know how much longer he could hold out without a flow of cash. He would not have to pay his newly hired workers until after the harvest, and he had no intention of touching Aubree's generous allowance. Somehow, the expenses of these next months before his ship returned must be met.

One day flowed into the next as smoothly as the rivers run to the sea, and the month of August had nearly disappeared before Aubree remarked its passing. She had ridden into the village with Anna and Maria to purchase some shirt material for her rapidly recuperating patient, when she realized the wheatfields had already turned yellow. She gazed at them in dismay, knowing it was only a matter of time before the harvesters came, and then it would be October. Summer had nearly gone, and she was no nearer her goals than before.

Anna caught her expression with curiosity. "Do you see something in that field?" she asked, scanning the yellowing seeds with stronger eyes than Aubree's.

"Only my life passing," Aubree murmured inaudibly. Out loud, she disguised the transition threatening her with platitudes. "Summer is nearly gone. I will be returning to London soon. Perhaps you could come with me."

Neither of her listeners heard the flatness in the countess's voice behind the excitement of the offer she made. To see London had been the dream of their lives. To see it in the company of aristocracy would be a dream beyond imagining.

Anna did her best to keep her head. "Heathmont might not be so appreciative of our company. And our father would certainly frown on it. We will miss you. Will you be returning for the holidays?"

Aubree kicked her horse into motion, averting her face to hide the tears threatening to cascade down her cheeks. "I have no plans as yet. We should begin working on your father. London is dull without the company of friends."

How easily words inspired hope, though there was no hope behind them. While Anna and Maria chattered happily of ways of turning their father's head, Aubree reflected on how easily that could be done. The news of the annulment of her marriage would most certainly turn the tide of the curmudgeon Sotheby's favor toward her. That was the extreme least of her worries.

In the village they met Geoffrey, who gallantly offered to buy them tea if they would honor him with their presence. When he understood the topic of the Sotheby girls' excited conversation, he steered a covert look in Aubree's direction.

She did not seem to be so excited about the possibil-

ity of returning to London, and he pondered over this
discovery for a while. Aubree had given him no opportunity for anything more than light flirtation throughout the summer. She had shown no sign of waning
interest in her lover as Harry had predicted, and Geoffrey had almost made up his mind to pursue Maria
despite Harry's warning. After all, his cousin could
not take both girls at once. There was no reason they
could not share alike in the Sotheby fortune.

But Aubree's dampened spirits were so unusual, he
could not help but reconsider the situation. Despite
the activity at the abbey, he knew from Harry's reports that Heathmont was as deeply in debt as ever.
Perhaps this match did not have the duke's blessing,
after all. And if Aubree grew bored with living in a
pigsty . . .

Geoffrey took the opportunity to single her out as
he escorted them back to the crossroads that would
take them their separate ways. As the Sotheby girls
waved their farewells, he lingered behind with Aubree.

"Do I mistake, or are you entertaining a fit of the
dismals today, milady?" he asked lightly.

Having forgotten he was still there, Aubree turned
to him with a start. After a summer in the country, the
young baronet was more sun-browned than usual, and
his light hair had developed a distinctly golden streak
just above the frown puckering his warm gray eyes.
She had forgotten what had once made her think him
suitable for a husband, but his quiet understanding
now gave her some clue.

She rewarded him with a forlorn smile. "When we
return to London, I shall have to play chaperone while
you carry on your pursuit of Maria. That seems most
odd, don't you agree?"

Wild hope trammeled through Geoffrey's mind at
these words. Surely she meant she regretted her marriage and his loss. Ever the gambler, he could see no
other reason for this statement.

"You must know, if there were ever any chance for
me . . ." he began.

Aubree smiled and dismissed this piece of gallantry.
"Maria does not have a husband and I do, but thank

you for the reminder that I am not beyond the pale yet. Jamie will see me home."

With this abrupt dismissal, she reined her mount toward home and galloped off as if she left the devil behind.

Geoffrey stared after her thoughtfully. All was obviously not well in the Earldom of Heathmont. Perhaps a spark of flint might light a fire to speed things up.

Austin stared at the remains of his burned-out wheatfield and turned on his heel toward home. He could not let himself contemplate the depth of this loss or the fit of black depression would overcome him with the force of hurricane winds. He had too much to do and too much to lose by letting this set him back. Even though he'd gone into debt over the fences and the poisoning of his prize bull last week had deprived him of a valuable source of cash, he could survive the loss of the wheat harvest if his ship returned with the cargo he had planned. He would be further behind than he had hoped to be, it would mean more risky runs through the French blockades of European ports, but he would not be defeated.

Aubree ran to meet him, her golden face upturned with concern as hazel eyes searched his face for hope. Finding none, she threw herself into his arms.

She could smell the smoke of the fire still on him as he gathered her into his arms and held her there. She knew he did not think of her as he hugged her close for comfort, but she gladly offered what consolation she could.

"John says it happens sometimes, that the fields become too dry and the sun too hot and it is like tinder. It did not spread farther then the hedgerow, did it?"

A black smile darkened Austin's brooding features. The hedgerow marked half a mile of grain, beyond it lay only uncultivated field. He would gladly have seen the field laid waste, but these "accidents" never had a silver lining. Still, he preferred that she had no understanding of the deliberateness of these unfortunate occurrences. One day he would discover the culprit and put an end to his mischief. In the meantime, there was no point in clouding Aubree's natural sunshine.

"No, it did not spread farther than the hedgerow, halfling. And you will be happy to know that all the rabbits from the wheatfield now call the next field their home, if you wish to visit them sometime," he jested lightly.

Though he tried to keep his words light, Aubree heard no banter in them. He had not been able to hide his fears from her any more than he could have hidden these multiple disasters that had befallen them. She heard and saw more with her heart than her eyes and ears could perceive. She suspected there was more behind these "accidents" than he would admit, but she was no closer to his thoughts than she had been a month ago.

"The rabbits will have to wait. You smell like a smokehouse. Come, Matilda is drawing a bath. You will feel better for a good soak."

Austin resisted the temptation, setting her feet back on the uneven cobblestones. "I must find someone to relieve Michael in the sheep pen, and John needs help with the animals. It will be a while before I can come in."

Having seen the painful limp with which he had arrived, Aubree bit back an angry retort. He tried to conceal the swollen inflammation of his knee on days when he worked himself too hard, but she had pried the information from John. She had supplied the groom with a liniment to use, but no potion in the world would work if Austin did not rest that leg and soak it occasionally. Since he would allow no mention of his injury, she must work around it.

"One of your new field hands has gone out to the sheep, and Michael is in the kitchen eating. The horses have been curried, and Jamie and John are taking care of the livestock. If you are to be a wealthy man someday, you must learn to share your burdens. No man can do everything himself."

As that was exactly what he had been doing since a very early age, Austin recognized the truth of these words as something of a revelation. The first glimmer of sunshine broke through the storm clouds that were his constant companions, and he stared into her upturned oval face with a mixture of chagrin and relief. He had seldom thought of her as little more than a precious ornament in his life. That she should share his burdens was practically heresy. Yet the knowledge that his chores had been anticipated and completed without effort on his part lifted an unseen weight from his shoulders.

"Aubree, my little one, there are days when I believe you are an angel in disguise. When I am king, you shall be queen. Where is that bath you promised?"

Joy illuminated hazel eyes to green. As Austin wrapped his arm around her shoulder and used her as a walking stick back to the house, Aubree let her mind leap from one impossible dream to another. She would learn to work by his side until he could not work without her. When he went to sea, she would sail beside him. She would heal his leg, save his reputation, make him wealthy. He could not send her away then.

Unaware of the impossible hopes he had created, Austin sank into the tub of hot water with gratitude and relief. He had not yet grown accustomed to the luxury of being waited on with such speed and efficiency. It had never occurred to Louise that she ought to see to any wants but her own. He had always looked after himself. Perhaps he grew old and soft to so enjoy this luxury now.

Despite the uncivilized life he had led these past years, Austin had always dressed for dinner. When rising from his bath to discover only his dressing gown laid out instead of his coat, he frowned in puzzlement. Surely he had some clean coat somewhere he could don.

A knock from Aubree's door sent him hastily into the dressing gown without time to search out breeches or shirt. Perhaps one of the maids had taken them to be pressed and Aubree was returning them.

At her husband's call to enter, Aubree stepped smilingly through the doorway. Garbed in a gold satin robe that set off her tawny coloring to advantage and wearing her hair in a simple ribbon at her nape, she, too, had obviously just stepped from a bath.

"I thought, perhaps, since things have been so hectic, you might prefer we dined in our chambers. Your mother is entertaining this evening, so Cook prepared us a simple meal. Joan can serve us anytime you are ready."

The idea of struggling into tight breeches and boots and traipsing down to that cold dining hall seemed suddenly unappealing to Austin in this light. The opportunity to put his leg up before a warm fire and watch candlelight dance across crystal and silver while he contemplated this enchanting creature seemed infinitely preferable. Austin smiled in agreement.

"I should not encourage your mischief, milady, but I cannot resist your invitation. Shall we dine?"

The meal was more successful than Aubree had hoped. The bleak lines on Austin's face seemed to dissolve as he sipped his wine and relaxed before the dancing fire. Not once did he mention the day's disaster or give the impression that he worried over its results. Instead, he recounted anecdotes of his cavalry days and schoolboy antics, while Aubree offered tidbits of the mischief she had achieved to earn her reputation as an incorrigible monster.

He roared with laughter over her tale of the day she had dared Alvan to race their horses through the gallery at Castle Ashbrook as their ancestors were said to have done. The image of the golden-haired imp with curls flying dashing down that stately hall on horseback followed by a bespectacled and outraged Alvan nearly unseated Austin from his chair, and Aubree smiled in satisfaction.

"I cannot believe your father survived your childhood. It is no wonder that he never remarried to raise another heir." Austin set aside his emptied dish of fruit compote and reached for the snifter of brandy so conveniently placed at his elbow.

"He would never have known about that escapade if someone had not locked the French doors at the other end of the gallery. We were forced to turn the horses around and ride back, and my pony left his mark of disfavor upon the carpet. I suppose the gallery would have been carpeted in rushes back in the first duke's time. Much more civilized for horses."

The satin of her robe gleamed warmly in the candlelight, but the rich material was no match for the creamy smoothness of throat and shoulders rising above it. A golden curl teased at the skin above her breast, and Austin longed to lean over and touch it, but that would disturb the temper of the evening. He wanted to forget problems, not create them.

Gallantly, he resisted temptation. Lifting his glass in toast to Aubree's beauty, he drank of the brandy and not of the fine liquor in the golden container across from him.

"Your father's coat of arms would not include a lion rampant, would it?" he murmured as he set down his glass and watched her delicately sip of hers.

The mischievous gleam of green eyes above her glass nearly pierced his heart.

"It does, but I shall not tell you the family motto. You would have been wiser to investigate our family as thoroughly as my father did yours. Why did the Atwoods choose a hawk for their arms?"

Replete with brandy and good food, relaxed in the warmth of a lovely woman's company, Austin allowed the bleakness of this past day to dissolve beneath the tranquillity of the night.

"The Atwoods have always been more at home in the forests and fields than in civilized society. A hawk is a fierce bird not much partial to company. He'll fight when attacked, kill to feed his young, but he does not seek to kill for killing's sake. Your lion prides himself on his ability to outkill any of the herd. I suppose that is why your family succeeded to a duchy and mine never climbed higher than an earldom."

Aubree smiled at the aptness of this observation. The Bereford ambition was no secret, but she suspected her father was the last of the breed. Her Uncle John had no ambition beyond winning a nap every afternoon, and Alvan's intelligence had other outlets besides politics. Only her brother might have carried on the family tradition, or any child she might conceive.

That thought made her eyes glow warmer. A child of Austin's would be as fierce and proud as any Bereford, but the Bereford ambition would be tempered by the Atwood love of nature and family. Austin's father had been a poor example of Atwood tradition, but a woman's instincts told her Austin would be as fierce in his protection of his young as any hawk. For the first time she had a full realization of what it meant to choose a husband. She must not only choose a man suited to her nature, but one who would best raise her children as she wanted them to be.

"If it were left to me, I would settle for a country squire who loved animals and children. Of what benefit are titles?" she asked quietly.

Austin knew he trod a dangerous path, and he took it cautiously. He did not believe she would be suited by a country squire like her friend Everett, nor would she be satisfied forever by a rural life of poverty or even genteel comfort. She had moved in high, fast circles all her life, and never realized the difference. Someday she would have to learn.

"Your title and your wealth represent a world of responsibility, Aubree. Soon, you will have to learn that. You have been pampered and protected all your life. I am in no position to continue offering you that same protection. You are going to have to grow up sometime, halfling, and learn what life is all about."

Reluctantly, knowing by the rebellious look on her face that he had gone too far, Austin rose from the table. The evening had come to its only possible conclusion.

"I am not a child, Austin." Aubree rose to confront him, her chin held proudly high.

"You have a woman's body, Aubree, I'll grant you that." He gazed wistfully on the full curve of her breasts beneath the clinging robe. "But you have no more idea of what it means to be a woman than a newborn babe. There is a world out there that you belong to; you cannot hide yourself behind your pets and mischief forever. When you learn the responsibility that goes with your name and breeding, then you

will be a woman. I'm not a fair teacher of that lesson.
Good night, my love."

This endearment and the kiss he placed upon her
forehead were no substitutes for what Aubree had in
mind, and she raged inwardly as the door closed behind him. What did she have to do to make the man
see her as a woman and not a child? Take a lover?

That did not seem a very probable solution, and she
went to bed no wiser than before.

20

September brought rain and cooler weather, and the
blackened wheatfield soon developed a haze of green
growth. Austin set one of his newly hired men to
plowing under the stubble in preparation for planting
turnips. The barley and oats had already been brought
in and now it was time to plan his winter crops.

He had sufficient fodder to get the livestock through
the winter without buying feed, but his need for cash
continued to mount. Wool sales had been declining
lately; perhaps he should consider selling some of the
flock. The sheep did not profit here so well as they did
in the hillier regions. The pastures could be turned to
better use.

The sun came out and warmed the chill from the air
as Austin rode out over the land, overseeing the last
of the harvest and the beginning of plowing. The letter
he had received the day before had served to dispel
the remainder of the cloud of gloom left from the fire,
but now he had other thoughts to occupy his mind.
Austin wrestled with the problem as he rode.

The news that Adrian had been located—still alive,
thank God—had set wheels of thought in motion.
Soon Aubree would be eighteen and all terms of their

pact would be met. He would have to release her as soon as his ship returned and he could refund the duke's dowry. He knew it was in Aubree's best interest to let her go, but the thought of passing this winter without her ate heavily at Austin's heart. He could not imagine a time beyond that.

His mind traveled back over these past months, remembering Aubree's laughing exuberance as they raced their horses over empty grasslands, seeing her golden face shining in the sun as she watched a hawk overhead, watching as she nursed a lamb injured by a fall. He had seen her in silks and satins with golden curls swept up in a sophisticated coiffure to rival any lady's, and he had seen her in dirty muslin with her hair in tangled rivulets down her back as she returned from berry-picking in a downpour. He had admired the childish mischief in her eyes as she teased him from the doldrums, and felt the pang of remorse when she regarded him with a woman's desires. In these few months she had become as much a part of his life as the sun over his head and the land beneath his feet. Somehow he would have to learn to survive without her.

From a distance, Aubree watched the tired slump of her husband's shoulders as he turned his mount toward the heavy undergrowth of a trickling stream. John had told her that his lordship most often took his lunch in the seclusion of a shallow pool beneath the willows. This must be his hiding place.

She dismounted and led her horse quietly through the grass to the stream's bank. She had often stopped to admire the flicker of birds' wings in the branches overhead and the call of their mating songs during the summer. The place was relatively quiet now. The last of the summer flowers were fading away. A few stalks of goldenrod added their color and soon fall berries would begin to ripen, but at the moment, the wild tangle of undergrowth shimmered in the deep greens of grasses and ferns.

Austin's stallion whickered a greeting as Aubree came nearer, but she saw no sign of Austin until she had carried her basket through the wild thicket of late-summer blackberries and past overhanging wil-

lows. He lay sprawled along a grassy area at a point
where the stream's trickling waters had backed up
behind a jam of logs and tree roots to form a quiet
pool. In the summer, it would be ideal for swimming,
but Austin only appeared to be idly contemplating the
whirring of insects over the pool's surface.

He glanced up in surprise as a twig broke beneath
Aubree's foot, and he leapt to his feet to help her over
the stepping-stones. She could not decipher the look
in his eyes as they hovered over her, but she was glad
she had come.

Without comment, Austin spread the blanket she
had brought over the grass and set her basket of food
beside it. He watched silently as she spread her white
muslin skirts upon the seat he made for her.

Suddenly shy, Aubree gazed up to his tall figure and
felt her insides inexplicably lurch. His hair had not
been trimmed in months, and it hung in tangled chestnut curls over his collar. He had evidently thrown
water over himself to cool the heat of the day, and his
linen shirt still clung wetly to broad shoulders and
wide chest. She did not dare look beyond his trim
waist and narrow hips. She was already too aware of
his masculinity for modesty's sake.

Careful of his stiff knee, Austin lowered himself to
the blanket beside her, still unable to believe this
golden creature had stepped out of his thoughts and
into his presence. The sun peering through the branches
overhead sent sparkling prisms of gold along her bare
arms and flowing hair, and his first thought was to
touch her to assure himself of her reality.

His next thought was to cover his foolishness with
the mundane. Lifting the towel covering the basket,
Austin inspected its contents. "You won't mind sharing, will you?"

Relieved, Aubree laughed, a low trill much like
birdsong. "No. I packed all that to feed the fish, and I
am certain they won't mind."

Austin broke off a crust of bread and flung it toward
the pond. "There, they are fed. Now it is my turn. I
had no idea I was so ravenous."

She watched with amusement as he helped himself

to large slabs of bread and ham and a jug of cider. "I send food out to the fields when the men are too far to return home. Do you not eat any of it?"

Austin finished chewing his mouthful before replying. "My timing was wrong today. I left the fields before the food arrived but knew I did not have time to return to the house to dine with you. How did you find me?"

A smile crinkled the corners of Aubree's eyes. "Talent and instinct. And John," she added honestly. She accepted the cider he poured in her glass and drank of it thirstily.

"I think it more likely I have spoiled a lover's tryst. Which of your suitors has an appetite ravenous enough to consume all this?" Austin inquired jestingly.

An impish grin twitched at her lips. "Ahhh, you have caught me out. I'll not give his name, but he is dark-haired and handsome and a wily rogue. I have seen him consume more than his share of dessert many a time."

Since she had just raised a fuss the night before over Austin's sneaking into the last of a plum cake she had intended for Michael, he had no doubt to the identity of the wily rogue. Austin grinned. "Rogues like that are not to be trusted. Beware he does not steal more than you wish to lose."

She stuck her tongue out at him. "Rogues like that will be fat ones if they continue to eat like starving pigs. Now leave that tart alone and finish up the ham. It won't keep until teatime but the cherries will."

Austin mumbled something decidedly wicked but set the tart aside while rummaging for the last slice of ham. He tore it in two and placed one piece between a buttery roll and handed it to Aubree. "Let us grow fat together."

She accepted the offering and contentedly munched on the makeshift sandwich while he finished off the remainders of lunch. Another glass of cider was called for, and he poured a generous amount into her tumbler before gulping down the dregs.

Even in the shade, the sun felt deliciously warm, and Aubree lay back against the blanket to watch the dancing motes of light through the leaves. The cider warmed her and stirred bubbles of well-being in her blood. A breeze blew off the water to cool her brow, and she gave a sigh of contentment. Days like this were too rare to waste.

Austin settled beside her, placing the cherry tart above her head where she could not reach and plucking one of the fruits from its center. He held it temptingly above her lips, blue eyes laughingly daring her to deny it.

Like a baby bird, Aubree parted her lips and he dropped the succulent fruit between. While she savored the sweet, he helped himself to the tart.

"Austin Atwood, you greedy gudgeon, that was for tea," she complained as he complacently sprinkled crumbs of pastry over her. "The least you could do is share it."

Since he had just swallowed the last mouthful, Austin considered this admonition sorrowfully, then with a wicked gleam in his eye, he bent over her recumbent figure and laid his lips to hers.

The taste of cherries was still sweet upon his breath, but the jolt of electricity that shot through them at this playful contact swept away all thought of stolen desserts. Instead of simply teasing at her lips as he had originally intended, Austin found himself deepening the kiss while lightning bolts careened through his blood at her response.

Bound together by this electrifying current, they explored the sensation cautiously. Aubree's arms tentatively reached out to grasp Austin's shoulders, and her fingers wrapped in the curls of hair on his collar as his kiss pressed her back into the grass-cushioned blanket. With uncertain touch, Austin traced the smoothness of her cheeks, trailing his fingers along the firm line of her jaw as she parted her lips to accept his need to be a part of her.

As their breaths mingled and Aubree felt Austin's heavy weight move over her, pressing her to the ground, she felt a small *frisson* of fear. But he touched her so tenderly, with such gentleness, that she could not help but give in to her body's natural responses. She re-

turned his kiss eagerly and arched into his embrace as
his hand moved lower. A thrill of excitement surged
through her as her husband's strong hand moved to
cup her breast.

Austin went slowly, savoring each delicious morsel
as it was offered. The smooth curve of her breast had
tempted him too long to refuse this opportunity, and
when she bent against him, he could not resist tracing
the supple lines of her back and hips. From there, he
was lost, and there was little turning back.

Aubree had little awareness of the direction of this
innocent passion. She knew only that the electricity of
his kisses excited her and that she craved the touch of
his hand with a hunger she had never before acknowledged. When Austin loosened the drawstrings of her
gown and chemise and the breeze blew over her bare
flesh, she gasped with the sudden freedom of this
sensation. It seemed only a natural extension of their
kisses for his hand to explore where no other man had
been before, and she reveled in the sheer delight of it.

But another, less innocent excitement built within
her as Austin's kisses grew more urgent and his fingers
plied her breasts to aching, sensitive peaks. The pressure of his hard body along the length of hers stirred
smoldering embers into licking flames. Aubree became fully aware of the danger only when Austin tore
his lips from hers and gazed down on her with a
burning question in his eyes.

She felt no shyness of her near nakedness as Austin
searched her face for answers. She would gladly have
unclothed herself had he asked. She wanted his desire
as she wanted him, and she would pay any price to
attain her goals. As he read her answer in the quiet
joy of her expression, Austin bent in relief to drink of
the nectar of her lips once again.

His need was too great to linger long, and Aubree
cried out in wonder and delight as his lips fastened on
the sensitive crest of her breast. The flames of fire
licked higher and she writhed beneath him, wanting
more than he was giving.

Austin willingly obliged by sliding his hand along
her thigh, raising the frail muslin up above her hips.

This baring of her flesh was almost Aubree's undoing, but Austin calmed her with his kisses and taught her to welcome his touch with the warm caress of his hand. Aubree succumbed to the lesson, rejoicing in the tenderness of her husband's touch even as the flames licked roadways through her lungs and stomach and found a harbor in the place where his fingers played urgent games.

As she instinctively arched against him, pulling him closer so she could spread hungry kisses across his cheek, Austin groaned her name and covered her fully with his weight. Aubree cried out her hunger and frustration as her skirts rode up about her waist and his clothing still separated her from the soothing solace of his flesh, but she did not cry in vain.

Austin quickly unfastened the flap of his breeches and the hampering cloth fell away. His kiss smothered Aubree's gasp of surprise at the heated hardness suddenly pressing against the coolness of her thighs, and he waited until she relaxed again before proceeding.

His fingers again played their teasing games, and Aubree moaned as the fire burned a vast hollow within her. Her hips rose repeatedly to meet his exploring fingers, begging for what they could not supply. When Austin moved to meet her with his own need, she opened willingly to his thrust.

Aubree cried out as the pain of his penetration seared through her, but Austin had done his job too well. Her body moved instinctively against him, seeking the satisfaction he promised.

Austin took her as gently as his hunger would allow. He bellowed his own satisfaction as he found himself within her at last, and he could scarcely control his desire to stake his claim at once. Sensitive to her pain, however, he moved slowly, until he felt his rhythm build within her, and she followed him to the pinnacles that promised long-denied relief.

Aubree's fingers clutched at the linen of Austin's shirt as he plunged deep within her and claimed her with his seed. She trembled beneath the hurricane forces of their passion, tears trickling down her cheeks as he collapsed against her, and she realized how fully they had become one. She could feel him stirring within her even now, and the sensation sent new prickles of excitement along her belly.

Austin took her in his arms and rolled over so that Aubree's slight weight pressed against his side. His hand sought and found the softness of her buttocks and caressed them gently as she buried her face against his shoulder. Her breasts heaved against him in silent sobs, but he could not answer her accusations until they were made. He waited silently, holding her tightly in his embrace, comforting her within the circle of his arms.

Finally, Aubree rested quietly against his chest, her tears drying on the soft linen of his worn shirt. He had smoothed her skirt down below her hips and covered his own nakedness; now he reluctantly slid the bodice of her chemise and gown into place. With one hand, he could not tighten the drawstring, and the full roundness of her breasts and the shadowed valley between continued to tempt his gaze.

Now that her sobs had subsided, Austin gently lifted her in his arms and carried her to the pool's edge, where he dipped his handkerchief in the cool water. He mopped the tearstains from her cheeks first, rubbing the dust from beneath dusky eyelashes as she gazed at him wonderingly. Then, having regained her trust, he slid her rumpled skirt above her stockings and applied the damp cloth to her thighs. Aubree gasped at these intimate ablutions, but after a brief struggle, she relaxed and gave in to the pleasure of them.

"Little hedonist," Austin murmured as he spread the cloth out on the grass to dry, and she curled up contentedly in the shelter of his arms.

"Ummm," she purred, not quite daring to look him in the face yet but enjoying her newfound status. "Why did you not tell me before what I was missing?"

Austin choked back a roar of laughter that nearly brought tears to his eyes. Guilt had built up inside him until he had nearly burst from the effort of guarding it, and this little brat wanted more!

He swallowed his laughter, but his mirth was evident as he spoke. "You still do not know what you are missing, little goose. Like everything good, lovemaking takes practice, but I will admit, you show a natural aptitude for it." ·

At this, Aubree dared to peek up at him, and her heart missed a beat at the sight of the laughing man gazing down on her. The hard years had faded from his face, and he was a boy again, a boy with an engaging grin and a blatant look of admiration in his eyes.

"Is that good?" she asked dubiously, uncertain of the reason for his laughter.

"Not if you wish to be a nun," Austin answered with a straight face, "but for someone bent on having a dozen children, it is a very convenient talent, indeed."

Aubree blushed crimson and buried her face in his shoulder again. "Does this mean I will have a baby now?" she asked timidly.

Austin sobered a little at this. He held her close and wrapped his fingers in a long, golden curl. "No, I do not think so. It very seldom happens on the first try. But if your monthly courses do not begin when they should, I want you to tell me immediately. Do you understand?"

At his grave tone, Aubree understood she had touched upon a serious subject, but the idea of a child made her happy, not solemn. She did not understand his attitude, but she understood his command. She nodded silently.

"Good. Then I had better take you back to the house or we will find ourselves rolling in the grass again."

Aubree peeped up at him through one eyelash. "Would that be so bad?"

Mixed exasperation and amusement tinted Austin's reply. "The next time I make love to you, halfling, it will be in a proper bed like any wedding night. And in the meantime, you will do well to learn not to lie down with men anywhere unless you wish to end up as you have done this day."

Confused by the tone of his voice and his words, Aubree straightened her skirts and disentangled herself from his hold, turning her back on him as she fastened the strings of her gown. "I see nothing wrong with what we have done this day," she replied defensively.

Austin rose to stand behind her, not daring to lift his hands to touch her. "As man and wife, we did nothing wrong, but we both know those were not the terms of our agreement. I cannot afford a wife, and you are not yet ready for a husband. We should never have started down this path."

Aubree swung on him in a sudden gust of fury. "Speak for yourself, milord. I have done nothing I regret, and if you are not ready for a wife, I am most certainly ready for a husband. If you will not be him, then I shall find another."

She stormed off, leaving Austin to gather their blanket and lunch basket. To her humiliation, she could not mount her horse in this gown and without a mounting block. She had begun to lead Dancing Star across the field when he caught up with her and lifted her into the saddle.

Keeping his hands on her waist, Austin gave his angry reply. "Right now, milady, *I* am your husband, and you'd damned well better remember it."

Aubree gave no answer but spurred her horse into a furious gallop.

21

Austin didn't return for dinner, and Aubree dined alone in her chambers. She should have sought other company but her thoughts, but discovered this too late. Every minute, every word that had passed between them came back to her with aching clarity. She could still taste the cider and cherries, smell the warm musk of Austin's skin, feel the way he cleaved to her as if he would never let go. She would not change a second of that for all the coins in the world, though it may have cost her more than she could afford.

She threw herself into the lonely comfort of her bed and rewrote their conversation afterward a thousand times. She could have said so many things, but would any of them have changed his heart? If she had told him she loved him, told him she wanted him for husband and no other, would he have been any less adamant about sending her away?

She feared not, and it was this thought above all others that kept her from sleep, kept the tears spilling from her eyes and down her cheeks long into the wee hours of the morning. He had taught her the meaning of love, but he did not love her.

Austin not only did not want a wife; he did not want *her* for wife. Just as her father had rejected her, so did her husband. She could not bear the awful pain of it, and her muffled sobs filled the pillow until she had no strength left for more.

Somewhere in the dark hours well before dawn, noises drifted up to her from the stable yard, but she had reached a state beyond consciousness and could not rouse herself to investigate. She could not remember if she had heard Austin return home, but she tried not to think of that. How many times had he not returned home, times spent in some other woman's arms, making love to someone like Blanche in the same way he had made love to her today? The fickleness of a man's affections made her cringe, and she buried herself beneath the pillow and refused to hear.

But by dawn, Aubree's painful thoughts had worried her into a frenzy that could not tolerate inaction. She hastily donned her riding habit and slipped through the gray mist of dawn to the stables.

To her surprise, there was evidence that most of the field and stable hands were already up and about. Burned-out candles sat upon the table and straw littered the entranceway. None of the work horses or mules remained in the paddock, and she found neither Jamie nor John to help her saddle her horse. Austin's stallion, too, seemed to be missing.

With irritation and no small amount of worry, Aubree set about saddling her horse herself. She had done it often enough, when she had wanted to go riding but had been forbidden the stables. Where there was a will, there was a way, and she had swiftly seized the opportunity to learn this task when offered one summer by one of her father's grooms.

Carefully checking the cinch, she led Dancing Star to the mounting block and gained her seat. Second sense led her through the open paddock gate and down the path toward the sheep pen. Since the "accidents," Austin had set men to guarding the fields and patrolling the grounds at night. The paddock gate should have been padlocked last night. The gates to the sheep pen should have been checked at intervals throughout the night. But both stood open as she crossed the field from one to the other.

Uneasiness wormed its way through her thoughts as Aubree noted the trampled path through dew-wet grass in the direction of the rock quarry. The original stones for the abbey had been mined from that pit centuries ago, but it had become only a jagged reminder of generations past in recent years. Heavy undergrowth sealed the ugly scar from view, but animals and curiosity-seekers had beaten paths through the weeds to gain access to the dangerous ravine. Austin had fenced it off after his wife's death, but fences seldom held back the persistent.

As she drew closer, she could hear the low murmur of voices through the dawn air. She could tell nothing by them, and she urged her mount into a canter. Even from this distance, she could see something was amiss with the back fence of the sheep pen. Her stomach lurched violently. From here, she should be able to see some sign of the flock. She heard an occasional distant bleat, but none of the familiar gray-matted beasts came into sight.

The back fence lay in dismantled pieces in the thick grass as Dancing Star carefully picked her way over them. A thick grove of ash trees hid the quarry from view, but the trampled weeds and grass and muddy

ground from the pen to the wooded undergrowth spoke
volumes. Sick with fear, Aubree forced herself on.

Her mare whickered and danced reluctantly at the
shady entrance to the ash grove, and in almost instant
response, John appeared on his pony. He looked
alarmed at Aubree's appearance and gestured frantically for her to halt.

"No, milady. Don't go in there. Go back to the
house," he pleaded as he successfully read the determination in the countess's eyes.

"Is my husband in there?" Aubree demanded.

"His lordship said to keep everyone out. Please,
milady, it is no place . . ."

Aubree ignored his plea and pushed past him down
the trampled path. Forced from the pen, the sheep
could have gone no other direction, though they would
have trampled themselves in trying to do so. Hanks of
matted wool littered thorny branches, but the underbrush had given away beneath hundreds of sharp
hooves. The path was quite clear as she followed it to
the opening ahead.

The stink reached her first. Nausea rose in her throat
as the odor seeped through the damp air. Worse than
rotting logs, it permeated the small forest, reeking of
death. The bleats she had heard earlier were few and
far between now. Sheep were not known for their
survival instincts.

Even though she had mentally prepared herself for
the sight, Aubree retched violently as she came out
upon the ledge overlooking the quarry. John came out
behind her and grabbed for her reins, but Aubree
hastily gathered them up again.

The rocks below were littered by the broken bodies
of hundreds of sheep. Once over the edge, there was
literally nowhere else to go but down. Even those who
fell only to the first level of boulders were crushed by
the remainder of the herd, which either piled up at
this level or bounced and slid and tumbled to the
bottom depths far below. Men scrambled through the
grassy hillocks on the cliff's edge, searching for signs of
life around the top of the ravine, with little luck.

A pen had been hastily erected of saplings in a

nearby hollow, and the few surviving members of the flock had been herded in there. The sheep stood silently in the comforting confines of this makeshift safety. The occasional bleats came from injured animals below.

Sick with grief, Aubree slid from her mount and cautiously stood at the cliff's edge. She saw no sign of Austin anywhere, but the men obviously had avoided the impossibility of the quarry in order to search the safer grounds of the woods. Austin would not lead his men into the dangerous boundaries of the sheep-strewn quarry.

Still, she could hear the pitiful call of some maimed animal somewhere in that first level of boulders. In places, a ledge had been chipped from the stone, a walkway to the bottom at one time, perhaps, or a collapse of the wall. She could see no sign of life among the carcasses littering this narrow path, but she heard it.

To tear one life from this senseless waste became a fixation. One life was all she asked. Somewhere, there must be rhyme or reason for this slaughter, but she would ask no more than to rescue just one life.

Before John could halt her, Aubree had found a firm hold in the side of the quarry and began to scramble down. She heard John's panicky yells above her head, but she found this part of the path surprisingly easy. Her feet were small and found footholds without much difficulty. The wall did not go straight down, but offered large flat boulders and handholds for easy passage.

Once on the ledge, she had greater difficulty walking among the broken bodies of the murdered sheep. Rage built within her at the cruelty that had caused such a painful end to harmless lives. Who could have conceived of such destruction? Her hatred was such that she could easily imagine shoving such an abomination from the face of the cliff to join the cold bodies below. She prayed for the strength to control herself should she ever be faced with the culprit.

Austin's hoarse cry echoed from just above as Aubree found the lamb trapped against the cliff by the solid wall of carcasses around it. Gingerly, she bent over the foul-smelling bodies to pat the lamb's head, comforting it with her touch. The lamb responded frantically, trying to reach this source of heat.

Aubree stood and scanned the cliff's edge. Austin was already working his way down the path she had taken, and she frowned in consternation. If he had been up half the night or more, his leg would be stiff and swollen by now. He was too large to make that descent comfortably, and not agile enough. Fear for her husband outweighed her fear for the lamb, but it was too late now to stop the logical progression of events.

To Aubree's relief, Austin made it safely down. She could cope with the fury darkening his face. He had a rope wrapped around his shoulder, and she suspected he half-meant to use it on her, but she could put it to better use.

"Do you think John can pull the lamb up if we tie the rope around it?" she inquired calmly when he was within a comfortable range of her voice.

"Aubree, my God, I ought to shake you until your teeth rattle or your brain wakes up," Austin gritted out between clenched teeth as he reached the shelf of rock on which she stood. "Do you think one lousy lamb in all this slaughter is worth risking your life?"

She contemplated him gravely. "I did not think my life had much value to anyone but myself, and it would be worthless to me if I could not use it to help those who cannot help themselves. Did you come down here to yell at me or help me save the lamb?"

Faced with this unarguable logic, Austin had to give in, at least until he got her back to safety once more. "Let me get by so I can reach the damned animal," he grumbled.

After communicating to the men up above what he intended to do, Austin fastened a rope sling for the terrified animal and knotted it carefully to a rope thrown from above. The sheer face of the cliff at this point would ease the lamb's ascent, and he signaled for his crew to haul the rope up.

As soon as the rope began to move, Aubree began

picking her way over the rocks and corpses back to the path up the cliff. The stink and the depression had taken its toll, and she wanted only to carry the lamb to the green pastures and sweet air of Atwood Abbey. She could not abide another minute in this foul valley of death.

Austin kept a careful eye on her as she climbed upward, but once down here, he felt obligated to search for other signs of life. It would be cruel to leave a maimed animal to suffer the slow death of suffocation beneath the bodies of others. There had been too much cruelty this night to suffer more.

Aubree did not realize he had not followed her until she was nearly at the top. She rested on a flat rock and watched as John lifted the lamb over the edge into Michael's waiting arms, then she looked down to follow Austin's path across the sheep-littered ledge. He had poked and prodded his way through all the cold, still bodies within his reach, and now found his footing on the narrow path upward.

What happened next etched its way into Aubree's memory to haunt her dreams for months and years thereafter. He had almost reached her level perch, was just within a hand's grasp of her ankle, when he shifted his weight to his game leg to enable him to climb the next step in the path. Aubree watched, aghast, knowing even as he must at that moment, the excruciating pain that lanced through him. As the leg gave way, she grabbed frantically for his hand and screamed helplessly as Austin tumbled backward and slid and bounced to the rocks below.

Her hysterical screams brought men rushing from all directions, but none was so swift as Aubree as she scrambled back down the cliff side to the inert body on the ledge. They tediously made their way down the treacherous path while Aubree crouched beside her husband, holding his bruised and bleeding head in her hands.

Afterward, she remembered very little of the hours spent hauling Austin's unconscious body up the deadly cliff. Had he fallen an inch farther, he would have missed the ledge and joined Louise on the jagged rocks at the quarry bottom. As it was, he was still breathing when they reached him, though Aubree swore he would never survive the ascent to the cliff.

When they reached the abbey, she moved in a daze, ordering hot water and cold compresses, bandages and towels. The one thought that stood out in the confusion was that she could not call the only physician in the area.

After she examined the mangled state of her husband's injured leg, she knew he would not survive without a physician, a good one, and not the quack in Exeter. It might be days before even the fastest mail coach could carry her letter and return with a doctor, but she could not wait and helplessly watch him die. She ordered horses and scribbled a frantic note and sent Jamie with her urgent pleas to London. If her father weren't at Ashbrook House to receive her letter, her Uncle John or Alvan would have to find the man she required.

With the help of Austin's loyal groom, Aubree divested her patient of his clothes and bathed his battered body in water mixed with soothing herbs. John had cut the tight breeches from Austin's swollen leg, and for modesty's sake, a sheet was draped over the lower half of his body, but Aubree was very much aware of every muscle beneath the skin she massaged. With gentle fingers, she worked liniment along the bruises of his shoulders and back, discovering from Austin's incoherent groans the places where ribs were cracked. With relief, she realized no other bones had broken, although she told John his master's hard head had apparently softened the fall. John gave her a wry grin at this small jest and anxiously followed her every command.

The leg was another matter entirely. Aubree bit back a gasp of dismay as she turned back the sheet and examined the limb she had bathed just an hour before. In that time, it had swollen to uncomfortable proportions, and the vivid discolorations had grown more pronounced. She could have no idea how it looked under normal circumstances since she had never seen Austin completely naked before, but the ungainly appendage she saw now was barely recognizable as a leg.

Gingerly, she began rubbing the liniment into the toughened muscles of his thigh and working downward. Austin's groans grew sharper as she reached his knee, and she halted her massage while her fingers gently searched for damage. If the kneecap were there, she could not discover it as such, but blood-covered gashes where it should be seemed to be oozing unhealthy fluids.

She soaked a cloth and began to wash at the wounds, wondering how he had succeeded in doing so much damage to the one weak point in his otherwise healthily strong body. She had never really understood the differences between the bodies of men and women before, but examining the hard carved muscles and tendons beneath her hands brought the differences to clarity. She suspected Austin's work-hardened physique was stronger than that of most gentlemen, but that fact only heightened her interest.

As her fingers came in contact with a sharp fragment jutting from one wound, a vividly explicit curse split the air. Aubree jumped and John turned crimson as he sent her an apologetic glance. They both turned to stare at the man stirring painfully on the bed.

Aubree hastily dropped the cloth in the basin and gestured to John to grab the pillows she had stacked beside the bed. The men had carried Austin to his rightful chamber and not the antechamber he had occupied since Aubree's arrival. The massive bed held him comfortably, but caused Aubree some difficulty in reaching both sides of him.

John obediently slipped a pillow to her and lifted Austin's head so she might prop him up more comfortably. A scowl puckered Austin's dark features, but in a moment he forced open one eye. At discovering Aubree's worried face hovering over him, he forced open the other.

"My God, what did you hit me with?" he moaned as he tried to turn his head to focus his gaze more clearly.

Aubree exchanged a look of relief with the groom. He at least retained his senses.

"Go tell Lady Heathmont her son's hard head is not entirely broken yet," Aubree murmured, dispatching the good tidings in the only manner she could without tears.

John nodded understanding over Austin's wince of pain and left obediently.

"Are you quite certain it's not broken?" Austin muttered miserably. "It feels like its shattered in a million tiny pieces."

"Your head's not that big," Aubree retorted. "As a matter of fact, you use it so seldom I doubt that it would hurt to have it removed. Any man fool enough to clamber down that cliff on that leg . . ." Her throat choked with tears and she could not continue, but turned away to fill a glass with brandy for him.

When she turned back, Austin had maneuvered his head into a position where he could watch her more closely. He ignored the proffered brandy and studied her tear-begrimed face.

"You're a mess," he declared finally, revealing none of his thoughts.

"And you're not?" she answered sharply, shoving the glass in his hand. "Shall I bring you a mirror?"

"If my pretty face is scarred for life, it's no major loss," Austin assured her, grimacing as he tried to sit upright. "But I damned well would like to sit upright again in the not-too-distant future."

Aubree gently slid another pillow behind him and sat on the bed's edge to steady the glass while Austin situated himself uncomfortably. She could tell the extent of his pain by the way the glass shook, but he would never speak of it out loud. She ought to ring a peal over him for his stubborn pride, but she could barely speak sensibly. Tears glittered in her eyes as she watched him move. The fevered flush of his skin and the brightness of his eyes did not bode well for the coming hours.

"I do not think there is anything seriously broken, if that's what you're asking," she replied quietly. "Do not move too abruptly or your ribs will revenge your haste. I have some liquid here I would like you to drink if the brandy has strengthened you. It is not so pleasant-tasting, but it will ease some of the pain."

Austin glared at her suspiciously. "Not laudanum."

"Only a small amount," Aubree assured him.

"None," he commanded firmly, returning the brandy glass.

Aubree set her lips determinedly to prevent the tears from falling. "The pain can only grow worse," she pointed out. "I only wish you to rest comfortably while you can."

"No laudanum," he repeated. Relenting at the sight of Aubree's tear-swollen eyes brimmed with moisture, Austin added in some explanation, "My father was an addict, halfling. It's too easy an escape."

She nodded, vaguely understanding his fears. "I'll not use it against your wishes. But I cannot bear to see you suffer so."

"Never mind that. How's my leg? It feels like someone's tearing at it with a dull hacksaw." Austin moved the limb tentatively, choking back his cry of pain as the metal shards beneath the skin ground against bone.

"It is still there. That's all I can say for it. I was trying to examine it when you woke."

As the worst of the pain from his movement subsided, Austin realized he wore nothing beneath the skimpy sheet. He sent her an odd look at this mention of her examination.

"I should think John would be a more appropriate nurse, halfling. He has tended me before. Why don't you go hold my mother's hand and let me sleep this off? I will be fine in a few days' time."

Aubree favored him with an angry glare. "I believe you must already be delirious. Sleep will not heal you this time, milord. John's skill is limited to tending a horse's legs. It will take all my limited knowledge to prevent infection from setting in before a surgeon arrives. From the looks of it, the infection was already there before this fall. For an intelligent man, you certainly play the part of fool well, Austin."

Austin's head pounded like the hammers of hell, but even he could sense the alarm behind her angry words. He had lived with the fear of losing this leg for years. It seemed damned inconvenient for it to happen now. Still, worrying would not solve the problem.

"Do what you can, lass," he murmured wearily, closing his eyes. "Just make certain the men keep to their rounds every night. I'll not have that bastard getting any nearer the house."

These disjointed words were hard to follow, but Aubree assumed they made some reference to the criminal who had torn down the sheep pen. "Who is it, Austin? Let me send the sheriff after him."

"No proof. Have to catch him. Hang him when I do. Bastard murdered Louise. Stay away from him, my love."

He slipped into unconsciousness, leaving Aubree to grasp at nameless fears. Who was he calling his love? Louise? Surely, he would not refer to herself that way in this brief moment of honesty. Yet he feared somebody, and she could not shake the uneasiness of his allusion.

22

Lady Heathmont arrived late that evening to persuade Aubree from her unflagging vigil.

"Let me sit with him while you rest, dear. There is little we can do while he is like this." Beneath her cap of white hair, the dowager's bright-blue eyes regarded her daughter-in-law with worry.

Aubree lifted a cooling sponge to Austin's heated forehead and smiled gently at this suggestion. "I am not tired. I will rest here when I am."

Lady Heathmont's brow puckered into a concerned frown as she tentatively broached her major concern.

"You need your rest, dear, especially if there is a child to be considered."

Aubree looked up in surprise. "A child?" she asked with confusion.

Her mother-in-law managed to appear slightly embarrassed. "I know I promised Austin not to interfere, but it seems if he can go announcing it to half the county, we should be able to talk of it."

"Announcing? A child?" Aubree decided her brain must be more tired than she imagined.

"The day at the market," the widow continued doggedly. "The maids told me what Austin said about an heir."

A rush of embarrassment flooded her cheeks at this memory. So that was why everyone had been treating her with such care lately. Even Mattie had made her climb down from the footstool when she had tried to reach one of the kittens in the bed hangings. Austin had served a twofold purpose with that wicked declaration.

Aubree shook her head decisively. "Austin was simply getting even with me for embarrassing him. He meant nothing by that statement."

Lady Heathmont's face sagged sadly. "You are certain? There is no chance?"

Aubree suddenly realized how much a child meant to the dowager. If anything should happen to Austin, he had no heir to carry on the title. There were no brothers, no other line of Atwoods to call on. The abbey and its lands would revert to the crown. All rested on one very slim hope.

She offered what hope she could. "There is always a chance," she admitted softly.

The dowager nodded with a small measure of relief. "I had feared . . . So many rumors follow Austin about. My correspondents in London said your father forced the marriage. I could not believe Austin could be forced to anything, but his insistence on separate chambers . . . I was worried."

She had every right to be worried, but Aubree did not have the heart to tell her that. "I would not listen to gossip, milady. Your son is overly concerned about my welfare, perhaps. There is the difference in our ages."

"Fustian!" Lady Heathmont announced, rising from her chair and preparing to leave the young bride to her bed. "Austin did not turn a score and ten until last spring. A green girl with no one else to guide her needs a man with more experience than she. And he needs your youth to remind him he is not an old man yet. I shall leave him in your good hands."

Aubree blinked back tears as the dowager departed after quite effectively dismissing what Aubree had considered to be the insurmountable problem of age. Now if only Austin could be convinced that he did not need an older woman, or that her wealth was not a handicap, or that her inexperience could be overcome . . . The list seemed endless, but one factor weighed more important than all: before Austin could be convinced of anything, he must recover.

Austin's unconscious groans and thrashings haunted the upper-story halls the next day. Solemn faces bent to their tasks, never far from the countess's call. She was seen belowstairs only once, when the young man from Sotheby Manor came to call.

Aubree greeted Harley in the small salon but made no effort to sit and linger long.

Harley acknowledged her nervous impatience graciously. "I just heard of the accident, Aubree." He ignored her title for the first time, speaking to her as friend to friend. "Is there anything I can do? We can do? Anna and Maria offer their aid, too. At times like these, neighbors cannot let old grudges come between them."

Aubree stalked nervously up and down the worn carpet. Free of the sickroom, a dozen things came to mind, but she hesitated mentioning any of them. Austin had all but acknowledged that the recent string of disasters was no accident, but she could think of no one who would hold so strong a hate for him but the Sothebys. She could not believe Harley guilty of such heinous crimes, but after all, he had been the one who had kidnapped her in the first place.

"Can you not, Harley?" she asked irritably, too

tired to be diplomatic. "Can you tell me your father knows nothing of these little 'accidents' that have all but destroyed Austin? Who else would enjoy bringing him down and making him suffer like that?"

Harley looked startled. "You are telling me what happened the other night was not an accident? Austin's fall—I heard . . ."

She swung to face him. "Austin's fall was an accident. An inevitable one, perhaps, but an accident. No, his tormentor does not mean to kill him quickly, it seems. He would prefer to drive him to his grave in misery, just as your sister died. Louise committed suicide, Harley. You didn't know that, did you? I wonder if your father does? I have seen Austin suffer so, I cannot help but wonder what keeps him from taking his own life. Maybe that's what his tormentor intends. What do you think, Harley?"

She said unforgivable things, things she had never even thought of until this very minute, when driven to desperation. Someone out there hated Austin; she was never so sure of it as now, when it all began to come together. Austin had hidden the knowledge of Louise's death, but it seemed the safest, fastest way to free him from the prison he had been buried in. In truth, there was power.

Harley stood, stunned, unable to cope with this barrage of facts all at once. Little by little, he picked up the pieces and began to fit them together again.

"I don't think even my father knew how Louise died, Aubree. He and Austin have not spoken since her death. He's a blind, bitter old man, but I cannot imagine him taking his vengeance on Heath. They were friends once, and I think his bitterness stems from what he considers Heath's failure of his trust. I have never heard him call Heath a murderer."

Aubree stared unhappily out the window. "Then I must believe he has other enemies. I do not know what to do, Harley. I must go back up to him in case he wakes."

She turned to leave, but Harley intervened. "You are certain the sheep and the wheat and all the other little incidents were not accidents?"

Aubree stared at him coldly. "I know nothing of what happened before I came, but sheep can't fly and wheat can't play with fire. I thank you for your kindness, sir, but I must be going."

She was every inch the regal countess as she swept from the room, despite the fact that curls escaped her chignon in unruly order and a kitten trailed at her heels. Harley accepted his dismissal with understanding, but she had given him food for thought. If Austin had actually been innocent all these years, the Sotheby family owed him a great deal, indeed.

As the next day wore on with no signs of improvement, faces around the household grew longer. Aubree seldom stirred from Austin's bedside, and for lack of any proper staff structure, John and Matilda were left in charge of running the house and estate. They struggled valiantly with the day-to-day problems and delegated all other mishaps to the dowager and Aubree, neither of whom paid great attention to detail.

Mattie stared in dismay at the mounting stack of mail Aubree had sent back down, unopened. There were several official-looking seals and an assortment of personal notes that really shouldn't be left lying around, but Aubree had glanced at them all in disinterest and sent them away. If she only had a proper secretary, like she ought . . . But there again, a house with no butler could scarcely be expected to have a secretary.

The plump lady's maid left the letters in the study and sailed into the kitchen. At least a scullery maid and a cook had been acquired, though they spent more time gossiping than working, it appeared. They jumped guiltily from their seats as Matilda soared in.

"How is his lordship?" the young scullery maid asked eagerly, too inexperienced to treat her betters with deference.

"No change that I see," Mattie replied gloomily. "Can you fix me something light for her ladyship? She doesn't eat enough to keep a bird alive."

"The poor, wee bit of a thing. It was lovely watching the two of them together, just like in the stories.

Anyone with half an eye could see how they adored each other," the new cook declared grandly, to no one in particular.

"And to think me mum said he'd beat her," exclaimed the little maid. "Why, his lordship would no more lift his hand to her than to these pots." She shook the blackened skillet she had been scrubbing for emphasis.

"Fools people be," Mattie grumbled as she set napkins and utensils on a tray for Aubree. "There's those who ain't no better than they should be, but where are those who raised him up from a lad? Why don't they step forward and say it's all brazen lies, that his lordship could not hurt a lady, and put a halt to this nastiness? That's what I want to know." She slammed the tray down on the table, set the bowl of broth on it that Cook gave to her, and sailed out of the kitchen again.

The kitchen servants gazed at one another guiltily. They all knew people who had worked at the abbey in the past, and never once had any of those former servants had anything hard to say about the present earl. Yet none of them had stepped forward to defend him, either. Maybe it was about time.

Aubree clenched her teeth and grasped the stubborn sliver of metal as firmly as she could. Telling herself it worked on the same principle as a splinter, she grimly tried to ease the shrapnel from the wound in Austin's leg. He groaned in pain, but she ignored the sound, knowing he was not conscious of anything.

The metal gave way with great difficulty, and she felt sick to her stomach as it seemed to saw through muscle and tissue in its path. But at last, it came free, and she stared at it in disgust and satisfaction. This scrap of iron could have naught to do with a fall from a cliff, but much to do with Austin's lameness. She wondered how many more of the nasty pieces lay embedded somewhere in that swollen mass of flesh?

The wound began to drain and Aubree hastily bent to the task of cleansing it. So far, she could find no signs of the infection spreading, but she lived in dread of the day when she might. If Austin harbored doubts about taking a wife under present circumstances, he would most certainly refute their marriage if he should lose a leg. For her sake, as well as his, the leg must be saved. She prayed the doctor would hurry.

It was late afternoon of the third day before an exhausted Jamie rode into the courtyard, trailing an equally fatigued gentleman on a blooded stallion. The gentleman's hat had become grimed with dust, and a layer of topsoil appeared to coat his elegant riding coat and buff breeches. As he swung down from his mount, a flurry of youngsters flocked to take his reins and help him with his instrument bag.

Somewhat alarmed by this ragtag reception instead of the usual liveried footmen, the physician scanned the worn stone walls of Atwood Abbey's impressive facade. It was no doubt the residence of nobility, but the broken panes and boarded openings in the unused portions of the rambling structure told a tale of lost wealth. Remembering the comfortable mansion he had just left, the physician made a mental note of this decay.

A somewhat harried maid answered his knock and greeted his card with relief. His short strides could scarcely keep pace with the maid's quick ones as she led him up the stairs, without so much as an offer of a rest or washcloth.

He understood why when he came face to face with the lovely Lady Aubree. He had known her as a child, watched in admiration as she grew up through adolescence. The woman who stood before him now was even more lovely than her youth had promised, but all trace of the lively spirit that had set her apart had disappeared. He noted the black circles beneath her eyes with alarm and seriously contemplated sending for a carriage immediately to return her where she belonged.

But Aubree recognized her childhood friend and her eyes lit with an emerald glow of relief and delight. "Dr. Jennings! Oh, thank goodness. You will know what to do. I am so grateful for your coming. I hope it has not been a serious intrusion." She turned to Mattie without giving her guest a chance to comment. "We must give Dr. Jennings some time to rest. It's an abominable journey and he must have made it in incredible time. Did you have one of the bedrooms cleaned as I asked?"

Mattie nodded curtly and turned to lead the doctor from the room, but he set his bag upon the chair and moved to wash his hands in the basin.

"Actually, I was in Hampshire when the message arrived. Luckily, the lad stopped at Lady Clara's to rest and caught me before I left. Your father and aunt send their regards, Lady Aubree. There are other messages, but they can wait. Let me take a look at the patient first."

He moved swiftly and efficiently, examining the wound on Austin's head, looking into his eyes, carefully searching out the damaged ribs, before uncovering the swollen leg. Aubree hovered near at hand, searching anxiously for some clue to the physician's thoughts.

The patient groaned and moved restlessly beneath the physician's thorough scrutiny, but he did not regain consciousness. Finally, Dr. Jennings shook his head and covered the leg.

Panic-stricken, Aubree confronted him. "Is there no hope, Dr. Jennings? Can we not do something? He has fought so hard to save that leg . . ."

The doctor was of no great stature, and his eyes met Aubree's on an even level. He regarded her gently and with sympathy. "I will do what I can, my lady, but I make no promises. He must have suffered much to carry such wounds with him for so long. There are very few doctors on battlefields, and they cannot have time to remove all the debris that is lodged in a wound such as that one. Generally, it is easier to amputate. Your husband must have fought as well off the field as on to come away with that leg whole. Those pieces of shrapnel must be removed, however, if we are to stop the infection. Let me wash and change, and then I shall see what I can do."

Aubree nodded nervously and gestured for Mattie to take the physician to the room prepared for him.

Then she sat on the chair beside the bed, folded her arms on Austin's pillow, and buried her face against them. She prayed as she had never prayed before. She did not pray for herself, but for Austin. If only he could recover, she would accept whatever fate brought her, but she could not bear the thought of a world without this gentle, cynical man. He had to live. There were too few men like him out there. He deserved life, a healthy life, some happiness from the poor lot he had been given. Somewhere, someone had to hear prayers.

By the time Dr. Jennings returned to the earl's chambers, Aubree had restored herself to respectability and looked relaxed and confident. He dared not comment on the change, but hesitated when she made it evident she intended to stay.

"I would prefer it if you would send his valet or a footman or someone with a strong stomach, my lady. I cannot recommend an operation such as this to one of your gentle nature. I will not have time to hunt for smelling salts should you faint." He spoke a trifle acerbically.

"Then I would recommend my services over the others you named," Aubree replied placidly. "Not one of them has had the courage to remove the slivers that have come to the surface. They have left that task to me."

He looked dubious, but consented to her unusual demand.

Aubree worked diligently at the physician's side as he probed and located the jagged slivers of debris forced to the surface by Austin's fall. Others still lay embedded closer to the bone, but these, too, were removed with tedious meticulousness. The water in the basin grew stained with red and had to be replaced, but Austin lay mercifully unconscious throughout the proceedings.

They worked by candlelight as the last piece of metal was removed from the gaping wound. Aubree felt her hands shaking with weariness and horror, but a small ray of hope kept her going. Austin lay quite peacefully as the wound was neatly stitched and Dr.

Jennings rigged some ingenious invention to drain the remaining fluid.

"What are the chances of saving his leg?" Aubree inquired softly, admiring the physician's skill.

"I cannot say, my lady. Such a wound invites putrefaction. You must be very careful in tending it. He must not move it until it begins to heal, and then only a little at a time. It would not do if the wound reopened."

Aubree suspected the worst of the ordeal lay ahead, when Austin regained consciousness but could not be allowed out of bed. He was too active to lay still long.

She made mental notes of the doctor's instructions as he finished and they began to clean up, but something the doctor had said on his arrival had stayed with her, and she questioned him now.

"You said my father sent his regards? Was he in Hampshire, too?"

The physician continued his methodical ablutions. "Visiting your Aunt Clara. He had a busy summer and was in need of a rest." He reached for a towel and diverted the subject. "Your cousin's child is due any day now. They were hoping you would return for the lying-in."

Aubree was still trying to deal with the thought of her father needing a rest and barely noted the remainder of his words. Her father never rested. There had been times when she wondered if he ever slept. And the fact that Dr. Jennings had been there with him created further suspicions.

"My father is not ill?" she demanded anxiously.

"I recommended that he rest. He will not listen to me for above a week, but that is sufficient time for him to worry your Aunt Clara to death. I may have to send her somewhere to recuperate afterward. They were hoping they might persuade you to accompany me back to London for the remainder of the Season." The physician knew the mention of London sent the thoughts of most ladies trotting obediently down a social path.

Not so Aubree. She dismissed the suggestion with a brief gesture. "You must explain the seriousness of

Austin's accident to them and give them my apologies. I would dearly love to see Alvan's babe when Austin is better. But if my father is ill, I would like to know about it."

The physician had always known that beneath Aubree's blinding loveliness and careless attitude lay an intelligent woman. He only regretted that she saw free to exercise her perceptiveness on him now.

"My lady, if I think you should be notified, I will, but you have a husband to look after now. Let someone else worry about the rest of the world."

That did not satisfy her, but Aubree saw the wisdom of his reminder. Even if her father were ill, she could do nothing. And he obviously wanted her to do nothing. Feeling sick with grief that she and her father had grown so estranged, she nodded her understanding.

"I thank you, Dr. Jennings, and I will trust you to keep your word. My father is a stubborn man, but I love him. Perhaps I have not shown it in the past, but I am trying to mend my ways. As soon as Austin is well, we will go to see him."

Dr. Jennings nodded in relief. "You must get some rest now. Shall I call for one of the maids?"

Aubree glanced at Austin's still figure and felt the weight of weariness dragging her down. But the dowager and all the servants waited below for some news, and she could not let them down.

"John will be waiting outside. He will sit with Austin while I go below. I don't know what we would have done without you, Doctor."

That wasn't the answer he had wanted, but he had no authority to overrule a countess. He watched her descend the marble staircase and shook his head in dismay. The duke had his heir right there. 'Twas a pity the courts and society did not recognize a woman.

23

The next morning, Dr. Jennings removed the bandage on Austin's leg and nodded encouragingly.

"The swelling has gone down and there is no new sign of infection. I shall give it one more day, then I will carry the news to your father. He has been most concerned about the two of you."

Aubree handed him a clean bandage in silence. She began to understand better why one of the country's best surgeons had traipsed to this wilderness at her plea for help. Her father had paid him well to carry news of her well-being and to spy on Austin's behavior. She could not complain if it resulted in Austin being able to walk again, but she wondered how high a price she would have to pay in return.

After Dr. Jennings left the chamber, Matilda brought up the latest collection of notes and letters. Aubree found notes of sympathy and concern from some of the neighbors she had never met, but she did not stop to marvel at these. For all she knew, they thought Austin on his deathbed and wished to impress his widow-to-be. She had grown as cynical as Austin in this respect.

She recognized Geoffrey's handwriting and discarded those letters without opening. He could have nothing to say that would interest her anymore.

Austin began to stir and she dumped the remainder of the stack on the tray for Matilda to take back. She had no time for answering letters or invitations. She would take care of them at a later date.

But another intrusion later in the day could not be so easily ignored. Joan came to the door, nervously twisting her fingers as she passed on her message.

"H'it's the sheriff, milady. 'E wishes to speak to 'is lordship and 'e won't go away, milady."

Aubree continued fitting the cold compress to Austin's fevered brow, but her forehead puckered into a frown. "Whatever on earth could the sheriff be wanting? Surely he must know Lord Heathmont is not well."

"I told 'im, milady, but 'e don't believe me. 'E 'as to see for 'imself."

Joan's grammar had a tendency to slide under pressure. Aubree could tell she would be of little use in this situation. Sighing, she handed over her duties to the girl.

"Keep this cold, Joan. I will go down and speak to the man."

Meekly, the maid obeyed, though sending Austin's prostrate form a terrified glance, as if he would rise and demand explanations for her presence. Aubree ignored the maid's nervousness. Checking her hair and gown in the mirror to be certain she had not let herself become too disreputable, she impatiently left the sickroom for the hall below.

Joan had left the man standing in the gloomy hallway, and judging by the muddy state of his boots, that was better than he deserved. Aubree threw the abominations a disdainful glance before turning her haughty glare to this brash intruder. She knew well how to intimidate when necessary, but her adversary did not cower as well as hoped.

Not bothering to introduce herself, she jumped into the fray fighting. "Joan tells me you wish to speak with my husband. That is quite impossible, under the circumstances. If there is a business matter that must be discussed, you will have to deal with me."

The sheriff was a fairly well-built man of middle age and he looked down upon this dainty girl with near-total astonishment. He had seen Lady Aubree from a distance, gowned in her fashionable riding habits and hats and surrounded by well-dressed gentlemen and ladies. Never before had he seen her as he did now, her golden hair pinned in an unsophisticated chignon and her slender figure draped in simple blue muslin, but her proud carriage and haughty air effectively clarified the distance between their places. She did not need fashionable gowns or company to prove her status as a lady. The title was as inherent as the color of her hair.

The sheriff successfully concealed his admiration, however. He disliked dealing with the gentry and had delayed as long as he could. He wished to end the ordeal now, without a return trip.

"It is a legal matter, milady, and it must be to his lordship that I speak. I have heard that there has been an accident and he is resting, but I will gladly wait until he wakes." That was the best offer he was willing to make.

Aubree regarded him coldly. "Then you may wait until he is six feet under, sir. The chances of that are as good as of his waking."

The sheriff's ruddy color paled a little as he realized his mistake. He had not considered the earl's accident a serious one. If this frail girl were about to be made a widow, he had, indeed, made a major error. The earl's history was a black one, but the countess appeared genuinely distraught. Perhaps he had been overhasty in his judgments, but he still had a duty to do.

"I apologize, milady," he began humbly. "I had no idea 'twas so serious. But they say the maid that died was used to work here . . ." They said more than that, but he could not utter such defamations to this lady.

Aubree grew suddenly still, finally listening to the words behind the sheriff's uneducated speech. "What maid?" she demanded.

"Blanche Shaughnessy, milady. Her brother's been with you as a stable lad, they say. She was found dead in yon quarry."

Aubree felt a sharp pain in her midsection at the thought of that willful girl and her unborn child at the bottom of the terrifying crevasse. It would not do to dwell on the matter.

Gathering up her courage, she replied coolly, "I doubt if my husband can help you. The girl was sent from here last spring and has been seen here seldom since then. And since my husband has been bedridden for some days, I can assure you that he can provide no details of her death. He nearly lost his own life in that same quarry. It is a dangerous spot, but there are those who insist on destroying the fences and ignoring the warnings. Perhaps you would do better to go after those, Sheriff."

He waited patiently through this tirade. "I made certain of the dates, milady. His lordship's accident was four days hence. Blanche died the night before."

Aubree paled. The night before the accident, Austin had never come home. But there was no reason this man need know that. She kept her quaking fears to herself.

"I do not see how that affects my husband. In any case, he is in no position to talk with anyone at the moment. You may find Michael in the stable, if you care to speak with him. He is a good lad, perhaps he knows more about his sister than I. I bid you good day, sir."

She swung around and nearly walked into the short, stout figure standing behind her. Nodding a greeting to the doctor, Aubree skirted around him and walked blindly toward the stairs.

As the sheriff seemed ready to protest this dismissal, Dr. Jennings strode abruptly forward. "The lady has asked you to leave, sir. I would advise you to do as bid."

The sheriff was nearly twice the physician's size, but he knew when he was beaten. Grudgingly, he turned his muddy boots out the door.

The doctor watched him go with growing qualms. What kind of household had the duke sent his gently bred daughter to? Had the powerful Duke of Ashbrook been bested by a country earl? Or had he lost some of his keen sense of character judgment? Surely he could not know the conditions under which Aubree must live. To think that a country-bumpkin sheriff dared confront a countess with his gory tales! It showed a singular lack of respect, and after some of the gossip he'd heard about Lord Heathmont, a definitely suspicious mind. The duke needed to be told.

The matter of Blanche's death had so sorely shaken Aubree that she could scarcely concentrate on anything else for the remainder of the day. The care of Austin came automatically, without thought, but all else fled her mind. How had Blanche come to be at the bottom of that pit on the same night the sheep met their ruin? Had she fallen? Had she been the perpetrator of these "accidents" and been caught in her own trap?

Aubree found it difficult to believe these possibilities. Louise had deliberately flung herself from the rocks, providing the impetus necessary to miss the rocky ledge and travel to the bottom. But as Austin and the sheep had exhibited, any object simply falling from the cliff tended to remain on the ledge. Blanche would have had to have deliberately dived from the rocks, and in her unwieldy condition, that would not have been easily done. Or she could have been thrown or shoved roughly.

It took most of the day to come to the same conclusion that must have taken the sheriff some days to arrive at. In all probability, Blanche had been murdered. The thought sent chills of cold fear down Aubree's back.

Luckily, Austin's fever began to subside late that afternoon, and she became occupied with keeping him still and spooning broth between his lips. Dr. Jennings inspected the wound a final time and pronounced it improving, though how he could tell from the sight of that mutilated flesh, Aubree did not know. She was only grateful that the signs of spreading infection had not appeared.

She quit worrying about Dr. Jennings' report to her father and dismissed all other concerns while she immersed herself in the task of aiding Austin's recovery. First things first.

Lady Heathmont came up to sit with her for a while, again offering to help with the nursing chores, but Aubree only smiled away the suggestion. She had taken to sleeping beside Austin at night so that she could be there whenever he needed her. She would not give up her place beside him so another might assume the chore of caring for him.

"You are helping greatly by keeping Dr. Jennings occupied. There is little enough to entertain him here, but he seems quite impressed by the quality of the card games you and your friends offer. He is a good man to know, and I would hold his favor."

"He's a trifle too sharp, if you ask me, but if he heals my son, I will not complain. If he is any example of the whist players in London nowadays, I may have to visit the city again. My finances could always use a little improvement."

On that tantalizing remark, she swept from the room, leaving Aubree with a small smile on her face. Lady Heathmont was not the mother she would choose, had she a choice, but the widow had a delightfully practical view of life.

After this emotionally exhausting day, Aubree retired early. She slipped between the cool sheets next to Austin's fevered body and listened to the sounds of his shallow breathing. How strange that she had come this far, from unwilling bride to lover. She could not say wife—that required the consent of two, and she was not at all certain Austin would be willing to accept her as wife. Somehow, she had to persuade him, but as yet, she had come upon no plan.

In these last days she had come to learn Austin's body as intimately as her own. The knowledge took much of the fear from the act they had so hastily committed a week ago. That knowledge, combined with these newfound sensations he had taught her, made it easy to think of becoming a wife and mother. She had dreaded the idea before, but she looked forward to it eagerly now—if only Austin could be her husband.

Clasping his wide, capable hand between her fingers, Aubree gradually drifted off to sleep.

To be awakened by a loud clatter and Lady's hysterical barking not long after.

Groggily, Aubree reached for Austin and found him sleeping peacefully. Prying herself from sleep, she began searching for her dressing gown. She had assigned

Lady a bed beneath the stairs in the front hall, and that seemed to be the general direction of the pounding. With the servants asleep in the attic and stables and the good doctor probably still losing his wealth at the Dower House, there was none to hear the noise but Aubree.

By the time she had wrapped the robe about her, she was more thoroughly awake and not a little frightened. Men's voices shouted up to her, and she could hear the unmistakable clatter of steel. Had the sheriff sent for the military to arrest Austin? Whatever else could be happening?

With pounding heart, she crept downstairs. Lady barked frantically, racing back and forth between door and mistress. Aubree contemplated seeking out the old musket in Austin's study, but it sounded as if there were too many of them for one gun to be effective. Setting her chin, she defied the fates and threw the bar to the wide oaken door.

She caught her breath in astonishment as the cool night air struck her and she took in the sight on her doorstep.

Four uniformed officers of the British navy returned her stare with equanimity. Between two of them hung what appeared to be a pile of rags or a scarecrow. Only when the limp figure groaned and moved its head did Aubree recognize it as human.

By this time, John and a number of the farm hands had come racing around the house with pitchforks and shovels in hand. The farm hands stopped short at the impressive sight of gold-braided regalia, but John lowered his shotgun and came to stand at the foot of the stairs.

The officer in the front stared at the slight figure with flowing golden hair confronting him and puzzled over how best to handle this situation. He had been told this was the estate of the Earl of Heathmont and had expected to be greeted by a sleepy footman. Not only was this creature not a footman, he could not identify her as a maid or any other person likely to be throwing open an earl's door. How to address her was the most pressing problem.

"Is this the home of Lord Heathmont?" he finally inquired.

"Yes, this is Atwood Abbey. What brings you here?" Aubree sent the ragged figure clamped between steely arms a concerned glance. Surely the navy would not be so far inland catching smugglers?

"We have orders to deliver one Adrian Adams to the door of Lord Heathmont. Is his lordship here to acknowledge that these orders have been carried out?"

Aubree's shocked gasp was quickly followed by the sound of John's boots on the steps. He had thrown aside his gun and now bent to take the limp prisoner on his shoulder. Aubree awoke instantly to the situation and fury raged through her from the tips of her toes to the roots of her hair.

As arrogantly as the noble duke himself, she commanded, "John, leave him be! These *gentlemen*"—she emphasized the word with scorn—"may carry Mr. Adams to his room."

"Lady, my orders are to . . ." The officer tried to protest.

Aubree had already hurried toward the stairs, now she swung on him with a scathing glare. "Your orders are to carry him upstairs, Captain. Any less than that, and the duke shall hear of it. He shall most certainly hear of the state Mr. Adams was in when he arrived, so do not compound the felony. My father is not a gentle man."

Finally understanding his position in relation to this raging lioness, the captain gestured for his junior officers to carry the unconscious man toward the stairs. John hurried to follow, glancing inquiringly to Aubree.

She caught his question instantly. Dr. Jennings occupied the only decent spare room, where should he take this newest patient? The answer was an easy one.

"Take him to the small chamber next to mine and fetch Dr. Jennings. It will be easier that way."

John nodded and hurried away, leaving Aubree to deal with the apologetic officer.

"I am sorry, milady. I did not expect . . . I was just following orders. It wasn't my ship. I'm with the coast patrol. My orders were to board the brig and take one

Adrian Adams into custody and deliver him here. No one told me . . ."

Wearily, Aubree waved away his apology. "It is not your fault, then, Captain. Perhaps the fault lies higher up than you or I can achieve. Let me offer you and your men some refreshment before you go."

The captain relaxed his stiff stance to a degree. "I thank you for the offer, milady, but we must return to our duty. We have word of a large shipment of smuggled goods heading toward Exeter. We must be there before the smugglers."

Aubree absorbed this information with a quiver of foreboding, but displayed no emotion. "Then I must leave you, sir. I am needed upstairs. Please make yourself comfortable, and I will send your men down to you at once."

Dr. Jennings was hurrying up the back stairs from the servants' hall when Aubree returned to her chamber. She greeted him with a nod and watched silently as the uniformed sailors hurried down the marble stairway. Men just like those had brought a proud man to the sorry state of the scarecrow they had just carried in. Her stomach churned with the unjustness of it, but she knew there were many more out there, and unlike Adrian, they had no powerful friends to save them. That was true unjustness.

Bringing her thoughts back to the practical, she followed Dr. Jennings to Adrian's bedside. John had already begun the tedious process of stripping filthy, blood-caked rags from Adrian's emaciated body. Aubree used her candle to set the tinder in the fireplace ablaze and with a poker, she lifted the verminous cloth into the flames.

When that was done, she returned to the bed, but Dr. Jennings shook his head warningly. "Do not come any closer, Lady Aubree. He has a pestilent fever. It is possible you could carry it to your husband. Go back and scrub yourself thoroughly. Your man and I will stay here for the night."

Aubree stared in horror at the striped mass of bruised and bloody flesh that was the remains of her brother-in-law's back, and nodded her understanding. Tears sprang to her eyes as she wondered if they might not already be too late. How could any man survive such torture? How could he live with the horror if he did?

She spun on her heels and hurried out. They said troubles came in threes, but she had lost count long ago.

24

After spending the night doing what he could for the injured American, Dr. Jennings departed early the next morning. He refused Aubree's offer of the carriage, understanding by this time that she could scarcely spare a man to drive it.

He held her hand briefly, looking into tired hazel eyes with concern. "I trust Lord Heathmont continues to improve this morning?"

Aubree's eyes lit momentarily. "The leg seems much improved and his fever seems less. He has been sufficiently awake to take some broth. We owe you a great deal, Dr. Jennings. If there is ever anything . . ."

He waved away her gratitude. "I will admit I considered the case a professional challenge. My success is my reward. I wish I could offer you more help with Mr. Adams, but his case is entirely different. He will live, if he wants to. I cannot be of much help to him there. Keep him cool, feed him liquids, particularly citrus ones, and keep his wounds clean. No more can be done for him than that. Perhaps it would be best if I sent someone experienced in nursing to help you. I know several capable people in London."

Aubree shook her head. "They cannot do the job so well as someone who loves them. John and my mother-in-law will look after Adrian, and I will tend to Austin. We shall be fine, though I thank you for your offer."

Dr. Jennings shook his head at the monumental task she set herself, but he could not argue with a countess. She would have to learn on her own. A house and estate of this size needed work to keep it running smoothly. To operate from a sick chamber seemed the height of foolishness.

By the time night came around again, Aubree had almost reached that decision by herself. Harley had stopped by and found the field hands munching apples in the shade of a tree. He had set them to their tasks and stayed around for a while to be certain they kept at them, but he advised her that a farm manager would be needed soon. Austin would not possibly be able to ride out for many weeks, maybe months, and he risked all to allow the farm to lie idle now.

Aubree stared out at the yellowing leaves of the trees and tried to imagine them bare or covered in snow. Somehow, she could not quite hold the image. Her birthday was little more than a week away. Soon, Austin would be well enough to realize their bargain was complete. What chance would she have then of staying into winter? Very little, she suspected, unless his ship did not return.

She could not wish that disaster on him, though last night's uneasiness returned briefly at the thought. Smugglers were common enough along the coast. She had no right to think in terms of further disaster.

She checked to be certain John needed no help with his patient, wished her worried mother-in-law a good night, sent Jamie and Michael to make rounds of the estate as she had promised Austin, and returned to allow Matilda to dress her for bed. The candle had nearly guttered to its end before she climbed beneath the sheets.

Exhausted, she still slept when dawn rose the next day, but the stirring of the man in bed beside her brought some semblance of wakefulness. He took her hand and she curled closer beside him and slept again.

The next time Aubree woke, she became instantly aware of the masculine physique pressed against hers, and her lashes flew open. Clouded blue eyes met hers with gravity.

"You are exhausting yourself, halfling."

These words filled her with senseless joy. She stretched voluptuously, distracting Austin from his gloomy thoughts before turning to rest her hand against his warm brow.

"Not nearly so much as you, milord. You have slept this week away."

Austin schooled his body to peace as soft breasts brushed his side, and his hungry gaze rested on the inviting valley between as she bent over him. His hand ached to reach out and take what was rightfully his, but the pain in his leg made him aware of the difficulty of possession. He submitted to her ministrations with mixed emotions, at best.

"If you have slept beside me all those nights and I did not know it, I must have been unconscious," he muttered as she moved away to a less-promising position.

"Something like that," Aubree agreed, eyeing him with satisfaction. "But if you behave sensibly, the worst is over now."

Austin attempted to drag himself to a sitting position but found himself too feeble to complete the effort. He settled for another plump pillow slipped comfortably behind his back. "Behave sensibly?" He lifted one eyebrow inquiringly.

"The leg must not be moved until it begins to heal. Then you may move it only a little at a time, to keep it limber while the wound closes. You are a prisoner in this room for some time to come."

Austin groaned and turned his eyes heavenward. "Is there no justice?" he asked the heavens. "Trapped in bed with a beautiful woman, and I cannot even move to still her saucy tongue! Was there ever such a misfortunate man as I?"

Grinning, Aubree bent a kiss to his brow, then slid hastily from his reach, groping for her dressing gown. "I can send your mother to tend to you, if you prefer. I am certain she will loan me a bed in the Dower House, should I ask."

"Preserve me from my mother, please. She will bring out her cards and take what little money I have left. But how is it that I am in your bed? Could you not as easily have taken care of me if we were in separate chambers?"

Aubree threw him an uncertain look. She would rather not remind him of their bargain by naming Adrian, but he had to be told. He was still too weak to protest much, she decided.

"That might be arranged, if you wish one of us to share a bed with your brother-in-law. Shall we draw straws?" she asked helpfully, taking the brush to her hair while waiting for Matilda to arrive.

"Adrian?" Austin asked in astonishment. "You have Adrian stowed in that other chamber? How is he? How long has he been here? I need to see him . . ." He stirred restlessly, testing his leg for reliability as he made as if to remove his bedcovers.

"I shall send him out to the stables if you make any attempt to do any such foolish thing," Aubree reprimanded him sternly, swinging to face him. "I have not worked myself to the bone to save your wretched leg only to have you throw it all away out of sheer perversity."

Austin fell back against the pillows and closed his eyes. He was weaker than he had thought, but he detested being at the mercy of this pint-sized termagant. He groaned more with the misery of his position than the pain in his leg, but the effect was electric.

Aubree instantly dropped her hairbrush and rushed to examine his leg. When Austin clung to the covers and refused this intimacy, she placed her hands on her hips and glared at him.

"My Lord Heathmont, I have tended to that leg every day for a sennight. You do yourself no favors by being stubborn now."

"I am fine," he insisted mutinously. "I need a chamberpot and breakfast, in that order. And I want to know about Adrian. Right now."

She flushed and relented. "They brought him night before last. He is in poor condition, but Dr. Jennings says he will live. John is looking after him."

Matilda rapped on the door, at last, and Aubree called for her entrance with relief. A wakeful Austin was quite likely to be a chore well beyond her ability to cope.

But nature had a way of taking care of these things. Soon after he had eaten, Austin fell asleep again, and slept off and on for some days afterward, slowly regaining his strength. He ate ravenously when awake, complained vociferously of his confinement, but fell asleep soon after Aubree brought him some task to keep him occupied. She watched with love and fear as he slept, knowing each passing day brought them to the point of a decision she did not want to face. Soon, too soon, he would be well enough to realize he had a wife he did not want. How could she make him change his mind?

A letter from her father to Austin arrived some days after Dr. Jennings' departure, and Aubree added it to the mounting stack on the study desk. She did not quite dare destroy it, but she made no effort to take it to Austin, either. Whatever her father had to say could wait.

When another letter from the duke arrived addressed to Aubree, she frowned at it. She could not so easily ignore her father's imperious handwriting as she had the other stacks of unopened messages. Inside, she found what amounted to a royal command to attend Peggy at her lying-in. Since Alvan had resisted being torn from his books, it meant going to London for the occasion. Aubree had no intention whatsoever of obeying. She had seen all of London that she wanted to see. Her place was here.

She ripped the letter into tiny pieces and threw it on the fire before returning upstairs to Austin.

He was alert and restive when she entered. He had gained the strength to sit up by himself, and he had done so now. He threw aside the book he had been trying to read when Aubree entered.

"I can't sit here any longer, Aubree. Call John and hand me my walking stick. I want to see how Adrian fares."

The commands were peremptory, but Aubree made no effort to obey them. She drifted to the window overlooking the stable yard and stared at the falling leaves. Maybe there would be an early snow. Maybe it would be a terrible winter and it would be unthinkable to return to London until spring.

"They say the stockingers are rioting in the north. They've no work since the public has started buying machine-made stockings, and their families are starving. They are holding demonstrations and threatening to overthrow the government. Do you think there could be a revolution here like there was in France?" she asked absently.

Austin stared at her as if she were crazed. "Dammit, Aubree, if there is one, I'll be the first to join, but unless you're intent on fomenting one in this room, I want my walking stick. Do you want to see a grown man crawl across the floor to get what he wants?"

Caught by the drift of dust down the road, Aubree continued gazing out the window. "Adrian's fever has not improved. It would do you no good to catch it. Your mother and John are doing everything they can, but there is little life in him. I am sorry, Austin. If you think it will help, I will take over your mother's duties and do what I can. The doctor said it would not be wise for me to go back and forth between the rooms, so I would have to teach your mother to clean your wound, but you are starting to heal. It would not be difficult."

The lack of emotion in Aubree's voice was not natural, and Austin stared at her worriedly. Perhaps they had all asked too much of her, expected too much. She was accustomed to being waited on, not to doing the waiting. Guiltily, he realized how difficult he had been on her. She had given everything he asked and more, and he had offered nothing in return.

"You should have told me, halfling," he replied softly. "I am strong enough to take some of the decisions out of your hands. No one expects you to wreak miracles. If my mother and John cannot cure Adrian, neither can you. You have had your share of invalids; I will not ask you to take on another. But do not keep things from me, Aubree. It is my leg that is crippled, not my head."

Remembering for the thousandth time the tale she

had not yet told him of the sheriff's visit, Aubree kept her face averted. Perhaps now was the time.

Fortunately, a carriage pulled in off the road as she watched, and her thoughts gratefully found another direction. The carriage was a large and handsomely appointed barouche, but there was no coat of arms on the door. Who could possibly be coming to visit this lonely outpost without word of warning? Guiltily remembering the stacks of unopened letters below, Aubree followed the carriage's progress with curiosity.

"There are times, my lord, when I am quite prepared to believe the opposite, but we will leave that matter for another day," she responded to his earlier observation. "Who do you know who owns a splendid barouche with four matched grays and has yellow livery?"

Austin contemplated the question with interest. He had grown so bored with lack of activity that he would welcome almost any society at all.

"I have some friends in Exeter whose servants wear yellow. I cannot remember their traveling equipment, but I should think it would be in London at this time of year. Can you not see the occupant?"

"I can now." Aubree raised her eyebrows at the flurry of activity taking place in the courtyard. The carriage had not pulled into the grand drive at the front, but pulled familiarly up the side entrance that the family generally frequented.

"Whoever it is is making quite a grand entrance. There are a dozen footmen bowing and scraping, and the driver is ordering Jamie about as if he owned the place. How odd. The passenger seems to be female and traveling quite alone. I do not recognize her."

"Traveling alone with a dozen footmen?" Austin asked sardonically. "That is an incongruous statement."

"Footmen don't count," Aubree insisted. "A lady should be escorted by her father or husband or accompanied by a companion. She is quite regal, for all that. How eagerly she scans these windows! Austin, you do not have another wife you have not told me about, do you?" Aubree asked, only half-jestingly. The woman did, indeed, appear to act like she owned this place.

"My God, Aubree! What would I do with two of you?" Austin protested. Then Aubree's description began to make sense, and he thought he recognized a pattern. "This regal lady, does she have hair darker than mine? Above average tall?"

Aubree nodded, fascinated despite herself as the lady impatiently waited for the footman to announce her. The woman's near-black hair was styled in a complicated stack of curls that did not resemble the artful Greek simplicity of fashionable London. Despite her regal posture and expensive traveling equipage, the woman wore a full gown with a low waistline that had been outmoded for years.

"Who is she?" Aubree demanded as Austin groaned at her silent agreement with his description.

"My sister!"

Aubree stared aghast at this beautiful, self-assured woman, then dived for her wardrobe. "I cannot go down like this! Look at me! I am wearing my old housedress and my apron is all smudged and my hair . . ."

Austin began to chortle. "Shall I pretend you are the housemaid instead of a duke's daughter? I thought I played the part of secretary very well for your friends."

Aubree sent him a scathing look and did not deign to answer. She hastily scrubbed her face and rearranged the pins in her hair to capture straggling curls. She threw off her apron and gazed in dismay at the drab muslin she had donned for her housekeeping chores. She could not meet her sister-in-law wearing these rags. Whatever would she think!

The sound of shoes clattering up the steps warned of Joan's approach with the news of their guest. Aubree wailed her distress and began struggling with the row of buttons at her back.

"Come here, I will do them." Austin spoke soothingly, though a trace of laughter remained behind his words.

Aubree dropped to the bed beside him and his nimble fingers made quick work of the fastenings. She jumped up to answer Joan's rap at the door, told the maid she would soon be down, closed the door, and hastily stepped out of the dreary daydress.

Austin watched his wife's chemise-clad figure with admiration as she darted to the wardrobe and removed a pale-yellow muslin with ribboned inserts. The short waist emphasized her high bosom and the cap sleeves revealed shapely golden arms. Within minutes, she had transformed herself from housemaid to lady. It was a performance he would not have missed for all the gold in England.

"You do realize, once Emily learns her husband is here, she won't notice if you are wearing a cow suit?" he warned her laughingly.

"First impressions matter," Aubree insisted. She threw him a linen shirt. "Garb yourself. She will wish to see your worthless hide, too, I should imagine."

"Then I should ungarb myself, if hide is all she wishes to see," Austin chuckled as Aubree threatened to send his hairbrush to him in the same manner. He hastily stripped off the old nightshirt she had made him wear for decency, and reached for the clean shirt.

Unnerved by the sight of that bronzed torso emerging from the folds of cotton, Aubree hastily lay the brush on the washstand beside him and headed for the door. While he was her patient, she could deal practically with his nudity. Like this, when he talked to her as husband to wife, she became very conscious of his masculinity. She did not need to be any more flustered than she was.

Not that the cool, poised young woman who entered the drawing room to welcome her guest appeared in any way flustered. She smiled cordially, held out her hand, and greeted her lovely visitor by name.

"Oh, my, you must be Lady Aubree!" Emily stepped back and gazed at her hostess with incredulity and admiration. "Austin said you were attractive, but he never said you were a diamond of the first water. And so young! You must tell me how you did it. I thought my brother had determined to be a crusty old bachelor. I have been terrified of meeting you. Where is Austin? Is he well?"

Aubree's smile warmed beneath the onslaught. "He is recovering from an accident and cannot come down to meet you. I will take you to him when you are ready. One of the maids is on the way to the Dower House to notify your mother of your arrival. If I had known of your coming, I would have prepared a chamber for you. Your room will need some freshening. Have you trunks?"

Emily shook her head impatiently. "I left everything in Exeter. I did not know what sort of reception to expect here. Take me to Austin. I very much want to know what he has heard of Adrian. I could not wait for another letter. If he is to be brought here, I wanted to be waiting when they came. Do you know anything of it?" she asked anxiously, near turquoise eyes searching Aubree's face for truth.

Aubree had hoped to give their guest a moment's respite before plunging into the news, but that had been a foolish thought. If Austin had been the fevered man upstairs, she would want to know immediately.

"Adrian is here," she answered gently. At Emily's excited leap of joy, Aubree touched her arm and warned, "He is very ill. He does not recognize anyone. I believe John is with him now. Would you prefer to rest before I take you to see him? Your journey has been such a long one . . ."

"Now. Take me to him now," the woman demanded firmly, though tears rimmed her eyes.

"Of course," Aubree replied understandingly, and led the way to Adrian's room.

John had been warned in advance and had managed to cover the invalid's disfigured back with a light linen sheet before they arrived. Still, Emily gasped in horror at the emaciated man lying so pale against the sheets. John had trimmed and washed his matted, filthy hair and beard, but the result still did not resemble the handsome, cheerful sailor he had once been.

"Oh, my word," Emily whispered as she dropped to her knees beside the bed and stroked Adrian's fevered brow.

Emily's perfume permeated the close air of the shuttered room. Aubree did not recognize the scent, but the man in the bed evidently did, even in his fevered dreams. He moaned and stirred restlessly and her name whispered past dry lips.

Aubree could scarcely control her own tears as Emily wept helplessly beside the bed. She beckoned to John and they left the room, closing the door on the private scene inside.

25

Austin gazed at his sister with sympathy. She had washed the tears from her face and combed her hair, but her eyes were still swollen and shadowed, and she curled in the high-backed chair like a lost little girl. The beautiful, haughty lady who had arrived earlier had been reduced to a weeping child.

He loved his sister, but he could not help comparing her emotional state to Aubree's cool determination in the face of adversity. Aubree might weep and rail and curse the fates, but it never took her long to recover and face the practicality of any situation. He could imagine Adrian preferring a woman who would turn helplessly to him in times of trouble. For himself, he preferred Aubree's stubborn independence.

"It will take time, Emily, but Adrian is one of the most courageous men I know. He will recover now that you are here, I am certain of it," Austin soothed. "Where are the children? Did you not bring them with you?"

"Of course I brought them," Emily replied a trifle tartly. Austin was the least comforting of men, sometimes. "I left them in Exeter with the Travers' nanny."

"Oh, but you must bring them here, Emily," Aubree interrupted excitedly. "Adrian will want them here when he wakes, I'm certain. It might even help him to wake. I'll admit, the accommodations are not grand, but . . ."

Emily began to look a little more enthusiastic. "You

would not mind? I hate to intrude, I know you and
Austin are only recently wed and this dreadful barn of
a place is impossible to manage, but I will help in any
way I can. It would be like coming home to me, and I
am certain the children will be thrilled. Austin and I
used to have the grandest adventures . . ."

Austin frowned. "The old wing has been barred off,
Emily. It's become much too dangerous. Whatever
you do, don't tell the children about our 'adventures'
there. We were lucky we didn't kill ourselves."

"Austin, I declare! You're getting old. But I suppose you're right. There is plenty-enough mischief for
the rascals to achieve without sending them in there."

Apparently cheered by the prospect of bringing her
children to their ancestral home, Emily left the room
with a more stately tread than she had arrived.

Austin turned an inquiring eye to his remarkably
quiet young wife. "In addition to my sister and ill
brother-in-law, you would add two extremely young
children to your list of tasks?"

She looked suitably shocked. "You would leave them
elsewhere? You are a callous man, milord. Besides, I
shall enjoy their company."

"It will be the first time I have seen them, and I will
admit I am eager for their arrival, but I will not be the
one chasing them down the hallway. Perhaps we ought
to borrow the Travers' nanny?" Austin tried to gauge
what went on behind his wife's lovely face, but she
revealed nothing of her thoughts with her reply.

"Don't be ridiculous. You scarcely need my care
any longer, and Emily will attend Adrian. Your mother
and I will quite enjoy having the children to amuse
us."

Before he could question further, Aubree stood up
and swept from the room.

The children made Atwood Abbey a home again.
Aged three and two, they could not go far without
supervision and were thus constantly underfoot, but
Aubree would have it no other way. She smiled in
satisfaction as they romped with Lady and piled on the
bed to demand that Austin read them a story. He was
good with them, and it relieved some of the tedium of

his long confinement. But Aubree knew it was only a temporary respite.

There were no more demanding letters from her father, but she realized it was only a matter of time before the duke enforced his commands. If she could believe Austin would fight to keep her at the abbey, she would not be so worried, but she knew Austin well enough by now to know he would take her father's side. He had intended to send her away from the first. She suspected he only waited until his ship returned or he was well enough to carry out his commands, or both. She doubted if Austin had communicated his desire for an annulment to her father, and she wondered how the duke would react to that. After Dr. Jennings' report, he might even agree without a fight. It did not sound at all promising.

However, Aubree's birthday passed without notice, and her spirits lifted somewhat. There were legal letters to Austin she felt certain concerned her inheritance, but she knew better than to remind him of the subject. They joined the stack of things to be done when Austin recovered.

The sheriff had apparently been temporarily embarrassed into staying away, and Aubree stopped worrying about passing on the information about Blanche. Austin would certainly have some alibi for that night. Perhaps the sheriff had already learned of it and would not return. There were more important things to worry about.

Adrian's condition rapidly improved with the arrival of his family, as Austin had predicted. By the first week of October, he was not only awake, but consuming everything the kitchen prepared.

He greeted Aubree cheerfully as she carried in his two youngsters for a kiss before sending them off to bed.

"You'll have them spoiled rotten, milady. Their nanny won't take them back, and we'll have to leave them here with you." Adrian laughed as the mischievous duo screamed their approval of this prospect.

"You are more than welcome to do so. This place will be empty without them." Aubree caught the smallest one as she tried to climb onto her father's still-painful back.

Adrian claimed his daughter and held her firmly as he tickled her belly. But he turned his smiling gaze to his hostess. "I should not think it will be empty for long. Austin never struck me as one shy of fatherhood."

Aubree hid her blush by removing the Adam's heir from the bedpost and propping him on her hip in preparation to carrying him off to bed. "Austin is more interested in increasing his herd than starting a brood. This accident has been a severe setback to him." She scooped up the second child and turned to leave, but the note in Adrian's voice halted her.

"Lady Aubree, I do not mean to pry, but is all well with Austin? There is no chance he will yet lose his leg? Or perhaps the estate? I know he has been in precarious finances, but surely all that is over. Yet I feel there is something I have not been told."

Aubree hesitated, sensing this man was much more than friend. As Austin had done for him, so Adrian would do for Austin. But there was nothing she could tell him, really. Only time could return Austin's wealth and reputation, and time was something she did not have.

"His leg heals and should be better than before," she reassured him. "I know little of the estate, but I cannot think him in danger of losing it. He does have some friends, and they would all gladly help should there be the least danger of the abbey lands being lost. There is truly nothing for you to be concerned about."

"Perhaps you're right." But Adrian did not seem at all certain as he let her go.

Aubree went to bed that night dissatisfied with her own inability to put an end to their problems. If she could persuade Austin to accept his fate as a husband, then the income from her inheritance would easily solve the estate's financial difficulties. But Austin was much too proud to accept that. And she wasn't certain she would be happy if he did take her on those terms. She wanted him to want her for herself, not for her money.

Which solved nothing. She lay awake long after the man beside her began to breathe evenly. Out of loneliness, she curled closer to his sturdy warmth, wishing to feel his arms around her once more. But of course, that was impossible. Just for Austin to turn on his side involved a great deal of pain, though naturally he tormented himself with this maneuver whenever he thought her not around. Aubree smiled at this remembrance of his perverse stubbornness, and gradually she found sleep in her husband's closeness.

Dawn brought the nip of fall to the unheated chamber, and Austin moved instinctively closer to the source of heat warming his bed. It did not take long for him to wake to the tickling of golden tresses and the discovery of rounded buttocks rubbing softly against his hip. The sheer silk separating her flesh from his was an impediment he strongly desired removed. Without another thought, he eased the silken gown gently upward until his fingers came in contact with warm flesh. Smiling triumphantly, he gave the gown another tug until it lay in a bundle about Aubree's waist, and his hand could explore at will.

Aubree stirred restlessly in her sleep, and Austin hastened to tug a blanket over her hips, but their combined warmth soon heated cool flesh. He turned on his side, easing his injured leg into a comfortable position as he found his wife well within his reach at last. With satisfaction, he circled her waist with his arm and brought her closer, igniting all manner of small fires between them.

As the flames spread, Aubree squirmed sensuously against him. Encouraged by this response, Austin allowed his hand to travel higher, sliding beneath the hampering silk to sample the full softness of her womanly curves. Aubree moaned lightly and pressed against him where he wanted her most.

He could take her like this, Austin realized, and she would not be able to stop him. He ached to do so, and someday he intended to have the right to follow his impulse, but that someday was not here. What he wanted now was her consent. He wanted that more than he wanted relief for his loins.

Austin kissed her ear and gently manipulated a rising nipple into a tempting peak. Aubree groaned and leaned back against him before waking sufficiently to discover her indelicate position.

Her eyes flew open to find Austin leaning over her, blue eyes dark with desire as his hand caressed her to readiness. Momentary panic dissolved quickly as she discovered the gaping hollow within her, waiting to be filled. She leaned further into his embrace, and he pressed her back into the pillows, his lips eagerly seeking the approval of hers.

Aubree drank of his excitement and rejoiced in the life he brought to her body. For the first time in weeks, she felt fully alive, and she turned hungrily to meet his caresses. She could feel the thrust of his manhood between her thighs, but did not know how to bring him closer.

"Austin, this is madness," she whispered. "Your leg . . ."

He tore his lips from the enjoyable task of devouring her earlobe and smiled wickedly on her. "If my leg is all that concerns you, that can easily be remedied."

With a swift strength that caught Aubree completely by surprise, Austin rolled to his back and carried her with him. She found herself curled upon his chest and flat belly in a most abandoned manner, and she ducked her head in embarrassment, hiding beneath a fall of thick tresses as she buried her face against his shoulder.

"Austin, what . . ."

But before she could even form her question, he caught her lips with his and effectively silenced her. As she drowned in the exquisite pleasure of his kiss, Austin firmly lifted her hips and showed her what he desired.

Though shy at first, Aubree understood instinctively, and the sensations he aroused in her quickly took command. Her gasp of surprise as Austin quickly took possession of her was soon followed by cries of pleasure as she learned his rhythm and realized this time there would be no pain.

Laughing and crying as Austin carried her on the tide of his passion, Aubree took the first steps in the direction of learning what it meant to be a woman. Their need had been denied too long to linger over this joy, and as Austin exploded deep inside of her, Aubree wept at the power she possessed and he controlled. She collapsed against him, the salt of her tears mingling with the perspiration beaded on his chest.

Austin cradled her close, not knowing the meaning of her tears, understanding only that he had not yet taught her the full pleasure of this joining. That would come with time, when he had more control and she learned to relax and accept his lovemaking. As it was, his body was growing ready for yet another taste of this heady liquor.

Gently, Austin rolled on his side and lowered her to the bed, but Aubree resisted his attempt to roll away. She clung to him, her kisses sweet with tears as they covered his face. He grew strong within her again, his body craving the delights she promised.

This time, Aubree was ready for him. His slow movements fanned the flames of desire to unbearable heights, until all sight and sound dissolved and melted, and all that remained was the pulsating roar of passion joining them as one. They reached a crescendo together, and Austin's final thrusts brought them to a crashing finale. Aubree shuddered as he buried his seed deep inside her, and a prayer formed in her heart.

They lay in silence for some while, letting the morning air cool the heated embers of their passion while the pounding of their hearts meshed and slowed to beat together. Austin gently stroked the full curves of silken draped breasts, tested the narrowness of the valley at her waist, and lingered on the swell of rounded hips. Aubree settled for exploring the rough mat of hair traveling down a bronzed hard chest, sighing with the pleasure of finally being allowed this liberty.

At last, Austin finally admitted, "I should not take advantage of you like this, halfling. Once we start down this road, there is no turning back."

Aubree slid her bare leg along his teasingly. "I don't believe in looking back. I'm ready to follow this road wherever it goes."

"When is your birthday?" Austin asked abruptly, disentangling her teasing leg from his and firmly setting her from him.

Aubree smiled. "Last week."

Austin turned to stare at her with suspicion, read the truth in her face, lay back, and closed his eyes with a groan. "I knew I should have pried that date from you. We've got to get you up to London somehow. Damn, what a time to be laid up in bed!"

"There is no hurry. I'm certain the lawyers enjoy counting the money and will willingly wait. If they grow too worried, they can send someone here. I'm not going anywhere until you are well again." Aubree stated this with a decisiveness that hid her sinking hopes. He still thought to send her away. What did she have to do to make him understand?

Before her despair could make itself known, she got up from the bed. A dressing screen had been located in the attics, and she had had it set up in the corner around the commode for privacy. She was grateful for its protection now.

"Many more mornings like this, and the cure may kill me," Austin yelled after her. Her laughter from behind the screen did nothing to relieve his torment. In one way, he was relieved that she did not insist on beginning the process of annulment now, for he had no intention of relinquishing her. But he also realized he had made it much more difficult to send her away, as he surely must do until he could keep her in safety and comfort.

He lay debating his alternatives long after Aubree had brought his breakfast and disappeared in the direction of the nursery. Her looks had attracted him, but her high spirits held him in thrall. Just listening to her infectious laughter relieved his pain and chased away the clouds of despair. But to keep her here in the gloom of poverty, cut off from society, would certainly destroy those high spirits in time. And the danger of leaving her within reach of the creator of these "accidents" was too great to risk. He must send her away until he found some means of resolving these problems, if only he could solve the problem of how to do it without turning Aubree against him.

But he could solve nothing while lying abed with a crippled leg.

Austin threw off the covers and gingerly slid his leg over the side of the bed. He would lose more than his leg by staying in this bed. He would rather take his chances on losing the leg than losing Aubree.

He waited until he heard his sister leave the room next door. Then using his cane and keeping the motion of his injured leg to a minimum, he limped to the connecting door and threw it open.

Adrian looked up from his breakfast tray with a satisfied grin. "Damned well time, old fellow."

Austin's black frown only served to fuel his friend's amusement. Adrian watched in anticipation as Austin lowered himself awkwardly into the first available chair.

"Will you quit grinning like a damned looby? At least, I've dragged myself from my sickbed. That's a damned sight better than you've managed," Austin grumbled.

"Your language grows must foul with age," Adrian admonished cheerfully. "Besides, I am in no hurry to relinquish the tender loving care of your ladies, old boy. After these last months, I wallow willingly in luxury."

"Luxury!" Austin scoffed. "Sloth, mayhap. How's your back healing? From the description Aubree gives me, you must have raised a few tempers in H.M.'s Royal Navy."

A scowl quickly replaced Adrian's engaging grin. "Don't start me on the subject, Heath. You know when I go back, I intend to raise all the gates of hell until an end is put to that infernal British practice of stealing men to feed the insatiable maw of your bloody navy! His majesty's glittering jewel is more than a trifle tarnished."

Austin watched him gravely. "I'm aware of that, and so are others. Not enough, perhaps. A navy that can produce a Nelson cannot be insulted easily. I would have you go to London and describe the conditions rather than back to your hotheaded countrymen. War now would aid neither of us."

"Who would listen?" Adrian demanded scornfully. "I can trace my family back to William the Conqueror, but without a title, I cannot bend the ear of the lowliest lord. No, thank you, my mighty earl. I'll hasten back to people who listen to common sense."

Austin shook his head but did not argue. "If I could take my place in the House, I would have your story told. I can only relay the information to my father-in-law. He has more than a passing interest in our relations with America. I would ask that you speak to him if I can command his attention."

Adrian looked dubious, but his curiosity made him cautious. "Emily tells me your wife's father is a duke. Aubree is a strong-headed little brat, but I find it difficult to believe even she could fight a father as powerful as a duke. So you must have managed to get in his good graces somehow. I assume he must be the one who negotiated my release. Are you certain he has any further interest in me?"

Austin tapped his walking stick thoughtfully against the floor as he pondered how best to answer all his friend's unspoken questions. "I cannot say that his grace and I are on the best of terms. Perhaps I should say that we understand each other. When it comes to politics, we are better suited. I shall write him at once, but first, there is another proposition I would offer you."

The man in the bed smiled his agreement. They dealt well in business matters, and he was growing bored with the monotony of confinement. The challenge of negotiating a deal with the tightfisted earl suited his needs of the moment.

As Austin set about explaining what he had in mind, Adrian's smile became a frown of concentration.

26

Aubree recognized the writing from the address and flung the note in the fire without opening it. Geoffrey's impassioned pleas had ceased to amuse her long ago. Once, she had thought them romantic, but now she recognized their foolishness. She could not imagine why he persisted in pursuing her after she had made it clear she had no desire for dalliance, but she would not worry over the matter. Surely he would give up soon and return to London for the Little Season. It was already October. He did not have much time left.

A letter from an unknown firm of solicitors joined the ones from her father's lawyers. No doubt they spoke of her inheritance, but she could not interest herself in legal terms. The matter would wait until Austin could handle it for her.

Her hand hesitated over a letter addressed to Austin in a crude, hurried hand. Uncertain of the origin, she thought it best to take it to Austin for handling, but a feeling of foreboding made her cautious. She had never known letters from strangers to bring good news.

At the maid's arrival in the study entrance, Aubree lay the missive back on the desk.

"The sheriff be back, milady," Joan whispered, bobbing a curtsy while trying to look back over her shoulder at the impatient harbinger of bad tidings in the hallway.

Muttering a mild curse to herself, Aubree hurried out to forestall the inevitable. Austin grew irritable enough as it was. The sheriff's news could only make him impossible.

As she hurried out, the purring kitten that had perused the mail with her leapt to follow. With a swish of his black-tipped tail, he sent the stack of letters floating from the desk. They settled comfortably about the uncarpeted floor, slid along the waxed planks to take up residence in shadowed corners, or disappeared beneath cobwebbed furniture. The draft from the open door scattered them again, securing them in unreachable corners.

Carrying a washbasin and a pitcher of warm water, John hesitated outside his lordship's chambers as bits and pieces of the spirited conversation drifted up to him. With a slight frown of consternation, he shook his head and gently eased open the chamber door.

Wielding two walking sticks and hobbling back and forth across the bedroom floor, Austin welcomed his groom with an irascible scowl. "It's about time. If that damned wife of mine sees me up, she's apt to cripple me again. Lay it down by the bed. That way she won't know what I've been about."

John remained appropriately solemn at his employer's tirade. He had never thought to see the day when the devil-may-care earl came under the thumb of a piece of fluff, but he had to admit he enjoyed the sight. Without Aubree, the madman would have been downstairs and racing his stallion by now, and crippling himself for life. No, Lady Aubree had spun magic and twisted the earl in her net just in time.

However, there were limits, and John shifted nervously from one foot to the other, trying to find some gentle means to broach the subject. After laying the basin and pitcher down where indicated, he hesitated instead of leaving.

Austin gave him a black scowl. "Out with it, man. I'm not likely to start caning you for impertinence at this late date."

"It's the sheriff, milord," John stammered out. "He's belowstairs, asking to see you. Her ladyship is that much set against it, I fear he will take offense."

Austin snorted. "He won't be the first. She'll teach him to mind his manners right enough. But I assume you're telling me I need to hear what the fellow has to say." At the groom's barely discernible nod, Austin shrugged. "Go fetch him. Aubree's been spoiling for a fight for some time."

John bit back his thoughts and hastened to do as told. Her ladyship wasn't the one spoiling for a fight. The earl had all the gentleness of a caged tiger these days.

Aubree held her tongue as John conveyed his message to the sheriff, but she followed right on their heels as the two men traversed the marble staircase to the upper hall.

She hid her surprise and vexation as she discovered Austin ensconced on a settee in the musty, unused sitting room. She had been allowing him to exercise the injured leg but had feared letting him place any weight on it until the wound had closed more thoroughly. That he had taken it upon himself to walk the length of two chambers raised her ire.

"What is it you wish to see me about, Fletcher?" Garbed in an old maroon dressing gown and a pair of loose-fitting trousers, his dark hair curling about his collar and falling forward in disheveled curls upon his forehead, Austin scarcely dressed the part of earl, but the man before him watched him with wary respect. The cold intelligence of the earl's blue eyes commanded obedience.

"The maid, Blanche, milord. When was the last time you was to speak to her?" the sheriff inquired nervously.

From Austin's startled look, the sheriff judged his lady wife had told him nothing of the earlier visit, and he sent the countess a baleful glance. Interfering women did not rate high in his book.

"Blanche?" Austin asked in disbelief. Then following the sheriff's glance, he turned on Aubree. "Is there something you should have told me, my dear?" His tone was quietly ominous.

"It is of no consequence," Aubree replied haughtily, staring down the sheriff. "I have already sent our regrets to Mrs. Shaughnessy and made arrangements for the girl's funeral. I have allowed Mr. Fletcher the freedom of making inquiries among the servants. To insist on questioning you is an insult that I will not countenance."

John gulped and edged closer to the door as a frosty green gaze came to rest on him, but it swept on by to freeze the sheriff in his place. Royalty would have thought twice before arguing with this petite tyrant.

"I see," Austin murmured in the silence following Aubree's reprimand. He gave his wife a sharp look that warned of trouble to come but did not make his complaint public. "I collect that Blanche has met with some untimely end and you wish to inquire into my whereabouts at the time, Fletcher?"

The coldly forbidding lift of the earl's eyebrows made the sheriff flinch inwardly, but he held his ground. "It's my duty, milord."

"Of course, Fletcher. I cannot recall having spoken to the girl since last summer. Just when did she die, if you will allow me to ask?"

His sarcasm went unnoticed by its intended victim. "The night before you met with your accident, milord. The same night as your flock went over the cliff, the same place more or less."

Only Aubree could discern the slight tensing of the muscle along Austin's square jaw, and her stomach churned uneasily. She had known instinctively that only trouble could come of this confrontation. Now she could see no way out of it.

"You are saying Blanche died in the same manner as my first wife, Sheriff?"

The ominous chill in his voice finally penetrated the man's density, and he shifted uneasily. "More or less, milord," he repeated himself. "If you could just give me the name of some people as was with you that night . . ." He threw a hopeful look to Aubree's frozen features.

Austin intercepted the look and shook his head forcefully before Aubree could utter a word. "I was out riding my fields, Fletcher, trying to prevent further attacks on my property. As you can tell, I was not successful. I haven't enough men to work them both night and day. No one was with me."

Aubree's tiny exhalation of disappointment went

unnoticed. She had hoped he would say he was with the men. She might even have accepted it if he'd said he was with another woman. That he did not lie and claim he was with her proved his honesty in her eyes, but she feared it condemned him in all others.

"I'm sorry, milord. The magistrate's been hard after me. He'll be wanting to know everything you say. Did you not see anyone that night?"

The muscle over Austin's jaw grew tight with rage, and with the help of his walking stick he drew himself to his full height. He met the sheriff's gaze on equal terms. "You may tell Sir George to issue any warrants he desires, but he'd damned well better stay out of my business until he does. Do you understand me?" Before the sheriff could answer, Austin gestured to his groom. "John, show this man out."

Aubree hastily hid a tear as the solemn manservant led the hulking intruder from the room. Not until he spoke did she realize another had witnessed this scene.

"Well done, old fellow. Antagonize the law, they'll love you for it."

Adrian strode into the room with only a slight hitch to his stride as he confronted his furious brother-in-law.

"That damned Featherbottom should have been impeached long ago! The man is an ass. Sending that damned poor fool here to harass me. That's all I need, all those old stories dredged up . . ." Austin turned accusingly on his wife. "Why didn't you warn me?"

Before he could attack further, Adrian interfered. "Yelling at Aubree won't help. You know as well as I do the best way to put an end to those tales."

Austin's bronzed features darkened another shade as he glared at his friend. "I will not give the old fool the satisfaction. It will serve no purpose."

Aubree leapt to her feet and grabbed Austin's hands, pleading with him. "Tell someone, Austin. If not the magistrate, tell Mr. Sotheby. He was your friend. It will come easier if he hears it from you. Then Harley can go to the magistrate and tell him that you cannot possibly be guilty of your wife's death and that Blanche's death is surely an accident."

Over Aubree's head, Adrian watched with anger and sorrow as the proud earl shook his head in refusal.

"Let Louise lie in peace. Resurrecting that tale will solve nothing. I can no more prove I killed no one than they can prove I did. I have warned you before, Aubree, do not interfere in what does not concern you."

The tone of his voice was worse than a slap in the face, and tears rimmed Aubree's eyes as she turned away without a word.

When she walked out, Adrian gazed at his friend scornfully. "Well done, brother. Do you wish the rest of us to leave you, too?"

Austin's broad shoulders slumped wearily as he shook his head. "I cannot keep her, Adrian. She is as free to go as you. More so, because you are in my debt, but I am in hers. Do not ask, I cannot explain."

He waved away Adrian's questions and dragged himself back to his chambers. He had known it was only a matter of time before his past caught up with the present. He had hoped there would be time to provide a better buffer against the shock when it did, but he could see such hopes were groundless. He had meant for Aubree to return to London for a Season, at least, in any case. He could foresee it being much longer than that. He refused to think "forever."

Aubree avoided her husband for the remainder of the day, until the dowager caught her troubled expression and demanded explanations. When they were reluctantly given, Lady Heathmont shook her head in exasperation.

"It has been seven years since Louise died in that dreadful pit. Austin was barely more than a boy then. I cannot feature anyone but that curmudgeon Sotheby actually believing Austin capable of such an atrocity. And to blame the death of that wretched maid on him is the work of fools. But then, Sir George was always a nodcock and that witless Fletcher only a step better. Ever since Austin threatened to have him impeached over some bit of nonsense about land rights with Squire Eversly, Sir George has been eager to find fault with him. It's trumped up hubble-bubble, is all it is. Don't you worry yourself over it. Austin is angry now because he's feeling helpless. Let him get back on his feet again and all will be well.''

Aubree did not have the same confidence as Lady Heathmont, but she could not avoid Austin forever. If he meant to send her away, she had given him a good excuse, not that he needed one. Still, she didn't think he could forcibly throw her in the carriage and drive her away. She felt certain such an action would raise more than a few protests and make life very uncomfortable for him.

Only slightly relieved by this train of thought, Aubree wandered outside instead of upstairs. She had given the guinea pigs to young Michael, and she would see how they fared. And perhaps she would visit with Myna and Dancing Star for a while. It had been a long time since she had given any attention to her less-than-human friends.

Michael was delighted with the visit and attempted to apologize for the sheriff's actions in his sister's death. Aubree waved away his stammering explanations and steered the subject to her pets. Before long, the youth was happily chattering and showing her the lambs they had saved from the carnage.

It grew dark early now, and the sun had already set by the time Aubree wandered back into the brisk air of the yard. Harley had told her the harvest was in, and the scent of freshly cut grain bore out his words. In a few months, frost would set the ground and it would be Christmas. Surely Austin would not send her away at Christmas?

She was back to where she started, and she kicked idly at a pebble on the cobbled drive. A horse snorted and stomped his hoof somewhere in front of her, and Aubree glanced about to see who was out so late.

Instead of one of the workmen she expected, Geoffrey stepped from the thick overgrowth of trees and hedge lining the drive. His golden hair gleamed briefly in the candlelight from one of the windows, but otherwise his features were blurred and indistinct in the dusky light.

"Aubree, will you let me speak to you?" he pleaded.

Aubree stared at him as if he were a phantom from another world, as indeed he was. Geoffrey was the embodiment of the London society she had left behind, the beauty and unreality of a world foreign to this one she meant to carve out here. She had a family inside that crumbling old house. That was her world now.

But she had too much innate courtesy to turn her back on a friend. "Of course, Geoffrey. Won't you come in?"

He shook his head and lifted the reins of the horse he had led up the drive. "I am on my way elsewhere, but every time I pass, I try to see you. Do you read none of my letters?"

Aubree shrugged indifferently. "I have been unable to accept any invitations since Austin's accident, so I have set aside my personal correspondence for a better day. Surely there can be nothing urgent for you to say to me?"

Sadly, Geoffrey shoved back a lock of hair and shook his head again. The look of uneasiness in his eyes was hidden by the dark.

"I only wished to reassure you that I am still here should you need me. There are those who say your husband will hang for this latest deed, but I have never heard of the courts hanging an earl over a housemaid. But if anything should—"

Aubree cut him off sharply. "Don't speak fustian, Geoffrey. Austin might be capable of slaying an armed man in a fair fight, but he would never lift a hand in anger to any other. If that's all you wished to say, then I bid you good night."

She turned to walk away, but Geoffrey stopped her. "Wait, Aubree! I didn't mean it to sound like that." His voice contained a hint of panic as he hurried to amend his error. "There is something else I wished to speak to you about. Will you listen?"

Aubree turned impatiently and waited.

"The Sothebys are having a dinner Saturday evening. My cousin and I are invited, and Maria and Anna would very much like you and Emily to attend. They've been hoping Emily would visit while she is here. They were once very close. And I promised my cousin to introduce you to him. He's a neighbor of yours, Harry Eversly. I've been staying with him, and I rather owe him one, you see . . ." He shrugged offhandedly.

"You know better than that, Geoffrey. I will tell Emily of the invitation, of course, but I will not go where my husband is not welcome. Now, if that is all . . ."

Hastily, Geoffrey held her back. "No! That's just it, Aubree," he improvised rapidly. "Sotheby is starting to soften, and we thought if you and Emily could come and show him how wrong he's been . . . The girls have planned it so carefully, Aubree, and I promised I'd persuade you. For old times' sake, please . . ."

Aubree sighed and contemplated this audacious proposition. If Sotheby could truly be persuaded that Austin had no part in his daughter's death, it could easily sway the tide of public opinion. And, of course, if Emily went, there would be no impropriety in her attending. It would serve Austin well to sit and stew while she went out for a while. They had been too much in each other's pockets lately.

She nodded a curt agreement. "Very well. Have Anna send me a card with the time and I'll see to it that Emily joins us. I am trusting you, Geoff. Don't let me down again," she warned.

"I won't," he agreed eagerly, kissing her hand. "Seven on Saturday. I'll bring my cousin's curricle. Do not forget."

But Aubree was already striding rapidly for the welcome warmth of the abbey.

From a window above, Austin watched as the two figures in the courtyard parted. He could not see their expressions, but he had seen Aubree's nod of acceptance and Geoffrey's joyful response. When the young lord swung confidently into his saddle and rode away, Austin cursed and closed the curtains. He had thought that young pup long since vanquished. Now he had one more worry to add to his collection.

27

When Aubree slipped into their bedchamber, she discovered Austin sitting in the light of a candle, staring at the household accounts, quill in hand. He set the books aside and rose from his chair at her entrance.

"I thought you would be in bed," Aubree murmured, hurrying for the escape of the dressing screen in the corner. Now that Adrian was healing, she really ought to move him to another room so they could have separate chambers and privacy once again.

"I'm not an invalid," Austin replied, more sharply than he intended.

Aubree halted and swung to face him, her anger having reached its limits. "Fine, then you do not need me anymore. There are clean linens in the blue room, I'll sleep there. You can have your bed back."

Before she could reach the door, Austin caught her arm and held her still. "Aubree, you are more than a nurse to me." The compelling plea of his eyes gave a different meaning to the abruptness of his tone.

Aubree gazed up into his dark face, searching for some sign to give her hope, but finding none. The harsh angle of his jaw seemed even sharper in this half-light, and no smile softened his lips as he stared at her. Only some spellbinding current in his gaze kept her from replying in scorn.

"Am I?" she demanded quietly.

Austin knew the reply he needed to give to keep her, but he could not afford to give it. Until he had something to offer her, he could not ask her to stay. To offer words of love without the promise of a lifetime to share it was not the kind of game he enjoyed. Reluctantly, he released her arm.

"I will only cause trouble if I must explain myself. Don't let me make it worse, Aubree. Stay tonight and let us discuss this more reasonably in the morning."

Now that he had released her arm, more than ever Aubree wished he would hold her again. She didn't want to talk, reasonably or otherwise. Only when he held her in his arms did she have any confidence in his feelings, and she knew that sensation to be illusory, at best. He had held many women in his arms and kept none of them.

Still, she gained nothing by walking away. She met his gaze with a troubled stare, but nodded a silent agreement.

With relief, Austin stepped aside to let her pass.

They exchanged no other words as Mattie hurried in with warm water to help her mistress undress and wash. Austin watched impatiently as one article of clothing after another flew over the screen or dropped to the floor. Mattie bustled about, tidying up as the sounds of water splashing came from behind the screen. At last, the long, white nightdress was brought out. He moved about restlessly, banking the small fire, pinching out the bracket of candles on the wall, and heartily wishing Mattie would depart.

In the semidarkness, Austin's black countenance appeared thunderous, and Mattie scurried from the room. The earl was a fair man, but she knew Aubree could try the patience of a saint. The maid sent up a silent prayer that the night would bring an end to the strained atmosphere between lord and lady. Sometimes, a good bedding could work miracles on young lovers.

As Aubree slipped from behind the screen, golden hair streaming down her slender back, Austin pinched out the last candle. The banked fire sent a flickering red gleam upon the opposite wall as Austin moved to join his wife behind the curtains of the bed.

She knew as soon as he joined her that he had no intention of leaving her alone. His dressing gown had been discarded, and even in the darkness, she sensed the heat burning in his eyes. She could escape, but she had no desire to. Whatever differences they might have, they found common ground in this.

As pale arms slid over his shoulders to greet him, Austin growled in satisfaction. He had meant to have her one way or another, but he preferred this way. His lips found the sensitive skin beneath her earlobe, and he pressed his advantage as she writhed beneath him. The throbbing in his leg only served as counterpoint to his pounding heartbeat.

He took her almost savagely, as if fearful of delay. Firelight sent eerie shadows dancing across the bed curtains in company to their rhythm. Aubree lost all control of the situation as he overpowered her, carrying her heedlessly along terrifying heights, proving beyond any doubt that she had much yet to learn and he would be her teacher.

When the moment came and the thunder broke and rolled over them, Austin let her feel the jolt before gathering her in his arms and sheltering her from the storm. The tide of passion swept over them, rocking them in its wake as they clung together.

"I need you, *chère amie*," Aubree thought she heard him whisper before thick clouds of contentment engulfed her. His kiss brushed her lips as sleep reached out to claim her.

Aubree woke in the morning to discover she had lost whatever small power she had gained during Austin's illness.

Austin had sent for Harley before breakfast, and they spent the morning closeted in the small salon discussing the amount of the harvest and the work left to be done. Instead of being dumped in the study to await Aubree's dilatory inspection, the post was immediately carried up to Austin, who perused it thoroughly. Aubree watched anxiously and breathed a sigh of relief as he disposed of the few letters without question.

She found herself excluded when Adrian entered, and she joined Emily in the nursery as the two men delved into a discussion not meant for her ears. She would have given a quarter's allowance to know what was being said, but she had too much pride to pry.

Emily and the children greeted her with pleasure,

however, and Aubree found contentment in their company and the plans they made to brighten the dreary walls of the nursery. The wainscoting had suffered much damage from generations of thrown toys and dirty fingers, but a coat of fresh paint could work wonders. With the addition of the children's multicolored artwork, the room came to life again. It was nearly as satisfying as watching a bed of carefully tended flowers come to bloom, and Aubree enjoyed every messy minute of it.

When Aubree returned to her chamber to check on Austin before going downstairs to oversee dinner preparations, she overheard Adrian's voice raised in anger and impatience from behind the door.

Aubree stepped back into the shadows as the door opened a crack and Austin's voice came floating clearly through.

"You'll relieve a goodly portion of it when you take that ship off my hands. I expect to hear from it any day. Give me a good price, and I'll have the money I need to do what I must, and you will have a ship at your disposal to return you home."

Aubree coughed loudly and clicked her heels against the hardwood floor as she approached the door.

Adrian spied her and opened the door wider, greeting her with a grin. "It looks like you've been entertaining the terrible duo." He whipped out a handkerchief and scrubbed at a paint spot on the side of her nose. "When next we visit, I trust you and Heath will have a few of your own so they can entertain one another instead of us."

Aubree looked anxiously to Austin, but he leaned against the mantel with a carefully noncommittal expression. She felt he studied her, waiting for her reaction, but she could not determine what he expected. She smiled apologetically at their guest.

"I realize I have been a poor hostess these past weeks, but now that you are well again, we should arrange suitable entertainment for you. Surely you are not thinking of leaving already?"

Adrian gazed down into her golden face, admiring the fading sprinkle of freckles across her nose and the anxious sincerity in upraised hazel eyes. She was too young to be as cynical as Austin, but too intelligent to be ignored. Austin did not give her intelligence sufficient credit.

That was not his problem, however, and Adrian attempted to soften the blow as gently as possible. "We will be leaving as soon as I can find a ship to take us home. The good weather is almost gone. The delay might mean waiting until spring. I am sorry, my lady."

Disappointment and some other emotion akin to fear swept over her. Her anxious gaze returned to Austin. With his sister gone, he would be free to send her away. No one but Lady Heathmont would be left to protest. He planned it that way, she felt certain. That was why he met her stare so boldly now. The shock of it bounced off her heart and rippled to her toes. With the ship sold, he could return her dowry. The bargain would be met.

She felt the tears welling up in her eyes and she hastened to hide them. "I will miss you," she whispered, and ran away.

Adrian watched her go with sorrow, then turned one last scornful look on his friend. "The years have hardened your heart, Heath. Too much pride is not healthy."

"It would be worse had I too little." Austin reached for the brandy decanter on the mantel. "This way, she will have some choice. To hold her here would be selfish."

"What fools these mortals be," Adrian muttered, stalking out and slamming the door after him.

Austin insisted on dressing and dining downstairs that evening, and for the first time, the entire family—minus the nursery—dined together. Despite Lady Heathmont's happy chatter and Emily's excited planning, the evening was a dismal failure. Aubree's laughter was forced and brittle, and Austin's brooding countenance spread gloom like thunder clouds over the sparkling candles.

When they finally retired, Aubree came out from behind her dressing screen to discover Austin rubbing at his aching legs. Immediately, she bent to unwrap the bandage. She examined the wound and found it healing as the doctor had promised. A scar would remain, but with care, it should not interfere with the use of his knee. With gentle fingers, she began rewrapping the wound with clean lint.

"The fall did you more good than harm, it seems. 'Tis a pity you did not fall on your head."

"I vaguely recall mention of some such earlier. Do you wish me to return and try again?" Austin asked wryly of her bent golden head.

A sparkle of mischief brightened her eyes as she glanced up at him. "It might be worth trying. Or I could simply take one of Patience's iron skillets to your pate. I think I would prefer the latter."

"You would." Austin lifted her from the floor and settled her on his good knee. She perched there, ready to flee again as she once had before they were married. He had lost her trust already. It saddened him, but he had no alternative. "We have not talked. Why did you not tell me your father had written?"

The swiftness of his attack left Aubree unprepared. She attempted to rise from her precarious position, but Austin's grip only tightened. She wore no robe, and the heat of his hand where he held her burned through the flimsy cloth of her gown.

"You have a fever and I forgot about it. Where did you find it?" she asked guiltily, wishing she had cast the letter into the flames.

"John brought up the stack of letters from my desk. Those cats of yours have been playing in them. There could have been important correspondence in there. Have you read none of it?" Austin watched her with curiosity. Notes of condolence and sympathy had been interspersed with invitations and legal documents. He had not enjoyed such popularity since his first marriage, and he could not imagine what inspired it now, but it was Aubree's reaction to it that puzzled him.

"I read anything addressed to me that looked important. I would not pry into your affairs," she answered stiffly.

Austin eyed her skeptically. "And not telling me of their existence is not prying into my affairs? Do you have any idea of what was in that letter from your father?"

"I do not care," she said crossly, again struggling to escape. "Let me down, Austin. I will not be scolded as if I am still a child in leading strings."

"I ought to turn you over my knee, but this will be simpler." He lifted her abruptly and flipped her over on the bed with her legs dangling over the side and her derriere arched toward the ceiling. She screamed in dismay, but the sound was muffled by the bedcovers as he held her down. "Will you promise not to interfere in my affairs again?" Austin asked threateningly.

"I did not!" she protested, wriggling to escape this ignominious position. "Let me go, Austin," she screamed, fruitlessly.

"If you had any idea how tempted I am to thwack that pretty bottom of yours, you would not annoy me this way, Aubree Elizabeth. I owe you much, but you need to be taught some discipline as well. You knew what was in that letter, and you deliberately kept it from me. How many others did you hide? Is there more I ought to know? Tell me, Aubree, or I will give you the thrashing your father should have done years ago."

Aubree grew still and turned her head to glare defiantly at him. He held her hands behind her back so she could not scratch his eyes out, but her look should have scarred. "Do that, Austin. Prove your reputation."

If she thought that would deter him, she erred. With a murderous glare, Austin swatted her soundly. She wore nothing beneath the silken gown and the sound of the slap seemed to echo in the partially furnished room. The feeling so revolted him, he could not raise his hand to repeat it.

Aubree waited for the next blow, but when none came, she turned and discovered the look of horror and disgust on Austin's face. When he released her hands and started to rise from the bed, she scrambled to right herself and pin him down.

"Don't, Austin," she whispered, fearing the terrible self-loathing she read in his eyes. Her arms flew about his neck and he caught her by the waist, burying his face against her breasts. "I won't do it again, Austin, I promise. I just didn't want you to worry. You worry about so many things. I wanted you to be happy for a while. Please, Austin, don't be angry with me. I hate it when you're angry with me."

And he knew she spoke the truth. She was like a child who wished only to please. She craved his attention and sought it in any manner she could find. He should be relieved that she had outgrown the habit of riding her horse through the gallery.

"I'm not angry with you, I'm angry with myself, widgeon. Don't cry, please. I just don't know how to teach you that I can take care of myself." Austin pulled her into his arms and cradled her against his chest, kissing her cheek when she turned her face away from him. He could taste the salty track of her tears and his arms closed tighter around her.

"Not against my father," came her muffled reply.

"You are my wife, and he cannot take you away without my consent. Now look at me, Aubree," Austin commanded.

She wiped her eyes on his robe and peeked up at him suspiciously.

"Tell me you trust me." He spoke gruffly, with the authority of the military officer he had once been.

She wanted to. With all her heart and soul she wanted to. But she had heard enough of his conversation with Adrian earlier to know trust meant one thing to her and another to him. Trust was a two-way street and he had not set foot upon it.

"You will send me back to my father," she accused him.

"You are a wealthy heiress and can go wherever you wish. I cannot send you anywhere," he explained patiently. "But I should think you would wish to see Alvan and Peggy and the baby."

"Will you come with me?" Aubree sat up slightly and regarded him warily.

Austin debated the matter. "I might. But I could not stay long. Your father is concerned about your welfare, and rightly so. You must reassure him, while

I must stay here and rebuild the abbey. If you would only trust me . . ."

Aubree deliberately ignored his plea. He meant to send her away as her father always had, but she would teach him the foolishness of such thoughts. She squirmed slightly against his muscled thigh and tightened her hold about his neck so that her breasts flattened against his unyielding chest. She nibbled teasingly at his earlobe and ran her fingers down the back of his neck.

"Don't talk anymore, Austin," she whispered against his ear. She could feel his arousal rubbing along the place where he had spanked her, and her excitement grew. Surely he would understand now.

Austin knew he was being manipulated, but to have her come to him was a novelty he wished to explore. With one fluid move, he rolled her back against the bed and leaned over her. Cat's eyes stared up at him, challenging him. Candles still flared all about the room, and he could see her clearly. His hand rose to stake possessive claim of one full breast.

"Is this what you want?" he demanded, his hand sliding beneath the silken material to ply the rising peak. When she nodded silently, his hand caught firmly in the neckline of the gown. "Will you trust me?"

A hint of fear leapt to her eyes, but she nodded defiantly. When he ripped the gown away from her, the torn material fell away in shreds, leaving her completely exposed to his hungry gaze. Aubree reveled in his stare, however, and arched to greet him when he bent his head to suckle at her upturned breasts. The thrill shot through her like a thunderbolt and all caution evaporated.

Aubree caught both her hands in Austin's thick hair and tugged until he came to her, their lips meeting with an urgent hunger that betrayed their bodies' passion. But they delayed, exploring with lips and fingers, playing lovers' games, postponing that moment of union when promises meant more than words.

Fully naked, with no darkness to hide their doubts and fears, they finally succumbed to what they had tried to deny for so long. Austin took her with a tenderness so painstaking that Aubree nearly cried with the joy of it. Whatever words he might use later, he could never deny what his body spoke to her now. She had made her claim as thoroughly as he had claimed her. She could see it in his face, the ecstasy in the brilliant blue of his eyes, the tenderness of his touch, the relaxing of taut muscles, and the contented smile on his lips. She brought him happiness. She knew that with every fiber of her being and was content, for now.

Afterward, Austin strode about the room, snuffing out guttering candles. When he returned to bed, Aubree curled like a kitten beside him, warming his bared flesh.

He pulled her close and whispered against her hair, "God forgive me, but I never meant this to happen, halfling."

"I did," she murmured sleepily.

Austin did not question that bold declaration. He was firmly convinced this slender brat in his arms was quite capable of almost anything, including fomenting revolution. His only problem now was how far he dared let her run with their lives. And the answer would not be a popular one.

Aubree laughed at the antics of the children as they played with Lady beneath the trees. The day was warm for October, and the sky was unbelievably cloudless. For the first time in weeks, she allowed herself to relax and enjoy the moment.

Emily noted the glow of color in Aubree's cheeks and smiled approvingly. Austin's young bride was meant for sunshine and laughter. Her spontaneous affection spread ripples of warmth wherever she went. She was the ideal choice for returning love and light to Atwood Abbey and its neglected owner, but for a while Emily had feared the gloom would be the winner. Apparently, Aubree needed Austin as much as he did her. The night had worked wonders.

"I wish we could take you back with us, Aubree. We are all going to miss you," Emily murmured, expertly twisting a knot in her embroidery.

"And Austin?" Aubree glanced at her companion with a twinkle in her eye.

Her sister-in-law shrugged. "My big brother has ever been too self-important. I cannot imagine how so proper a gentleman has managed to get himself into so many improper scrapes. He will never leave the abbey."

Aubree laughed at this description of the rogue she had married. Austin's main goal in life may well be the restoration of the abbey and its estates, but his method of achieving that goal had certainly taken some strange paths. She laughed, remembering the time he had climbed the vines outside her window. Emily knew nothing of prim and proper if she thought that appellation belonged to Austin. Someday, she must introduce her to Alvan.

That path of thought led to another, and she hastened to broach a new subject. "Anna and Maria! I had forgotten. They are eager to see you before you leave. We were supposed to receive an invitation for dinner this evening. Have you seen it?"

Emily bent a quizzical look at Aubree for this odd tangent to their conversation, but she shook her head negatively. "I have not seen one. Could we not invite them here? I would love to see them again, and I'm certain they would like to meet the children."

Aubree gave a ragged sigh. "If it were only that easy . . . Geoff said Mr. Sotheby might be softening toward Heath. I had hoped . . ."

A flash of understanding leapt to Emily's proud eyes. "Surely he cannot hold Austin responsible after all these years! Louise was always the wild one. Why, Austin—"

Aubree interrupted hurriedly. "Here's Harley. Let us ask him. We certainly cannot go if we are not welcome." She waved at the young gentleman striding eagerly down the walk in their direction.

"Lady Aubree! Emily! It is good to see both of you outside that gloomy house for a while." He clasped their hands warmly, his open face a portrait of delight as he gazed upon them. His auburn locks took on a burnished sheen in the sunlight. "By Jove, Emily, I still cannot believe I allowed that cursed American to carry you off."

Delighted with this pretty speech, Emily laughed and gestured toward the romping children. "You would change your tune quickly if you stayed in the company of those two for very long. Besides, you were more interested in war than me, if I recollect rightly."

"Fool that I was," Harley agreed. "Have you hidden those two dull fellows away so you might walk with me?"

"They are talking politics, ships, and farming. If you wish to discuss any of those, we will not walk with you. However, if you wish to tell us how we might see Anna and Maria, you are welcome to join us." Aubree rearranged her skirts so that their visitor might sit between them on the garden bench.

"They are terrified you will return to London and Emily to America before they ever see you again. I have almost convinced them they will have to brave our father's wrath and come here as I do. Unfortunately, they are rather timid creatures."

While Emily scolded Harley for this insult, Aubree puzzled over the information he had imparted. Harley had said nothing of expecting them for dinner, and the reference to his father's wrath did not sound as if Mr. Sotheby had softened his opinion in the least. But why should Geoff make up such a tale? A suspicion of uneasiness crept over her.

"I understand Geoff and Squire Eversly will be dining with you tonight," Aubree ventured during a lull in the conversation.

Harley looked surprised. "Whatever in the world gave you that idea? Geoff is an amusing fellow, but I have warned the girls not to encourage him. He has not a feather to fly on, you know, and though he does have some claim to the title of baronet, the family is neither old nor well-respected in these parts. And as for Eversly . . . well, if you will pardon my language, ladies, he is a rake and a scoundrel. In his younger days I understand he was considered handsome and likable enough, but he's a rag-mannered brute in my book."

Momentarily stunned by this knowledge, Aubree stumbled over her words, thinking faster than she could speak as a quiver of alarm began to ring. "Not a feather to fly on? I don't understand . . ." She hesitated, searching her memory. "I understood he possessed estates somewhere north of here. And he is always dressed like a Bond Street beau. Surely, there is some error."

Harley regarded her with amused patience. "Heath is right. You are an innocent little goose. And do you believe the Beau himself is wealthy and possesses name and title because he carries jeweled snuffboxes and was courted by Prinny? Half London lives on credit, gudgeon, and I swear the other half lives on Dame Fortune. Why do you think Geoff has spent his summer here? His creditors are threatening him with Newgate, and his cousin offers him free room and board. I know you are fond of the twit, but you really must learn the facts of life, my girl."

Thoroughly confused and definitely uneasy, Aubree still had the grace to blush. She had assigned Geoff different reasons for spending his months in this desolate place. Even knowing he was not to be relied on, she had allowed him to continue making a cake of her.

"I remember Eversly," Emily mused when Aubree made no reply. "Mama would not allow me to dance with him. We were at a ball in Exeter, I believe. She said he would not be welcome in polite society, which did not impress me much since my father was not very welcome, either, as far as I could discern. But what did impress me was the ugly look he gave me before he walked away. No one had ever looked at me like that before. I felt as if I were a worm he would gladly crush. Now that I think back on it, I believe he was quite tipsy."

"When was that?" Aubree inquired abruptly.

"Oh, I had just come out, so it must have been about a year after Louise's death. Austin had gone off to war and we had no money, so Exeter was the height of my fancies, then. Why?" she asked, suddenly realizing the oddity of the question.

Harley looked at her, too, and did not like what he saw. The golden girl of a moment before had grown pale and her laughing eyes had turned dark and worried.

"Aubree, are you well?" Remembering the rumors circulating in the village, he felt a vague anxiety. He had no experience with expectant ladies, if the rumors were truth. "Shall I take you back to the house?"

Aubree gave him a look of exasperation. "I am quite well, thank you. I simply dislike being lied to and cannot conceive of any reason for it."

Harley shook his head to clear the cobwebs and gave her a puzzled frown. "Are you accusing me of lying to you?"

"Emily, I believe the children are climbing the mulberry," Aubree observed calmly, diverting the subject.

"Oh, my word!" Emily darted in the direction of the daring duo, leaving Aubree alone with Harley.

"If you are lying, I'll have Austin cut your tongue out," Aubree replied absently to the momentarily startled Harley. "But if everyone starts lying to me, how will I ever know the truth? It is so very confusing."

"Aubree, sweeting, you are making absolutely no sense. Have you had too much sun, perhaps? I understand the inhabitants of sunny climes are all a trifle mad."

Aubree giggled at this exasperated reply. "Tell that to Adrian. He curses our fogs and rain most vehemently." She grew serious again, keeping an eye on Emily to make certain she was not overheard. "It is Geoffrey who is acting strangely. He told me that Emily and I were invited to dinner with you this evening and that he would stop by to take us there. What purpose would he have in saying such a thing except to get us away from here?"

Harley did not look so alarmed as she. He shrugged. "It is typical of him. If he arrived with you in tow, we could not possibly turn him out. He undoubtedly thought the enormity of such an occasion would turn the entire establishment into confusion and no one would notice the discrepancies. And he's quite likely right. Do you mean to say you would actually come to dinner if we sent an invite? I shall go home at once to send one."

She shook her head. "He spoke as if your father might have had a change of heart. I was so eager to mend fences . . . No, Harley, something is wrong. I know it. I just cannot put a finger to it. But how can I tell Austin of my fears? He will go all cold and haughty and advise me to go with Geoffrey if I so desire."

Harley looked into her troubled face and read more there than he wished to see. He, of all people, knew the details of Austin's marriage and Geoffrey's courtship. He did not like the part he had played, although he could not help but applaud the ending. Still, he owed Austin a grave debt for the injustice done him over the years. Somehow, the wrong must be righted.

"Let me handle it, my lady. I would not risk you with Geoffrey, so stay home tonight. That might stop any foolishness. But there will be extra eyes about, just as a precaution."

Normally, Aubree would have hugged his neck, but Emily approached with the children in tow, and she settled for a demure squeeze of the hand.

"And if you're lying . . ." she teased.

"I'll cut my own tongue out." He grinned.

28

Certain now that Aubree's feelings on the matter of an annulment were akin to his own, Austin approached his plans for the future with more confidence. His talks with Adrian had convinced him much could be done to improve his finances within a short period of time. There were still the matters of his reputation and her youth and inexperience to overcome, but they did not seem so insurmountable as before. Austin's greatest fear was that his young wife would grow bored and resentful as his first wife had, and in Aubree's case, with more reason than Louise ever had. For that reason alone, he must be certain of her feelings.

It would not be easy. Her father had already rolled the warning drum, but Austin felt confident he could outreason the duke's complaints. Knowing Aubree intended to stay changed everything. Money would be found to increase the staff and make the main living quarters of Atwood Abbey inhabitable again. There was this damned problem over Blanche's death and the accidents he felt certain were aimed to bankrupt him, but he suspected both those problems could be solved with a well-laid trap. He had never bothered before, but he had sufficient reason to try anything now. He had only to convey his intentions to the duke to silence the drums, for a while.

Austin felt like a schoolboy again as he searched the downstairs for his wandering wife. Up until now, he had not allowed himself to think deeply on the possibility of Aubree actually staying here as his wife. There had been too many obstacles preventing such an occurrence, but her words of last night had blown them aside with the force of hurricane winds. To have her at his side for a lifetime, laughing and dazzling his days away, warming his nights, sharing his thoughts, and someday, bearing his children, was a dream of such magnificence that it nearly carried him from the floor. He needed her to share it with him, to reassure him he was not dreaming.

Unable to find her downstairs, Austin dragged his still-uncertain leg up the stairway to the upper floor. He still needed to use care in his movements, but he could feel the knee growing stronger with each passing day. Part of his dream was to carry his golden wife down a dance floor in a graceful waltz with all the world looking on. Then he would know for certain that the world acknowledged his claim.

He grinned to himself at the spectacle they would in all probability make if unleashed upon polite society. Aubree would no doubt insist on some ailing animal accompanying them, and he would spend the evening alternately stepping on toes and rescuing the animal from beneath chairs, or worse. He could not imagine any ballroom being stuffy that included Aubree among its occupants.

Austin found her in their bedchamber, pensively staring out the window overlooking the stable yard. Her mood was so distant from his, he hesitated, wondering if he had only dreamed what had gone between them. He had not dared make any mention of his feelings, nor his hopes, for fear obstacles he could not foresee would intrude, but surely she understood that. She who communicated so well with mute animals could surely see his predicament and wait patiently while he extricated himself from the past.

Silently, Austin crossed the room and slid his arms around Aubree's slender waist. They fit together so perfectly, her head at just the right height for his cheek to rest against, her hips curving softly to mold against his thighs. She relaxed into his embrace without reserve, and he muffled a sigh of relief.

" 'Tis scarce half-past seven, halfling. Have our demands grown so tiresome that you must escape our company early?"

Aubree leaned back against his strength and let the pleasure of his touch chase away her fears. Austin's hand drifted upward to cup her breast, and she smiled at the sensations engendered by just this gentle caress.

"On the contrary, everyone seemed so engrossed in their own pursuits that my presence seemed superfluous. Adrian and Emily are behaving like newlyweds, and your mother is telling dreadful tales to the children. And I assumed you and John had found some new venture to embark upon."

He kissed her hair, breathing deeply of the scent of lilacs. It was all but impossible to carry on a practical conversation in this position. He calculated it might take another twenty years before he could utter two coherent thoughts in a row while Aubree rested in his arms like this.

"There is business I must tend to if I am to have my way with you as I want. I would not like to think you spend those hours in lonely contemplation." Beneath the layers of muslin and silk that separated his hand from her flesh, Austin could feel the peak of her breast harden beneath his touch. This involuntary sign of how her body reacted to his pleased him inordinately.

The joy of these words swept through Aubree like a warm breeze on a spring day. She tilted her head backward to better observe the bronzed countenance of this man who had stolen her heart and given nothing in return. She knew he thought her too young to be his bride, and she knew his pride would not allow him to accept her wealth, but if she could only touch his heart, she could win him.

The smile on his lips increased her hopes. "I have not been lonely once since I came here, milord. There is so much I could do, if you would let me."

"You are a little fool and I believe you deserve your fate." The blue of his eyes was as cloudless as a sunny day as he pronounced this indictment. Gently, Austin bent to kiss the troubled pucker of rose-pink lips.

This kiss spoke promises more than passion, and Aubree greeted it joyously. Austin was a man of some consequence, a man unlike any other she had known, and she respected his judgment more than her father's. To win his respect and convince him to keep her as his wife were goals she had never dared voice. She almost wished they were single again so she might hear him say the words out loud, but she would not test the fates. She still remained uncertain of his decision, understanding only that she had received some reprieve.

When his kiss wandered to her cheek, Aubree wrapped her arms around him as if she would never let go. Her eyes opened to search his face as she asked, "You will not send me away?"

Austin kissed the tip of her nose. "I think, for a while, you must go. Peggy needs you, and so does your father, whether you understand that or not. I want you to have time to think and be very certain of your decision. I am terrified that you may be too young to know what you really want."

He reassured her and worried her at the same time. Did he love her? Did he truly want her to stay? Or did he simply find it more convenient to have a wife and she was as good as any? Aubree did not dare dwell long on these thoughts. She had been sent away so many times in the past, she had learned not to dwell on doubts. She must keep going forward and trust that her instincts did not lead her astray. Instinct told her now that he was protecting her at the cost of himself. It seemed like a foolish waste of time, but if it would make him happy in the end and speed the process, she would have to acquiesce.

"Austin, I am not the fool here, but I will do whatever it requires to convince you. Must it be soon?" she asked wistfully.

He grinned and moved his hand to cover her belly. "If these last nights are any measure, it had best be soon or you will be plump as a partridge and there will be no choice left to be made. I warned you once what would happen if we started down this path."

Aubree did not return his grin but regarded him seriously. "What happens if it is too late? Would you be terribly displeased?"

Austin's dark features showed no sign of displeasure as he kissed her brow. "Louise and I were not so blessed in two years of marriage, so it is not very likely, my love. You know the answer to your question without being told."

She understood, and her eyes glowed from within as he bent to silence any further questions with his kiss. She read his answer in the hunger of his lips and the possessive caress of his hands as they slid from her breasts downward, forcing awareness of the use her body was meant for. She could not imagine allowing any other to use her in such a way, but with all her heart, she wished to bear Austin's child in that empty place blossoming within her now.

As if sensing the intensity of her need, Austin half turned her to study her face more carefully. "Aubree . . . ?" His hunger blinded him to all else but his desire to bed her right here and now.

But the worry that had brought her here in the first place had not completely left her, and when Aubree opened her eyes to meet his question, they fell on a more terrifying sight.

"Fire!" she breathed, not quite believing the truth of that evil flicker in the darkness outside.

Austin lifted his head to look out the window at the

sight that held his wife's gaze riveted. Before he could react, Aubree had spun from his embrace, grabbed the bedcovers from the bed, and started out the door.

"The stables!" he heard her scream. "They're burning the stables!"

His stiff stride took him quickly after her, but not quickly enough. Already doors were opening and confused voices echoed down the passageways in response to Aubree's cries. Only half-dressed, Adrian met him on the stairway, and Austin had to hurry past, gripping the stair rail to keep his balance as he chased after his fearless wife.

"Stop her, dammit," he roared as servants popped into the hallway below. "She's heading for the stables."

Not quite understanding the disaster this would portend, everyone raced to do as told, and Austin found himself almost the last one out as the household streamed down the drive toward the cobbled stable yard.

By the time they reached the side of the house, the smell of smoke was so thick that explanations were not needed. Somewhere, someone had begun to peal the giant iron bell in the abbey wall. The sonorous alarm rang out over the cold night, awaking the countryside to danger as it once had pealed of matins.

Cursing bitterly, Austin hurried toward the stable. The eerie light was confined to the rear of the half-stone, half-timbered building, but the upper level was filled with recently harvested hay, and the light already cast shadows on the racing figures below.

John came out leading two terrified carriage horses, their uneasy whickers generating frightened responses from the animals still inside. The stallion could be heard rearing in its stall, pounding at the ancient oak walls, his cries echoed by the whinnies and bleats of the other trapped animals.

Smoke belched from the rotting timbers of the roof as Aubree's slim figure appeared out of the black hole of the stable entrance. Beside her, blinded by wet blankets thrown over her head, quietly walked the high-strung Dancing Star.

Immediately understanding what she had accomplished, Austin gave orders for more blankets to be found. A line of bucket wielders had already formed between the pump at the horse trough and the back of the stables. He ordered one line to soak down the front of the building while the other worked at the impossible task of quenching the back. Giving thanks to the original architects who had designed a courtyard distancing the highly volatile barn from the main structure of the house, Austin soaked a blanket and headed after Aubree.

He never seemed to quite catch up with her. Helping John steady the wild-eyed stallion long enough to cool and blind him with the drenched blanket, Austin caught sight of her leading out another of the carriage horses. When he led the stallion out, she had disappeared again. A terrified Michael, clutching the pet guinea pigs, pointed toward the smoking entrance of the stable when questioned about Aubree's whereabouts.

Containing his own fears, Austin directed the lad to carry the animals to the kitchen and be certain all the cats and the dog stayed inside. He could well imagine Aubree racing back after some missing animal at the risk of her own life.

The yard began to fill with animals not his own. Wagons and carriages rattled to a halt on the broad lawn as the nearest neighbors poured into the courtyard to lend their backs and hands to the bucket brigade. He noted even his elegant sister hauled water beside the dim-witted Patience, and his mother's haughty French cook dipped the household linens in the trough to pass out to those leading the animals to safety.

He followed Adrian's raw, scarred back into the inferno of screaming animals and nightmare smoke. The flames only crackled in the rear, but the smoke had become so intense it scorched the lungs. He searched for Aubree's pale muslin gown in the blackness, but he could see no farther than the hand before his face.

Commanding all he passed to detain Aubree outside if they saw her, Austin fought his way as close to the flame as he could, freeing the stall doors and smacking the skittish animals into a trot in the direction of safety. Plowhorses, oxen, the ponies his men rode, all were quartered in this massive structure that had once held some of the finest thoroughbreds in the land. At least these less elegant animals possessed more sense of self-preservation than the high-strung thoroughbreds as they stampeded toward the door.

He followed them out, throwing open stall doors as he went. He could no longer see if there were animals behind any of them. Austin's lungs felt as if they filled with acid and each cough tore a piece of flesh from its mooring.

Outside, the air was little better. The cold stung the heat in his lungs, but the stench remained. Flames leapt from the roof now. It was only a matter of time before the hay set the whole loft afire and the entire structure would come tumbling down.

Austin searched for some sign of Aubree. The pandemonium in the courtyard had reached fever-pitch and few could hear his hoarse questions. He was aware of more carriages arriving but paid them no heed as he grabbed John's coat. The groom was heading for the inferno of the stable, though all the animals appeared to be milling about the yard, gradually being herded toward the paddock in the rear.

At Austin's shouted question, John pointed back to the stable entrance. A small white figure flickered briefly against the belching smoke and was quickly engulfed.

Never before in his life had Austin experienced such terror. He had met the charging brigades of French soldiery with fatalistic fear, watched Louise dive to her death with a horror he never wished to repeat, but the sight of Aubree walking into the flames of hell twisted him into demented terror.

Alerted by some common thread of fear, others turned in time to watch Aubree disappear into the cloud of smoke. Not until Austin's roar of rage and anguish drowned the cacophony around them did they finally realize the peril.

A timber at the back of the stable slowly began to

creak and sway, shooting sparks of fiery debris into the night. A woman screamed as Austin broke into a run, shoving aside the men who jumped to intercept his path.

A man hurtled from one of the carriages that had just drawn up, but Adrian caught him in midstride and held him back.

"Don't, Harley. There's nothing we can do but pray." They watched in paralyzed horror as Austin disappeared into the flaming building.

"My God, I never thought they'd strike so close," Harley whispered, aghast.

"We were all wrong. Go move your father from danger. We've got to wet down the rest of this place before it spreads."

Beneath Adrian's shouts and curses, the line again took up its mechanical pumping, this time concentrating on the burning timbers nearest the door. They could no longer reach the tower of fire groaning and spurting flame at the rear.

The hoarse cry of a raven and its inhuman cackling of curses flew from the burning timbers overhead. All eyes again turned to stare as the black shadow perched in a tree limb over their heads. Furtive signs of the cross were made as the bird rained diatribes upon their heads.

But instead of an ill omen, the raven preceded good fortune. As the rear timber crackled and snapped and fell backward into the dusty, unused sheep pen, a figure in shirtsleeves staggered from the smoking entrance carrying a seemingly lifeless burden.

A cry of excitement rang around the walled enclosure as Austin blindly worked his way from the smoke through the crowd. Without being told, Mattie handed her bucket to another and raced to the house in advance of Austin's slow movement. The bucket brigade went to work with new vigor, though whispers circulated up and down the line, reporting every movement made—or not made—by the stricken earl and his unconscious young wife.

Anguish screamed from another source as a new

arrival fought his way through the milling animals and people.

"Aubree!" The cry ripped from Geoffrey's throat. "My God, what have you done to her? Damn you, you promised me . . ." Shouting incoherently, the well-dressed gentleman stumbled over sheep and toes in his effort to reach the couple disappearing in the direction of the house.

Instantly alerted by the sound of his voice, both Adrian and Harley halted what they were doing and shoved their way to intercept the newcomer. Before they could reach him, however, a shadow stepped from behind one of the carriages, catching the panic-stricken Geoffrey by his high collar. Geoffrey fought against the shadow's grip, ignoring the whispered words of warning hurtled at him.

"Damn you, let me go! I'll never forgive you for this. Never! My God, she could be dead and you've killed her!"

This last was uttered with a piercing shriek as the shadow flung his prey to the ground and began to blend into the maze of carriages.

Too late, however. A cane came smashing down from one of the vehicles, catching the intruder on the side of the head, sending him sprawling along the cobblestones.

"Harley! Come fetch this rascal and tell me who he is. Make him speak louder. I want to hear his voice." This querulous demand came from the depths of the Sotheby chaise, but Harley was already racing to the scene, with Adrian close on his heels.

They caught Geoffrey before he could follow Austin's weary path, and Adrian held him while Harley leaned over to jerk at the sprawling figure on the ground. A small crowd began to form, circling the chaise and the combatants.

"It's Eversly," Harley announced with disgust, dragging the squire to a half-sitting position. "What in hell are you doing here?"

"Make him speak up, boy. I thought I heard him a moment ago. Eversly, is that you?" The elderly man in the carriage leaned forward, unable to discern the darkness outside from the darkness within. Only the dying embers of the fire made a pattern across his clouded eyes.

"Who wants to know?" a hoarse voice croaked in defiance.

"Damn you, man, I knew you when you were young enough to steal the apples from my trees. Stand up and speak like a man."

Eversly threw off Harley's imprisoning grip and stood, arrogantly dusting himself off before answering. His collarless, loose-cut coat had received a recent tear, and his buckskin breeches reeked of an odor not easily placed in a barnyard. He threw his frantic cousin a malevolent look.

"I cannot imagine what we have to speak about. I have not darkened your door since you threw me out of the garden when I was no more than a hungry lad."

The old man turned livid with rage.

Coming up behind Adrian, Emily pushed her husband aside to hurry to the carriage. Sotheby waved her aside.

"Don't lie to me, you young whippersnapper! I may be blind, but I'm not deaf! Harley, fetch the sheriff! That's the man that killed your sister!"

A gasp of shock went up from the crowd beginning to gather. Austin's farm hands began to edge in closer while someone else went in search of the sheriff. Emily gently urged the enraged old man from the carriage, while Adrian and Harley stared at each other over their prisoners' heads. Whispers filtered through the crowd, growing to ugly murmurs.

"I think we'd better take them into the house." Adrian spoke with decision, followed by action. Shoving Eversly in the direction of the abbey, he gestured for Harley to follow with the frantic Geoffrey.

The crowd made a path and watched them pass in the same direction the anguished earl had traversed only minutes before. The mob's suspicion had found a new subject, but their anger grew silent, waiting.

The glowing embers of the burned-out stable made bright-red stars against the cloudless sky. The remaining men in the yard continued to douse the last dying flames, while others completed the task of herding the straying animals into the paddock.

Atwood Abbey had brought the scattered occupants of village and countryside together again. But at what cost?

29

Tears streamed down his soot-begrimed face as Austin gently carried his unconscious burden up the stairs. She did not move within his arms and he could not feel her breathe. It seemed only moments before she had been warm and vibrant in his embrace. Now she lay cold and still, and he could not bring himself to think of the disaster this might portend. The fates could not be so cruel as to rob his world of its only sun.

Mattie quenched a scream of horror at the sight of the earl's tear-streaked face as he lay his burden upon the bed. Had it not been for his motion, she would have thought him as lifeless as the woman he carried. His features had grown cold and hard, and tears soaked the maid's face as she understood the anguish he so ruthlessly controlled.

A slight movement from the bed returned fevered hope to midnight eyes, and Austin grabbed the cool, wet cloth from Mattie's hand. Mopping gently at Aubree's sooty face, he was rewarded with a choking gasp, followed by a long bout of harsh coughing. He could feel his heart tearing from its mooring with each ragged breath, but he could do no more than hold her and pray.

At long last, the worst of the coughing subsided, and long lashes swept upward. Green eyes stared into a dark countenance coated in filth and wet with tears, and only the familiar flare of blue told her all was well. With a sigh of relief, Aubree's eyes closed again. "You're safe," she murmured indistinctly.

With a blaze of joy Austin clutched her closer to him. The coughing resumed, but it sounded as music to his ears. She was alive. Nothing else mattered.

Choking back sobs of relief, Austin barked at the helpless maid. "Tell them below to help themselves to the ale in the cellars. There's cause for celebration."

The earl's eyes were glassy with tears and relief and weariness, and Mattie nearly wept to see the happiness reflecting from behind their mirrored surface. Rumors to the contrary, there was no doubt in her mind that the melancholy earl had found love at last. She hastened to do as bid.

Gently, Austin removed Aubree's grimy clothes and soaped delicate skin with the cooling cloths Mattie had prepared. Aubree's violent coughing prevented conversation, but he worked patiently, holding her tightly while great, wrenching heaves shook her slender body, then tenderly caressing her skin with scented soap and cool water until she relaxed in his arms again.

Until that time he sensed she rested comfortably, and all his pent-up anguish surfaced and spilled over in painful fury.

"Why, Aubree? Why did you go back in?"

Her golden-brown lashes looked dark against the drained pallor of her skin as she rested against the heap of pillows. A spasm of coughing shook her as she fought to regain her speech.

"Looking for . . . you," she finally gasped out.

Appalled at the implications of these few words, Austin lifted her in his arms, wishing he could breathe for her as she gasped for air. She seemed to rest more comfortably in this position, and he cushioned her head against his shoulder and held her there.

"I let the animals out, Aubree. Why would I go back in there?"

"They said . . . you did. Heard Myna . . . thought, maybe . . ."

The coughing was less violent, but Austin held her

silently, offering a sip of wine when she recovered sufficiently. He could barely control the ghastly progress of his thoughts as he took these words and carried them to their logical conclusions. Someone had deliberately sent her back into that inferno. He was certain of it.

The bird puzzled him. The raven should have been the first one out when the doors opened, but instead, he had found it screaming haunting cries over Aubree's unconscious body. He might never have found her in time had it not been for the raven. From these few words he could not determine whether he owed the bird her life, or if the bird had nearly cost it.

"Aubree, you must know your life is much more valuable to me than any animal's. If I discover you went back in to find that bedeviled bird . . ."

She shook her head restlessly against his shoulder. "No. I did not know. He was caged. Why?"

Anger began to build within Austin, an anger even more compelling for its futility. To cage that bird had to be an act of madness, or deliberate bait for a deadly trap. But to prove either would be an impossibility.

"I don't now, Aubree. All is well now. Don't worry over it. You frightened me, my love. I apologize." He held her close as she sipped at the wine.

But when the coughing had dwindled and color began to return to her cheeks, Austin kissed her forehead and loosened his grip. "I must thank those who came to help us, my love. Will you rest comfortably if I leave you here?"

Her eyes flew open to scan the dark circles of his eyes, the weary lines about his mouth, and she shook her head. "You cannot go down those stairs again, Austin. You will reopen the wound, if you have not already."

Ruefully, he realized she had regained her speech. It would be difficult to deny her, but he had to speak with the others.

"They are in the kitchen, halfling. I need only stand on the balcony to speak to them. The acoustics were designed for a reader to be heard throughout the kitchen, so I daresay my bellow will reach them well enough."

She had forgotten the speaker's passage in the back hall. Chapters of the Bible had once been read from this vantage point above the silent monks dining in the kitchen. In later days, it had been opened out so that musicians might play above the great hall. The passage was little used now, but useful for the purpose. He would not have to descend the stairs to speak to the people waiting below.

Almost shyly, she inquired, "Might I go with you?"

Austin's eyes lit as if he had just been gifted with his one desire. "You feel well enough?" He asked anxiously, attempting to hide his eagerness to display her in the role for which he had chosen her.

"If you can walk to the end of the hall on that leg, then I might manage," she retorted. The cough that followed did nothing to reassure, but she had recovered sufficient spirit to fight for what she wanted. And she wanted to stand beside her husband in this moment of disaster—and triumph.

For triumph it was. Aubree could see it in the faces shining below them, hear it in the lusty cheer that rattled the smoked timbers of the kitchen as they appeared in the upper balcony. Austin had to wait for the cheers to die down before he could convey his thanks to the neighbors who had come at a time of need, despite the gossip that circulated of him.

The people below had other reasons for cheering. They had come to respect the young countess who had defied their obstinacy and forced them to realize rumor was not fact, though they would not put those words to their feelings. They only knew this bit of girl stood by her husband's side without fear and loved him without shame. It had made them wonder at their own foolishness. And now, watching the lord and his lady together as they had this night, even the strongest of disbelievers had to set aside their doubts. Their earl had risked the jaws of hell to return his lady to life. Whatever his faults, Heathmont forced them to respect his courage and devotion.

Austin kept his speech brief and to the point. "I want to thank all of you for your help this night. Without you, our loss would have been much greater, more than I care to imagine." The crowd grew silent at this reminder of what might have been. "I realize Atwood Abbey has not been the best of neighbors for quite some time, but with your help, I would like that changed. With the mines closing and shipping down, we are in for a long, hard winter. But winter is a time for rebuilding and plowing and planning next spring's crops. That's what I intend to do, with the help of any of you who might offer their services. There is enough work to be done in this place to employ half the army should the French fall and Wellington bring our boys home."

Another cheer rang around the kitchen at this senti-ment, and though more needed to be said, Austin wisely chose to wait for another time. He knew too well the poverty of the countryside surrounding him and the backward superstition that kept it that way. One step at a time was all he could take.

The crowd quieted as Aubree stepped from her husband's shadow to indicate she would speak. Her blue velvet dressing gown fell to her feet like a royal robe and the upsweep of golden hair above it created a shimmering crown in the candlelight. Despite her youth and lack of stately attire, they looked upon her with the respect deserving of a Countess of Heathmont.

"I regret that our wedding feast was held elsewhere and gave me no opportunity to meet all of you good people. Circumstances have prevented any cause for celebration since then, but my husband permitting" —she threw Austin a mischievous glance that rated catcalls and feet stomping from below—"we should welcome the new year with a suitable feast. And if the stable is rebuilt, I should think a country dance or two would not be amiss. I have not yet seen my husband dance a jig, but perhaps we could persuade him."

Austin grinned as their audience roared with laugh-ter and applauded their approval. He had thought to win them cautiously through their pocketbooks, but Aubree had thrown aside caution and aimed for their hearts. From the sounds of the melee below, she had won them, too.

To the tune of laughter, Austin gave his wife a

hearty buss and led her away. Too much success would empty his coffers as well as his kegs. And there were other matters waiting that had a more serious flavor to them. Celebrations might be premature.

He waited until Aubree slept to slip down the front stairs to the lighted study below. Although his concerns had all been for Aubree, he had not failed to notice what went on about him. And the absence of Harley and Adrian at a time like this hardened his suspicions. He would see what their fracas had uncovered.

The group of men scattered about the musty study turned at Austin's entrance with varying degrees of relief and apprehension. The comfortable leather chair at the fire had been given to Mr. Sotheby, who had turned at the sound of the door opening and waited for a voice to identify the newcomer. Harley leaned against the mantel near his father while Adrian stood commandingly in the center of the room, his scarred back hastily covered with an unfastened shirt. At Austin's entrance, he turned to reveal the center of argument.

Geoffrey and Harry Eversly sat upon the ancient couch with Sheriff Fletcher close at hand. The sheriff looked uneasy and out of place and received Austin's presence with a mixture of fear and relief. He would have to follow the earl's orders. His responsibility ended there.

"How is she?" Adrian spoke before any of the others.

"If you heard the crowd in the kitchen, you would know," Austin replied curtly, his gaze falling upon the men at the couch. "But we owe no thanks to the man who sent her in there. I'll see him hung for that."

Eversly coldly returned Austin's stare, but Geoffrey choked and turned pale and looked ready to flee. The sheriff's broad frame blocked all escape, however.

"There's your culprit, Heathmont. Would to God that I could watch him hang." The old man by the fire spoke forcefully.

Austin turned his gaze to the frail old man who had once been his father-in-law. His sturdy frame had dwindled to a shadow of itself, but the merchant vibrated with much of the vigor he had once possessed. He punctuated his words with a sharp rap on the floor with the same walking stick that had brought down his prisoner.

"It's good to see you again, sir, though I regret the circumstances. Did you wish to make a formal accusation against these men?"

Sotheby glared in the direction of the couch. "Don't know the young whippersnapper. It's Eversly you want. He killed Louise. Don't doubt that he tried to do the same for your new bride."

"Don't be ridiculous," Harry drawled. "I have never even met the present lady. Why on earth should I want to kill her? Or Louise? Why do you keep protecting this bastard? It's obvious he's a Bluebeard."

Austin caught Adrian by the shoulder before he could fly into the insolent squire with both fists. "He's not worth it. A judge will decide his fate, if any have proof." He turned back to Sotheby. "Sir, Eversly cannot have killed Louise. This much, I know. Do you have evidence of the other charges?"

"Don't tell me what he did or didn't do," the older man grumbled irritably. "You've paid for your neglect, but this bounder has escaped scot-free until now because I could not put a name to him. He had not a man's voice when last I heard him, but I should have known. I forbid Louise to see the cad when she mentioned he paid her court. I married her off to you thinking that would put an end to it. But no, you had to go bounding off over the seas instead of taking her away from here. I could hear them in the garden when you were gone. I thought p'raps 'twas some stranger who would take his leave and leave none the wiser. The servants protected her, damn their black hearts. But he came back. He kept coming back. They thought I would not know because I was old and blind, but I heard them. They laughed at first, like young lovers. And then they fought, as only Louise knew how to fight. That girl could have cut a sword to ribbons with her tongue."

Austin shifted uneasily, not wanting to hear more

but unable to silence a man he held in respect. He pulled the brandy bottle off the shelf behind his desk and poured himself a glass, nodding toward the tray of glasses sitting on the table to indicate others help themselves.

Harley was the one who approached his father with remonstrations. "Father, we cannot relive the past. Louise is dead. There is no need to resurrect her faults." He stood behind his father's chair, uncertain how else to ease the tension building within the room.

"I'm only telling you so you know I'm no crazy old man. I knew my daughter, I knew her faults. She was a good lass, too wild and high-spirited, mayhap, but a good lass. But someone led her astray, and I'm telling you it is that man over there. I cannot tell you how long it went on, if it started before or after she married Heath, but that is the man who killed her."

"A man can't be hanged for adultery," the sheriff interrupted. "It's no proof he killed her." He gave Austin a look as if to say it would be reason enough for the husband.

Austin felt no emotion at learning the name of the man who had cuckolded him. He had suspected as much for a long time, and he could answer Sotheby's question as to when the affair began. Louise had been no virgin when she came to his bed, but it had not mattered then and it meant less now. What mattered was whether this same man had set his stables afire and nearly killed Aubree in the process. That he would give up all his worldly possessions to know.

"Let Mr. Sotheby speak," he commanded curtly, sitting himself in the desk chair with his brandy and waiting.

Sotheby gave the floor another rap in satisfaction. "I hold you guilty of neglect, Heath. She was no more than a child, you should have kept tight reins on her. I cursed your name every time I heard those two together. I tried to warn you, but you would have none of it. Young and stubborn as a damned stone wall. Then when I heard the whispers about the beatings, I thought you had finally found her out and gone too far. I was livid with rage, but I held my tongue. She was your responsibility and I knew you to be fair, if a trifle hotheaded. I thought that would be the end of it. But it wasn't."

The fight seemed to have gone out of him, and he stared sadly into the flickering light of the fire, his voice growing weaker. "When you took that last trip, I didn't hear them so frequently. I thought she had cast him off, and I was relieved. But I heard her scream one day. The sound was quickly cut off, as if someone had slapped a hand across her face, but I knew then. And I could do nothing. I tried to persuade her to stay with us while you were gone, but she enjoyed her freedom too well. She only used the garden to escape the abbey's loyal servants.

"I cannot know for certain what happened at the end. Mayhap you can persuade the brute to it. I heard them fighting one day, and he hit her. The sound was unmistakable. I think she hid from all of us after that. I heard you had returned, Heath, and I waited for your visit. I wanted to tell you I would pay for a house in London if it would get Louise away from that obsession of hers. But the next I heard, she was dead, and it was too late."

Harley put a hand on his father's shoulder and threw Austin a pleading look. The story had thrown the other men into respectful silence—all but the accused, who looked bored and cut at his fingernails with a small knife from his pocket.

Austin rose and poured another brandy into a clear glass, taking it to Mr. Sotheby. "Perhaps we all failed her, George, but in the end, she failed herself. You know I would have raised the child as my own. She had no need to do what she did." It was as close as he had ever come to admitting the truth of Louise's death to her family.

Sotheby seemed to accept it with understanding, but surprisingly, Eversly reacted with a growl of anger.

"Now that's a damned lie if I ever heard one. The mighty Earl of Heathmont raising another man's bastard. Don't make me laugh. You killed her and you'll never prove otherwise."

Geoffrey sat silently and uneasily beside his cousin,

watching the reactions of the older men around him.
He had always believed Harry's tale of Austin's seducing his lover. The romantic tale of a beautiful
woman and wealth won and lost had appealed to him,
and Austin's brutality and violence had been common
knowledge for years. This new side to the story seemed
equally believable, however, and fear for his own hide
left him in a dilemma.

Austin ignored the interruption. "But though you
have proved Eversly's a coward and a rutting bounder,
there is nothing to show he is responsible for tonight."

Adrian took the floor as if upon cue. "Your wife
and I and this dandy might help along those lines,
Heath."

At the mention of Aubree, Austin swung around to
confront his friend. "How?"

"Your dandy here tried to persuade our wives to go
with him this evening, gave them some trumped-up
invitation. After talking with Harley, Aubree became
suspicious, but since you hadn't seen fit to inform her
of your opinion of Eversly, she did not know the
danger. Harley carried her suspicions to me, and I took
the liberty of disposing your men and Harley's about
the estate. We never suspected the bastard would strike
so close."

Austin sensed Adrian held something back and understood it was not yet time to reveal it. He turned his
controlled fury to Geoffrey.

"I have borne your impudence out of respect for
Aubree's attachment to you, but I will not tolerate it
any longer. What explanation have you for your
behavior?"

Geoffrey seemed to melt beneath the vitriol of these
accusations.

Harry was the one who answered. "The pup is guilty
of nothing more than advancing his cause. You have
nothing to hold us on, and I resent the treatment we
have received at the hands of your oafish accomplices.
I would demand satisfaction, but I hold the line at
cripples and wife-beaters."

Austin grew very still. His bronzed features hardened into a cold mask that emphasized the aquiline

flare of his nose and the strong jut of his jaw. The dark lock of hair upon his forehead did nothing to conceal the blazing blue of his eyes as he fought for control of his temper.

"Sheriff, if that man opens his insolent mouth again, I intend to take that horsewhip over in the corner to him. I would suggest you find some means to shut him up before that occurs."

The horsewhip alluded to was a particularly nasty specimen Austin had ripped from a man's hand one day after catching him using it on an unbroken yearling. He had thrown it in that corner some years ago. Since then, someone had found a hook for it and hung it on the wall, but it remained there as a souvenir—and a threat. Austin's fingers ached to put it to good use now.

The sheriff did not doubt his intentions. After what had been said here this night, he suspected Eversly would be fortunate to live out the week. But he would rather not witness the method gentry used to exterminate one another. Dueling was illegal.

"Squire, I have to ask you to hold your tongue unless spoken to, else the matter will come before the judge. This here be his lordship's land and you be trespassin' to be found on it."

"Thank you." Coldly formal now, Austin returned his questioning to Geoffrey. "Why did you wish to take Aubree away from here this evening?"

Cornered, Geoffrey glanced for help from his cousin, who gave him a look of disgust before turning away. Still uncertain as to where he stood, Geoffrey evaded the question. "What did you mean when you said someone sent Aubree in that stable?"

"Just as I said. Someone caged that damned bird of hers, and when its cries weren't sufficient to draw her back, they told her I had gone in to fetch it. The bird had been hung in the rear, where the fire started. I would never have found her had the bird not stayed with her when she freed it."

Austin watched with stony gaze as Geoffrey absorbed this information. The young dandy grew pale above his high white cravat, but he carefully avoided looking at his cousin. "I cannot believe that," he whispered hoarsely. "There is no reason . . ."

"Except to a man who wishes to murder his wife for her wealth," Harry agreed coolly. "Sheriff, I prefer to be heard by the judge than a murderer. May we go now?"

"One moment." Adrian stepped in front of Austin before he could make a move toward the other men. "Can you explain your presence here tonight? I understand your land lies some distance from here."

Harry rose and gazed at him with contempt. "There is a public thoroughfare at the end of the drive. Will you pardon my traversing it and hearing the alarm? Half the bloody county must have heard it."

"At what time was this?" Adrian asked without hesitation.

"How in the devil do I know?" Harry exclaimed with irritation. "What time was it when the old curmudgeon tried to bash my brains out? I had only just arrived shortly before."

Satisfied, Adrian turned with a smile toward the officer of the law. "Sheriff, the man lies. It was nigh on to ten of the clock before we hauled him in here. The alarm sounded some two hours earlier. It could not possibly have been heard two hours' ride from here, but I have men outside who are prepared to swear they saw this man passing the main drive shortly after seven in company with his cousin, and another who swears Eversly never passed the far gate. The first two men will also swear that Sir Geoffrey here never left the grounds after he was turned away at the door. He turned his curricle down the south road and stayed there. When the alarm sounded, he tried to spring his horses but the wheels had become enmired. It was some while before he could reach the drive again."

Austin squeezed his friend's shoulder in gratitude, then nodded in the direction of his sullen prisoner. "If that is not enough, Sheriff, I recommend you save his trousers for the judge. They reek of coal oil. Now take him out of here before I lose my temper and do something we shall all regret later. Leave the other here. I would have a word with him."

Geoffrey buried his face in his hands as the sheriff led his cousin away.

"Sit up like a man and tell me why the bloody hell you went along with him," Austin roared as the door closed upon the representative of the law.

Geoffrey shook his head and looked everywhere but up at the earl's forbidding figure. "Harry's a bit of a bounder when he's in his cups, but he's my only kin. I had no reason to believe he lied to me. I believed him when he said you stole his intended like you stole Aubree from me. I could have made her happy. All she wanted was a place in the country with her animals. Her dowry would have bought that and enough for me to get by on. I'm not a greedy man."

"Enough!" Austin looked as if he would have liked to shake the pup, but he refrained. "What has that to do with destroying me? It would not win Aubree back."

"Harry said it would," he replied defensively. "He said you would beat her and I had to get her away from here, but she wouldn't come with me. So he said if you lost the abbey, you would take to the sea again and Aubree would be safe. I knew I'd lost her, but I had no reason to doubt Harry. It was common knowledge you killed your first wife, and he was right about your smuggling, although with a duke for a father-in-law, they'll never arrest you."

Adrian and Austin exchanged looks at this piece of information, but both held their tongues.

Geoffrey wandered on without urging. "But when Harry said he meant to fire the stables, I worried. Aubree's peculiar about animals. I didn't want her to see it. I didn't think she'd come with me, but I thought if I asked for her sister-in-law, too, she might agree. And it would have worked, too"—he looked up defiantly—"if you had not kept me away."

Austin raised a languid eyebrow to his accomplished brother-in-law. "How did you manage that?"

Adrian shrugged. "I borrowed John. Told him you had given express orders not to allow the ladies out with this man. Poor fellow never got past the gate. Damned fine groom you have there. Ought to employ him more frequently."

"If Aubree found out, he'd be a dead groom," Austin replied impassively.

Harley intruded quietly. "Geoff's never been terribly bright, Heath, but I don't think he ever meant any harm. Harry's the one who put me on to you, too. He had me believing you were out to debauch Geoff's fiancée like you destroyed Louise. He knew how I felt about you. Geoff was only looking for a diversion so he could play hero. I doubt if he even knew Harry had brought me to London."

Austin ran his hand through disheveled curls and gave a ragged sigh. "At this moment, I am prepared to hang just about anyone who looks at me crooked. I think, perhaps, you had better get out of my sight and stay there until my solicitors send for you. Then you had best bear witness against your cousin or leave the country. I'll not stand for any less."

Geoffrey looked miserable as he rose and glanced at the implacable faces around the room. With only a nod for answer, he gathered what pride remained to him and walked out.

When the door closed behind him, the voice at the fire inquired querulously, "Smuggling, Heath?"

30

The stench of burned wood and leather hung low in the moisture-laden air as Austin inspected the damage the next morning. Wearing only shirtsleeves and waistcoat against the chill wind, he picked his way cautiously through the ruins. A small group of men gathered in the stable yard as he tested the stone walls and burned-out timbers. The threat of rain hung over them, but they waited patiently.

He had no choice but to rebuild if he were to house

the animals this winter. The high-strung thoroughbreds had already been taken to a neighboring farm,
except for Austin's stallion, which watched the proceedings with a baleful eye from the paddock. A temporary shelter would have to be erected for it if he
were to go anywhere this winter. The splendid new
carriage in the adjoining coach house had received
extensive damage and would not be usable for some
while. All this would cost more than he possessed,
until his ship returned.

Hiding his apprehension about the whereabouts of
his ship, Austin calmly strode out to the stable yard to
interview the men waiting for him. With the price of
wool going down while costs soared, small sheepfarmers
found themselves driven out of the market. These men
were just a few of those who had found it impossible
to feed hungry mouths on what little they could earn
on animals and tilling their soil. Most were not carpenters by trade, but they would have to do. He could not
complain when six months before he could not have
hired the devil himself.

As he talked to the men, Austin recognized the lone
rider ambling up the front drive on his superannuated
gelding. Sheriff Fletcher was a slow man and a poor
one. He did not take well to horses. But he was
basically an honest, dutiful fellow, and Austin was
eager to hear what he had to say of their prisoner.

Setting John in charge of his newly hired helpers,
Austin strode through the yard to where the sheriff
waited. The muscles in his leg had not quite returned
to normal, and the wound had partially reopened during the night, but he could walk without the aid of a
stick and made a practice of doing so. He had too
much to accomplish to be delayed by a game leg.

The look on the sheriff's face was glum as he stood
beside his mount and watched the earl's quick stride
from the burned-out barn. He did not like dealing
with the gentry, and he had spent more time here
these last days than in all his prior life. He didn't
expect to be thanked for this trip either.

"Sheriff," Austin greeted the man curtly. His leg
throbbed and his mood was none of the best as he

calculated how far back the cost of a new stable would set his plans.

" 'Mornin', your lordship," the sheriff replied awkwardly. "Thought I'd best bring you the news before some other did."

Austin nodded permission for him to continue.

"The magistrate let Eversly go free without bail this morning. Said 'twasn't enough evidence to hold him, and he would bind the case over to the next session. Sir George warn't too happy that I didn't bring you afore him. He's a hard man when crossed."

"My God." Austin felt his shoulders sag beneath this additional burden and automatically straightened them. They were none of them safe if Eversly were out free. Sir George had a maggot between his ears.

The sheriff waited for some additional instruction besides a plea to the Almighty. Prayers were useful, like knocking on wood and throwing salt over your shoulder, but he had always found it easier to do things himself rather than wait on luck or the heavens.

Austin quickly came to certain conclusions. He could not tell the sheriff he intended to kill Eversly the moment the man set foot on his land again. The only thing left for Eversly to harm was the house and its occupants. He could not imagine the man mad enough to return, but he could afford to take no chances.

"There's some chance the man will seek some retaliation for last night, Fletcher. I'll need a man to keep an eye on the place at all hours. If you know of anyone, send him my way. I would appreciate it if you would keep me posted as to Eversly's whereabouts. If he retains any sense at all, he will be halfway to the coast by now, but I cannot rely on that."

The earl spoke with a certain degree of detachment that puzzled the sheriff. He had expected curses and threats, but this cool assessment of the situation seemed more sinister. Still, there was little he could do. The sheriff watched as a carriage turned into the drive at a breakneck pace, spattering mud on the elegant livery of the footmen. There could be some clue to the earl's detachment, but Fletcher felt himself dismissed and did not dare linger.

With a few muttered words concerning the guard to be hired, the sheriff meandered off, eyeing the arriving carriage with curiosity. Such equipage was uncommon in this rural area, and the crest on the side spoke of nobility. Nobility very seldom came this way anymore.

Austin knew his visitor before the carriage turned up the drive, and his heart sank. From the condition of the carriage and the pace at which it arrived, he judged the duke had been traveling the better part of the night. That did not bode well in the least. He glanced up at the window where Aubree still slept, and his heartstrings tightened a notch. He had not wanted to let her go so soon, but the news about Eversly made it imperative that she do so.

Austin stood silently as the footmen leapt to fix the stairs and open the door for their noble employer. The duke stepped out with no other ceremony. He appeared thinner, his face more drawn than when Austin had seen him last, but there was nothing weak about the snapping gaze he sent his son-in-law.

"Where's my daughter?" the duke demanded immediately, not offering his hand to his host but striding across the yard to the front entrance.

"Sleeping." Austin made no haste to keep up with him, forcing the duke to swing around and glare at him until he caught up.

"What in hell is she doing in bed at this hour? She never sleeps late. What's been going on here?" he added in afterthought, catching another glimpse of the burned-out remains of the once-enormous stable. He had noticed it earlier, but his anger had prevented any polite introduction of the subject. Now it seemed pertinent to his goal.

"A small accident," Austin replied wryly, leading the way up the front stairs. "We were up late, and I told the maids not to disturb her."

He threw open the wide oak door and gestured for the duke to enter.

"Well, tell them to bring her down here immediately with her bags packed. She's going with me." The duke stalked past Heathmont and into the towering great hall. Ignoring the soaring Gothic architecture, he glanced around, and spying a fire burning in a room off to one side, he stalked toward it.

A wide-eyed Mattie stood on the lower steps and Austin gave a curt nod in her direction. "Wake Lady Aubree and bring her down when she is dressed." He gave no opportunity for questioning, but followed his father-in-law into the study and closed the door behind him.

"You will give me some explanation of this visit?" Austin inquired dryly, avoiding the brandy bottle left from the prior night. A good gulp might be beneficial, but it was morning yet and such an act would certainly not impress Aubree's father.

"You need ask?" the duke roared, staring at him with incredulity. He gave the cracked leather of the fireside chair a dark look and remained standing.

"I can think of nothing I have done that you did not already know about. I believe at the time that I made it devilishly clear that I could not offer Aubree the comforts to which she is accustomed, nor the society. I painted my case in quite bold colors, I believe." Austin's leg ached, but while the duke remained standing, he could not sit.

The duke snorted. After inspecting the other poor specimens of furniture the room had to offer, he lowered himself into Austin's desk chair, leaving his son-in-law to sit on the couch with his game leg sprawled across the mottled upholstery.

"I figured you to have some damned-fool notion about not using Aubree's income, that is why I settled a sizable dowry upon you. What in hell have you been using it for if not to make this moldering ruin more comfortable for her?" the duke asked indignantly. "The damned rumors never bothered me if they didn't bother Aubree, but there's no end on them. What is this business of your murdering one of your housemaids? That is taking it a bit too far."

"If you give me time, I will explain, but I see no need to call Aubree into this. The argument is between us, and she will only be hurt if she is made to stand in the middle."

"She will be standing in her own room in Ashbrook House within the week! Admittedly, I would like to hear explanations of why you betrayed my trust, but no explanation will satisfy this." The duke jerked a packet of papers from his coat and slammed them down upon the desk.

As Austin slowly lowered his leg to the floor so he might reach for the packet, Ashbrook waved at him impatiently. "You need not read them now, I'll tell you what they are. They are warrants for your arrest on charges of smuggling. Would you care to explain those away?"

Austin leaned back against the couch and closed his eyes against the pain throbbing everywhere. There did not seem much point in arguing.

He had known since last night that something must have gone amiss. He suspected Eversly had his hand in this new disaster, too, but he had only himself to blame. He had been in a hurry to replenish his fortune, and he had taken risks he should not have taken. They had seemed justified at the time, when he had only himself and his land at stake. He had not meant for Aubree to become involved until he had established himself. Now the risk loomed enormous and unforgivable.

"Where is the ship and the captain?" Austin inquired wearily.

"The ship is impounded at Exeter. The captain's been taken to London for questioning. He held out as long as he could, but without a battery of barristers to protect him, he was forced to reveal your name. Not very sporting to let the man suffer on his own," the duke growled.

"I knew nothing of his capture." Austin thought of the letters that had accumulated during his illness and wondered what other bits of disaster had been lost to him. It was too late to worry now. "I have a buyer for some of my land. I will see the man defended."

"Hmph." The duke leaned back in his chair and glared at his son-in-law. "I daresay he can afford to defend himself once you find where he's hid your gold. The ship and the goods for the return journey are on board, but naught was found of the proceeds from the first sale. I daresay the profit was considerably higher than the investment on board."

Considerably, but the knowledge weighed little against the packet of papers on the desk. Consorting with the enemy was a hanging offense. He might get off with transportation to the Australian colonies. Did they send lords of the realm there? Or perhaps he would just molder in the Tower for the remainder of his life. Austin reflected on these fates with black humor. None of them left room for the dream he had so recently allowed to grow.

"I would rather Aubree did not know until she is safely away from here." Austin tried to think how best to break the news to her, but his mind refused to function with any degree of practicality. He kept seeing those enormous green eyes of hers staring at him with bewilderment and hurt and he could not make them go away.

"I had no intention of informing her of my poor judgment in men. Stay away from her, and those writs will go no farther than my pocket. I had hoped to see her well-protected before I die, but I can see I must rely on family for that. My brother is an indolent fool and his son is a dreamer, but between them, they should be able to keep her content. I should never have been fool enough to wish her happy."

Austin opened his eyes and stared at the once-proud duke. "You thought to make her happy by forcing her to marry me?"

The duke shrugged uncomfortably. "I introduced her to all the men I had chosen for her, and she could scarcely remember their names when I asked her of them. I couldn't have her pining after a country squire or a damned court card. She seemed to favor you, for God knows what reason. My men could find no truth in the rumors about you. You came highly recommended by men I respect. I knew you would never offer for her, and after the scandal the two of you managed to create, I could persuade none of the men I preferred to marry her. You left me with little choice. I regret it now. I am not dying so rapidly as the

physicians hoped. There might have been more time
to allow her to grow up, to find a more suitable match.
It's too late for that now. Just stay away from her, and
I'll see to her care."

"If the physicians give you so little hope, that will
be difficult to do," Austin replied dryly. "And you
forget, I am her husband. I cannot wish her married to
a felon, but neither can I wish her any of half a dozen
other fates. I will keep my distance if that is the
penalty I must pay, but only so long as I think her safe
and happy." Even that might be a difficult feat; Austin almost preferred swift death or imprisonment to
the thought of Aubree just within his grasp but out of
his reach. But Aubree's future must come first. A
husband and wife who did not live together was not an
odd circumstance in their circles, and preferable to
the first scheme she had offered of annulment or
divorce.

Piercing gray eyes studied the man across the room.
The cynical, self-contained earl who had argued his
case so selfishly last spring had lost some of his arro-
gance these past months. His bronzed coloring had
faded somewhat with his confinement, and the hostile
set of his jaw had lessened. The tactical defensiveness
with which he had protected himself had been breached;
the Earl of Heathmont was now as vulnerable as any
other man. The duke had chosen his moment well, but
he did not like the sour taste of this victory.

A knock upon the door prevented any further comment on the dubious wisdom of Austin's warning. The
duke barked a command, and the door swung open to
reveal his daughter's delicate grace. Jade eyes fixed
upon him immediately, but she stood in the doorway
without any sense of urgency. Her golden hair caught
a sunbeam from some obscure point of the hall, and
her delicate sprigged-muslin gown set off her rich coloring to perfection. The green ribbon of her bodice
picked up the colors of her eyes and the small jade
pins she had affixed to her curls. But it was the seren-
ity with which she gazed upon them that severely
rattled the duke's composure. His daughter was a

woman now, and an extremely self-confident one. He had the feeling only half the battle had been won.

"Father, what brings you here?" Aubree drifted into the room, closing the door securely behind her. She could tell by their faces what had brought the duke here, but she would not acknowledge her fear. "Has Peggy had the baby? She is well, isn't she?" She could not hide her concern as she noted her father's gaunt appearance, but she knew that was a topic the duke would not allow discussed.

"I have just come from there. It's a boy, and Alvan's crowing as if he were the first father to have a son. Peggy's a bit frail, if you can imagine that. I'm to take you back with me."

Austin had risen at Aubree's entrance and offered her a chair near the desk. She declined it by grasping his hand and standing beside him, saying nothing as her glance took in his impassive countenance. She felt a moment's anxiety, but he had said to trust him, and she did. To a point.

"Austin, will you be well enough for such a trip?" she asked innocently, probing for the truth.

Caught by her gaze, Austin had difficulty finding his tongue. He had reached for the sun and found his wings melting. He could feel himself plunging to the ground as he disentangled their hands and returned to his seat upon the couch, his leg sprawling across the cushion to prevent further intrusion.

"I cannot go, Aubree. There is too much to do here. You will want to see Peggy and the baby, and the Little Season is in full swing. You need to get out and about some. Didn't you promise the Sotheby sisters a trip to London?"

He was grateful for that last thought. The Sothebys were eminently practical young ladies and would keep Aubree on an even keel and well-occupied for a while. And they might write and tell him how she fared upon occasion. He could ask for no more than that.

Aubree's gaze grew mutinous as it rested upon him, but she saved her wrath for her father. She swung to face the duke.

"How soon will you return me here if I go with you?" The edge in her voice revealed her scorn.

The duke returned her glare but kept his voice neutral. "Peggy needs your company. Your Aunt Clara misses you. The holidays will be here shortly and you will wish to be with your family. Do not press me for dates."

Though appearing as some golden goddess sent from the heavens, Aubree leaned her hands on the desk and spoke with the wrath of the gods. "Do not give me your faradiddle! I will visit Peggy and pay my respects to Aunt Clara, but I am a married woman now, and my place is with my husband. If he cannot come with me, I will go to him, and you cannot prevent me."

A step from behind startled her, and Aubree noted her father's relieved expression as Austin's hands closed upon her arms. She turned to look on him with hope and fear, and the light died in her eyes as she read his expression.

His hands held her in a crushing grip as he gazed upon her with all the blackness of his soul. "You will do as your father tells you, Aubree. I cannot keep you any longer. My ship is lost and I will be selling the abbey to repay my debts. It is better this way."

Aubree's eyes clouded with tears and her fingers clenched into fists of rage as she searched his face for truth. There was something totally impenetrable about the mask that met her gaze, and she wanted to beat against it with all her puny power, but if he could turn her away like this, he could not want her. The tears spilled over and her fists went limp.

"You bastard," she murmured, still staring at him. "Do you really think it is money I want from you? Have you that little thought for me?"

Austin dropped her arms and walked away. "You are too damned young, Aubree," he answered callously. "Go back to your father's house and your pets where you belong."

Her voice shook as she replied. "You're no better than he is, after all. You don't want me to get too close, to interfere with your life, to get in your way.

Well, damn you to your own bloody hell, my Lord
Heathmont. I'll not ask for your company again."

Tears streamed down Aubree's face as she strode
out, but her shoulders were straight and her back rigid
as the door slammed behind her.

Austin continued staring out the murky window to
the unseen landscape below.

BOOK THREE

Absence diminishes commonplace passions and increases great ones, as the wind extinguishes candles and kindles fire.

　　　　　　　　　—Duc de La Rochefoucauld,
"Réflexions, ou Sentences et Maximes Morales"

31

Aubree sat in the weak sunlight of the front salon of Ashbrook House, meticulously opening the stacks of invitations upon the secretary with her gilded letter opener. The heavy linen paper and vellum crackled in her fingers as she casually inspected each notice and set it in one stack or another.

Near the warmth of the small fire, her companions complacently occupied themselves with poetry and embroidery until the afternoon round of visits began. Appearing for all the world as London fashion plates instead of the country girls they had arrived as, Anna and Maria still retained their abilities to amuse themselves rather than waiting for others to amuse them. They awaited Aubree's decisions on the morning's post with curiosity and eagerness, but little outward animation.

Aubree's cry of satisfaction brought them to attention, however. Both pairs of calm, gray eyes turned to watch their hostess.

"Lady Jersey invites us to tea! She wishes to make your acquaintance. You have caught the attention of the *haut ton,* ladies, and soon the world will be yours for the taking." If her inflection contained a hint of sarcasm, Aubree was sincere in her happiness for her guests. She had been uncertain of her ability to carry out the maneuvers necessary to conquer fashionable London, but she was not her father's daughter for nothing.

Anna smiled with pleasure at this news, but Maria gave a moan of despair.

"Lady Jersey! I shall disgrace myself, I know it. I

shall drop my scone in my tea and splash the Duchess of Somewhere or the Other. Or spill jam upon Princess Charlotte. We shall have to hide our faces in Devon for eternity," she wailed.

Aubree laughed and presented the invitation to Miss Sotheby. "She undoubtedly will expect nothing less from guests of mine. I was invited there the first week I came up from Hampshire. I informed the entire company of my very latest discovery, that my pet guinea pigs were male and female and were about to have babies. I told them how I discovered it, too."

Anna quietly choked on a comfit she had just bit into and Maria fell into a fit of the giggles.

"You did not!" she cried. "And what did Lady Jersey have to say to that?"

Aubree helped herself to one of the candies. "As I recall, after she persuaded Aunt Clara to crawl out from under the sofa, she thanked me for the informative lecture and asked if my father were returning to London any time soon."

Both girls were choking with laughter by now, and satisfied that she had dispelled all anxieties about the upcoming tea, Aubree returned to her battle plans. Even the Little Season required a masterful grasp of military tactics, from provisioning the troops to leading an attack into the war zone. She had very little experience, but a strategic turn of mind and a title that made the enemy cautious. The inquiries about her husband and marriage had been overpowering at first, until she had learned to maneuver her limited weapons. She had more confidence in her ability to field insulting questions now.

An invitation to a fete at Lady Bessborough's seemed the ideal opportunity to introduce the Sotheby sisters to a large number of unattached males. They had resided relatively quietly these last weeks, refurbishing wardrobes and easing into society's momentum gradually with afternoon teas and morning calls and occasional rides in the park. The November weather had turned wicked lately, however, and the end of the Season would come soon. They would fit in what they could before the Sothebys returned home for Christmas, and be a step ahead of the debutantes when they returned in the spring.

After Aubree announced these plans, even the placid Anna contrived to appear anxious.

"We shall not suit, Aubree. We are nobodies and cannot change that fact as we have our gowns. It has been pleasant seeing sights we have only heard about before and moving in circles that would never have been open to us without you, but we are only daughters of a merchant, and not particularly young or attractive daughters, either."

Aubree looked at her friend in astonishment. True, Anna Sotheby would be twenty-five within the month, which nearly made her a spinster, but Aubree could not apply the word "unattractive" to her. Her carroty-red hair was not fashionable, perhaps, but her large, wide-spaced gray eyes were set off by fine, high cheekbones and softened by a particularly lovely smile. And Maria was but twenty-two, and though not a diamond of the first water, her features reflected her lively friendliness, and her strawberry-blond hair was a jewel to behold. She shook her head in vigorous denial of Anna's protests.

"Utter fustian!" she announced. "Austin has told me your family dates back to the very beginnings of history. If they have fallen on hard times recently, it is through no fault of your own. Harley is accepted in all circles, why should you not be? Besides, once it is known you come accompanied with large dowries, you may have your pick among titles. Wealth is ever more important than beauty or family." This time her sarcasm very definitely shone through, but her companions showed no shock.

"Harley went to school with his acquaintances," Anna reminded her. "It is easy for him. I cannot be convinced I will accomplish more than adorning the woodwork. I am not certain I could bear the humiliation."

"Coward!" Maria flung at her. "I shall certainly take my chances. I cannot think there is nothing more for me in life than riding about the fields of Devon and tatting shawls in front of the fire. Perhaps there is some short, balding man out there who will not care if I have freckles or come from merchant stock. We can live merrily in Scotland and visit Italy when the war is over and I shall be content. All society cannot be Lord Heathmont and Harley, or Geoffrey and Eversly. There must be some in between.''

Aubree turned away and allowed the sisters to carry on the argument between themselves. The mention of Austin's name twisted a knife in her heart. She would have been content to ride the fields of Devon and sit beside the fire for the rest of her life if only Austin could have accompanied her. She had been a fool to think it was enough for Austin.

She tapped her quill against the ink pot and wished for the words to draw her wrath on paper, but all previous attempts had failed. She had not quite believed it when her father had carried her off without a word of protest from her husband, but she understood it now. Her fury still kindled at the memory of his treachery. She was obviously no judge of character whatsoever.

She had never intended to stay in London. In her anger and self-pity, she had followed her father as commanded, but even on that tedious journey, plans for rebellion had gradually formed. She was eighteen and an heiress. She had the wealth to do whatsoever she wished without depending on anyone. And she detested London.

Her revolt was put down on that very first day her father had left her unattended. She had cooed over the third in line to the duke's title, idled away the hours with Peggy discussing the baby's feeding habits, all the while seething with the frustration of captivity. The baby was adorable. Peggy was her best friend. Even Alvan had come down off his high cloud to greet her with happiness. But misery ate at Aubree's insides with inexorable thoroughness. She wanted a home and family of her own, and if she could not have one, she would have none other. And the moment she was given the freedom of a carriage, she struck out.

Aubree brushed hastily at the tears as she remembered

that day. The carriage had taken her directly to the solicitors who had so reliably deposited her quarterly allowance into the bank. She had no word from them upon the occasion of her eighteenth birthday, but perhaps they waited upon her. She would discover just exactly the extent of her wealth and how far it would carry her. Austin and her father would rue the day they had conspired to destroy her happiness.

She had met her mother's man of business upon occasion before and had not been overly impressed with his surly attitude or condescension. He had obviously thought it a streak of madness that had allowed such wealth to accumulate in the hands of mere women, and he had difficulty dealing patiently with Aubree's inquiries. He was no better than she remembered when she arrived that day.

Informed rather coldly that the bulk of the estate was entailed and that only the income could be provided for her use, Aubree had demanded that a list of her investments and income be provided to her. She had then been informed that such information had been sent to her husband as the law required. As an unemancipated female, she could not be expected to approve decisions upon the investment of such sums. Furious by that time, Aubree had demanded to know to just what she was entitled, and the lawyer handed her a blow she had not recovered from to this day.

"You are entitled to the income from your estate, as I just explained to you, my lady," the man had replied insolently. "The first installment has already been deposited with your husband's man of business. As a married woman, you must apply to your husband for the use of those funds. The trust does not allow your husband to control your estate, but the law expressly provides that a woman's income belongs to her husband. A woman cannot be expected to deal in such matters herself. Now, if I have answered your questions, Lady Aubree . . ."

He had dismissed her as if she were no more than a child. His attitude had rankled for the remainder of the day, but Austin's betrayal had nearly destroyed her. No wonder he had seen to it that there was no

means for an annulment and had made no mention of
a divorce! He had all the funds he needed to do with
as he wished. Why should he rid himself of so lucra-
tive an investment! And without funds, she could not
seek the divorce herself. She could do nothing.

Aubree stared at the tapping quill as if she had no
control over it. She still could not believe she had
been so thoroughly deceived. She was virtually a prisoner of her father's whim while Austin made free with
what was hers alone, and all because she had been
fool enough to believe his loving lies. No, that was
wrong. Austin never spoke a word of love. She had
been the one who had thought such a thing existed.
She slammed the pen down and stalked out of the
room.

The Sotheby sisters exchanged glances. They had
accepted Aubree's invitation with excitement and gratitude, but they had come to understand she had offered it in some kind of desperation that they did not
understand.

Anna shook her head. "I cannot believe Harley has
the whole story. If his lordship feared Eversly's return,
Aubree would understand that. That does not explain
why she is so terribly unhappy. It is not natural," she
announced decisively.

"Perhaps Heathmont is mad like the hero of that
novel we read last week, and he sends her away for
her own safety." Maria had concocted any number of
other romantic theories, but this was her particular
favorite. It explained many things.

Anna made a wry grimace. "Well, I intend to write
the madman's mother and tell her Aubree is none too
sane, either, and her safety is endangered more by her
own hands than any other's. I have never seen her like
this. And she will not talk to me or anyone else. It is
most worrisome."

Maria grew serious. "You will not really tell Lady
Heathmont that, will you? I am certain she did not
expect such intimacies when she requested that you
write."

"On the contrary"—Anna set her lips firmly—"I
believe that is just exactly what she had in mind."

*   *   *

Adrian paced the study floor thoughtfully, whacking at dust motes with his riding crop. "I daresay I must be as mad as you, Heath, I cannot find any fault with the plan. Emily would have hysterics. I'm a married man now, a figure of responsibility. I shouldn't be indulging in any more theatrical escapades like this. But, by Jupiter, I want to do it!" He lifted his lean face to display a wolfish grin. "I owe myself this opportunity to thumb my nose at the English navy. You say she's schooner-rigged? How does she set in the water?"

"Like a babe. She'll have you home by the new year. I should never have told you of this. Emily will never forgive me." Austin stared out the dirty window to the still-green swath of lawn. The trees had lost their foliage, but the frost had not yet done its final damage to the summer. He imagined a slender figure garbed in white muslin running swiftly down that grassy hillside, her hat ribbons flying out over a golden river of curls, her eyes laughing. The pain of that image struck him more forcibly than the fading ache in his knee.

"Emily will never forgive your sending Aubree away. She is so furious she will barely speak to me when I try to explain. If she thought Aubree would welcome her, I believe she would be off to London tomorrow. As it is, she has nowhere to go once she gets there. If I don't do something to bring back your wife, I may well lose my own." Adrian flung himself into the cracked leather chair and stared at Austin's back.

"I can steal the ship," Austin drawled laconically. "There is no guarantee I can steal Aubree back. There is no guarantee I will even be able to find her once I am free to look. She has access to a fortune large enough to build a kingdom of her own on the other end of the world."

"Shades of Lady Stanhope! I cannot believe she is quite that mad, in any sense of the word. Didn't young Harley say his sisters went to stay with her?"

Austin shrugged. "I cannot imagine Aubree chaperoning two country sisters about society without some reason. She's still so green it is painful to watch. Alvan and Harley will have to look after her every minute."

"You do mean to fetch her back, don't you?" Adrian asked with concern. Austin did not speak as a loving husband.

His friend stood silently for a long moment before answering. When the words came, they echoed as if from the bottom of some deep well. "What are the chances of a convicted felon and murderer of asking a duke's daughter to marry him?"

32

Garbed in a hunter's-green riding habit, her hair simply styled *à l'anglaise*, Aubree descended to the downstairs hall to greet Harley. His gray eyes warmed with appreciation as she approached.

"With your hair down like that, you look no older than a schoolgirl," he jested lightly to hide his deeper sentiment. Had she not been wed to another, he would have been forced to give serious thought to ending his own bachelorhood.

Aubree did not respond with any degree of enthusiasm to his jest. His words had jarred a discordant note in an already exceptionally bad fugue that had been her morning.

"Thank you, sir," she replied acidly. "Shall you tell me next to return to my schoolbooks? I am certain you and Alvan would be much more comfortable if I were back in the schoolroom."

Harley had the grace to look decidedly uncomfortable. "I'm sorry, Aubree. I didn't mean . . ."

His apologies were interrupted by the clatter of his sisters as they hurried down the stairs to greet them, and the moment was lost.

"Aubree! You mean to accompany us, after all," Maria exclaimed happily, noting her friend's attire.

But Aubree had just been blessed with an idea of blazing proportions, its dimensions so many-sided that she wanted to enjoy the moment by herself. With the first spontaneous smile she had managed in weeks, she declined the invitation.

"No, Alvan will be along shortly. Perhaps we will see you a little later," she lied, dismissing them hurriedly, wanting to consider all the facets of her inspiration privately, although her mind was already made up.

Harley went reluctantly, suspicious of Aubree's sudden turn of humor and not remembering Alvan having mentioned any such outing. But he was not the lady's brother or husband, and he could do no more than urge her to accompany them. At her refusal, he departed.

Aubree took very little time to consider the pros and cons of her decision. This was something she had wanted to do for a long time, but never possessed the daring. She had all the courage of fury behind her now, and the delight of revenge, and no one to account to at the result. When all other outlets of freedom were denied to her, she must take advantage of the few remaining.

Remembering the name Lady Caroline had dropped at a tea one day, Aubree hastily penned a note and called for a footman. When he left on his errand, she bounded up the stairs to change back into her day dress. She prayed there would be no delay in response, her time was restricted by the demands of her schedule.

Obviously, the modiste understood the demands of nobility. She responded immediately. To have such a client as the Duke of Ashbrook's daughter increased her efficiency. Her clients were her only advertisement, and Lady Aubree would be an ideal subject.

Mattie screamed in horror as the modiste's hairdresser brought out her combs and scissors and laid them upon the vanity.

"My lady, no! Not your beautiful curls! You cannot!

Please, my lady . . ." Tears could be heard in her cries as Mattie begged for Aubree to rethink her decision.

Aubree sat determinedly before the mirror and began pulling out the irritating pins and bows that held her unruly hair in place. "You must watch, Mattie, and learn to do as Mademoiselle Francine does. I will need you to keep it neatly trimmed when we are not in London," she explained firmly.

Mattie bit her tongue on further protests. To mention father or husband at this stage would most likely drive the rebellious miss to demand it all shaved off. With tears in her eyes, she watched as the first golden curls fell to the floor.

When the hairdresser had packed her scissors and left, Aubree stared at the shorn image in her mirror. Style demanded Grecian simplicity. Lady Caroline had gone to extremes, as usual, by cutting her hair to nearly resemble a man's. But the stylist had created a much more artistic coiffure for Aubree. Golden curls hung in ringlets about her ears and at the nape of her neck and waved luxuriously at the crown of her head. The image looked no older than the long-haired lass of the morning, but Aubree felt as if a great burden had been lifted from her shoulders. She loved it.

As her maid tearfully tied a blue ribbon about the long, fallen tresses, Aubree turned and ordered, "Find a box for them, Mattie."

Wiping her eyes, the maid hastened to do so and watched in astonishment as Aubree neatly packaged the golden curls beneath sheets of tissue. She tied the parcel securely with ribbons and left the chamber for the study.

After penning Atwood Abbey's direction on the outer package, Aubree handed it to a footman and ordered it taken out on the next mail coach. With satisfaction, she contemplated Austin's reaction to such a gift. She might be wrong about his character, but she felt confident he had sufficient intelligence to understand this symbol of defiance. She was her own woman now and would act accordingly.

Deep inside, she harbored the hope it would hurt as much as he had hurt her, but practicality told her that would not be possible. A man with a heart as hard as his could feel no pain, only the prickle of pride upon occasion. Mayhap she would prick his pride somewhat.

When the Sotheby sisters returned from their ride, they were aghast at what Aubree had done, but after the first shock, they grudgingly admitted the style was most becoming. On Lady Caroline, the style had contrived to make her look more boyish. On Aubree, that was an impossibility. Her small face had been relieved of excess encumbrance, thereby emphasizing her overlarge eyes and slender jaw and high wide brow. It suited her lively personality and carefree outlook on life, or the personality and outlook she had possessed prior to returning to London.

That Aubree had acted with as much malice as delight, Anna recognized but did not understand. It had seemed a miracle when her father had actually begun speaking to Lord Heathmont again. The miracle lost most of its glitter when she learned the cost. She had listened to her father's explanations and understood the duke not wishing Aubree endangered by a man like Eversly, who would burn stables or worse. She wished her father had explained "worse," but he had been exceedingly reluctant to explain anything at all. Still, it seemed odd that the duke could not trust Heathmont to protect his own wife, or that Heathmont would allow Aubree to go without explaining his motives. If only the men would learn to confide in their womenfolk, it seemed to Anna that the world would run much more smoothly.

But until offered some opportunity to change the flow of things, Anna found herself carried along on the current of events with everyone else.

The fete at Lady Bessborough's proved mildly amusing to Aubree and educational for the Sotheby sisters. The masculine attendance found Aubree and her daring coiffure without flaw while her husband remained in Devon. Aubree was less impressed with the Corinthians and young dandies who hovered about her than they were with themselves, however, and she quickly drew the limit on the amount of time she would waste on them. She devoted what time she was allowed to introducing her guests to the more eligible bachelors in attendance.

Toward the end of what proved to be a tiring evening, Aubree discovered herself in the company of one of her father's acquaintances. Though nearing two score years of age, Lord Killarnon was still a fine figure of a man. He bent gallantly over Aubree's hand and smiled charmingly at her hesitation.

"Killarnon, Lady Aubree. I do not expect you to recall all the names that have crossed your father's portals. It is most pleasant to see you among society at last. How is your father?"

Relieved that she did not have to grope for coy or witty answers to flirtatious questions from a relative stranger, Aubree offered honesty. "Meddling, as usual, my lord. The uproar the Luddites have caused in Nottingham has sent him galloping northward. He would do better to bring them here. I can think of better things to destroy than looms."

Killarnon laughed. "I dare not venture to ask what those things might be, or like your father, you will tell me in no uncertain terms. It is a pleasure to hear a woman who speaks of other than ribbons and beaus. I do not suppose I would be so fortunate as to claim a dance from you before the evening ends?"

Since she was most obviously sitting out this one, he had every right to ask, but as he reached to study her card, Aubree shook her head negatively. "I am sorry, but they are all taken."

He looked at her in some surprise, his strong brow drawing up in a slight frown. "There is one last waltz unaccounted for. Do you expect someone?"

Aubree smiled at his reaction to this small blow to his conceit. It seemed even her father's polished politicians dealt in pride. "No, my lord, my waltzes are reserved for my husband, who unfortunately is not here. I prefer to spend that time in conversing. You are welcome to join me in that occupation if you wish."

She had practiced this line enough during the evening to have polished it to perfection. The reference to her husband made the young bloods more cautious and gave her breathing room. They did not necessarily consider a married woman beyond approach, but their tactics of pursuit changed. Tomorrow, they would retire to their clubs and make certain of Heath's whereabouts before approaching her more discreetly. It was a silly game, in Aubree's opinion, but it gave her the opportunity to appreciate those few who joined her in conversation and friendship.

The handsome man before her now smiled in approval at her reply. "That is the most refreshing comment I have heard this night. May I join you?"

Aubree found his languid characterization of her father's colleagues absorbing and looked up in surprise as Anna and Maria returned to her side at the end of the dance. Introductions were made, and Killarnon reluctantly bowed over farewells when the next set began.

"You will be at Almack's Wednesday?" he inquired before Aubree departed with her partner for the country dance.

"If Lady Jersey will be so kind as to offer introductions for my guests." Aubree nodded toward the Sotheby sisters, who were now being carried off by two elegantly clad gentlemen.

Killarnon's lips bent into that charming smile she had noted earlier. "I shall be there early enough to claim a dance then."

He disappeared into the crowd, leaving Aubree to follow her escort onto the dance floor and wonder if that were an optimistic remark or a promise. Moving in the Duke of Ashbrook's circle, Lord Killarnon had the power to ensure anyone's entrance into Almack's. But her father had never lowered himself to the level of concerning his time over such trivialities. She could not believe a mere acquaintance would trouble himself in such a manner.

Whatever the reason, the Sothebys received their highly prized cards at the beginning of the following week. Maria shrieked in ecstasy and Anna gazed upon the invitation with gratification. It was akin to receiving a school report praising one's accomplishments. Anna and Maria had passed all exams without fail. They could not help but feel delight.

"This never would have happened without your assistance, Aubree," Anna murmured.

Her hostess frowned, remembering her brief conversation with her father's friend. "Do not be so certain of that. I am not high on Lady Jersey's books, although she cannot afford to offend me. But Lord Killarnon, now . . ." She eyed Anna speculatively. "If he has taken some interest in you, you can be certain red carpets will fall at your feet."

"Lord Killarnon? We have only just met the gentleman, and he has certainly shown me no preference," Anna answered in puzzlement.

"He is a lifelong bachelor. You cannot expect him to act other than cautiously. He is a trifle older than I would normally consider desirable, but he is an intelligent man who appreciates women with minds." Aubree considered the possibilities thoughtfully. "A man like that has no need to lower himself to search for women with wealth or title. He can search for one who pleases him. I see no reason why you cannot be that woman."

Anna looked momentarily alarmed at such a notion, but common sense prevailed. "I can see many reasons, but we shall see. I will not deny that he is an attractive man."

Satisfied that she had opened Anna's mind to the suggestion, Aubree slid gradually back into her doldrums. She had received no response to her package to Heath. Perhaps he had set her so far from mind that he could not even remember the color of her hair. A letter came from Lady Heathmont, a cozy, chatty letter speaking of the new stables and the changes being made to the abbey now that winter had arrived and Austin had more time to turn to it. And more money, Aubree added bitterly. She burned the letter and made no attempt to reply.

As soon as they arrived at Almack's, Killarnon worked his way through the thinning crowd to greet them. Many of the *haut ton* had already left London for their country estates, but sufficient remained to make the chambers as uncomfortable as ever.

Aubree avoided an offer for weak punch and greeted Killarnon with a smile. "My lord, I cannot believe you find time from your pressing duties to attend these functions."

He bowed gallantly over her hand and retained possession of it as he smiled into her eyes. "The Season is almost ended and there are very few opportunities left to obtain that dance you promised. You will allow me?"

Pleased at this attention from one of her father's friends, she agreed, then opened the way for Anna. "You will help me introduce Miss Sotheby and Maria, won't you? I am quite terrible at names and I fear I will embarrass them terribly."

He agreed amiably, signing both their dance cards and waylaying several younger members of his club to offer for dances. The evening was off to an excellent start.

Aubree had every reason to believe the entire evening a success by the time they rode the carriage back to Ashbrook House. Anna and Maria had proved popular, and Killarnon had kept Aubree entertained with his talk of politics and society. He could not, of course, offer more than two dances to Miss Sotheby, but his attention seldom diverted from the chairs where Aubree and her friends kept court.

Though she knew her success, Aubree could not quite wring happiness from it. She was lonesome, homesick, and bored, and no amount of frivolity would lighten her humor. She refused to contemplate the cause of this feeling of disenchantment. She must look to the future and not the past and design what she could of it. Her problem was that she could find no future.

A letter came from the duke announcing his intention to leave Nottinghamshire and go directly to Castle Ashbrook, where he expected his family to meet him. Aubree consigned this missive to the fire also. She would sit in London alone before she returned to that place where she and Austin had wed.

They followed the slowing swirl of social functions, meeting Lord Killarnon frequently. He could coax a laugh from Aubree when no other could, and she began to anticipate his company. Anna could find no interest in him but was relieved to see her friend relax and laugh a little. Perhaps her fit of the dismals would end before the holidays.

Alvan appeared on their doorstep at the end of November, announcing Peggy now felt well enough to travel, and they would be removing to the castle on the following week. Aubree promptly ordered a footman to fetch the gaily wrapped parcels she had purchased for her relations.

When presented with the bundle, Alvan appeared bemused. "I can pack them in our trunks, of course, but would they not go better in the baggage wagon? Mattie could see to them along with your other things."

"Mattie and I are not going with you." Aubree settled into her favorite chair and picked up her needlework as if she had not just dropped a bombshell in their midst.

"Who are you going with?" Alvan asked, still puzzled. "I thought Anna and Maria preferred to return to their home for the winter."

Aubree gazed at him in exasperation. "Aunt Clara will not be at the castle, will she?"

Alvan finally gathered the drift of her thoughts. "No, now she has no reason to leave Southridge, she prefers to stay there. But your father is expecting you at his home, Aubree. You cannot disappoint him. He is ill, if you have not noticed."

"He was not so ill that he did not go riding off to Nottingham at the first hint of revolution. If he can ride there, he can ride to Southridge if he desires to see me. I cannot offer anything so exciting as revolution, perhaps, but I will be there. That is more than he can say most times. Don't talk to me of disappointment, Alvan. How many Christmases have I spent in that dreary place waiting for the festivities to begin? And how many Christmases has my father whisked in the day before, kissed us all on the cheek, and disappeared again the day after? Castle Ashbrook will be yours one day, Alvan, not mine. I want no part of it. Alexa and Everett are getting married and they beg my attendance. I will go where I am wanted."

Alvan could not argue with her. Though he tried, his heart was not completely in it. He no more understood the reason for Aubree's coming to London than did Anna. He had received a curt note from Austin asking him to look after her, but no other explanation. Perhaps she had made up her mind to go back to Austin and did not wish to reveal her plans. He supported that action wholeheartedly, but he could not leave her to act alone.

"How will you be traveling to Southridge?"

Aubree threw him a grateful glance at this surrender. "Harley is taking his sisters home. I will travel with them. So, you see, you have nothing about which to worry."

He nodded approval and departed soon after. He would speak with Harley to be certain all was well, but he did not doubt her word. She might travel farther than Southridge, but she was not foolish enough to do it alone when other opportunities offered.

Lord Killarnon called the day before they were scheduled to depart, and Aubree considered that an auspicious sign for her plans for Anna. Unfortunately, the sisters managed to be out doing last-minute Christmas shopping when he arrived. Aubree did what she could to retain him until they returned, but Killarnon had other plans.

"I just learned you will not be going with Beresford to Ashbrook, Lady Aubree. Are you returning to Devon for the holidays?" he inquired casually as he donned his gloves in preparation for departure.

"No, Hampshire, my lord. A friend of mine is getting married and my aunt is expecting me."

"Ahh, Southridge, that is but a half-day's ride from my place." He nodded knowingly. "Excellent. I don't suppose you could be persuaded to linger a while in Sussex before traveling on to your aunt's? I'm having a small house party at the end of this week and your refreshing honesty would add a good deal of spice to what might otherwise be a tedious time."

"That is scarcely a recommendation for my attending." Aubree laughed, but her mind had already leapt at the possibilities. She would like to see Aunt Clara again, of course, but without her pets, Southridge would scarcely be the home she had once loved. And Alexa's marriage wasn't until the new year. There was plenty of time for that. Time seemed to loom eternal over these next months. She would have more than she would know what to do with.

Killarnon recognized that he had not been rejected and played this opening well. "I will bestir myself to make the festivities bright if I know you are to be there. Bring your lovely companions and we will be merry together."

"You are going down this night?" Aubree ran rapidly over possible ploys to persuade the Sothebys to linger.

"You are my final farewell, my lady. I am off this moment. Say you will consider it and I will go with glad heart." He held a mocking hand to his heart in imitation of a romantic young suitor.

Aubree laughed at these dramatics. "You are a fraud, sir. Or must all politicians be actors, too? No matter. I will give it my consideration."

At this much agreement, he grinned, bowed politely, and departed.

Aubree paced the salon in thought until her guests returned. Killarnon had offered no invitation to Harley and she felt certain Harley would have no interest in stopping under those circumstances. Perhaps he could just take Anna and herself to Killarnon, and other transportation could be arranged for the journey. She found herself strangely reluctant to return home. Southridge was much too close to Devon for comfort.

When Aubree shared her invitation with the sisters, they showed no such reluctance. They were eager to return home now that all their plans were made. Anna remained adamant in her opinion of Lord Killarnon.

"He is a kind gentleman, Aubree, and I am grateful for his invitation, but there really is no chance of making a match there. He is charming, and I am pleased that he has taken the time to bring you out of the dismals, but he stirs no other interest in me, nor I in him, I believe. If you truly are set upon going, I will accompany you for propriety's sake, but I beg not for my own."

Aubree had a vague understanding of the Sothebys' need to return home. She wished she could feel the same way, but she seemed to lack the ability. Perhaps she could turn the situation to some advantage, though.

She stopped her pacing and smiled benevolently. "There is no need for that. I am an ancient, doddering old married woman now and Mattie will serve as sufficient companion. Since she cannot possibly accompany us in your brother's coach, I will use my father's landaulet." Before they could protest, she hurried to distract them. "I wish you would do me a great favor, though." She hesitated, waiting for a nod of acquiescence. When it came, she finished, "I miss my pets terribly. Do you think it would be possible, if I sent the landaulet with a footman after you later, that you could persuade Austin to part with Lady and the kittens? I do not believe Myna would travel without me."

Immediate anguish set in at this indication of Aubree's not returning to the abbey at all. Both girls clamored and protested, but it was obvious their arguments were useless. Without access to Aubree's thoughts or reasons, they could do nothing but agree.

33

Winter twilight had already descended by the time the landaulet sped up the tree-lined drive of Lord Killarnon's estate. Her father's driver knew the way and they had made good time, but Aubree suffered a weariness that was not eased by the sight of this unknown abode. She wished she had never agreed to this excursion, but it was too late to retreat now. It should be preferable to staying at an inn, in any case.

The disapproving frown on Matilda's brow throughout the day had not eased Aubree's guilt in any way. Married woman or not, Aubree was but eighteen, and the old-fashioned maid had her own opinion of such gadding about. She had scarcely spoken a word throughout the journey, and Aubree had been left to contemplate her rashness in silence.

But she climbed from the carriage with determination, blessing the footmen who hurried to greet her with a smile. Thoroughly chilled by the evening air these last miles, she was eager for the warmth of a fire. With just the promise of her smile, the servants hastened to make her comfortable.

Inside, she learned the other guests were either still out hunting or in their rooms preparing for dinner, and she greeted this news with relief. She was not yet prepared to greet a crowd of strangers.

The chamber reserved for her was modishly styled in the Egyptian motifs made so popular with Nelson's defeat of Napoleon off those foreign shores. Aubree had never learned to like the heavily carved mahoganies and rosewoods with their grotesque sphinxes and crocodiles, and she had thought the style on the wane—but not so in the country, it seemed. She glared at a sphinx staring down at her from the towering dresser and threw her pelisse over its head.

Mattie helped her undress, and Aubree tried to lie down awhile before dinner, but a chill was in her bones and no amount of covering seemed to warm it. While Mattie went about her tasks of unpacking and scurried in and out with garments to be pressed in the kitchen, Aubree closed her eyes and tried to sleep, but her mind would not be stilled.

Half a day's journey closer to Devon and already she felt the pull more strongly, as she had feared. She wondered where Austin was now, what he was doing, what he was thinking. Lady Heathmont had said nothing of his selling the abbey, and she wondered if somehow his ship had returned to give him some reprieve. For Lady Heathmont's sake, she hoped so, but she would wish Austin in hell if she could.

By the time Mattie returned, Aubree's head felt as if it might split in two, and she had no desire at all to join in the small talk about the dinner table. She had no desire for dinner, for all that mattered. But the alternative was to stare at four walls and contemplate murdering Austin, so there was nothing left to do but rise and dress for the evening.

Lord Killarnon greeted her effusively and whirled her around the room, introducing the other guests. Aubree had met most of them at one time or another—most were closer to Killarnon's generation than her own—but she smiled obediently and repeated polite phrases learned since childhood. Her head throbbed, but etiquette must be observed.

Aware of the odd looks she received as various of the guests recognized her or whispered the latest gossip about her separation from Austin, Aubree chose to ignore them. She spent all her concentration on enduring each passing moment.

Killarnon led her into the dining hall and set her on his right, not only the position of the guest of honor but the one due her rank. None of the other guests could claim the title of countess or descent from a duke. Unimpressed with this fact, Aubree struggled to listen pleasantly to his lordship's slightly racy jests and bottomless lode of gossip. She understood how others considered him a charming host, but she longed for silence, or at least a sensible topic.

With relief, she withdrew into the salon after dinner with the remainder of the ladies, leaving the gentlemen to their port. The baroness who had served as Killarnon's hostess approached, and Aubree noted the wary light of dislike in her eyes, but she took no heed of it. The baroness was of the type of fading beauty who did not age well, and Aubree very likely presented a challenge to her, but Aubree had not the strength to rise to the fray.

She immediately grasped this opportunity to offer her apologies and make her excuses. Even the scorn of four walls seemed more appealing than making polite chatter another moment.

The baroness's eyes narrowed as Aubree murmured her excuses, but the girl's pale cheeks and black-edged eyes eliminated all suspicion. The older woman promised to pass her message on to Lord Killarnon and even offered the services of her maid, who was apparently adept at curing aches.

Aubree escaped with some difficulty and closed her chamber door behind her with relief. Surely, in the morning she would feel better, and then the holiday could begin. She simply didn't have the heart for it now.

Mattie hurried to help her into her nightdress, a look of distress replacing her earlier frown. Aubree seldom fell ill; it seemed a bad omen for the visit. When the better part of dinner came up shortly after Aubree retired, Mattie made it a point to stay in her mistress's chambers rather than retire to the attic. Someone had to stay by the foolish girl's side.

A scratch at the door sometime later disturbed Aubree's stupor, but Mattie hastened to answer it, and she drowsed again, leaving her maid to deal with the intruder.

Lord Killarnon met the maid's stern gaze with some astonishment but managed to conceal it quickly.

"I have come to inquire about Lady Aubree. Is she still not feeling well? Shall I send for an apothecary?"

He gave every appearance of an anxious host, though his eyes seemed to search the space beyond the servant's shoulder.

"My lady is sleeping. It would be best if she not be disturbed. I shall tell her you inquired, milord, and if she requires a physic, she will let you know," Mattie replied stiltedly, in her best imitation of her betters. She might never make a lady's companion, but she would not shame her mistress by being any less than she could be.

Killarnon nodded uncertainly. "Call me if her ladyship worsens. Otherwise, give her my regrets and tell her I shall see her in the morning."

He departed hurriedly, and Mattie noted his direction with cynicism. The servants' hall was rife with gossip, and she already knew the hoity-toity baroness was Killarnon's mistress. His direction now proved it. What worried her was the other rumors, the eager questions she had received about her own mistress. What kind of evil minds would think her innocent young ladyship would consent to bed with that smarmy old man? Mattie shook her head in astonishment and firmly closed the door.

Austin slumped into the old leather chair and stared at the crackling fire, oblivious to the pounding of hammers and curses of workmen in the great hall and salon. The stables had been resurrected with the improvement of a cozy room just for Aubree's litter of animals, and the renovation of the abbey itself was well under way, but he could find no interest in it.

His gaze returned to the vellum letter propped against the inkwell on his desk. Addressed to Aubree, the letter held him fascinated as a snake does its intended victim. The workmen had disturbed it from its hiding place while they tore out rotting floorboards and replaced damaged paneling, otherwise, under present housekeeping arrangements, it could have lay hidden for years. Austin knew he should forward it, but he could not bring himself to it just yet.

He knew its contents. The familiar scrawl from his solicitors told him that much. He had made all the arrangements when he was last in London, then set them from his mind. It had never occurred to him that Aubree had never received the letter, designed to be delivered on her eighteenth birthday, more than two months ago. She must think him a royal cad, indeed, but to offer her the freedom promised by that letter now would decimate what remained of his hopes.

Still, except for that taunting package of rebellion, he had heard nothing from her since she had left. Perhaps she had decided the freedom of a married woman was preferable to that of a scandalous divorcée. In that case, the letter would give her the wealth to do as she pleased, which would most likely be to go as far from him as she could.

Austin stood and crossed to the bottle of brandy on the table. It was morning; he shouldn't be touching spirits so early. He stared at the glass in his hand and reluctantly placed it back on the table. He knew better than to follow the example his father had set for him. He needed to make this decision with a clear head instead of reacting impetuously in the heat of anger—or liquor.

Swinging on his heel, Austin stalked toward the window and stared blindly onto the lawns. With Adrian's aid, he had stolen back his captured ship, and it should safely be on its way to the Americas now with its precious passengers on board. He missed the sound of the little scamps giggling in the hallways, and the old house seemed to echo without Adrian's shouting laughter or Emily's scolding jests. He didn't allow himself to dwell on the golden ghost that disappeared behind doors wherever he walked. The ship was gone, and he remained.

It had taken a small sum of gold to see his captain released, but it had been worth it once that reliable man had revealed the whereabouts of the profits of their smuggled goods. Now with the sum Adrian had given him for the ship and its cargo, Austin had emerged from financial difficulty long enough to contemplate his empty future.

He watched as Harley Sotheby strode up the newly laid walkway to the front door. The young man seemed perturbed about something, and remembering that he was expected to return from London with his sisters last evening, Austin hurried to greet him. The letter could wait.

Harley grasped his friend's hand with relief. He had not spent an easy minute since his sisters had revealed Aubree's intentions, and he had great difficulty facing his lordship with the news. But Heathmont's stern features demanded information, and he, alone, had the right to act.

"Your sisters are well?" Austin questioned politely, leading the younger man toward his study, out of hearing of nosy servants.

"Quite well. Their tongues did not stop once on the entire journey." Harley entered the study and heard the door close behind him. He looked up to meet Heath's anxious gaze.

"And Aubree?" the earl demanded.

Harley met his gaze with sympathy, but no fear. "She stayed behind, or so I thought, until Anna informed me she had accepted another invitation. It seems an old friend of her father's invited her to his home in Sussex for a house party."

Somehow, those words did not relax the tension in Heath's taut shoulders. He shoved the lock of hair from his forehead and waited impatiently for the rest. "The man's name?" he inquired evenly.

"Killarnon."

The name resounded like a curse spoken in church on Sunday, and the reverberations of Austin's response sent the spiders in the rafters into retreat.

Harley attempted to calm the furious earl. "He is a friend of the duke's, you cannot deny that. His intentions very well could be innocent."

"The most notorious rake of the century and his intentions might be innocent! Don't be a damned fool, Sotheby. The only thing that can be said about the man is that he leaves marriageable women alone. I'll have to go get her." Austin threw the glass from the table at the fire and strode toward the door.

"Heath, curse you, wait!" Harley hastened to intervene. "What can you do? Isn't Eversly still at large?"

Austin had scarcely given that worthy a thought since his disappearance and did not linger on him now. "He's not been seen. He's out of the country by now, which is where Killarnon will wish he was when I get through with him."

"I'll go with you, then." Harley grabbed his hat and hurried in the earl's lunging footsteps.

"I'll travel faster alone."

With angry impatience, Heath brushed aside all protests from both his neighbor and his groom as the eager stallion was saddled. Sussex was a long, hard ride from Devon. He had very little chance of making it in time, but he would have the satisfaction of grinding Killarnon into the ground when he got there.

Though weak and looking wan, Aubree felt better in the morning, and she descended the stairs in full determination of enjoying her day thoroughly. The sun had even condescended to shine, howbeit weakly, and it was an ideal day for a jaunt across the countryside.

The other guests were not so partial to that entertainment, but Killarnon and several of the younger gentlemen agreed a ride would be pleasant, and of necessity, several of the ladies fell in with the scheme. A picnic basket was prepared, and the party planned to make a day of it.

The cold drove them in by midafternoon, but spirits were high. Card tables were produced for the whist players, backgammon boards for those so inclined, and another group provided entertainment at the spinet. In front of a cozy fire with cups of hot toddy or something slightly stronger for the gentlemen, they made a merry company.

Except for Aubree. The toddy made her head spin, and the familiar pangs of nausea struck again. She concealed her distress, but by dinnertime she was prepared to call it a day. Only by gritting her teeth could she force herself to change into evening dress and join the other guests.

By delicately picking at the ample array of delicacies presented at the table Aubree managed to keep rein on her rebellious stomach. Perhaps the nervous strain of first London and now this new setting had conspired to upset her normally healthy system. Or perhaps Killarnon's cook used spices more liberally than she was accustomed to. Whatever the reason, by the end of the evening Aubree was fully determined to return to Southridge the next day. Home was the only place to be when feeling ill.

Lord Killarnon spent the evening in solicitous attendance on his young guest and bent lingeringly over her hand when she announced her intention of retiring early.

"You are absolutely correct, my dear. When in the country, we must certainly learn to keep country hours. The day has been a long and pleasant one and we must all think of our beds with pleasure. I trust you are feeling better tonight?"

Aubree murmured something reassuring and escaped. She disliked causing a scene by announcing her intention of leaving in the morning. Perhaps she could speak to his lordship privately before then. She certainly could not do it while all the guests stared upon her as they did.

Without the need to untangle and brush and plait her hair, Aubree was prepared for bed quickly. Matilda's hovering solicitude had a depressing effect, and she sent the maid away. After the prior night, the poor woman needed her sleep.

Aubree snuggled beneath the down comforter and tried to push all else from her mind. The room was warm and the bed was soft and she should need no assistance in seeking the welcome bliss of sleep. Her stomach stirred uneasily, but not so badly as the night before. Yet sleep would not come.

Those nights she had spent beside Austin came back to haunt her. While she was awake, she could ignore the memories of his lean frame lying next to hers or the touch of his bare leg, but when she drifted toward sleep, she would search out the comfort of his strong arms and wake instantly at the emptiness encountered.

Near tears at the impossibility of ever finding comfort again, Aubree heard the scratch on her door with dazed bewilderment. Without any other warning, the door eased open and a shadow carrying a bed candle slipped through, closing the door gently behind him.

Aubree nearly cried out until she recognized the face in the candle's glow as Lord Killarnon's. Still puzzled but not frightened, she made room for him to sit on the edge of the bed as he set the candle on the bedside table. He was in his dressing gown, and without the props of high collars, starched cravats, and padded shoulders to hide his sagging flesh, he appeared nearly as old as her father. Aubree smiled at the comparison. The duke had never come to sit at her bedside when she was ill.

"Lord Killarnon, you really did not have to concern yourself about me. I will be quite fine in the morning."

His lordship paid little heed to this nonsense. The lace of Aubree's gown barely concealed the swelling globes of her breasts, and only with great difficulty did he raise his eyes to meet hers.

"You are of great concern to me, my dear. I have watched your father's neglect of you with sadness, but he is an unhappy man, and I did not interfere. But now I see you without your young husband, and I cannot help but offer you my sympathy. So often these things do not work out, but you must learn to make the best of them."

His hand stroked her hair, and he sat uncomfortably close, but Aubree found nothing wrong in this. Here was a friend who would listen to her plight and perhaps explain what best she ought to do. If only she knew where to begin.

"I am honored by your thoughts, sir, and I would be most grateful for your advice. Could you arrange some time when we might speak alone in the morning?" she inquired.

Killarnon chuckled and gazed down into the innocence of those great green eyes. "You have so much to learn, young one. Let me teach you."

His head bent to sample her lips, and his hand tightened its grip on her shoulders as he pressed her closer.

The shock of this embrace held Aubree momentarily frozen, but she recovered quickly. Jerking her head away, she shoved at his chest.

"Sir! I am a married woman!" She struggled to elude his entrapping hands but Killarnon held her firmly.

He smiled gently and raised his long fingers to her slender jaw. "I know, my dear, that makes you free to enjoy your pleasures where you find them. Don't you see?"

His grip was relentless as he tasted of her lips again, holding her head firmly so she could not escape him. Only moments before, Aubree had been longing for a man's arms around her, but her stomach churned in revulsion at this corruption of her dreams. She twisted her head away, but now his knowledgeable fingers came to rest on her breast, kneading it with rapturous longing.

She opened her mouth to scream, but he pushed her back among the comforters, smothering her with his kisses.

"Do not cry out, dear one. The scandal would only reach your husband's ears and delight the gossips. Relax, and let me show you how good I can be to you."

He groped at her bodice and the touch of his scaly fingers against her skin gave Aubree the strength to shove him away and roll out from beneath his clutches.

She flew toward the door, but her bare toes caught in the loose rug, and she started to tumble.

Strong arms caught her up, and she found herself pressed full length against Killarnon's barely clothed body. As his hand pulled aside her bodice, she started to scream.

34

The immense bay stallion carried its weary rider to the grove of trees opening onto the great lawns of the mansion ahead. Both horse and rider had reached the extremes of exhaustion after covering the frozen ground of the width of England in less time than either had ever attempted before. The damp cold of the night air was scarcely noticeable through the heat of their sweating bodies.

Austin gazed in dismay at the brick walls rising vertically from sculptured grounds. Killarnon's country house was of recent vintage, with none of the charm of the older estates. Its raw walls sported no sturdy vines or protective shrubbery. Only one sturdy oak remained of the forest that had once existed here.

The blank gaze of rows of symmetrical windows presented an insurmountable problem. Austin had no idea behind which one Aubree might lie. He had not even the chance of throwing pebbles against the panes to attract her attention. That left only one alternative and not a promising one.

Glancing down at his rumpled, sweat-stained clothes, Austin wondered what the butler would say when he pounded upon the doors demanding entrance. He would most likely send for the local constabulary, particularly since it seemed the household had retired for the night.

Given no other choice, Austin marched up the lawn, favoring his weaker leg only slightly after the exertion. The thought of that decrepit old man holding Aubree in his arms gave him the strength to move mountains if necessary. He would dismantle the place brick by brick to find her.

The scream that split the air caused Austin's heart to lurch violently and sent him scrambling in the direction of the side of the house. Austin did not need to stop to identify the source of the scream. In his state of mind, there could be only one source. And it came from one of the rooms shaded by the old oak tree.

Holding her tight against his length, Killarnon forced Aubree's head back and muffled her screams with the thrust of his tongue. His rapacious fingers found the soft peak of her breast and played it with skillful aplomb. He had much experience in taming skittish fillies and had no doubt that he could bring this one into hand. Few men possessed the patience to woo a woman properly, and he found most women remarkably eager to accept his favors once they learned his skill. Already, he felt this one weakening.

Aubree fought not only Killarnon's invading hands, but her own nausea, and she was losing both battles. As the bodice of her gown slipped downward beneath nimble fingers and he moved the heat of his breath from her mouth to her throat, the remains of her dinner surged upward in a river of burning bile.

Austin chose that moment to kick his boot through the paned window. He had watched Aubree's struggles with growing fury as he climbed to the end of the tree branch and was fully prepared to murder her molester with his bare hands. The sight that greeted him as he entered the room presented a different predicament.

Killarnon had stepped away from his victim in disgust, giving Aubree the opportunity to run to the chamberpot. The sound of her retching provided the background music to Austin's entrance, and Killarnon scarcely lifted an eyebrow in surprise. He merely glanced down at his ruined robe and back to the furious earl.

"It seems the lady bears your brat." He spoke with repugnance, eyeing Austin coldly. "I ought to make you pay for that damned window."

Weary to the bone, wrung dry of emotion, Austin contemplated his antagonist with icy cynicism. "I ought to make you pay for my damned wife."

Killarnon shrugged, his gaze taking in the younger man's broad shoulders and knotted fists. The old kerseymere coat and faded breeches fit their owner with snug assurance that no padding disguised muscular arms and legs. He knew better than to argue.

He nodded toward the growing sound of anxious voices in the corridor. "Call me out and your wife's name will be on the tongue of every gossip-monger in the city."

The sound of retching had ceased, and out of the corner of his eye, Austin could see his wife rising to the washbasin. Curtly, he ordered, "Leave us."

Killarnon strode to the door and went out. From the bedchamber, the occupants could hear him reassuring his guests that the lady had been taken ill, and the murmur of voices drifted away.

Unable to assimilate all his thoughts into cohesive action, Austin turned what remained of his attention to Aubree. She had stripped herself of her nightclothes and now vigorously scrubbed at satin flesh with lilac-scented lather. Remembering Killarnon's words, Austin's gaze traced her lovely contours for some indication of motherhood, but none came readily to his eye. In the flickering candlelight, her breasts seemed fuller, heavier perhaps, as she leaned over the basin, but it had been two months since he had seen her like this. His memory and his wishful thinking could easily lead him astray. The hollow between her hipbones did seem rounder, and even in his weariness, his loins responded hungrily to the image, but that was no proof. It was much too soon to tell to the untrained eye.

Austin rummaged through dresser drawers until he found a fresh gown. He lay it on the bed beside her, removed the chamberpot to the corridor, and stuffed the broken window with spare blankets. Then he began to doff his soiled clothing.

Aubree buttoned her shift and stared at her husband with suspicion. She said nothing but moved out of his way as he approached the washbowl. Shivering, she climbed beneath the covers while Austin soaped at his skin. Bronzed flesh gleamed with moisture in the candlelight, and the ripple of muscle beneath his skin took her breath away. She watched with fascination as a soapy rivulet ran through the dark curls of his chest while he dried his back, but he caught it with the linen towel before it trickled below his belt.

The next thing she knew, he had blown out the candle and finished undressing and climbed into bed beside her. All the wrongs he had ever committed came instantly to mind, and Aubree darted out from beneath the covers on the other side of the bed.

"Aubree, don't be a fool. Come back to bed," Austin ordered wearily.

"Not while you're in it," she stated flatly, retreating to the settee beside the fire.

"I have been on horseback for nigh on to two days, and I'm not about to sleep on the floor. I'll be a hell of a lot safer bed companion than Killarnon."

Aubree dragged a blanket and pillow to the settee and arranged them around her, stubbornly refusing to reply.

"You cannot continue to behave like a spoiled brat if you're carrying a child, Aubree. Get up from there before I must drag you back." Austin had his eyes closed and one arm thrown over them, but he knew the mutinous expression on her face without needing to see it.

"Child! What child? Do you think in your enormous conceit that you have fathered a child after those few nights together?" Aubree scoffed. "You may forget your hopes of an heir, milord. I'll not give you the opportunity to try again."

So much for Killarnon's wisdom. He should have known better than to even hope after his experience with Louise. With his luck, he was sterile, and there would never be an heir to Atwood Abbey. Under the circumstances, regardless of his virility or lack of it, there would never be an heir to the abbey. Austin was too tired to argue with the minx.

Amazed by his silence after her challenging cry, Aubree waited nervously for some reaction from the man in her bed. After many anxious minutes, her worries dissolved under the sound of a light, rustling snore from the bed. She punched the uncomfortable pillow and curled up on the tiny cushions and slept.

Austin woke in the middle of the night, his muscles cramped and aching, and tried to orient himself. Memory returned instantly at the sound of light breathing across the room. The fire had gone out and the room had grown cold with the chill from the broken window. He moved noiselessly from the bed and stalked naked across the room.

Without disturbing Aubree's sleep, he lifted her from the settee and carried her to bed. He'd be damned if he'd let the stubborn chit take pneumonia rather than sleep in his bed. After the journey he had just made, he was none too certain he'd let the brat out of his sight again. His hand brushed the cropped curls on the pillow beside him, and he fell promptly to sleep cradling her in the curve of his body.

Aubree woke in the morning to the pangs of hunger in her stomach and the heat of a man's body at her back. She had no vision of Killarnon at all but knew Heath's hold too well, and fury and tears mixed in her heart. Rolling free from his grasp, she snatched the pillow from under his head and beat him roundly with it until he raised a hand in sleepy self-defense.

"You beast! You great, unnatural beast! How dare you! Get out of my bed! Get out of my life! Begone with you!"

Bemused, Austin unfolded himself slowly, the morning sun blinding him to the golden virago railing about his head. He lifted the pillow beside him and wielded it sleepily for a shield as he rolled from the comfort of the mattress.

"You want me to go and leave you with Killarnon?" He yawned, groping for the reason for this attack. A hail of small pillows and clothing greeted this inanity.

"What makes you think you can send me away and then climb in my window and start all over again? Who do you think you are?" Aubree vented weeks of pent-up wrath as Austin staggered toward her. Still holding the pillow, she pummeled furiously at his head and shoulders as he approached.

Austin riposted her blows with his own feathered

shield, finally grasping the grounds for this duel.
"Aubree, if you would only calm down, I could explain everything." His voice was less than calm, though,
its irritation sounding loud against the cheaply constructed walls.

"Explain? I worry myself half into the grave over
your worthless carcass, and you turn me away like a
servant girl you've tired of! Don't explain, clothhead!
Depart!"

Austin swiped harder at the bag of feathers nipping
at his shoulders like a buzzing gnat. A corner of his
pillow burst as it hit the bed, but he paid no heed to
the spray of feathers flying into the air as he swung it
to his defense again.

"I'm your husband, Aubree Elizabeth, and I'll
damned well depart when I've a mind to! You're the
peagoose who got tangled up with that rake Killarnon
in the first place. If you haven't any more sense than
that, I'll be damned if I'll let you out of my sight
again," he roared.

Both pillows had come loose at the seams and the
air was rapidly filling with a snowstorm of tiny white
goose down. They found no purchase on Austin's bare
flesh but clung to his tousled dark hair and brows and
settled in drifts upon Aubree's golden curls and lawn
gown.

"If you hadn't sent me to London in the first place,
I would never have met the cad. Don't preach to me,
Austin Atwood! Get out of my room before I scream
the house down."

Since that was exactly what she was doing, and
looking extremely ridiculous while she did it, this statement struck Austin as immensely funny, and he nearly
doubled up with laughter until she hit him broadside
with her pillow, sending him crashing to the floor. Still
chuckling infuriatingly, he rose and grabbed another
pillow from the settee. With glee, he boxed her ears
soundly with his feathered weapons, disturbing settled
drifts into a blizzard. Aubree screeched in outrage and
renewed her attack.

A small crowd began to gather in the corridor outside. The shrieks and curses muffled only by a thinly paneled door would have attracted attention in any proper household, but the fact that they came from the room of the Countess of Heathmont doubled their curiosity. She had arrived alone. So whose was the male voice resounding so forcibly from within?

Door after door along the corridor opened as the voices within and without disturbed the other sleeping occupants. The small crowd whispered among themselves, the women in shocked, delighted tones, the men with concerned cowardice. Someone ought to interfere; it sounded as if they were coming to blows.

One of the other maids warned Matilda, and she came hurrying down the back stairs from the attic. Recognizing Austin's voice at once, she clasped and unclasped her hands nervously. She had been taught never to disturb her master and mistress when they were together, and rightly so, but never before had they railed at each other like this.

"Damned if that don't sound like Heathmont," one gentleman murmured after one loud male outburst. "We ought to come to the lady's rescue if he's up to his old tricks."

A general murmur of agreement moved through the crowd. Mattie hid her irritation at this stupidity and eased herself into a position at the front of the crowd. She could scarcely be blamed if the gentry intruded, but she could certainly block their views as much as possible with her broad frame.

One brave gentleman grasped the latch and swung open the door, revealing the Earl of Heathmont, clad only in his birthday suit, swinging his deflated pillow ineffectively against the irate blows of his slender countess. Even as they watched, Aubree's pillow split to send a snowstorm whirling about her husband's head.

A drift of feathers blew across the floor in the draft from the open door, and Austin turned to give their audience a lazy lift of his eyebrow. He greeted the maid and her accompaniment nonchalantly.

"Good morning, Mattie," Austin answered her wide-eyed stare without inflection. "Tell the others we'll be down directly, and close the door behind you, there's a good girl."

Aubree had dropped her pillow at Mattie's entrance. Now she stared at the discretely closing door with momentary consternation, until laughter rose in her throat. She gave Austin's long, lanky, and very naked frame a quick glance, and giggles erupted like effervescent champagne.

The sound was balm to his soul and Austin bathed in its beauty. His gaze rested warily on his wife's golden-cropped head. "Does this mean we can kiss and make up?" he inquired hopefully.

Aubree held her mouth to contain her laughter, but she freed it long enough to reply, "Certainly not," before erupting again.

"Right," Austin agreed. Snatching up a sheet, he wrapped it around himself and hollered at the closed door. "Mattie, if you're still there, you can come in now."

Hesitantly, the stout maid peered around the door's edge. The room seemed to have been hit by an early snow, but at least the earl had garbed himself to some extent, and Lady Aubree seemed her normal, cheerful self for a change. Matilda entered cautiously and awaited her orders, leaving the crowd to dissipate in disappointment.

"Has John arrived yet, Mattie?" Austin roamed about the room, snatching up his strewn clothing.

"Just this past hour, milord," Mattie acknowledged.

"Ask him to purloin some clean linen for me, then he can sleep it off and meet up with us later. And if you would, Mattie, see if anything can be done with these. I didn't come attired for a formal visit." He handed her his travel-stained garments.

"Yes, milord." Mattie bobbed a curtsy and hastened to do as commanded.

Aubree stared after her traitorous maid with astonishment. "Anyone would think she was in your employ instead of mine."

"Isn't she?" Austin asked cryptically, searching the washstand for anything that might resemble shaving accoutrements.

"With my money!" Aubree replied indignantly.

Austin lifted an eyebrow and shot her a speculative glance. "Is that where your protest lies?"

"You know that is only part of it." Huffily, she threw open the wardrobe to inspect the gowns Mattie had so carefully pressed for her the day before.

"You had best choose a traveling gown," he warned. "We are leaving for Southridge as soon as we break our fast."

Aubree defiantly contemplated a dainty confection of primrose silk and lace, but common sense overruled. She had no desire whatsoever to stay in this abominable place. Austin would most likely make her travel in whatever she wore, and she would freeze to death. She might desire to murder him, but she held no such death wish for herself. She chose a sensible merino of rich gold with which she could wear the perky bonnet with the dashing feather. He would look like a country squire next to such extravagance.

Mattie reappeared in time to help her mistress dress. She carried freshly laundered linen for Austin and a newly cleaned and pressed coat and breeches. A large staff could work miracles, and John's efficiency in procuring clean clothing wherever he was dated back to their days of traipsing through Portugal with Wellington. It was that particular trait that had elevated John from groom to occasional valet.

Respectably clad at last, Austin swept his gaze approvingly over his wife's attire. The soft wool bodice molded nicely to high, firm curves, but the high neckline prevented any sight of the temptation beneath. If he could not touch, no one else could even look, he thought with satisfaction. The golden tresses curling loosely about her face and throat accentuated her innocent features, but there was nothing innocent in the way she glared at him.

Chuckling, Austin touched a hand to her curls. "I like your hair that way. I can see your face better, and it makes your eyes bigger."

Bewildered, Aubree stood rooted to the spot as Austin turned to open the door to escort her out. She had wanted to make him angry, to hurt him as he had her, but he accepted all her slings and arrows with patience and even admiration. She didn't know whether to be furious or suspicious.

Austin offered his arm, and warily, Aubree accepted it. They had an audience to play for and it would be easier to play it this way. With Austin at her side, she could move through the whispers and stares with self-assurance and composure. His strong arm beneath her fingers gave her all the strength she needed.

Below, as Aubree had feared, many of the guests had gathered in anticipation of their appearance. Austin greeted each by name, a mocking smile on his lips for the prepared quips on the morning's joust.

"Yes, I recommend it highly," he drawled in reply to one such jest. "Always beat your wife with a pillow. Entertaining, educational, and decidedly beneficial. Isn't that so, my dear?" He cocked his head in Aubree's direction.

Her stiff smile melted into a mischievous grin as her eyes met Heath's laughing ones. "Oh, decidedly, my dear," she said mockingly. "Every goose ought to be plucked regularly."

The roar of laughter following this riposte set the mood for the table, and for the first time since Louise's death, Austin was allowed to sit comfortably in the company of his peers. This was not the company he would have chosen, but Killarnon's worldly guests would soon circulate the tale of this episode and generate the first shreds of doubt about his guilt. He had no means of proving himself innocent, but neither was there any evidence of his guilt. Gossip would favor the more interesting story.

However, he steered Aubree from the party with little reluctance. Killarnon had retained the sense to stay out of the way until they departed, and Austin had no intention of lingering for a confrontation. Once Aubree's bags were packed into the landaulet, warm lap robes wrapped tightly about the passengers, and Matilda settled in the open seat beside the driver, Austin gave the signal for them to depart. John would follow later after he and the horses had rested.

Without an audience to entertain, the couple fell into silence. Austin threw his wife surreptitious glances, wondering what went on beneath that pert hat of hers, but he was no closer to the truth now than ever. He understood the reasons for her anger, but he could not fathom her deeper emotions. He would have a price on his head should the duke find they were together. Would that make her happy? Or even angrier? She had certainly showed him no sign of affection. Had he only imagined her feelings earlier? Or had they faded with her stay in London? Perhaps she had learned to enjoy the temptations London had to offer. How did he go about approaching her to find out?

Aubree took his silence for indifference. He had made it evident he did not intend to let her stray, but for what purpose? He showed no interest in her now, asked no questions, did not even scold her for her behavior. He had her money and evidently had no interest in her company; why had he ridden himself to exhaustion to prevent another having her? His question of the night before provided the only clue. He wished to be certain he sired his heir before he allowed her the freedom of a *mariage de convenance*.

Her chin jutted stubbornly at this conclusion. She would not bear a child simply for the sake of his lineage. That could very well mean she would never have children. The thought of Peggy's gurgling baby and the two delightful Adams cherubs brought a teardrop quivering to her eyelash. She wondered if Adrian and Emily were still in Devon, if she would ever see them or their children again. She would have to make herself more at home in Alvan and Peggy's house, perhaps. That meant enduring family gatherings that included her father and his various and assorted haughty relatives, but she would have to learn to be docile if she wished access to her nephew.

But as the carriage rolled on and the churning in her stomach returned, another suspicion gradually began to replace Aubree's previous unhappy thoughts. Austin had told her that he and Louise had not conceived a child in nearly two years of marriage, that relations on just a few nights had very little chance of being fruitful. Alvan and Peggy had been married nearly a year before Peggy became pregnant. And one of the first signs of her pregnancy was morning sickness. So this churning uneasiness every evening could not possibly be what Austin had accused her of. She could not possibly be pregnant.

But if she were not, then something else must seriously be wrong with her. Aubree tried desperately to remember the last time she had needed linens for her bleeding, but she could not. These last months had been such a jumble of ups and downs, it was not surprising if she were a little irregular. But the nausea burning at her stomach and rising in her throat was more than irregular.

As the carriage lurched into a particularly bad rut, Aubree turned green and signaled desperately. Austin yelled for a halt and quickly lifted her from the carriage, awkwardly holding back her skirts and pelisse as she bent beside the road and brought up the remains of their late breakfast. He had been considering stopping for tea, but there seemed little point in it now.

Mattie rushed to moisten cloths in a nearby stream, and between them, they managed to settle Aubree comfortably in the carriage again, none the worse for wear except for the embarrassment. The driver watched the road with more heed, and they proceeded with less haste than before.

Inside the carriage, Austin considered his wife's pale cheeks with concern. "You did not seem prone to travel sickness the last time we made this journey. Perhaps I should send for a physician when we reach Southridge."

Curling up beneath the warmth of the furred robe, Aubree considered her husband's countenance through lowered lashes. Her nausea had all but disappeared again, but now Austin seemed visibly distracted. Poor man, he was probably unaccustomed to watching ladies lose their meals. But he had been heroic in his efforts to help, so she ought to reply with civility.

"I am fine now. I think something I ate the other day must have disagreed with me. I am sorry if I disturbed you," she murmured.

Austin ran his hand through his hair and looked at her with indecision. She was pale, but there was no fever in her bright eyes. A suspicion of a smile lurked at the corners of her mouth, and he wanted to shake her until he had the truth from her, but he was in no position to demand confidences.

"We'll let your aunt decide. She's more experienced than I at these things. You have not been feeling like this for long?"

"Only since I left London," she reassured him. "I am quite well. Please, will you tell me of your sister and her family? Are they still in Devon?" As long as he was talking, she would extract what information she could from him.

"No, I'm sorry, they sailed last month. I had hoped to keep them for the winter, but circumstances . . ." Austin stopped and started again. "They left a letter for you. I thought my mother sent it on."

"Perhaps you did not explain to her that I would not be returning to read it," Aubree suggested mildly.

"No. Yes. Confound it, Aubree." Austin stared at her distractedly, his hair now in a rakish tangle upon his forehead as his eyes burned blue and fierce. "We must talk."

"About what? About how you had to use my inheritance to save the abbey? I really don't feel well enough for such a discussion. I think I will nap awhile, if you don't mind." She turned her head away from him and closed her eyes. She really did not feel well enough to handle such a topic. She would prefer to do it with ax in hand.

"Very well," Austin answered curtly, "but if you would overcome your childish habit of ignoring what doesn't please you, such as letters from solicitors, then other unpleasantness might be avoided. Sleep on that thought, my dear."

And of course, she couldn't.

35

Lady Clara welcomed them warmly, but she showed a particular delight in Austin's arrival. She clucked and bustled and smiled happily as she ushered her guests to their respective rooms.

Pleading weariness, Aubree retired shortly after dinner, leaving Austin to catch up on family gossip with Aunt Clara. Once Aubree was safely out of the way, her usually befuddled aunt turned serious.

"What has his grace done this time?" she demanded of the handsome earl as he entered the drawing room. "I thought certainly that Aubree had chosen a husband who would not cater to Ashbrook's whims, but it seems I was wrong. Am I?"

Austin leaned against the lovely Adam mantel and gazed in bemusement at the gray-haired lady primly reposing in the straight-backed chair by the fire. Her soft, fluttery exterior evidently hid a spine of steel. No wonder she, alone, had kept Aubree in line.

"There is more to it than meets the eye, my lady. I must act in what I believe to be Aubree's best interests," Austin replied stiffly.

Clara gave a muffled noise of disbelief. "Have you consulted Aubree about your decision?"

"It was my decision to make. I told her all she needed to know. To tell her more would be more painful than helpful."

"Oh, fustian! You are protecting his grace from his daughter or vice versa, no doubt. There is no winning that battle. They worship each other and show it by fighting like brother and sister. It is Ashbrook's fault, I suppose. After he lost both his wife and his son, he cut himself off from everyone, including Aubree. He cannot bear to think of losing her, so he attempts not to think of her at all. Quite impossible, I must say, but the duke is a stubborn man."

Lady Clara swung her fan nervously. The heat from the fire reddened her cheeks, but she remained seated where she could stare at her niece's husband.

Heath gave a shrug of acknowledgment. "That may be so, but I see no way out of it. I am not even certain Aubree wants out of it. She has asked for her pets to be returned here."

Lady Clara grew indignant. "Don't you dare! That child needs you more than those animals. She adores you. Her letters from the abbey were the happiest I have ever received from her. If you have sent her away, you have done the worst possible thing in the world for her. Do you have any idea of how many relatives she has been placed with in her brief life? I daresay I could list half the aristocracy in England. They all sent her away for one spurious reason or another. And, of course, her father does nothing else. You are her husband. If you don't find some way to keep her, I think I shall be tempted to take a horsewhip to the both of you."

Austin chuckled slightly. "I don't doubt that in the least, my lady, but it is not so easy as you make it seem."

"How much difficulty is there in marching up those stairs and telling Aubree why she cannot return to your home?"

"I am not so certain she will listen." Austin grew thoughtful, trying to picture the outcome of such a confrontation. "And if she did, I am not so certain that she will react wisely. You truly do not know what you ask."

"Do you love her?" Aunt Clara demanded abruptly, her old eyes following Austin's every expression.

He smiled sadly. "I can answer that one without hesitation. I love her too much to wish to see her hurt in any way, but I am given only a choice of pains to inflict upon her."

"Then let her make the choice." She laid her fan down with finality.

Austin nodded, accepting this wisdom. He gazed upon Aubree's elderly aunt with respect and affection. "Your judgment is sounder than mine when it comes to Aubree. We are both lucky to have you."

Clara's cheeks grew a little pinker, and she waved a dismissal at him. "Go on with you, then. If that girl does not choose you over her father, my judgment means nothing."

Austin bowed out and took the steps to their chambers two at a time. He had been wanting to talk to Aubree about his predicament for some while. The opportunity would never be better, and her aunt's words gave the encouragement he needed. He had no desire to antagonize Aubree's family or alienate her from them in any way, but Lady Clara was right. The choice was Aubree's.

He knocked lightly at her door, not wishing to wake her if she slept already. When he received no reply, the disappointment weighed heavily on him, and Austin could not resist at least reassuring himself that she slept well. He eased the door open and stared blankly at her empty bed. Untouched. Her nightdress neatly laid across it.

Austin swore to himself, but only a second's consideration was needed to realize her whereabouts. With flying feet, he raced down the corridor, taking the back stairs as the fastest route, nearly knocking down one of the maids in the servants' hall as he rushed out. She grinned at his haste. The sight of an earl leaving by the back door would make a fine tale to repeat in the kitchen.

Austin walked hurriedly down the unlighted garden walk. Bare branches scraped against the garden wall and tossed about overhead in the chilly wind. In the summer, this had been a dense haven of greenery and shade, but now only a few stubborn leaves clung to twigs of bushes and trees, frost already tracing a pattern of white along their skeletons. Austin saw none of his surroundings, but focused on the small light flickering in the window at the end of the path.

The Southridge stable was not nearly so elaborate as the abbey's. During the summer, all sight of it was obscured by the garden greenery. But its dark solidity loomed ahead against the winter sky, and the small candle flame in the window told of wakeful life.

Austin paused in the partially opened doorway, not wishing to startle the stable's occupants. Propping his hand against the doorjamb and allowing his racing heart to quiet, he watched the scene inside with quiet joy.

Aubree sat amid the straw in the first box, a lap full of kittens crawling about her skirts and up her shoulder, batting at the fringe of her shawl, tumbling over each other in play. These weren't the proudly bred Siamese she had left in Devon, but simple tiger farm cats, accustomed to barn life. The mother cat sat nearby, tail twitching watchfully, but not protesting this invasion. Candlelight illuminated Aubree's golden curls as she bent to untangle one of the furry balls from her shawl.

When she looked up again, she smiled a welcome at Austin's long shadow framed in the doorway. She could not see his face, but the wide shoulders in their unfashionable kerseymere coat and the long legs forever sprawled in some casual attitude betrayed him. She held a purring kitten against her cheek and gestured for him to enter.

"You were looking for me?" she asked softly, her eyes gleaming in the semidarkness.

The mother cat rose anxiously as Austin entered the stall and lowered himself to a seat on a bale of hay, but when he did not object to her lying across his lap, she made herself comfortable there. Austin scratched absently at her head while he gazed upon Aubree. How did one go about broaching a subject certain to cause argument in a setting as peaceful as this one?

"You are feeling better?" He evaded the issue a little longer, wanting to seal the serene expression on her face in his memory.

"I am well," she replied politely, betraying no curiosity.

"Your Aunt Clara tells me I have wronged you by trying to protect you. She seems to think you are strong enough to make your own decisions."

That awoke a flicker of interest behind those great green eyes, but her expression remained unfathomable. "You have already made your position clear. You think I am too young. Everyone's entitled to their own opinions."

What he wanted to do was to take her in his arms and hold her tight and whisper words of love in her ear and forget all else, but Austin could not afford even this small luxury. He had hurt her very badly, and now he must pay the price. Only caution now might keep him from paying forever.

"You are young," he agreed slowly, "and in some things I may have more experience than you, but you are the only one who knows how you feel or what you want. I have no right to take those choices from you."

Aubree cuddled a kitten in her arms and returned his gaze with suspicion. "Isn't it a little too late to discover that?"

Ignoring this, Austin plunged on. "Your father is carrying a warrant for my arrest, Aubree. If he discovers I am here with you, he can have me charged with smuggling and locked behind bars."

She showed no sign of shock, only a small frown of anger. "Why would my father want you arrested?"

"Didn't you hear what I said, Aubree? I'm a smuggler, a felon in the eyes of the law. On top of everything else, you're married to a criminal, Aubree." Austin strove desperately to make her see the seriousness of the situation.

"I know that," she answered calmly. "I'm not totally naïve. How else would one go about making a fortune in six months' time with a ship? Everyone would be sailors if it were that easy. I believe I knew it when the navy officers delivered Adrian and said they must return to catch a smuggler. But if you were not on the ship, how can they arrest you?"

Austin brushed his hair from his brow and stared at her perplexedly. "It doesn't bother you that at any moment you may be exposed to society as the wife of a smuggler?"

"Austin, half society is engaged in immoral flummery of one sort or another. I neither condemn nor condone it. The only sin seems to be getting caught at it. As far as I am concerned, there are far worse crimes than smuggling. If Napoleon is fool enough to think he can keep us out of Europe simply by saying we can't use his ports, then he must be all about in his wits. And you would certainly think the navy would appreciate fine wine from France, and I'm not averse to good lace and silk myself. What I do object to is your endangering your life and my father involving himself in what evidently is none of his business. Now tell me how he can have you arrested?"

Austin heard this speech with varying degrees of astonishment, laughter, and delight. She was still delightfully naïve, but certainly not stupid. "Have I ever told you how much I love you?" he offered inanely in reply.

This time, Aubree nearly did fall over with the shock, and she searched his face hastily for mockery. Midnight eyes held hers with no evidence of ridicule, and their intensity burned a searing path to her soul. She gulped and sought frantically for some response.

"You are quizzing me," she murmured, looking away.

"I am not," Austin denied firmly. "I daresay I have loved you from the very first moment I laid eyes on you. I cannot think why else I made such a cake of myself as to walk out with a green girl onto a dance floor. But I never really thought about it until you sent me that package of shorn hair. I nearly died. I thought for certain you had done something abominable like taking a boat to India or a camel to the Orient or Lord only knows what. I really ought to thrash you for scaring me like that, but I'm not certain I have that right anymore. I wanted to wait until I had earned the right to ask you to be my wife, but it has become too important to me to know how you feel right now. I am not wealthy, Aubree, but it is my money rebuilding the abbey, not yours. You may put yours in trust for your children for all I care. I cannot offer you a lavish home, but it is mine. You know the worst about me by now, Aubree. Do you still wish to be my wife?"

During this speech, Aubree had slowly tucked the kittens, one by one, into their box, and the mother leapt from her perch to join them. Her mind whirled helplessly beneath these words she had never hoped to hear, could not believe she was hearing now. There was so much left unsaid, so much to be explained, but somehow none of it seemed important any longer. He was asking her to trust him, and she loved him too much not to. If she could not believe him, she could never believe in anything or anyone again.

With wonder, she finally gazed up into his eyes. She had once wished she could hear him ask her to be his wife and had wondered how he would do it. She had never dreamed it would be in the stable among the straw, but she should have known. His eyes seemed to see nothing but her, and she had to smile at his typical single-mindedness.

"I have never stopped wishing to be your wife, Austin, only I want to be a wife who stays by your side." She ducked her head and stared at her hands. "I know I am too young and have not the experience you prefer in a woman, but I want to learn. Austin, I . . ."

Before she could finish her sentence, Austin had slid to his knees and wrapped his arms around her, forcing her to look up to meet his gaze. "Do not tell me what I prefer, halfling," he whispered fiercely. "You are what I want and I will take no other."

Aubree's arms flew about his waist as he kissed her, and tears flooded her eyes as he held her where she belonged, at last. She tasted the hunger in his kiss, but also the love and the longing, and she returned them full measure. Her fingers clung to the corded muscle of his back as he pressed her close, and she could feel the wild pounding of his heart next to hers.

"I have loved you for so long, Austin," she whispered almost incoherently as his lips finally released her to spread their heat across her cheek and hair. "I sometimes thought you didn't even know I existed."

"Little fool." He could feel her slightness in his arms, trace each curve and count every rib beneath the light wool of her gown, so well did he remember the feel of her. They had not come to the end of their problems, by any means, but he could endure anything in the security of her love.

He ran his fingers into her tousled curls and tilted her head back. His smile bathed her face as he gazed down upon her with no small amount of wonder. "Knowing everything you do, you will still agree to be my wife?"

Aubree smiled at his doubt. "Until death do us part, milord, and most likely into the hereafter. I am a very stubborn person when I make up my mind."

Austin grinned briefly, then sobered. "It is very possible that I will end up in the Tower, my love. Until I straighten things out with your father, perhaps you had better stay here with your aunt. I have no fear of prison, but I would not heap more scandal on you."

"How you will persuade my father to tear up those warrants is your decision to make, my lord, but whether I care to risk scandal or not is my decision. You once yelled at me for interfering in your affairs, but it seems I have equal right to protest if this is your reason for sending me away," she reminded him.

Gently, Austin stood and lifted her to her feet. His hand held hers, fearing to let it go. "Perhaps we should come to an understanding, then. From now on, we will not hide anything from each other, but let each make his own decisions based on all the facts. Agreed?"

"Agreed." Daringly, Aubree lifted her hand to his bronzed cheek, caressing the hard knot of his muscle along his jaw. It relaxed beneath her touch, and she stood on her toes to kiss his cheek. "Now will you give me all the facts?"

"Witch." Austin caught her up and kissed her thoroughly before returning her to her feet. "Let us confer somewhere warmer, if you please. Your nose will soon be turning an enticing shade of blue if we do not."

She stuck her tongue out at him and, lifting her skirts, ran unerringly over the crumbled stones of the garden path toward home. Hampered by the need to close up the stable and pick his way along unfamiliar paths, Austin did not catch up with her until they had almost reached the house. The sound of her giggles lifted his hopes more than her words of affection.

Words might lie, but Aubree's laughter came from the heart. He swung her up in his arms and proceeded to carry her past the shocked footman up the stairs to their chambers.

It was long into the night before Aubree had all the facts of the impounding of Austin's ship and his reckless stealing of it from beneath the navy's nose. With the evidence gone, the arrest warrants might be moot, but Austin feared the worst unless he had time to mend his bridges with the duke.

With concern, he traced the black circles under Aubree's eyes. He had not dared take her to bed, not yet, not until she knew the full extent of the problem. If, as she said, she were not pregnant, it would be better if they took no chances yet. Aubree might decide she could live with a jailbird, but their child would have no such choice. Instead, he sat in a chair beside the fire, and Aubree curled sleepily in his lap, her head upon his shoulder.

"There is still the chance I might lose the abbey, my love, and spend the rest of my days behind bars, or worse. You must see that it would be wisest for me to persuade your father of my suitability as a husband first."

The weight of these last few months had flown, leaving Aubree light-headed. She did not think she could rise from Austin's arms had she wanted, and she did not want to. The desires he had taught her were there, but buried beneath a layer of drowsiness and well-being. If he would but touch her breast, she would turn eagerly into his arms, but she enjoyed the moment as it was. Perhaps she ought to tell him what she suspected, but the time did not seem right.

She yawned and curled closer to his warmth. "If my father has not answered your letters before this, he will not do so now. You might catch him at Castle Ashbrook if you wish to make the journey, but I cannot imagine how you will prove your suitability without me or the abbey. If the sheriff has dismissed the charges against you in Blanche's death, and you are restoring the house, and you have no ship left, I cannot see how he could object to our marriage. We will flee to the Americas if he insists on being stubborn. Live in a cottage by the shore," she finished sleepily.

"You would, too, wouldn't you?" Austin brushed her brow with his lips and lifted her in his arms prior to rising from the chair. "And I daresay you'd make footmen of the Indians and train turkeys to talk." She giggled softly as he stood up and carried her toward the bed. "But in the meantime, you had better sleep on this decision. I will not leave until you are ready."

"I want to go home," she murmured as he lay her upon the bed.

"Then so you shall, my love." He kissed her eyelids and hurried from the room before his resistance weakened.

36

They rose and met in the garden so early in the morning that the house still seemed asleep. The frost on the grass crackled beneath their feet as they walked lightly down the lane toward the vicarage, and their breaths froze in the air.

Aubree swung her husband's hand as they hurried through the morning air. All signs of the prior day's illness had disappeared and her eyes sparkled with merriment as she met Austin's.

She came to a halt and slid her arms unashamedly about his neck and stood on her toes to kiss him fully.

Austin clapped her small, bundled figure close and warmed his heart on the intensity of her love. To have her come to him like this was too new and exciting an experience to not savor every minute of it. But when he set her down on the ground again, his expression was grave.

"You are certain the vicar will not object?"

"No! Why should he? He enjoys sounding pompous before an audience, and it is not often he has an earl to preach before. And if you are worried I am having second thoughts, you don't know me very well."

Since that was just exactly what he was worrying, Austin gave her a sheepish grin and set his feet in motion again. He knew her well enough, all right, he just could not yet believe his good fortune. He wanted it shouted to the world. He could scarcely suppress the urge to go running through the streets yelling, "She loves me!" at the top of his lungs. He had never felt so thoroughly young and foolish in all his life. And he loved it.

Aubree swept Austin a brilliant smile as she tripped lightly over the stile and onto the vicar's grounds. His eyes had turned the sparkling summer blue she loved, and his teeth flashed white against his sun-darkened skin as he caught her stare. All traces of bitterness had melted from the lines upon his face, and he laughed with a new joy as he swung her up in his arms just for the sheer pleasure of it.

"I love you, Mrs. Atwood," he whispered against her ear before he set her down again.

"Fie on you, sir, to treat a poor girl so." Aubree made a pretty pout. "And it is time enough and past that you be giving me your name before the whole world knows what a wicked man you are." She darted from beneath his hand as he grabbed for her and ran laughing down the lane.

Alexa's father looked quite astonished when the servant led the laughing countess and her husband into his study, but he agreed readily to their request. Why should a couple not repeat their wedding vows? It seemed an excellent example for many. Perhaps he could make a sermon of it. There had been many a time he had wished to preach a sermon at the hoyden-ish Lady Aubree. He could no more resist this opportunity than metal could resist lodestone.

And so it was that the Earl and Countess of Heathmont stood at the altar of the small village church before a country vicar to repeat the wedding vows they had not meant to keep on the first occasion.

As the words, "Wilt thou love, comfort, honor, and keep her in sickness and in health, and forsaking all others, keep thee only unto her, so long as ye both shall live?" echoed through the tiny church, tears formed in Aubree's lashes. She could not deny the fierceness and intensity of Austin's eyes as they met hers and the forcefulness of his "I will" as it resounded through the room. This time, there was no doubt in either of their minds as they repeated their vows out loud. Whatever the future might bring, they would meet it as one.

Afterward, the vicar wanted to chat, but the couple had eyes only for each other. Reluctantly, he accepted the earl's generous gift and watched them walk away more slowly than they had arrived. The solemnity of the occasion had even impressed this irrepressible duo.

But as they drew closer to the welcoming warmth of Southridge, Austin's thoughts took another direction and he gazed hungrily upon his newly promised wife. Bundled up in a tawny-gold wool pelisse with fur trim that succeeded in hiding all her lovely curves, Aubree still managed to appear as delectably feminine as any man could desire. And the bewitching light of her eyes as she looked up to him told him her thoughts did not stray far from his.

" 'Tis a pity your aunt will be up and expecting us," Austin murmured regretfully.

Aubree nodded, her thoughts traveling on to another obstacle. "And that your son already has his days and nights mixed up and only leaves me comfortable in the mornings."

Austin came to a dead stop and swung around to stare at her, his eyes wild and uncomprehending. "My *what?*"

Remembering that she had not quite yet imparted that information to him, Aubree glanced slyly up at him. The look of sheer startlement upon his aristocratic visage was a joy to see.

"Well, it could be a daughter, I suppose, but the first one really ought to be a son, I believe. Boys are so devilish difficult, you know, I would prefer to concentrate on just the one for a while. Don't you agree?" she asked innocently.

"The devil, you say!" Austin exclaimed vehemently. "Aubree Elizabeth, you told me . . ." He stumbled, not certain at all what she had told him. Lost, totally bewildered, he ran his hand through the hair on his brow and stared at her with growing hope.

"I was mistaken," she informed him gleefully. "I have thought about it and thought about it and there can only be the one answer. Act-u-al-ly," she drew the word out tantalizingly, "if my calculations are at all right—and I never was very good with figures—it seems you might be a father by . . ." She mentally counted forward again, checking her fingers. "By June. You know what that means, don't you?"

Utterly flummoxed and beyond grasping even the simplest thought, Austin shook his head in confusion. June! By Jupiter, June! A father! By June. His mind whirled with the astonishment of it.

Aubree laughed, curling her gloved hand within the warm strength of his. "It means, my lord, that you never had a chance."

And as the sun came out from behind a cloud to shine upon his face and brighten the day to glorious gold, he understood. He'd never had a chance. Austin turned his face up to the sky and crowed with laughter as he hugged her to him. June! He must have caught her that very first time. Or she had caught him. Totally impossible. Absolutely outrageous. Preposterous and absurd. And perfect.

He swung her around until they were both dizzy and giggling as if they were tipsy. Then, after covering her face with kisses, Austin marched them toward the door. If they could not have their honeymoon until the early hours of the morrow, he would spill his joy to the world today.

But when they entered the house, the butler helped them with their coats and intoned mournfully, "Lady Clara sends her regrets but she has been called to town and will not be back until luncheon. She asks that you make yourself at home."

Austin's gaze flew to Aubree's and the ripple of

conspiracy between them was almost visible as he deadpanned, "That's quite all right, Bothwell. Lady Aubree is weary after our walk and needs to rest."

Beneath the butler's steady gaze, the earl offered his arm with supreme dignity to his lady, who could barely stifle her giggles. Austin bent her a severe look and formally escorted her up the stairs for the benefit of any watching. Arriving at his chamber door, he quickly glanced up and down the corridor, then flung open the door and swept her abruptly into his arms.

"Now, my lady," he whispered wickedly, "you are at my mercy." Her marched into his chambers and, slamming the door behind him, proceeded toward the wide bed.

Aubree shrieked with laughter as he tumbled with her to the mattress and began assaulting her face with kisses.

"Shush, my lovely, you will tell the whole household what we do at this disgraceful hour," Austin murmured as he nibbled at her ear and his hand located the tempting globe of her breast.

"Horrors," Aubree replied without fear. She drank in the wonder of his dark face hovering over her once more and slid her fingers into the tumble of his dark curls. As his hand nimbly unfastened the pearl buttons of her gown, she felt a familiar heat rise within her, and her cheeks colored at her eagerness.

Austin grinned at this evidence of maidenly modesty. "I think I shall enjoy teaching you to be my courtesan, my dear. You'll not remain innocent forever." His hand found the rest of the buttons and slid beneath the hampering cloth to cup her chemise-clad breast in his palm.

"If I am your courtesan, then you will need no others." Brazenly, Aubree plucked the knot from his cravat and sought the hardness of his chest beneath.

Austin's kiss was fierce and hungry as he took her mouth and plundered its treasures, claiming all for his own. Aubree surrendered gladly, knowing he had won her with the strength of his love. He carried her heart and protected it gladly, and for that, she would give him all he asked and more.

They undressed each other carefully, savoring each evelation uncovered. In the morning light, the roped muscles of Austin's shoulders and chest seemed some-ow more magnificent than she remembered, and Aubree traced their pattern beneath his skin with awe. She felt shy as Austin finally slid her chemise over her head, leaving her naked of all else but garters and stockings, but his gaze was worshipful as he touched her nakedness.

When he removed the last of her garments and she ay stretched beneath his half-dressed frame, Aubree elt the power of love rising within her and she basked n its flame. She wanted him to enjoy the new fullness of her breasts and the lushness that she felt already ounding her belly. As his hands and gaze spoke their admiration, she flourished beneath his touch, and her onging grew stronger.

"My God, you are so lovely, Aubree," he whis-ered in amazement, caressing the creamy satin of her skin, memorizing the perfect curve of her hip with his and. "I cannot believe I have all this and be blessed with what you carry here, too." His hands reverently troked the slight curve of her abdomen where his hild had begun to grow.

"I want to make you as happy as I am, Austin." Aubree held out her arms and he came into them and heir kiss removed any barriers that remained.

When Austin rose to remove the last of his clothing, Aubree could not help but watch in awe. In the bright unshine, she could see how magnificently he was made, and the sight made her tremble.

But as he lay down beside her and held her against is heat, the fear dissolved in her longing for the act of passion he had taught her. She kissed him urgently, er hands clinging desperately to his back as Austin ressed her close. He tortured her with his slowness, making her wait while he caressed those places that made her weep and beg for more, arousing a need within her so great she thought she might die from it.

And then he was inside her, righting her world and making it quake with the thunderous rhythm of his assion. She had not remembered the moment so clearly

as this, and the beauty and violence of it rose u
within her until she felt the explosion that sent he
beyond her body and into his, where they drifted i
some sweet bliss that could not be sustained foreve
but must constantly be renewed.

The aftershock was quite as nice, and Aubree smile
peacefully as Austin eased his weight from her, keep
ing her safe within the shelter of his arms.

"How did I ever live without you, my love?" Austi
murmured in wonderment, breathing in the scent o
lilacs. Her soft weight pressed against his side had a
amazing effect on his senses, among other things.

"With great difficulty, evidently." Aubree nibble
at his ear and pressed herself temptingly against him
enjoying the effect she had on him.

Austin groaned and twisted so that she lay sprawle
on top of him in a most compromising position. "I ca
see my difficulty has only just begun. You will becom
a demanding, greedy wench if I do not take seriou
steps to keep you in the traces."

"Atwood Abbey will never lack for heirs, then,
she murmured as she felt him harden against her thigh

Austin caught her hips and held her firmly as h
thrust against her. "I trust our son will be reasonabl
about this. I have lost too much time to make it u
quickly. It was most incautious of him to be in such
hurry."

Aubree bit her lip to keep from crying out he
eagerness as he teased her unmercifully with his hands
She was aware that his gaze rested on her breasts wit
fascination, and a slow blush of color rose betwee
them. "In a few months, I will be so unwieldy yo
will lose all interest in me," she announced defiantly.

A smile curved Austin's firm lips as his blue gaz
swept rakishly over pert breasts and tiny waist an
slender hips. He knew all of her now, but he wa
eager to learn more. The sight of her belly swellin
with his child was one in which he intended to tak
much pleasure. He chuckled and lifted her above him

"Do not count on that, milady," he murmured as h
thrust deep within her once more.

Aubree cried out her surprise and joy, and soon th

covers tumbled to the floor as the bed shook once more with their joining.

Lady Clara watched them descend the stairs for luncheon, and joy filled her heart at what she read in their eyes. As Aubree came up to kiss her cheek, Clara hugged her tightly, then turned to Heath to do the same.

"Bless you, my boy. I knew you would make her understand."

Austin hugged her in return and gave Aubree's questioning eyebrows a grin. "I believe it worked the other way around, my lady. She has made a believer out of me."

Clara stepped back and searched Aubree's face carefully, noting the quiet joy behind her eyes and the new maturity with which she held herself. The young hoyden had too much spirit to ever be a proper lady, but she gave every appearance of being a proper wife. Right down to the most important part. Clara nodded knowingly.

"Good. Your father can make no objections to this marriage now. I shall write him at once and tell him I have sent you home to be with the father of your child. See if that does not bring him running."

Aubree and Heath stared after the amazing lady as she regally led the way to the table. Then, grinning foolishly at each other, they followed. If all the world could read their secrets, they had nothing to hide.

When they retired to bed that night, Aubree curled up gratefully in the security of Austin's arms. Now that she had what she wanted, she had time to worry about the consequences. She had a child growing within her, and the responsibility weighed heavily upon her shoulders. And if her father should still he angry enough to have Heath arrested, how could she bear to part with him again?

She curled her fingers in the hairs upon his chest and her small sigh breathed across his skin.

Austin settled her more comfortably against his shoulder and covered her belly with the flat of his hand. "Is he causing trouble so soon?"

Aubree smiled, reveling in the gentleness with which he treated her. She had known he was a gentle man from the very start, despite deceiving appearances. All Austin had ever wanted was a home and a family, just as she had. If they could only lay all scandal behind them, he would settle down to be an excellent father and a loving husband. She could only pray the world would leave them alone.

"He is learning to behave. I think I shall be well enough to travel in the morning."

"Are you certain? We could stay here awhile until the sickness passes." Austin held her anxiously, also a victim of worried thoughts. She was too young to be having his child. He would never forgive himself if anything happened to her. He should never have taken her to his bed.

But lying here like this, entwined in each other's arms, he knew he could never have settled for any less.

"The sickness might stay for weeks or disappear tomorrow. No, I want to go home and see my pets and see what you have done to the abbey and let you give your news to your mother. And then we will come back here for Alexa's wedding. Your son shall have to learn to behave, for I don't mean to pamper him."

"I can't think all this gadding about can be good for you." Austin frowned.

"My decision, remember?" she whispered sleepily beneath his ear.

"That's what you think, madam," Austin informed her sternly.

But her soft giggles against his side left the matter open to conjecture.

37

The clouds lay leaden across the sky as Aubree rode down the drive toward the Sothebys' manor house, but a smile played about her lips despite the threatening chill of the weather. She had grown fond of the crotchety old man over these past weeks, and she looked forward to seeing Anna and Maria again. Although Austin had not quite been informed of it yet, they were planning a special treat for Boxing Day, a little surprise for the servants and tenants of the abbey, and a chance for a merry gathering for the rest of the neighborhood. They would put the finishing touches on the packages today and announce their plans when the Sothebys arrived for dinner tonight. Austin might be doubtful, but Aubree had full confidence his friends and neighbors were ready to support him.

A horse stood tied to a tree at the end of the drive, and Aubree gave it a curious glance. Guests generally rode up to the house and a stable lad would take their mounts in out of the cold. To leave one tied to a tree seemed somehow in bad taste, but perhaps this visitor was in a hurry. The Sothebys' servants were often lax. Anna was much too softhearted to reprimand them properly.

The abbey grooms had been busy, and since Aubree only intended to visit the Sothebys, little Michael had been appointed to accompany her. Away from the slatternly household he had been raised in, he was growing into a fine, strong boy, and he idolized Aubree. Normally, he was at her heels whenever possible, so she found it odd that he didn't dismount to help her as they halted at the entrance.

She turned to find him staring at the strange horse

with what seemed like worry and suspicion. Aubree dismounted impatiently and handed her reins to the mesmerized boy.

"Take Star back to the stable, Michael, and warm yourself until I send for you. I might be a while."

He started from his revery and shook his head violently, refusing to take the reins. "No, milady. Don't go in there. *He's* in there."

Aubree stared at him. "Who?" she asked in confusion.

"The squire, milady. He's not nice. Please don't go in there. We can come back another time."

"Well, if he's not nice, I shall send him away. Anna's much too easygoing to not know how to turn away unwelcome visitors." Throwing the rein to the worried lad, Aubree turned firmly on her heel and marched toward the house.

The door swung open when she lifted the knocker, and Aubree hesitated a moment on the doorstep. Something was not quite right here. The Sothebys did not possess an army of servants, but usually they had a maid who answered the door if someone knocked. It seemed extremely odd to find the door open in mid-December.

And then she heard the loud voices arguing in the front room, and indecision left her. It was really too much of some rude guest to harass a blind old man like Mr. Sotheby. He could barely rise from the chair on his own anymore. The disability made him irascible, but that was no excuse for this kind of behavior.

Swinging her riding crop angrily in her gloved hand, Aubree stormed into the house, turning in the direction of the voices. She was quite familiar with the house by now and recognized the room as one in which the family usually gathered. On this afternoon, they were probably waiting for her.

She slid open the parlor door and glared belligerently at the intruder in the usual family scene. A tall, swarthy man with a scar disfiguring the side of his face turned to stare at her. His eyes lit with some inexplicable delight that found no home on his terrifying demeanor.

"Run, Aubree," Maria squealed hastily before a word could be said by anyone else.

But it was already too late for that, Aubree decided even before the intruder spoke. The evil glitter of the pistol pointed at Mr. Sotheby's frail head told her that much. The sight of the maid crumpled on the floor in a corner of the room confirmed the fact. She could never run fast enough to outpace this brute.

"I'd advise against it, Lady Aubree," the stranger admonished pleasantly, gesturing for her to close the door. "I don't mean anyone harm, but my life is at stake, and I can't allow a slip of a girl to hang me. Come in, sit down, and tell your friends how foolish they are."

Slowly, Aubree did as told, her eyes never quite shifting from the gun in his hand. Mr. Sotheby sat with quiet dignity beneath its menace, but the white knuckles holding it in place trembled unsteadily. Any sudden motion might set off the trigger.

"I don't believe we've been introduced," she mentioned calmly, taking a seat near Maria and grasping her hand comfortingly.

"It's been so long since I needed manners, I've quite forgotten them. Forgive me. I'm Geoffrey's cousin, Harry Eversly." His grim face twisted upward in a tortured grin. "I'm in something of a hurry, so if you will persuade your friend there to do what is right, we'll be on our way."

He glanced toward Anna, who seemed frozen in the chair nearest her father. Her bright mop of hair had been pulled back sternly from her brow, and her features were pale and pinched as she stared at the man with the gun in his hand.

"I have told you," Anna spoke so softly her words were no more than a breath in the tense silence, "I will marry you, but I see no reason to involve my father and Maria. Let them go with Lady Aubree, and I will do as you wish."

"Never!" Mr. Sotheby roared, slamming his fist against the arm of his chair. "No daughter of mine will marry a monster. Shoot me, Eversly, my life is worth nothing."

Aubree noted with horror the look of hatred gleaming in cruel eyes beneath Eversly's lank, dark hair. He must once have been handsome, but a life of dissolution had done as much harm to his features as the scar. Unbathed and unshaved, he no longer could claim the status of gentleman, if ever he could have.

"Shoot you, I will, if necessary, and your daughter still will be mine, but I prefer a life of ease to that of fugitive. A brief sojourn in another climate is needed for a while until the hue and cry dies down, and then we can return and live a pleasant life just as you are now. You owe me a daughter, Sotheby. Anna can never be Louise, but she is the eldest. It's only fitting that the eldest marry first."

Aubree interrupted this monologue. "But Anna is already promised." She strove desperately to think of some suitably eligible young lord. "Lord Edgemont would be extremely distressed if his fiancée is spirited away, and since the dowry is already promised . . . I really think you would have to consider the legal ramifications."

Austin would have been highly amused at her totally fabricated legal expertise, but Austin was not here. Aubree desperately wished he were. The atmosphere in the room was too taut for any other to see her humor, and the squire seemed to be considering her announcement seriously.

"Edgemont? Bit high in the instep for a country spinster, ain't he? But he's got pockets to let. The dowry must have been a substantial one." Eversly glared at his captive. "Why didn't you tell me this from the first? Edgemont's only a viscount, but he stands to inherit the title from his uncle one day. A marquess in the family is nothing to blink one's eye at."

Anna looked vaguely startled, and Maria squeezed Aubree's hand as they watched their captor with some small vestige of hope. Aubree wished for some way to disarm the man, but she could think of none that would not endanger Mr. Sotheby. Surely, if she could delay long enough, a servant or someone would enter

Then perhaps there would be a moment of distraction. She must plan how to use it.

"He's a very good catch, if I do say so myself," Aubree agreed. "And he's quite fond of Anna. But you know, I can think of a lady who might just be perfect for you, Mr. Eversly. I do love matchmaking. She's the daughter of a marquess, as a matter of fact. I have not inquired into the particulars, but I understand she can expect a substantial dowry. Really, you must look at this reasonably."

The squire ignored her prattle this time. His gaze swung to fasten on Maria, who clung desperately to Aubree as she realized the path of his gaze. Aubree clutched her riding crop beneath her skirt, praying the man had forgotten she possessed it. If he dared come near, she would have no fear of using it.

"Maria is more like Louise, I believe," Eversly decided, his gaze traveling over golden-red tresses, resting momentarily on slightly freckled but pleasant features, and settling on the girl's modestly covered but well-developed figure. "I will have to be assured a dowry equal to Anna's, of course—perhaps better, since it can be assumed I will not be your favorite son-in-law and stand little chance of inheriting any portion of your estate. The quill's on the table there. Lady Aubree, if you will fetch the ink from the desk, we'll take care of the formalities."

Aubree knew she argued with a madman, but she had no idea what he intended to do once a marriage settlement was agreed upon, if it were agreed upon. It seemed far more likely that Sotheby would refuse to sign anything, thereby sealing his death warrant. She must stall, if only to give time for thought.

Hiding her crop in the sofa cushion, Aubree rose and began to search the desk for the inkwell. "Of course, you realize, Mr. Eversly, that Lord Agerton fancies himself madly in love with Maria. He's an extremely volatile young man." She found the inkwell and carried it carefully toward the unsteady squire. He stunk of ale, but did not seem quite drunk. Just fortified.

She cautiously stayed on the far side of the chair from him as she set the ink upon the table.

"He'll have forgotten her before we return," Eversly declared unfeelingly. "Come here," he demanded as Aubree turned to go back to her seat.

She turned and gazed at him questioningly. His eyes were dark unfathomable pools burning with an explosive passion that terrified her. He motioned for her to stand in front of him. When she hesitated, he gestured menacingly with the pistol.

"I will fare better with the old man dead. The girls will probably inherit equally, and there will be no one to stand in my way if I wish to take both of them with me. Do not tempt me more than necessary. Come here."

"Leave, Lady Aubree," Sotheby commanded firmly. "Take my daughters with you. This is between me and this villain. Let it remain that way."

Aubree understood what he meant. She could run now, dragging Anna and Maria with her, and they could possibly reach safety before Eversly caught up with them, but not before he killed Sotheby. Such a scene would keep Heath uninvolved and mark Eversly for the murderer he was, but she could not do it.

She stepped bravely forward to stand in front of Geoffrey's cousin.

Eversly struck her across the jaw with a blow that would have knocked a man to his knees. Aubree crumbled silently to the floor, the action freezing the other occupants of the room into brief cries of pain and stares of disbelief.

"That's for thinking you can stop me," Eversly announced to Aubree's inert form. Then, turning to Maria, he pointed to the spot beside him. "Stand here and we will see how quickly your father can write."

Terrifed, her gaze focusing on her unconscious friend, Maria did as told. A cold hand caught her waist and drew her close to Eversly's stench. She gave a cry of fear as he fondled her breast and gestured again with his pistol.

"Start writing, Sotheby."

Austin leaned back in his chair and propped his boots upon the desk as he gazed around his newly refurbished study with satisfaction. He had not intended to renovate this room as yet, but Aubree had insisted, arguing that she could not work on his books for fear of mice and spiders and other unmentionables. But with the fire crackling in the hearth and the thick carpet lying before it, Austin could think of other things he would rather do with her in here than keep books.

That thought aroused pleasant anticipation, and he glanced impatiently at his watch. The Sothebys were expected for dinner; he didn't know why Aubree had to visit them before they arrived. There would have been time to test the carpet for softness before dressing for dinner.

He let his feet return to the floor, and turning his thoughts back to business, he glared at the letter on the desk before him. The duke certainly didn't write like a dying man. The physician who had made that diagnosis must have been indulging in wishful thinking. Austin stared at the hostile slope of the words upon the page.

He could never agree to live like a virtual prisoner in Castle Ashbrook—even for Aubree's sake—as the duke commanded. He had to find some way to placate Ashbrook's fears before he grew impatient and issued the warrants for his arrest. Perhaps they ought to return to the castle just for a visit, just long enough to reassure her father that Aubree was healthy and happy.

But the journey from London had been difficult enough for her; Austin could not ask her to endure an even longer one. For all he knew, such a journey under these weather conditions could endanger Aubree and the child. Surely her father could understand those fears.

Picking up his pen, Austin began to write.

When his door burst open to reveal a dusty, gasping little boy, it so startled Austin he knocked the ink pot across the desk, blotting his carefully worded letter. He cursed and glared at the urchin.

"Lady Aubree! Come quick!" the lad gasped out between breaths, clutching desperately at the breeches bagging around his waist. His buttons had disappeared somewhere in his hasty flight, but he gave them no thought.

Austin was on his feet in a minute, rushing for the door. "Where is she? Has she been thrown?" Panic flooded his veins and the images crossing his mind nearly paralyzed him with anguish.

"The squire! At the Sothebys'!" Terrified by the scene he had glimpsed from the windows, Michael glanced around the room, searching for some weapon. He had wished for one before when Eversly had struck his sister, but none had come to hand. His gaze lighted on the iron poker on the hearth and he leapt for it.

The boy's words produced an instantaneous reaction in the earl. He halted in midflight, his mind suddenly cold and calculating now that images of Aubree lying broken and bloody upon the ground evolved into a much more subtle danger. This was a different kind of menace, an enemy that must be fought and outwitted. Austin, too, sought a weapon.

Cursing the optimism that had made him store his rapier away, Austin thought quickly. The collection of old hunting guns in the trophy room were nearly useless, so long had they sat there unused. He had never favored dueling pistols, even if he could have afforded them. His gaze fell on the whip still hanging from its nail in the corner. Not wishing to disturb his belongings, Aubree had left it there. Gratefully, he grabbed for it, and with the boy at his back, he flew out the door.

Shouting orders at the men in the stables, Austin mounted his saddleless stallion and spurred him on, leaving a confusion of activity behind him.

Even if fury and fear for his wife had not urged him on, Austin would have outdistanced every man in the yard with the galloping hoofbeats of his thoroughbred. As it was, they could only follow in his dust.

Aubree moaned and stirred groggily. Ignoring the madman at the table, Anna flew from her seat to gather the countess into her arms.

Eversly had been forced to allow Maria to sit at the

table and write out the document he dictated to her. The blotched scribblings of Mr. Sotheby lay scattered about the floor, fluttering in the draft from the fire.

Growing impatient, he paced the floor restlessly now that his goal was nearly at hand. Sotheby's signature on the marriage documents would fairly well seal their fates. He knew a vicar just outside of Exeter who would record the marriage for a bottle of brandy. He had bought the license some time ago. The marriage would be final enough for all legal purposes when he finished with the girl.

He glanced at Maria's pale face as she carefully penned her fate. She was not Louise, but he would have no problem bedding her. Once he had her wealth in his hands, he could look around for better.

His glance fell to the floor where Anna was helping Aubree to rise, and he frowned. He would dearly love striking at Heathmont where it hurt, let him know what it felt like to have his woman stolen away. Geoff had made a botch of it. But surely, there should be some way . . .

Aubree could not see the contemplative glance from behind her. She focused on righting herself, ignoring the rush of anger and fear that came with her memory of how she had arrived there. If there had ever been any doubt as to who had driven Austin's first wife to her grave, the bruise forming along her jaw resolved it. She owed this monster for more than the pain and humiliation.

Aware of Eversly's attention on them, Anna did not dare speak. But her father had no such inhibition.

"My lady, I have done your husband a grave injustice these past years, do not allow me to compound it. For you to come to harm at that man's hands would kill me as certainly as if you were one of my daughters. Leave while you may. He has only the one shot and he saves it for me."

With Anna's help, Aubree rose from the floor. The old man sat with his back to the long French windows, and the weak sunlight threw his features into shadow as she faced him. Eversly stood behind him, a crooked smile on his lips as he gazed upon Aubree's slender grace.

"If I wish to kill you, old man, I can do it without a shot. Run, Lady Aubree. I prefer moving targets."

Maria had stopped writing and stared at him in horrified fascination. Anna kept her arms protectively around her friend.

"Lord Heathmont would hunt you down like a rabid dog," Anna replied vehemently.

Eversly chuckled. "Heathmont would be hanging from a rope. Can't you imagine what would happen if the lady's body was found in the bottom of that damned hole? It would only be justice. Putting Blanche there didn't work, but another one of his wives . . ."

Sotheby struggled to rise, fury growling from his lips in incoherent curses. All eyes but Aubree's focused on him. From this angle, she could just make out the road through the windows. She cursed her inability to see clearly, but she thought she saw movement in the bushes beyond. Freeing herself from Anna's hold, she shoved the older girl toward her father.

"Go to him," she whispered.

Torn between her father's struggles and Aubree's protection, Anna hesitated, but Aubree gave her little choice. She stepped away, keeping Eversly facing in her direction, away from the window. The small family group stood between her and the madman, but if he were an expert marksman, he would have little difficulty reaching her.

"An excellent plan, Squire," Aubree spoke mockingly. "And what of the maid?" She pointed to the dazed girl in the corner. "Will you convince her that my husband killed me? Or do you intend to take the whole family and the maid, too, when you go?"

Eversly frowned, realizing he had not planned this thoroughly, but his desire to see Heathmont suffer overwhelmed rationality.

"I will think of something. With both you and Heathmont gone, we can return here much sooner than I had anticipated. I have no wish to stay among babbling foreigners longer than necessary." He gestured violently toward Maria, who had stopped writing. "Finish it, woman. I'll not have any more damned females standing in my way. Or do you find my handsome visage too unbearable to look upon?" He smirked as Maria winced and returned to writing.

Hefting his pistol thoughtfully in his hand, Eversly returned his attention to Aubree. She would not cower before him, and that irked him. He could not kill her like this. He needed some reaction from her first, some justification for what he intended to do.

"Louise did not find me so fearsome to look upon. Neither did your husband's other mistresses, my lady." He used the term with scorn, watching carefully for her reactions. "They called me brave after learning how the mighty earl scarred me for life."

Aubree could no longer see the movement outside the window and despair licked along her veins. Somehow, she must remain calm and handle this herself.

"Whatever Austin did to you, you must have deserved it," Aubree informed him coldly.

"His slut of a sister had no reputation to protect!" he shouted as if she had questioned his integrity. "Everyone knew she would sell herself to anyone with enough wealth. She proved it, too, marrying that upstart American. And for speaking the truth, your husband nearly blinded me! He has much to pay for, my lady. I've waited a long time for this, but I will have what is rightfully mine."

Before any other in the room could guess his intentions, Eversly lifted his pistol in Aubree's direction and took aim.

The room erupted in a cacophony of screams and shattering glass. The pistol exploded, filling the enclosed space with the stench of sulfur at the same time the ominous whine and snap of a whip crackled through the air. Aubree crumpled to the floor as the smoking pistol went flying from Eversly's hand. Austin's furious dark figure strode through the glass shards of the window, his whip sailing back and forth in lashing cracks that ripped tormented screams of pain from its victim.

Both Maria and Anna flew to the unconscious figure upon the floor as Austin took his rage out upon

the man who had done his best to destroy his life—
who *had* destroyed his life, if Aubree did not rise
again. Eversly's cries and pleas for mercy were music
to his ears as the whip connected again and again,
flaying its victim for the crimes committed against
Louise, against Aubree, against even poor Blanche.
The whip sung a vengeance that was bitter in Austin's
mouth as he kept one eye on the lifeless bundle of
blue upon the floor.

"Enough!" Sotheby roared, dragging himself from
his chair in the direction of the sounds of violence.
"Austin! Stop before you regret it!"

Startled by this intrusion, Austin hesitated, and
Eversly collapsed, moaning, before the hearth. The
blood-red rage that had pounded in Austin's brain
drained away as suddenly as it had come, and looking
at his adversary with disgust, the earl flung the whip
down and rushed to kneel beside Aubree.

The parlor door burst open and the sheriff hurried
in, followed by little Michael and half the men from
Austin's estate, filling the room with stomping boots
and the scents of sweating horses and leather. Austin
paid them no heed as he lifted Aubree's slight figure
into his arms.

Out of respect for the earl's grim, pale countenance,
the sheriff held his tongue and motioned for the men
to stand back as Austin rose with his precious burden.
Only Sotheby, unable to see this drama, dared break
the silence.

"Anna! What's happened? Where's your sister? And
Lady Aubree?"

Anna rose to stand beside her father, soothing him.
"We are fine, sir. Lady Aubree has fainted."

Even as she spoke, the still figure in Austin's arms
came to life, her lashes fluttering first, before she
moved restlessly in her husband's embrace. A sigh
raced around the room as jade eyes flew open.

Aubree gazed lovingly into her husband's worried
face. "Austin," she whispered ecstatically, "I knew
you would come."

"If only to thrash some sense into your interfering

hide, you damned little brat," he agreed, irritation
hiding the pounding fear of his heart.

Into the shocked silence, Aubree's soft reply fell
clearly. "You are welcome to try, my lord." She raised
her arms to a more comfortable position around his
neck and snuggled closer against his shoulder. "But I
cannot promise you will succeed."

Harley burst through the door just as the entire
room erupted in relieved laughter. He glanced from
Aubree's smothered giggles against the shoulder of
her rapturous husband, to his family wrapped safely in
each other's arms, and down to the sorry villain curled
moaning upon the floor with Michael standing merci-
lessly on guard, iron poker in hand.

"By Jove!" he cursed to no one in particular. "Late
again!"

Epilogue

The Earl of Heathmont stood on the edge of the
merry crowd overlooking the ballroom and dwelled
upon the differences the new year had brought. The
guests tonight had not quite reached the glittering
pinnacle of Holland House, and the ballroom's deco-
rations leaned in favor of holly and ivy rather than
crystal and silver, but over all, he preferred the company he found himself in at the moment.

His large hand covered the small one clinging to his
arm, and he bent a look of love and delight to the
radiantly lovely woman at his side. Aubree's golden
curls shimmered in a halo about her delicate face as
she gazed happily over the crowd of friends and relatives. The golden velvet clinging to her rounded figure
did not reveal so much as the froth of gossamer he had
first seen her in, but his knowing eyes could find the

soft swell where his child grew, and pride blazed in his eyes.

He followed the path of her gaze and reflected thoughtfully on the mesmerized couple awkwardly leading into the first dance. Everett and his new bride might not be the most graceful of dancers, but the happiness in the eyes of the young squire and the vicar's daughter blinded all watching to that fact. Remembering his own wedding reception, Austin again glanced at his entranced wife.

Before he could speak, a familiar figure intruded upon their privacy. Austin stiffened involuntarily, but Aubree's warm fingers continued to rest invitingly upon his arm.

"Heathmont, we need to talk." Having only just arrived from London, the duke was not appropriately garbed for the occasion, but his elegantly clad figure caused a stir throughout the crowd.

"I agree, sir, but here is neither the time nor the place," Austin answered comfortably. He hid his amusement at Aubree's beaming smile of approval.

"Dammit, man, the House has just received a formal letter of protest from the American government over this impressment business. I need your help if we are to make that gaggle of dunderheads understand the seriousness of the situation."

Austin quirked his eyebrow. "I doubt that I can call on Adrian at this late date, and my presence has not been welcome there for some years. In what manner would I be of use to you?"

The duke's gaunt face drew up tight with irritation. "The evidence presented in court on your Eversly fellow cleared you of those old charges. From what I hear, you're riding a tide of sympathy now. Flaying that bounder with a whip appealed to their sense of justice. Can't say I approve of protecting that first wife of yours at the expense of my daughter, but if she's not complaining—and I can see that she's not . . ." He threw Aubree's radiant face a softening glance. "Then I'll accept your excuses. Right now I'm more concerned about getting this bill written."

"You forget, there are still those outstanding charges of smuggling. They'll not sit well with our noble brethren." Austin drew Aubree closer into his embrace, quieting her restless eagerness to interfere.

His grace shrugged his indifference. "What they don't know won't hurt them. The evidence is gone"—he gave Austin a shrewd look—"and the charges are being filed away. I'm an old man, Heathmont. Don't make me any older."

Aubree could not resist this opening. She touched her father's sleeve and drew his attention away from her husband. "Should you not be resting, Father? Austin says you've been ill, but here you are, galloping about the countryside as if you had nothing better to do. Surely Dr. Jennings would not approve?"

The duke took his daughter's hand and gave Austin a scowl. "Quacks, all of them. Now Jennings says I'm too mean to die, tells me it was all a mistake. Mistake! If he only knew what he's put me through . . ." He returned his gaze to his daughter and his face softened. "I'll be around long enough to watch my grandson grow. Clara tells me you have wasted no time in making an old man's dreams come true. Your cousin is well enough when he takes his head out of the books, but he's got too much of his father in him. I'm counting on you and Heathmont to produce a true Bereford. I don't give a damn for the name, it's character I'm after. And if the two of you can't produce an heir worthy to follow in my footsteps, then this world has grown too soft for the likes of me. I'll not be resting yet, my dear. Perseverance is the Bereford motto. I'll wait to see what kind of son you raise."

Austin hid his amusement but he lifted a questioning brow, waiting for explanation. He remembered their discussion of family mottoes. She had informed him he should have been more thorough in discovering theirs. Perseverance had a solid ring to it. He could have thought of better for this ambitious and fractious family, but perseverance was certainly apt. He waited.

In a whispered aside, Aubree translated for him. "Perseverance is the censored edition. In the Latin on the fireplaces at Ashbrook, it translates loosely, 'Burn your bridges and damn the world!' Although, I think in this case, we burned the barn."

Austin choked on his laughter.

The duke ignored this frivolousness and stared impatiently at his chuckling son-in-law. "Well, are you with me on this? Can I count on your help when the session opens?"

Austin made his face suitably grave and gave a slight, formal bow as the first notes of a waltz began to fill the salon. "Sir, I can think of only one thing more important at this time."

His grace snapped irritably, "Well? What is it?"

"To dance with your daughter." Austin turned his gaze to Aubree, covering her fingers with his. "My dear?"

Her brilliant smile caused even her father to fall back out of their way.

Austin led her to the floor and swung her into his arms with the finesse of an experienced dancer. As they moved smoothly about the room in time to the lilting notes of the waltz, the crowd parted before them, opening to make way for the handsome couple floating so rapturously in each other's arms.

As the girl in gold and her adoring partner wove in and out of the dancers, all eyes turned to watch with admiration.

"If that's what beating does for them, I'll have to try it myself," one gentleman sniffed to his comrade as his gaze followed the pair.

". . . and they say he walked through *fire* to rescue her! Isn't that romantic?"

"I can't believe it's the same little hoyden who picked all my tulips not two springs ago!"

"Daresay it's his training under Wellington that's brought her into line . . ."

The duke lifted his quizzing glance to examine this last speaker. "That's my daughter out there, sir. A credit to the Bereford name. Married a fine chap. Atwood's the name. You'll be hearing more of him."

Totally entranced with each other, oblivious to the whispers and stares, the couple continued to circle the floor, their eyes only on each other.

About the Author

Patricia Rice was born in Newburgh, New York, and attended the University of Kentucky. She now lives in Mayfield, Kentucky, with her husband and her two children, Corinna and Derek, in a rambling Tudor house. Ms. Rice has a degree in accounting and her hobbies include history, travel and antique collecting.